DR
ALL...

BY
JOANNA NEIL

SUMMER WITH A
FRENCH SURGEON

BY
MARGARET BARKER

MILLS
BOON

DR RIGHT
ALL ALONG

BY
JOANNA NEIL

MILLS
BOON

First published in Great Britain 2012
by Mills & Boon, an imprint of Harlequin (UK) Limited.
Harlequin (UK) Limited, Eton House, 18-24 Paradise Road,
Richmond, Surrey TW9 1SR

© Joanna Neil 2012

ISBN: 978 0 263 89165 2

Harlequin (UK) policy is to use papers that are natural, renewable and recyclable products and made from wood grown in sustainable forests. The logging and manufacturing process conform to the legal environmental regulations of the country of origin.

Printed and bound in Spain
by Blackprint CPI, Barcelona

Dear Reader

There's something really special about college days, with young people so full of energy and sparkle, living life to the full. Everything takes on the brightest colours. Their lives are filled with music, deep, lasting friendships and the sheer joy of being alive and trying new things.

So when the four young people in my book get together to share a house things are bound to fizz. It isn't long before Jade and Ben find themselves drawn to one another… Things are definitely beginning to warm up but, as always, there are pitfalls along the way. Jade is cautious about getting involved—and anyway, what with all her studies, and working part-time at the café-bar in London, whenever would she find the time for a relationship?

And what of the other two people in the house? Well, Lucy and Matt are certainly a mismatched couple… Jade and Ben are well used to observing their frequent spats. But when they have to work together as well as live together, sooner or later things are bound to change.

I loved finding out how these young people interacted with one another. I hope you do too.

With love

Joanna

When **Joanna Neil** discovered Mills & Boon, her lifelong addiction to reading crystallised into an exciting new career writing Mills & Boon® Medical™ Romance. Her characters are probably the outcome of her varied lifestyle, which includes working as a clerk, typist, nurse and infant teacher. She enjoys dressmaking and cooking at her Leicestershire home. Her family includes a husband, son and daughter, an exuberant yellow Labrador and two slightly crazed cockatiels. She currently works with a team of tutors at her local education centre, to provide creative writing workshops for people interested in exploring their own writing ambitions.

CHAPTER ONE

'YOU'RE cutting it a bit fine, aren't you?' Matt Berenger frowned as Lucy hurried into the kitchen. 'Aren't you supposed to be starting your new placement at the hospital at eight o'clock this morning? That gives you less than half an hour.'

'Tell me about it!' Lucy groaned. She dumped her holdall down on a chair and ran her fingers through her silky golden hair, as though the action would in some way help to clear her head. 'I left my parents' home at six this morning, thinking I'd have plenty of time, but there was an accident on the road, and before I knew it I was in a tailback half a mile long. I hope whoever was involved will be all right. I passed a couple of ambulances, but I couldn't see what was going on.'

She opened a cupboard door and peered inside. 'I'm starving. I didn't have any breakfast before I left because I thought I'd be able to last until I arrived back here.' She frowned. The cupboard was practically empty.

'You forgot to get the groceries in before you went away for the weekend,' Matt remarked in a dry tone. He walked over to the coffeemaker and flicked a switch.

Lucy stared at him distractedly for a moment or two.

He was wearing dark trousers and a freshly laundered linen shirt, and he looked fit and ready for anything—a huge contrast to her sleep-deprived, travel-weary self. Long limbed, lean and muscular, his presence seemed to dominate the small kitchen. It was a little unnerving. She hadn't even expected to find him here this morning. She'd been sure he would have set off for the hospital well before she'd arrived home.

'We're out of everything,' he added, 'barring milk.'

She winced, coming back to earth with a bit of a jolt. 'Oh, heavens, I'm sorry…it was my turn to get the food in, wasn't it? I'll have to get a grip. I meant to do it, I know I did, but something must have come up.' She shook her head in frustration, causing her long tresses to sway and then settle in a shimmering cloud over her shoulders as she tried to remember what it was that had caused her to forget. 'It was Jade, I think…she told me she and Ben had bought a house, and she wanted me to go and see it with her. I was going to do the shopping on the way back, before I left for Berkshire, but…'

'But then I guess something else cropped up.' Matt poured coffee into a mug and handed it to her. 'Here, drink this. Perhaps it'll help you get your head together.' He studied her for a moment or two, his penetrating blue glance moving over the smooth lines of the dress that draped itself lovingly around her curvaceous figure. He blinked, falling silent for a while before giving himself a shake and bringing his mind back to the situation at hand. 'I thought you planned on coming back last night?'

She nodded. 'I did, but Mum and Dad invited family friends round at the last minute, and it would have been rude to leave since I'd not seen them in a while.' Hunger pangs clawed at her stomach and she stared in dismay at the cupboard once more. There was a fog clouding her brain and she couldn't think what to do.

'There's half a slice of toast left over from my break-fast,' he said. 'You might want to eat that. I was going to put it out for the birds, but I'm sure your need is greater than theirs.' He gave a wry smile and pushed a plate towards her. 'I'd have done the shopping myself but I was on call over the weekend. I didn't get home until late last night.'

She sent him a quick look. 'Thanks for this,' she mur-mured, spreading butter on the cold toast and munch-ing gratefully.

'You're welcome. It's a bit pale around the edge be-cause the bread slices are too big for the toaster—I had to hunt it out because the grill on the cooker isn't work-ing.'

'It tastes perfect to me.' She frowned. 'I'll have to get someone in to look at the cooker.' She bit into the toast once more, and after a while she said, 'You must be shattered. Do you have to go in to work again today?' From the way he was dressed, she guessed he wasn't going to be lounging around the house.

'I do. It's not too bad, though. I'm part of a good team—I'm being given the chance to do procedures we only practised in med school, and being on call means I get to take on a lot more responsibility. It's what I want.'

Lucy nodded, finishing off her toast and brushing the crumbs from her fingers. She swallowed the last of her coffee. 'This year's gone well for you, hasn't it? I suppose, with any luck, I'll be in the same position as you, a foundation-year doctor, by August…except that I have to get through my final exams first.' She thought about that and pulled a face. 'I'm really not looking forward to those. I'm spending every last minute revising.' Finding that time was becoming more and more difficult of late, though. Much as she loved her parents, she could have done without going home this particular weekend.

She hunted around for her bag, and said hurriedly, 'I have to go. What time do you have to be on duty?'

He glanced at his watch. 'Soon. I'll walk with you.'

'Okay.'

It was a strange feeling, being alone with Matt like this, and she wasn't sure quite how she felt about it. There were usually four of them sharing the house, but things had changed now that Jade and Ben were planning their wedding. They had been house hunting, and hadn't been around very much of late.

Perhaps that was why Matt had been acting differently these last few weeks. It was an odd situation. He'd been surprisingly laid-back about her forgetting to get the groceries, and that in itself was peculiar, given the way he usually enjoyed teasing her.

'You said Jade took you to see the house they'd bought,' Matt commented now, cutting in on her thoughts. They left the neat, Georgian crescent of houses behind them and set out along the London streets, heading for the hospital. 'I imagine that means they'll be wanting to move out fairly soon.'

She shook her head. 'It'll be some time before they do that, I think. With prices being what they are in London, they've settled for a house that needs quite a bit of work.

They have to rewire the place and put in central heating, and so on, and after that they'll be decorating.'

He pulled a face. 'That sounds like a lot of hard work.'

She smiled. 'I don't think they mind. It'll be a great house once the renovations have been done. And I guess, as long as they're together, they'll be happy enough. I suppose it could be fun, getting the place just how they want it.'

He gave her a sidelong glance, lifting a dark brow. 'Fun? Well, yes, it's the sort of thing I'd enjoy. I can see how it would be good to stamp your individual touch on a house, to make it well and truly your own, but I can't imagine you wanting to do hands-on stuff like that. With your background, I'd have thought you'd be more inclined to get the builders in.' The hint of a smile touched his lips as his gaze wandered to her beautifully manicured nails.

'Oh, here we go…' she remarked in a cross voice. 'Why does everyone assume they know me from a quick glance at the way I look? And you're a prime example. We might have lived in the same house for the last few months, but you don't know me at all, do you? You just think that you do. I'm perfectly capable of setting to and fixing things up if need be.'

Not that she'd ever been called on to do anything like that, but it didn't mean she wouldn't be capable if the situation arose, did it?

'Okay, okay…I take it back. There's no need to get yourself worked up about it. I didn't mean to ruffle your feathers.' His mouth quirked and she frowned, looking at him suspiciously. Was she overreacting? It had been a difficult weekend, one way and another, and she had to admit to being tired and out of sorts.

She was silent for a moment or two, thinking things through. It looked as though she and Matt would be on their own in the house for a good deal of the time from now on, and that could be difficult for both of them, without Jade and Ben there to deflect their arguments. They were opposites, after all. Matt was laid-back, easy-going, happy to strum on his guitar whenever the fancy took him, whereas she…

She had a lot to contend with, even more so of late since her father had decided to expand his business. The changes meant there was far more work to be done. Lucy was a medical student, but she'd always helped out with her parents' property development company, ever since she had been old enough to hold the other end of a measuring tape. She'd been round countless properties with her father and grandfather, and knew the jargon off pat—strengthen those joists, put in a new damp course, sand the wooden floors. Even now, her father regularly sent work her way.

'See if you can track down a supplier for those ceramic tiles I want for the old-cottage renovations, will you?' he'd said last week. 'And have a look on the internet to see if there are any likely properties in the neighbouring area. Find out how much the houses go for over there. You can fill me in on the details when you come over at the weekend. Your mother's looking forward to having you with us for Sunday lunch, and I want to show you the old farm cottage now that the work is almost finished.'

All these things took time, when she really ought to

be studying, but she didn't complain. After all, her father owned this house that they were all living in, and she, at least, didn't have to pay rent. No doubt Matt thought she was a spoiled daddy's girl, but in reality she paid her way by working as a researcher for her father.

It wasn't fair, the way she was judged. Just because she came from a wealthy family, and she happened to be blonde with a decent figure, people only saw the superficial, the outer packaging. They saw a golden-haired fashion model, and assumed she was only interested in looking good and keeping up with the latest fashion trends.

It was the same at the hospital. She had to work harder than anyone else to be accepted as the woman she really was, someone who would one day make a skilled and capable doctor.

That was what she hoped she would become, anyway. If she didn't get there, it wouldn't be for want of trying.

'You'll be working on Paediatrics for the next week or so, won't you?' Matt asked, sniffing the air as they passed by a café. The proprietors were setting up for the day and the appetising smell of meat pasties and hot bacon wafted through the air.

Lucy's mouth watered, and she thought longingly of food…crisp bacon, eggs with bright yellow yolks, and maybe a couple of hash browns to complete the meal… She groaned inwardly; the toast Matt had given her had only served as an appetiser. She didn't even like fried food, so why on earth was she obsessing about it now?

'Yes, that's right,' she said. 'Jade told me she had a

good experience on Professor Farnham's team, so I'm hoping things will turn out pretty much the same for me. I'm not sure how I'll cope, though, working with children.'

'I'm sure you'll be fine.' He laid a hand on the small of her back and urged her through the automatic doors at the entrance to the hospital. 'I must go and meet up with my consultant. Perhaps we'll catch up with one another later on?'

Even though he removed his hand, she still felt its warm imprint on her spine as they walked along the corridor towards the lift bay. It was a peculiar, intimate feeling, and she pulled in a quick breath to help her deal with the strange emotions that had suddenly overtaken her.

'Perhaps.' She nodded in agreement, though with any luck they'd go their separate ways. She still wasn't sure quite how to deal with this new-style Matt. Over the last few months, she'd become used to their frequent, fairly good-natured spats, but now that he was being halfway nice to her she didn't know how to take it.

She went straight to the children's ward and introduced herself to the registrar on duty and to the nursing staff.

'It's good to see you again, Lucy,' the registrar greeted her with a smile. They'd met before and talked occasionally whenever there had been a gig going on in the student union bar, and the last few times he had made a point of singling her out. James Tyler was tall and good-looking, in his mid-thirties, and she was sure he would be a catch for any girl but she wasn't inclined to get involved with him, no matter how much he pushed the issue.

She'd been bitten a couple of times before, and he had all the hallmarks of being like the other men in her life—seduced by the way she looked, and interested only in one thing. She just wasn't prepared to go down that route again, especially not at this particular time when she was completing the most difficult year of her medical studies.

'You, too,' she murmured, and listened attentively as he briefly outlined the case histories of the young patients in the unit.

'Professor Farnham wants you to check on all the youngsters, and make yourself familiar with their conditions, and their treatment, medications and so on. When you've done that, he'd like you to take a look at the baby in here,' he said, taking her over to the neighbouring bay. 'See what you make of him. He's ten months old.'

'Do I get to look at his notes?'

He smiled. 'Later. I think the professor wants to see what you come up with first.'

Lucy drew in a deep breath. 'Okay. I'll do my best.'

'Good. I'll leave you to it, if you don't mind. I have to go and see to a patient who's being admitted. The professor should be along in around an hour's time—he's been liaising with A and E over a ten-year-old who was injured in a traffic accident on the bypass this morning. We'll be looking after him. The boy has a splenic injury, but he may not need surgery if we can keep him on supportive treatment for a while.'

Lucy frowned. 'That must have been the accident I came across when I was on my way home from my parents' house, first thing. Do you know if anyone else was injured?'

'His parents escaped with minor injuries, and the driver of the other car has a broken arm. It seems they were lucky, all things considered. The boy was hurt when the side of the car was pushed inwards.'

'Well, I'm glad I found out what happened to them, anyway.'

He moved away from her and Lucy went to introduce herself to the children on the ward. Some of them were very poorly, whilst others were on the way to recovery and greeted her cheerfully.

When she had finished getting to know them, she went back to the bay where her special patient, the ten-month-old baby, was sleeping. She walked over to the cot and gazed down at the tiny, pale-looking infant. He was receiving oxygen through thin tubes inserted in his nostrils, and when she looked at the monitors, she could see that his blood oxygen level was very low. He was breathing fast, and even with the oxygen therapy it seemed as though he was struggling to get enough air into his lungs.

'You poor little thing,' she murmured. 'I'm going to disturb you for just a minute or two, poppet, while I listen to your chest.' She put the earpieces of the stethoscope into her ears and warmed the chest piece with her hands before running it over the baby's lungs.

'What have you managed to find out, Lucy? Anything interesting?'

She jumped as Professor Farnham suddenly appeared at her side. Even more startling was the fact that Matt was with him. She looked at both of them, wide-eyed, before recovering herself and sliding the stethoscope back around her neck.

'I—uh…' What was Matt doing here? He wasn't meant to be on this team, was he? The professor was waiting for an answer, though, and she hurriedly pulled herself together. 'There are decreased breath sounds bilaterally and I heard inspiratory crackles, suggesting involvement of the deeper lung tissues. He has a high fever, he's breathing fast and has shortness of breath. I'd say he was suffering from a severe chest infection, possibly pneumonia.'

The professor nodded. 'And what procedures would you carry out?'

She gave it some thought. 'Blood cultures, sputum sample and chest X-ray.'

'Good, well done. Keep that up and you'll get through your clinical exams without any trouble at all.' He beamed at her. He was a tall, slim man, in his mid-fifties, she guessed, with dark brown hair that was beginning to grey a little at the sides. His hazel eyes showed an alert, keen intelligence. 'The tests have already been done. Let's see what the lab came up with, shall we?' He moved over to the computer at the other side of the room, leaning over the table and pressing a few keys.

While the professor was otherwise engaged, Lucy sent Matt a narrowed glance. 'What are you doing here?' she mouthed silently.

'New rotation,' he mouthed back. 'Paediatric medicine and intensive care.'

A small surge of dismay flowed through her. He could have told her before this, couldn't he? As things were, it had come as something of a shock to discover that they would be working together, and she felt as though she had been completely wrong-footed. Why had he held back from telling her?

'I thought it might put you off your stride if I told you this morning,' he whispered, as though he had read her mind. 'I only got the placement at the last minute when someone dropped out.'

'Here we are,' Professor Farnham said. 'The test results are on screen. What do you make of them, Lucy?'

Discomfited, she hoped he wouldn't notice the warm colour that had flooded her cheeks. She hated being put on the spot like this, with Matt looking on.

She went over to the table and studied the lab report. 'It's a bacterial infection—*Staphylococcus aureus*.' She brought the X-ray film up on screen and studied it for a while. 'Definitely pneumonia,' she decided, 'though there's something else going on there.' She hesitated, unsure of what she was seeing. 'There appears to be some inflammation in the pleural space.'

'What do you think, Matt?' The professor waved Matt forward so that he could have a look.

'I think she's right. It could be an empyema,' he said, 'a collection of pus in the cavity between the lung and the inside of the chest wall. I expect that's why the baby is in so much distress.'

The consultant nodded. 'Usually, these things clear up with antibiotic treatment, but he's already been given that. We might be dealing with a secondary infection here. I don't think we can leave this one—perhaps you'd like to do the chest-drainage procedure? That should reduce the pressure and help the baby to breathe more comfortably. We'll get the sample analysed and then we can see what kind of antibiotic we need to add to the mix.'

'I'd be glad to do it.' Matt turned to look at the baby, his expression serious. 'I'll set up the equipment right away.'

'Excellent. Lucy can help you with that—in fact, it might be a good idea if she were to shadow you for the next week or so.' He sent Matt a querying look. 'It'll give her a good insight into what goes on in Paediatrics.'

Matt hesitated just for a moment, and then said, 'That's fine. I'm okay with that.'

Lucy held her breath for a second or two, trying to take it in. She was to follow Matt around? Her mind skittered, seeking a way out of the situation, before coming around to the inevitable conclusion that there was no escape.

She had to be professional about this, of course. Obviously the professor had no idea how she and Matt tended to avoid one another back at the house, if only for the sake of peace and quiet. Something that had been easy enough when Jade and Ben had been around, but now...? She was doomed. Not only were they being thrown together at home, now they were to work together, as well. How long would it be before they found themselves at loggerheads over something or other?

Matt looked at her, and for a moment their glances met, each of them keeping their innermost thoughts hidden.

'I'll leave things with you, then,' Professor Farnham said. 'Any problems, and James will be around to help you out.'

Lucy looked anxiously at the baby after the professor had left. 'He's so small and vulnerable,' she said softly. 'I'm glad it's not me having to do an invasive procedure on him. Are you okay with it?' She sent Matt a troubled look. She felt unnaturally queasy at the thought.

He shrugged. 'It has to be done if he's to get better,' he murmured. 'Let's take him over to the treatment room, and then we'll scrub up.'

She went with him and helped him to lay out a trolley with the necessary medical equipment. It was something she'd seen done many times, and she knew well enough how to clean the baby's skin and drape the chest area with dressings.

Matt sedated the baby, and all appeared to be well. Even so, her stomach lurched as he anaesthetised the area and prepared to make the incision. She didn't know what was wrong with her. It was odd, this feeling of being out of synch with everything. She was usually on the ball and quite happy to go along with whatever procedure was needed.

Matt carefully identified the area over the baby's rib and began to insert the chest tube. Lucy felt a wave of nausea swell up inside her. It threatened to overwhelm her, and immediately she began to panic. All of a sudden she felt hot, with beads of perspiration breaking out on her brow, and her heart was pounding so much that she could feel it in her throat. She felt faint.

This couldn't be happening to her, not here, not now. Whatever would Matt think of her if she were to disgrace herself by being sick, here in the treatment room?

'Are you all right?' he asked, pausing as he checked that the tube was in place.

'I'm fine,' she managed, keeping her head down. She handed him the collecting device and he connected the tube to it so that the drained fluid could be accumulated and made available for testing.

'You don't look all right,' he commented. 'You're very pale. Are you going to be sick?'

She shook her head and swallowed hard. She wouldn't allow herself to be sick. Heavens above, she'd seen this operation performed many times before, and it didn't make sense that now, of all times, she should want to throw up.

'We'll have to take him down to X-Ray to make sure that the tube is in the right place,' he said.

She nodded. 'I'll just… I'll… Excuse me a minute, will you?' The way she was feeling, she knew she wouldn't make it as far as Radiology, so she grabbed the opportunity to escape. Their work was more or less done here, and she wouldn't be missed for a minute or two, would she? All she could think about was getting outside and finding some fresh air before she made a complete fool of herself.

It was probably too late, anyway. Matt had already guessed that she wasn't feeling well, and he would come to the only possible conclusion, that she wasn't fit to be a doctor if she felt faint assisting with a commonplace surgical procedure.

She didn't wait for Matt to answer. Instead, she headed outside and made for the paved area set out in the L-shape created by the wall of the children's ward where it met up with the treatment area. Fortunately for her there was no one around, and she found a bench to

sit on, where she bent forward and put her head between her knees.

She stayed like that for a few minutes, only coming
up for air when the nausea had passed.

'Are you feeling any better now?' For the second
time that day, Matt startled her by arriving when he
was least expected.

'Oh,' she said, looking at him aghast. 'I thought… I
thought I was on my own out here.'

He nodded. 'It's okay. No one else knows but me.
How are you?'

'Better,' she admitted. 'Much better. I'm sorry I
rushed out on you. I don't know what came over me. Is
the baby okay? Does he still need to go to X-Ray?'

'I asked the nurse to take him over there.' He studied
her, his dark eyes brooding. 'I'm guessing you're not
likely to be pregnant, so the other explanation for you
feeling ill could be lack of food. Let's get you over to
the cafeteria, and you can get some proper food inside
you.'

She shook her head. 'I can't do that—I have to get
on. Professor Farnham wants to see my case notes. He'll
want to know where I am.'

He frowned. 'I doubt he'll be waiting with bated
breath. Did you eat properly while you were at your
parents' house?'

'Of course I did.' She looked at him, astonished that
he could think otherwise. 'Though…well, I missed tea,
because I went with Dad to look over one of his projects,
and by the time we arrived back at the house there were
visitors waiting for us.' She thought things through. 'I
should have made myself a snack for supper, I suppose,

but it was late and I was so tired I just wanted to crawl into bed.'

He raised a dark brow. 'I thought going home was supposed to be relaxing?'

She gave him a wan smile. 'You know how my father is. He never stops. He's always on the lookout for new properties to develop. And whenever I did get half an hour to myself, I switched on my laptop and did some work for my exams.'

'Lord help us.' He rolled his eyes heavenwards. 'You won't even reach first base as a doctor if you don't know how to keep yourself healthy.'

She mulled that over for a while. Of course, he was right. He must have a very low opinion of her, and she deserved it. It was very depressing, and all at once she was swamped with guilt for letting things get to this state.

'Come on,' Matt said. 'I'll take you along to the cafeteria.' He placed a hand beneath her elbow and helped her to her feet. 'And don't even think of asking for a salad. Jade told me you keep that perfect figure by cutting out pasta and fries, and anything else that might tend to add the pounds. That's a silly way to be going on. You have to be at the top of your game, for heaven's sake. You need nourishment.'

Jade had been talking about her? How could she do that with Matt, of all people?

'I know that,' she protested. 'If I don't eat those foods, it's because I'm not keen on them. It's nothing to do with watching my weight. I don't do that—I don't even think about it.'

He made a disgruntled, scoffing sound and urged

her on, walking with her through the entrance door and along the corridor towards the cafeteria.

'Sit down,' he said, when they arrived there and he had picked out a table by the window. 'I'll go and order for you.'

He started to walk away. 'Hey, hang on a minute,' Lucy called after him. 'You don't even know what I want.' She frowned, feeling unaccountably annoyed. Perhaps that was another side effect arising from lack of sleep and practically nothing to eat.

He turned and looked at her as though he was dealing with a recalcitrant child. 'I thought pancakes with strawberry syrup, and waffles with ice cream on the side. That way you get to eat and be cheered up at the same time. Those are your favourites, aren't they?'

'Well, um, yes…but…' How did he know that? She didn't even know that he must have been watching her over these last few months. Waffles and ice cream for breakfast? She weighed it up in her mind. Then again, why not? 'Oh, what the heck…' She gave up the struggle and saw the faint smile that tugged at the corners of his mouth.

Then he swivelled around, and she watched him stride over to the counter to place the order. He was still shaking his head as though he was trying to fathom how they had come to be in this situation. She hated the fact that she'd had to be rescued by him. It would have been so much simpler if they could have gone on passing each other like ships in the night. That way, neither one of them would have needed to try to understand the other.

When he came back to the table a few minutes later

he was carrying a tray that was filled with goodies, along with two steaming cups of coffee. 'That should do the trick,' he murmured, laying the dishes in front of her. 'Tuck in.'

She didn't need a second bidding. Only when she'd finished with the pancakes and was ready to start on the waffles did she look up at him and notice that he was working his way through a burger and chips.

'First rule of medicine,' he said. 'Make sure that you're fuelled up and ready to go.'

'I'll remember that,' she murmured. She smiled, relaxing for the first time that morning, and he stopped eating, looking at her oddly, as though he'd never really seen her before.

'I wasn't expecting to be working with you,' he said, after a while. 'That might take some getting used to for both of us.'

'Yes, I expect so.' She gave him a fleeting glance before turning her attention to the waffles, still warm from the grill, with ice cream slowly melting into the syrupy hollows. 'You said you were given this placement at the last minute. What happened to the one you'd already chosen?'

'I had to talk to the consultants about it. I really wanted to do Paediatrics, and the opportunity seemed too good to miss. I didn't think they'd go for it, but in the end they seemed happy to change things around, and so here I am.'

She nodded, finishing off her dessert and leaning back in her chair, a satisfied expression on her face.

'The colour's come back into your cheeks,' he said. 'That's good.' He looked as though he was about to say something more, but then his phone started to play its familiar tune, a lilting guitar melody, and he sent her an apologetic look. 'I'd better get this.'

He studied the caller ID, and then said, 'Hello, Mum. What's up? It's not like you to call this early in the day.'

He frowned as the conversation developed. 'Chest pains? How long has he been getting them?' There was a moment or two of silence while he listened, and then he said, 'Make sure he goes along to his GP. I'll come over to see you, if you like... No? Well, yes, you're probably right—but let me know how he goes on, won't you?' Another period of quiet followed, before he added, 'Yes, I know, but they're partners, and he was bound to take on the bulk of the work when the business started to expand.'

He cut the call a while later, and Lucy gave him a sympathetic glance. She wasn't sure whether she ought to intrude, but she was sitting here with him, and she hadn't been able to help hearing what had been said.

'Was that about your father?' she asked quietly. 'Is he ill?' There had also been something about 'the business' and that worried her, because Matt's father was in partnership with her father, and it sounded as though there was a problem of some sort.

Matt pressed his lips together, making them into a flat line. 'My mother's worried about him. He's been working too hard lately, and now he's getting twinges in his chest.' His gaze met hers. 'The trouble is, he always puts in a hundred and ten per cent. We've tried telling him to slow down, but he doesn't listen. He says he doesn't have a choice.'

'Because of my father? That's what you're thinking, isn't it?'

His shoulders lifted, but he didn't reply, and his expression was unreadable, leaving her at a loss. Of course he blamed her father. Martyn Clements was a powerhouse of energy, and the business meant everything to him. He drove himself and everyone else to give their utmost to make it succeed. He'd never come to terms with the fact that his daughter chose to study medicine rather than carry on in his footsteps.

'We should get back to the children's unit,' he said, his features grim and impenetrable.

'Yes.' She hesitated. 'What will you do?'

'Nothing, for the moment,' he answered. 'I'll go and see him at the weekend.'

She followed him out of the cafeteria and neither of them spoke. A wall had come down between them, and the relaxed atmosphere of just a few minutes ago had passed. The loss left her with a hollow feeling inside.

CHAPTER TWO

'It looks as though you've bought enough food to last us for a month,' Jade observed with a laugh, watching Lucy stocking up the fridge and freezer. 'I can't see how the groceries kitty would have covered us for that lot.'

'No...well, I was worried about leaving the cupboards empty, so I decided to get a few extras in. Nothing major, but a few things to tide us over in an emergency—dried milk, bread for the freezer, pasta shells and sauces, rice and curry spices and chicken pieces. That way we'll always have something to fall back on.'

Jade smiled. 'Ah...now I see the reason for the shopping spree. So Matt's been giving you a hard time, has he?'

'No, no...not at all.' Lucy paused, thinking about that. 'Actually, he's been remarkably quiet, lately. He hardly said a word when we ran out of everything at the weekend.'

'You're joking!' Jade's eyes widened. 'What's wrong with him? Is he not feeling well?' She chuckled as she helped to put away the packages. She was glowing with health, her long, chestnut-coloured hair gleaming like the copper pans that decorated the far wall, touched by the morning sunlight. Her green eyes reflected the happiness that came from being a woman in love and for a second or two Lucy envied her that feeling.

She sighed and brushed those thoughts away. Romance wasn't for her. Not now, not perhaps for some time to come. It was a disappointment, finding out how shallow men could be. Though that wasn't true of all men, of course. Jade's fiancé was a wonderful man. He thought the world of Jade, and they were truly blessed, but it wasn't likely that such a liaison would happen for her any time soon.

Why was it that every time she was halfway interested in a man, he was all over her and trying to hustle her into bed? She didn't want a brief fling based purely on sex, she wanted something more than that— something deeper and more meaningful, a man to love her, perhaps, and care for her, and not just be obsessed by her body. But it wasn't happening. So far, every man she'd met hadn't been able to get past the way she looked. Even Alex, whom she'd known for some years and whom she'd thought at one time might be the one for her, had let her down and left her disappointed.

She tried to shake off those negative feelings. 'I think Matt's on top form lately. I get the feeling he's really happy to be working in Paediatrics, and he doesn't seem to be fazed by anything. One minute he's doing chest drainage on a baby and the next he's playing *Air Attack* with a ten-year-old on the ward. I wish I could be as relaxed about the job.'

Jade nodded. 'It doesn't help that we have clinical examinations coming up next month, does it?'

Lucy gave a slight shudder. 'It's definitely stressful.

I've been trying not to think too much about them, but with them looming up ahead there's no avoiding it any longer. I just hope I manage to keep it all together, and that my mind doesn't go blank when the time comes.'

'Me, too.'

'Whose mind's going blank?' Matt joined them in the kitchen, casually dressed in jeans and T-shirt, the cotton fabric hugging his muscular chest and showing off strong, sun-bronzed arms that were covered with a smattering of dark hair. Lucy guessed he'd just come from the shower because his hair was damp and spiky, giving him a roguish, ready-for-anything kind of look.

'Mine,' she told him, and before she could add, 'we were talking about exams,' he started to nod.

'That figures,' he said, his mouth crooking at the corners.

She gave him a soft punch on the arm and he pretended to be wounded. 'Did I say anything about you being an airhead?' he grumbled. 'I mean, just because you forget the groceries occasionally and the cooker still hasn't been repaired, it doesn't have to mean there's nothing going on in there, does it? Anyway, you're blonde…it goes with the territory.'

She scowled at him. 'Don't push it, okay? That joke is wearing a bit thin. I hear it all the time, and I'm telling you I'm not in the mood. As to the cooker, the repairman's coming this morning.'

'That's good. We've only been waiting a week.'

'And that was hardly my fault,' she said in a clipped tone, staying on the defensive. 'I rang several companies, and this was the earliest anyone could come out.'

'Did I say it was your fault?' Matt raised dark brows.

'Okay, children,' Jade interrupted, smiling, 'I'm going to leave you to it. I have a lecture to attend this afternoon, but before that I want to spend some time in the hospital library, looking up clinical exam questions to see what sort of thing might come up.' She glanced at Lucy. 'Are you coming along?'

'I'd like to, but it depends how things go here. I asked the cooker man to come early, but he's already late. I'll catch up with you as soon as I can.'

'See you later, then.' Jade left, and Lucy returned to the task of putting away the last of the packages.

Matt added coffee to the filter jug and said, 'I could wait in for the repairman, if you like. I don't have to be at work until lunchtime today.'

Lucy turned around to look at him, touched by his thoughtfulness. 'Would you? That would be so helpful—I really ought to go to this lecture. It's not quite the same, looking things up on the internet. My head's been all over the place just lately, and a face-to-face meeting is so much better because you can ask questions and clear up niggling difficulties.'

He nodded, but just as she thought about getting ready to leave Matt glanced out of the kitchen window and said softly, 'Well, now, it looks as though we have a visitor. I wonder what that little lad is doing here?' He walked over to the sink to get a better look.

Lucy went to join him at the window, looking out on to the small garden.

'He must be the little boy from next door,' she said. Matt brushed up against her as he moved to get a better view, and for a while her concentration went to pieces

as she stared distractedly at the patch of lawn and surrounding flowers and shrubs.

'He can't even be three years old,' Matt mused, his
voice low. 'I wonder how he managed to get into the
garden?'

Lucy didn't answer straight away. Matt was so close
that she could feel the warmth of his long body seeping
into her, and as he lifted an arm to point out a small figure scrambling about in the bushes she was conscious
of his biceps lightly grazing the softness of her breast.
His thigh was gently pressuring hers, and a rush of heat
spread through her, firing up every nerve ending and
shooting her nervous system into a spiralling state of
heightened awareness.

'I…uh…I think he must have crawled in through
a gap in the fence,' she managed, her voice becoming
husky.

'Mmm.' Matt half turned, looking at her. 'I expect so.' He sounded distant all at once, and he shifted
slightly, so that she wondered if he, too, was overcome
by this same feeling of warm intimacy that was bothering her, where her soft curves were brought into mind-
shattering contact with his strong, firm body.

'Perhaps I should go and talk to him,' she murmured
breathlessly, making an effort to get herself together.
'His mother might be worrying about him.'

'Yes, I think you're right.' He moved away from her,
slowly, and it seemed as though his mind was somewhere else altogether. 'I'll come with you.'

They went out through the French doors into the garden, quietly, so as not to startle the little boy. By now,

he was sitting on a collection of pebbles that were lit up in a patch of sunlight.

'Hello,' Lucy said softly, bending down to be on a level with the child. 'Are you from next door? I don't think we've met before, have we? I'm Lucy, and this is my friend, Matt.'

'I'm Jacob,' he told her, unperturbed by their sudden appearance. 'I live over there.' He waved an arm towards the fence. 'I've never been here before.' He looked around, his grey eyes bright with curiosity. 'Is this your garden?'

'Yes, it is.' Lucy nodded.

'I like it here.' He pushed his fingers into the pebbles and laughed when the smaller ones fell through his fingers to the ground. 'These are good. If I had my truck, I could fill it up wiv these.'

Matt nodded, kneeling down beside the boy. 'I expect you could. That would be fun, wouldn't it? But perhaps we should find out if your mother knows where you are. She might be worried.'

Jacob shook his head. 'She won't be worried. She's bathing the baby.' He frowned. 'She has to,' he added knowledgeably, 'because she fills her nappy and gets stinky. Babies are like that, aren't they? They're smelly and they cry a lot.'

Matt laughed. 'I suppose so, but they're not like that all the time.'

Jacob screwed up his nose and pursed his pink mouth. Obviously he wasn't too sure about that.

From somewhere in the distance Lucy heard the doorbell ring. 'That'll be the man about the cooker,' she said, glancing worriedly at Matt. 'I ought to go and let him in.'

'Okay. I'll see to it that Jacob gets home all right.'

'Thanks.'

She smiled at the little boy. 'Bye for now, Jacob. I'll probably see you again sometime.'

He nodded cautiously. 'Prob'ly,' he said.

The repairman was nonchalantly looking around when she opened the front door to him, but as soon as he saw her, his eyes widened. He looked her up and down, taking in the clinging, cotton top she was wearing, and the skirt that hugged the line of her shapely hips.

'Um… Domestic oven service. You called our company out because your grill's not working?'

'That's right. I'm so glad you've come.'

He was a good-looking young man, in his mid-twenties or thereabouts, with dark, silky hair that had a natural wave. His glance moved over her once more, and he took a moment to bring his mind back on track before he said with a grin, 'Consider me at your service.'

'Come on in.' She was well used to men looking at her that way, so she ignored his stares and showed him into the kitchen. 'It's not lighting up or getting hot or anything,' she told him.

'I'll take a look.'

'Thanks.'

He opened up his kit box and began testing various parts of the cooker. 'Your element's had it,' he said after a while. 'I can fit a new one for you. There's one in my van.'

'Oh, good.' She smiled. 'That's a relief. I wondered if

you might have to send away for the part.' She shrugged. 'I suppose I couldn't expect it to go on working forever. It gets a lot of use, one way and another.'

He nodded. 'They generally do.' He gave her a thoughtful look and said cheerfully, 'The only way round that is to go out for meals. I'd be happy to take you out and free you up from all that cooking…if you're not otherwise engaged, that is?' His glance went to the fingers of her left hand, and when he saw that she wasn't wearing a ring, his confidence seemed to grow. 'There's a new place opened up in the city. I don't know what kind of food you like, but I've heard good things about the restaurant. We could go there this evening, if you like.'

Lucy smiled again, but shook her head. 'Thanks for the invitation, but I'm afraid I've given up on dating. I have other things to concentrate on right now…like my studies and exams.'

His mouth made a wry twist. 'That's a shame,' he said. 'An awful shame. Seems to me we should all take a break every now and again.'

He eyed her up once more before reluctantly leaving her while he went outside to his van. When he came back a short time later, he set to and fixed the new element in place, and then asked if he could wash his hands at the sink.

'Of course, go ahead.' She took a clean towel from a cupboard and handed it to him.

'You know,' he murmured, drying his hands and putting the towel to one side, 'it would be such a pity to give up on the dating game. You're gorgeous, absolutely stunning, in fact, and I can't believe you're content to stay at home and swot every night. Give me half a chance, and I could show you what you're missing.'

She shook her head once more and said lightly, 'Thanks for the offer, but no, thanks…I meant what I said. I'm not going to change my mind. Do you want to give me the bill, and I'll settle up with you?'

He pulled a face and wrote out the invoice, and Lucy handed him a cheque. 'I appreciate you fixing the grill for me,' she said. 'Thanks.'

'You don't need to thank me…just change your mind and come out with me this evening.' He moved a little closer and Lucy took a step backwards.

'I already gave you my answer,' she said firmly. 'I'm sorry, but I can't.'

'Sure you can,' he murmured. 'We'd be great together, you and I. A night on the town would do you a world of good.' He moved towards her once more, but this time Lucy stood her ground.

'I don't think you're listening to me,' she said, her tone brisk, but she was wondering what she ought to do about him. He was certainly persistent. In fact, if he came any closer, she might have to resort to drastic action, something a little more forceful than mere words perhaps since he didn't seem to be taking any notice of what she said.

'I believe she's already given you her answer,' Matt remarked coolly from the doorway. 'Or perhaps you don't understand that "no" means no?'

Lucy was startled. She hadn't heard the kitchen door open, but Matt stood there, broad-shouldered, straight-backed, formidable, his eyes glittering like steel, lancing into the man who was holding on to her.

The young man stared at him in confusion. 'Who are you? Where did you come from?'

'I'm the man who's looking out for her, and I live here. Do you have a problem with that?' He dared him to answer. Matt's jaw was rigid, his mouth set in a hard line that brooked no nonsense. Lucy had never seen him like this before, and she was astonished that the easy-going, laid-back man that she knew had suddenly turned into this granite-edged guardian.

He walked towards them, his long stride steady and determined. 'It looks as though you've finished your job,' he said, looking at the closed toolbox and the old element on the kitchen worktop. 'Now it's time for you to leave.'

'I… Yes, well, I…' the young man floundered, pulling his hands away from Lucy as though he'd been stung. 'I didn't mean anything by it. I was just asking her out.'

'And you had your answer. Now you should go.'

'Okay, I'm out of here.' He put up his hands in a gesture of submission and then hurriedly grabbed his toolbox. Matt followed him to the door and watched him get into his van and drive away.

Coming back along the corridor to where she was waiting, he glanced at Lucy and said calmly, 'I can't leave you alone for five minutes, can I? Men take one look at you and their brains fly out the window.'

She stared at him, dumbfounded. 'Is that my fault?' she said, feeling affronted. 'Do you think I like it that way? I hate that it always happens. I hate it that other women resent me for the way I look, but I can't do anything about it. I wish I could, but I can't…unless…' Her mind whirled. 'Perhaps I should scrape my hair back into a ponytail and start wearing baggy clothes.'

'I can't see that working,' he said with a wry smile. 'Anyway, I was just teasing you—you make it so easy for me because you always rise to the bait. You really shouldn't take things so seriously, you know.'

She frowned. 'No, maybe not. But just lately I can't help it. I feel as though I'm under pressure all the while, and you have a knack of turning the key and winding me up even more. I don't want to feel that way.' Her gaze flicked to him. 'About what happened with the repairman just now… There was no need for you to intervene, you know. I was handling things. I was perfectly able to deal with him.'

'Sure you were.' He draped an arm around her and led her back towards the kitchen. 'Anyway, forget about it. You have more important things to think about right now, don't you?'

She looked at him in consternation. 'Oh—the lecture, yes. I must get my head clear.' She dithered for a second or two, undecided what she should do first. 'I have to get my bag… And I need to sort out some paperwork for my father before I go—he'll be ringing to ask me about it later today and I need to have it to hand.' She frowned, trying to bring her thoughts into order. 'What happened about the little boy…Jacob? Is he all right? He didn't look as though he wanted to leave, did he?'

She realised that it might seem as though she was babbling, and she stopped talking, her mind in a whirl. Then she put a hand to her head and said raggedly, 'Why can't I think straight? What's wrong with me? I'm not usually like this, and I don't understand it. I don't know what's happening to me.'

'Hmm.' He was thoughtful for a moment or two. 'I think you should sit down for a few minutes before you do anything at all. I'll make you a milky coffee. That will help you to focus. Just try to stay calm for a while—you're always so busy, busy, busy, but I'm sure you don't have to fill every single minute of the day.'

He laid a hand on her shoulder and lightly pressed her down into a chair by the table. And that would have been good, she might have taken comfort in his gentle urging and given herself a few moments to gather her thoughts, except that her mobile phone rang and from the display she saw that it was her father who was calling.

She pulled in a deep breath before answering. 'Hello, Dad, what is it? I thought you were going to ring later. Is everything all right back home?'

'Of course everything's fine. But the work's piling up, and I need you to go and take a look at the house you mentioned to me at the weekend…the one that's coming up for auction. I want to know if the structure is sound. How much work needs to be done? How much is it going to cost me to bring it up to scratch and what price do I bid to make a decent profit? The auction's on Thursday, so you'll need to do it in the next couple of days.'

Her mind reeled at the influx of new instructions. 'I can't, Dad. I can't do anything more than the basics right now. I'm snowed under. Do you remember, I told you I've started my new placement? That means a lot of extra work, and I have exams coming up. I don't have any spare time. I can manage the internet research, but that's about it.'

'You have the evenings, don't you? You can't be studying the whole time.' He sounded affronted. 'Anyway, how long will it take for you to get over there? It's only a hop and a skip away from you.'

'No, but that's not the point, Dad. You're not listening to me. I have exams, and I have to study every chance I get. With the best will in the world I can't go checking out houses right now. This is my career we're talking about—I have to take the time to work at it.'

'You had a career all laid out for you back here in the family business.' His tone was blunt. 'I'm not asking for the world, Lucy, just a few minutes of your time. It's not beyond you to give me that, is it?' His tone was scathing. 'You know I can't get over there right now, with the accountants coming to see me.'

She sighed heavily. It was always the same. He never listened to her. No matter what she said, he would never understand her point of view. It wasn't important to him. All that mattered to him was the family business, the company that his grandfather had started and had passed on to his son, and which from there had come to him. She felt as though she was being pulled in all directions. She knew he wouldn't back down.

'All right,' she said with a sigh, giving in. 'I'll see what I can do…but I'm making no promises.'

He cut the call, after asking about the paperwork she had prepared for him, and she pushed the phone into her bag, staring into space, her thoughts bleak.

'Well, now we know why your mind is all over the place, don't we?' Matt said, sliding a coffee mug towards her across the table. 'It's the same thing he does with my father. He pushes and pushes and doesn't consider the effect his demands have on other people.'

Lucy winced. 'He's not a bad person. He just has so much drive and energy, and he can't understand why other people don't have the same priorities. I know your father works hard.'

'Too hard.' Matt was grim-faced. 'His team does all the building work for your father, and they're stretched to the limit to keep up with all the projects he's taken on. My father's recruited more men, but even so they can't pull in all the extra work. My mother's worried sick about him. She says he's not sleeping well and she thinks he has the beginnings of a stomach ulcer.'

Her blue eyes were troubled. 'It must be a huge anxiety for her.'

'Yes, it is. For me, too.'

Lucy's shoulders slumped. Was this problem with her father going to drive a wedge between them? She had to share this house with Matt, and she didn't want any bad feelings to blow up between them.

Things had been different a few months ago when the two families had rubbed along well together—after all, it was the sole reason that Matt was living here in the house with Jade, Ben and herself. Her father was very particular about who shared the living accommodation with his daughter, but he had been only too pleased to help out by giving his partner's son a place to live when Matt had been offered a job at the local hospital. But now it looked as though being in business together was going to have all sorts of repercussions, especially if it was no longer an amicable arrangement.

'Drink up.' Matt inclined his head towards her coffee mug. 'Once you get that down you, you should be able to make it to the hospital in time to sort yourself out for this afternoon.' As an afterthought, he added, 'And make sure you eat lunch.'

'I will.' She sipped her coffee and glanced at him over the rim of her cup. 'I almost forgot—what happened with the little boy in the garden? Tell me, did his mother realise he had gone missing?'

He smiled. 'Yes, she came looking for him. She thought he must have gone through the fence after the cat. He's a bit of a tearaway apparently—the boy, I mean, not the cat—and there's probably a smidgin of jealousy going on with the baby. I get the impression he keeps his mother on her toes.'

Lucy nodded. 'It sounds that way. I'd wondered about the white cat that keeps appearing in the garden. I don't think they've lived next door for long. The couple in the house before them went off to live in a detached property.'

She finished off her coffee. 'Thanks for that,' she murmured, getting to her feet. 'I must go.'

She fetched her bag from the worktop and then looked at him once more before she headed for the door. 'I should say thanks for stepping in to help me out earlier. I know you meant well but, as I said, I'm perfectly capable of handling things myself. If he'd come on too strong, I was thinking about kneeing him in the groin, but I'm not altogether sure how that would have gone down.'

'Ouch!'

'Yeah!' She gave him a light wave of the hand and

left the house, stepping out into the morning sunshine. The trees were in blossom all the way along the crescent, and a good many of the houses were decorated with brightly blooming hanging baskets. It was a glorious summer's day, but something was bothering her and, try as she may, she couldn't quite place what it was.

She walked along the street, ignoring the interested glance of the man who lived across the way. She was used to being avidly watched by the opposite sex wherever she went, and she did her best not to pay any attention. She frowned. Perhaps that was the source of what was playing on her mind.

Living together as closely as they did, Matt had never made a pass at her, and before today he'd hardly ever commented on the way she looked. Of course, she was pleased about that because it made life so much easier… but a perverse little imp was prodding and poking her, and prompting her to wonder about it.

Could it be that Matt saw beyond the superficial appearance and found that what was left was ultimately flawed? In his eyes she was her father's daughter, programmed to do his bidding, sometimes a little resentful of that but happy all the same to live on the proceeds of his wealth.

It was a disturbing thought.

CHAPTER THREE

'You look worried, Matt. Is anything wrong?' Lucy had come from the neonatal unit and was on her way back to the children's ward when she saw Matt waiting by the main entrance of the hospital. He was frowning, glancing occasionally at his watch and looking out through the glass doors towards the car park.

He shook his head. 'Not really. I'm waiting for my father. He has an appointment with the cardiologist this afternoon, and I want to make sure he's okay. I said I would meet him here and take him over to the department.'

Shocked, she looked at him in dismay. 'I'm so sorry.' She moved closer to him, laying a hand on his forearm in sympathy. 'I didn't realise things had come to that state. Has his condition become much worse?'

'Yes, it seems like it. He's had chest pains for some time, but now they're getting quite bad, and his blood pressure is too high, despite the GP giving him ACE inhibitors to bring it down. I've been working on him whenever I've had the chance to get him to go and see a specialist. His GP was happy to go along with that, but my father wasn't keen at all.' He pulled a face. 'He's always been a proud, strong man, never one to make a fuss. I'm pretty sure the only reason he's coming here at all today is to put my mother's mind at rest.'

A twinge of guilt tightened her chest. Had all this come about because of her father putting pressure on him? She said quietly, 'It's good that you're here to take care of him, anyway. Is your mother coming with him today? It's a bit far out of their way, isn't it?' It was odd that they hadn't opted to go to a hospital in Berkshire, where they had lived for the last forty or so years, but perhaps this hospital's reputation had been the deciding factor.

He nodded. 'That's true. It'll take them about an hour to get here, but they think it's worth it. We have a first-class reputation for Cardiology at this hospital, which helped sway his mind and, I think, when my father finally agreed, he wanted to be seen here because he knew I'd be near at hand to advise him.'

'Who is the consultant he'll be seeing?'

'Mr Sheldon.' He gave her a thoughtful look. 'You were on placement with him a few weeks ago, weren't you?'

She smiled. 'Yes. He kept me on my toes, but he's a brilliant doctor. I'm sure your father will be in safe hands.'

'Let's hope so. I've had a lot of input, persuading my father to do this, and I'm keeping my fingers crossed that everything will turn out all right.'

Lucy felt for him in his anxiety and she wished there was something she could say that would give him some comfort, but only an all-clear from the specialist would achieve that. The way things were, it didn't look as though that would be forthcoming.

Looking down, she realised that she was still holding on to his arm, and now she self-consciously let her hand fall to her side. His body was tense, the muscles of his arms rigid, and she wished she could do more than just sympathise.

'Will you let me know how he gets on?' she said. 'I have to go and look at a patient for Professor Farnham so I'll be on the children's ward for the rest of the morning. Good luck with your father.'

He acknowledged that with a nod and she left him, walking over to the lift bay, heading for Paediatrics. It bothered her, somehow, that Matt was looking so serious. It wasn't like him—he was usually so laid-back and calm—but it just went to show how concerned he was for his father's well-being.

Back on the children's ward, she went to check up on the baby who had been suffering from pneumonia, along with a pleural infection.

'Well, isn't he looking better?' she said, her mouth curving in delight as she came across the young mother, who was holding her son tenderly on her lap. The infant gurgled and gave Lucy a toothy smile. She let him grasp her fingers with his tiny fist, and asked, 'Do you think I could have a listen to your chest, young man?'

The baby seemed happy enough to oblige, allowing his mother to lift his vest so that Lucy could run the stethoscope carefully over his chest. After a minute or so she pushed the stethoscope back down into her pocket and said in a cheerful tone, 'That sounds good. It shouldn't be too long before he's able to go home.'

His mother beamed with relief, and Lucy left them a short time later and went to check up on the ten-year-old boy who had been admitted a few days ago after a traffic accident. His parents had also been injured in the accident, but they had been discharged after a couple of days, and now their child was their sole concern. He had been admitted with a spleen injury, and the professor was giving him supportive treatment, keeping an eye on the situation because he preferred not to operate if it was at all possible.

'How are you feeling today, William?' she asked. He was very pale and unusually subdued, and immediately she was on the alert.

He tried to sit up, but collapsed back against the pillows. 'I feel sick,' he muttered, and Lucy hurriedly reached for a kidney bowl and handed it to him.

'Breathe deeply, if you can, and try to stay still,' she told him. 'I'll just check your blood pressure, and see if we can find out what's happening.' She glanced at him as she wrapped the blood-pressure cuff around his arm.

'Did this come on suddenly?'

He nodded, and said briefly, 'After I got out of bed to go to the toilet.'

Lucy frowned. That hadn't caused him too many problems before, so what had been different about this time?

'Were you on your feet for longer than usual?'

He managed a sheepish half smile. 'I went to play with some of the toys across the other side of the ward.' Talking exhausted him and he closed his eyes.

'Until the nurse found him and shooed him back to bed,' his mother finished for him. 'He's not been well since then. I'd gone to get a cup of coffee, or I'd have

stopped him. He's always been too lively for his own
good.'

Lucy acknowledged that with a smile. Of course most
children, especially boys, were naturally adventurous,
and could stray into trouble from time to time. She kept
her thoughts hidden, but she was worried about the drop
in the boy's blood pressure and his increased heart rate.
His pulse was weak. Put together, they added up to signs
of imminent shock.

'I just want to examine your tummy, William,' she
said. 'I'll be as gentle as possible.'

Even so, it was clear that he was in pain, and his ab-
domen was distended, which made her even more concerned. There was an area of bruising under his ribcage
on the left side, in the region of his spleen, plus another,
more recent, reddened patch.

'Did you bump into something when you got out of
bed?' she asked quietly.

He pressed his lips together, and she guessed he was
unwilling to answer so she said quickly, 'You're not in
any kind of trouble. It's all right to tell me.'

'I tried to climb up on a chair to reach something,
but I felt dizzy and slipped and banged myself on the
seat.' Breathless, he fell silent once more and after a
few seconds he began to retch.

His mother helped him with the kidney dish and silently sucked in her breath while Lucy quickly jotted
down her findings on his chart. Everything was becoming clear to her now. Wasn't it likely that the fall would
have been the cause of his problems? An injury coming
on top of an already damaged spleen could have been
the final straw, causing an increase in the internal bleed-

ing from the initial injury, to such an extent that now it looked as though blood was building up inside his abdominal cavity. If she was right, this was extremely bad news—an emergency situation. Too much blood loss could be fatal.

'All right, sweetheart,' she murmured, keeping her tone calm and pacifying. 'I'll get the doctor to come and look at you and we'll make sure you're feeling better soon.' Turning to his mother, she said, 'He needs to rest completely, and lying back with a couple of pillows under his legs might be best. I'll be back in a minute or two.'

She moved away from the side of the bed, debating what to do next. What if she was wrong in her diagnosis and there was some other interpretation to be drawn from his symptoms? Even so, she sent out urgent pager messages calling for Matt and the professor to come and look at the patient, and then she went to find Mandy, the nurse in charge of the ward.

Mandy was startled to hear about the change in William's condition. 'He was fine just half an hour ago,' she said. 'I found him playing with the train set and took him back to his bed. I felt bad about doing that, but he's supposed to have complete bed rest—Professor Farnham's orders.'

She was a pretty young woman, fair haired, with a delicate rose-bloom complexion, and she was also very good at her job. Lucy had learned to rely on her in the short time she'd been working in Paediatrics. 'The professor's in an important meeting,' Mandy commented. 'He didn't want to be disturbed. Perhaps we ought to bring in the registrar, instead.'

Lucy winced. 'It's too late. I've already paged him, and Matt, too. Anyway, the registrar is busy with a baby in Neonatal. A three-week-old baby suffered a cardiac arrest this morning and he's trying to find out what caused it.' She pressed her lips together as she fought off her doubts. 'Don't worry, I'll take the flak if there's a problem. I was the one who decided it was important enough to fetch the professor out.'

Matt came on to the ward as she and Mandy were assessing the boy's vital signs once more. 'Something going on here?' he asked in a soft voice. He studied the monitors and then glanced at Lucy. 'Those readings don't look too good.'

'No, they don't.' By now, it looked as though the boy was going rapidly downhill, and she hurriedly explained the situation while Matt made a brief but thorough examination of the child.

'His pulse is weak and thready—he's going into shock,' Matt said. 'We need to get him stabilised.' He went into immediate action, putting in a fluid line to compensate for the blood loss and giving the boy oxygen.

'He'll have to go for emergency surgery, won't he?' Lucy asked. 'I wondered whether to alert Theatre, but decided against it. I thought, being a student, I might be presuming too much, especially if the professor was to arrive at any minute.'

'I'll do it,' Matt said. 'And I'll call for a surgeon to be on standby in case the professor is delayed. I don't think there'll be time for a CT scan. He could bleed out before it's finished unless we act quickly. We have to get the mother to sign a consent form.'

Lucy pulled in a deep breath. So it was every bit as bad as she'd feared, and now it was down to her to explain things to the mother while Matt and Mandy worked to prepare the boy for surgery.

William's mother was shocked by the seriousness of the situation. 'Will he have to have his spleen removed?' she asked, almost in a whisper so that her son wouldn't hear what was being said. 'That would be really bad, wouldn't it?'

'We won't know for sure what's going to happen until the surgeon has him up in Theatre, I'm afraid. If it's at all possible, he'll try to repair the spleen and stop the bleeding. You're right, the spleen is an important organ because it helps us to guard against infection, but if it has to be removed it means that we'll need to be sure William is always kept up to date with his vaccinations, and he may need antibiotics on occasions to prevent him becoming ill.' She waited for Mrs Bradshaw to absorb all that, and then added, 'I know this must be a worrying time for you, but we'll keep you informed all the way through. Don't be afraid to ask any questions. We'll be glad to answer them.'

By now, Professor Farnham had arrived on the ward, and quickly sized up the situation. 'I'll go and scrub in for surgery,' he said, with a nod towards Lucy. 'Well spotted.'

She was glad of the small words of praise, but they didn't really make her feel any better. All she could think of was that small, vulnerable boy, sedated now and being wheeled away towards Theatre, his life hanging in the balance.

She left Mrs Bradshaw with Mandy and went in

search of Matt. He was in the doctors' writing-up area, adding notes to the boy's computer file, but he finished typing and turned around to look at her as she approached.

'It was a good thing you acted when you did,' he said. He shook his head. 'It's hard to think I was playing computer games with him just the other day. I don't know how the parents cope. It must be such a shock when something bad like that happens to your child.'

'Yes…although I don't suppose you have any choice but to keep going and keep doing your best for them.' Her gaze was troubled as she thought back to how rapidly the boy's condition had deteriorated. 'I think that's partly why I decided to study medicine, because I saw that doctors could make a difference in people's lives. It seemed to me to be a much more worthwhile thing to do than anything else.'

He nodded. 'I feel much the same. I actually thought about specialising in A and E at one time, but I'm still divided between that and Paediatrics.' He gave a faint smile and sent her a thoughtful, assessing look. 'Mandy told me how you kept your cool,' he said. 'She thought you were brilliant.'

She felt a warm rush of pleasure flow through her at his words. 'That's good to know, though I can't say I felt all that confident,' she admitted. 'I kept wondering whether I was overstepping the mark, and I thought maybe I had things wrong, and I shouldn't really be calling the professor to come in.' She perched on the edge of the desk, crossing one long leg over the other without thinking until she noticed his blue gaze glide slowly from the tip of her pale suede kitten heels all the way up to the golden curve of her thigh where it met the taut hem of her skirt.

It was too late to undo the action. Her cheeks flushed with heat and she tried not to notice the spark of flame that kicked into life in the depths of the suddenly darkened eyes that were watching her. It didn't mean anything. It was a trick of the light, wasn't it? After all, this was Matt. He didn't pay any attention to the way she looked, did he? He was more likely to notice that she hadn't got around to emptying the washing machine, or that she was spending an indulgently long time in the bathroom. Not that he ever complained about any of those things…it was just that he had a way of teasing her about them.

She sent him an oblique glance. 'I paged you, but I wasn't sure whether you would be coming on to the ward today. I know you had some study time this morning, and of course you were with your father this afternoon. I didn't know if I would be disturbing you at a bad time.'

'It was okay.' He shrugged. 'The boy had to come first, anyway, whatever I was involved with, but as it happens I was already on my way back to the ward. My parents are on their way home by now.'

'Oh, I see.' He was perfectly relaxed, back to his calm, easy-going self, and she couldn't help but marvel at how well he adapted to different situations.

He had given no sign that anything was troubling him when he had come on to the ward, but had sprung into action straight away, assisting the child, notifying the theatre staff and arranging a surgical consultation.

'How did your father get on this afternoon?' she asked.

'Okay, but he has to go for more tests. Mr Sheldon suspects he has angina, so in the meantime he's given him a nitro spray to use whenever the pain comes on.' His expression became serious once more, his mouth flattened into a grim line.

'I'm sorry.' It was clear that he was still concerned about his father's condition, and she felt awkward about it because she knew in his mind he must be attaching blame and laying it squarely at her father's feet. 'I suppose he must have been ill for some time—I mean, these things don't come on suddenly without warning, do they?' It couldn't be entirely her father's fault, could it?

'I dare say...though my mother had a lot to say on that subject.' The clatter of teatime trolleys sounded in the corridor, and he glanced at his watch. 'It's time I was off duty,' he announced. 'What about you—you're about finished here, aren't you? Are you thinking of going straight home?'

She shook her head. 'I can't. I have to go and look over a property for my father. He mentioned it on the phone the other day. It's coming up for auction and he wants to know whether to go ahead and put in a bid for it. I'm supposed to suss out the condition of the place and find out what work needs doing.' She frowned. 'I know it's my turn to cook today, but I'll probably be late getting back. I've made sure there's meat and salad in the fridge, so you can all help yourselves.'

'I don't think Jade and Ben will be back for supper today,' he said. She raised a questioning brow, and he

added, 'Ben told me they're going to start work on laying new floors, back at their house.' He gave a wry grin.
'I think they'll be making do with a Chinese takeaway.'

'That's your favourite food, isn't it, next to pizza?'
She gave him an answering smile. 'Though now I come
to think of it, you'll scoff pretty much anything that's
going, won't you?'

He lifted his shoulders in a negligent way and she
studied him for a moment or two. For all he had a good
appetite, his whole body was trim, with not a spare
ounce of fat anywhere, as far as she could tell. Perhaps
that was because he was always on the move, always
up to something or other. He was well muscled, broad
shouldered, with a chest that tapered to a lean, flat stomach.

Her gaze wandered to his face. Come to think of it,
he was incredibly good-looking, with a strong, angular jaw and a well-shaped, perfect mouth. She specially
liked his mouth, that way he had of making a crooked
smile, and he would gaze at you with those blue, all-
seeing eyes and...

She looked away, heat rippling through her like a
tidal wave. What was she doing, letting her thoughts
wander like this? Where had all this come from? She
was at work, for heaven's sake, and she ought to be behaving in a professional manner, instead of getting carried away with increasingly intimate thoughts about her
housemate.

She slid down from the table, tugging on her skirt
as she straightened up, and hoped Matt wouldn't have
noticed anything amiss.

'Where is this house that you're going to see?' he asked. 'Is it close by?'

'About half an hour away on the train. It's a waterfront property on a small island on the Thames. I think that's what made me notice it on the internet. It sounded like an idyllic situation and perhaps I was a little carried away when I mentioned it to my father.' She winced. 'Anyway, I have to go and take a look, because the auction's coming up the day after tomorrow. I just hope I don't get it wrong and pitch the target price too low or underestimate how much work needs doing.'

'Would you like me to go with you? For moral support, I mean.'

She blinked, startled by his suggestion. 'Would you mind doing that? I mean—' she floundered for a second or two '—it might take quite a while to look around, if I'm to do a proper job.'

'I don't mind at all. In fact, I'd quite like to see something of how your father operates. I know he has developments going on all over the place, large and small, but this will give me an insight into how one tiny part of the business works.' His glance flicked over her. 'Besides, I thought you might like some company. You've been under a lot of pressure lately, and I know this is one more thing you could do without. Perhaps if you have someone to share it with, it won't feel so bad.'

'I… Yes, you're right. Thank you. I'd like that.' She was touched by his concern. She was seeing Matt in a new light these days. Since they'd been plunged into working together on a daily basis, she was learning so much more about him than she had in all the months they'd been living under the same roof.

He surprised her with his comments, though. She'd had no idea he was interested in the business but perhaps, with his father being ill, it was uppermost in his mind right now. 'Doesn't your father talk to you about his work?' she asked, curious. 'I mean, he's in partnership with my dad, so you must get some idea of what goes on.'

He stood up, and they walked together along the corridor towards the exit. 'Of course, but my father operates the building and actual development side of things. He doesn't choose which properties are going to be renovated or which sites are ripe for development. I guess he must have an opinion from time to time, but it's not his main priority.'

'No, I suppose you're right.' They went out of the Paediatric unit and headed for the main doors.

'I wish we knew more about how young William was getting on,' she said as they left the hospital. 'If I wasn't so pushed for time, I'd have stayed on to see him come out of Theatre.'

He nodded. 'I feel much the same way, but we can ring up in an hour or so to find out what's happening. We're not going to do much good waiting around, and it's pretty certain that as soon as he's out of the recovery room he'll be taken to the intensive-care unit. He's in good hands with the professor, anyway.'

They walked along the London streets towards the station, bathed in the late afternoon sunshine. It dappled the leaves on the trees that lined the thoroughfare, and Lucy felt the warmth of it on her bare arms. All the time she was conscious of Matt by her side, tall, long limbed, fitting his pace to hers.

Entering the station was like stepping into another world, cool, relatively noisy, full of busy people intent on making their way home. After a few minutes they boarded the train that would take them to their destination, and Matt slid an arm around her waist to shield her from the buffeting crowd.

It was a natural gesture, and it felt surprisingly good to have him hold her. She wasn't used to feeling this way about Matt, being at ease with him, sharing the everyday simple task of getting to and from work. It was a comfortable, pleasurable feeling, as though he was lifting some of the stress from her, and for the first time in a long while she began to relax.

They left the train about half an hour later, and walked the rest of the way, crossing a footbridge over the Thames to access the island.

'It's a very small island,' Lucy said, looking around, 'but there are about fifty houses on it. Apparently lots of people want to come and live here, so when a property comes up for sale, there's a lot of interest.' She frowned, thinking about that.

'Do you think your father might be put off by that?' Matt was watching her, gauging her expression.

'It's possible. It would push the price up.'

'And that bothers you?'

She pondered that for a moment or two. 'Yes, I think so. Somehow I would hate to miss out on the opportunity to buy a house in this area. It feels so—' she looked around '—tranquil here. I can't help thinking it would be good to come here at the end of the day, away from noise and hassle, and just steep yourself in this picturesque place and breathe in the fresh air.'

He chuckled. 'Sounds like you're a country girl at heart.'

She nodded, laughing with him. 'You probably have something there. It comes from being brought up in the Berkshire countryside, I suppose... All those green meadows and wooded hillsides. A little bit of me wishes I was still there, and this backwater—' she waved a hand towards the gently flowing river, with its lush green banks dotted with trees whose branches swayed in the soft breeze '—seems to fill that gap somehow.'

'You're personalising it,' he commented. 'The house won't be yours, and, anyway, you haven't seen it yet.' He walked with her, and together they checked the map to see which property was up for sale. 'It might be completely dilapidated and beyond repair—not such a haven after all.'

'Maybe.'

They found it some five minutes later, overlooking the waterway, a detached house, white-painted, with dormer windows and a lower, gabled extension.

'Oh, it's beautiful,' Lucy said, gazing at the house in awe. 'Imagine sitting out here on a summer's day, looking out over the river. It even has its own mooring and slipway.' She frowned and studied the paper that gave the details of the property. 'It says some of the rooms require attention.' She glanced at Matt. 'That could mean anything, couldn't it, from a quick splash of paint to a complete refit?'

'True. Let's go and find out, shall we?'

They went into the house and wandered through the rooms, and Lucy tried her best to look at them objectively, sizing them up and noting down the things her father needed to know. It was hard to keep a clear mind on the subject, though, because deep down she knew she had already fallen in love with the place.

'The fireplace will need replacing in here,' Matt said, looking around the living room. 'And the kitchen could do with a refit.'

'Yes, but look at that view,' Lucy pointed out, her voice tinged with excitement. 'How could anyone not be smitten by that landscape? Two whole walls of glass and a terrace where you can sit out and while away the hours. I can just imagine myself living here.'

'As if you have time to sit around. Being a doctor means shift work and ongoing study to keep up to date, and crawling into bed dog-tired.' Matt was smiling, taking in her absorbed expression, but even his gentle teasing couldn't bring her down to earth.

'You won't spoil it for me, no matter what you say,' she told him, shaking her head. 'It's cast a spell on me, and I'm hooked.'

'So much so that you forget your father will sell it on to someone else. What are you going to do, come and press your face up against the glass every now and again and mourn what you can't have?'

'Oh, you're such a spoilsport,' she said, turning to look at him. 'I'm not going to listen to you.'

'I didn't think you would,' he said, his mouth making a crooked line. His tone softened. 'I just don't want to see you hurt, that's all. Even you wouldn't be able to persuade your father to hang on to it. And you're not in the market for buying, are you?'

'I can dream, can't I?' She frowned, then turned away from him and went to open the patio doors and gaze out at the tree-lined bank opposite. She wouldn't let him burst her bubble. She wouldn't.

She sat on a bench on the terrace and jotted down everything that she'd observed. 'A golden oak kitchen,' she said, making a quick sketch, 'with an island hob and a range cooker set into the recess, and maybe an overhanging fixture for copper pans.' She scribbled some more. 'A tiled work surface—and upstairs we'd need to build in wardrobes and add an en suite bathroom to the main bedroom.'

'How about a new fireplace for the living room?' Matt suggested. 'A proper open grate with coals that look like the real thing.'

She nodded. 'Good idea. What about the floors? Tiles in the kitchen, or wood?'

He smiled. 'Wood throughout—honey-coloured oak, to give the feeling of warmth in the winter.'

She looked at him. 'You're good at this sort of thing, aren't you? Have you been practising? Are you thinking of buying a place of your own?' It was her turn to tease him now. He'd always seemed content to live in their Georgian terrace, close to the hospital where he worked. And though he got on well with lots of young women, she didn't think there was anyone special in his life right now, so why would he be thinking of settling down in his own place?

'You never know,' he said, taking her by surprise. 'I can't live in rented property for evermore.'

'No, of course not.' She hoped her feelings didn't show. It would be so strange not to have him living with them at the house. She was so used to his half awake, half asleep appearance in the kitchen each morning, his constant strumming on the guitar that caused her to glower at him occasionally when she was trying to concentrate on something. But how would she feel if he was no longer there? The house would be empty without him. *She* would be empty, somehow, drifting, like a boat that had lost its rudder.

She blinked and tried to push those thoughts out of her mind. He wouldn't leave. He had no reason to go... not yet, did he?

CHAPTER FOUR

Lucy walked into the neonatal unit and glanced around, conscious of a sense of anxiety weighing her down. She'd been in Paediatrics all morning, but every so often she was scheduled to work in Neonatal, and this afternoon was one of those occasions. She had mixed feelings about spending time in here, because all of the patients were incredibly small and hugely dependent on the care of the doctors and nurses and on all the complicated equipment that helped to keep them alive.

She brightened a little when she saw Matt at the far side of the room. Somehow his presence made her feel more confident, more at ease with the highly specialised nature of the department where she was just a minor cog. He was a friendly face amidst all this uncertainty.

He was looking after one of the babies, setting up a feeding tube and checking that all was well, but even so, he took time to acknowledge her with a smile and a nod of his head.

She waved back, then went over to the desk and glanced through the patients' files until she found the one she was looking for.

'Hi, there.' James Tyler, the registrar, came to stand beside her, greeting her with a cheerful smile. 'How are things with you? I saw you in the library with Jade at lunchtime, working at the computer. It won't be too long before you two take your final clinical exams, will it?'

'Oh, don't remind me!' A host of emotions flickered across Lucy's face as she thought about all the studying she still had to get through, and the battle she had with finding the time to fit it all in. She still had to figure out the costs involved if her father was to put in a bid for the house she and Matt had gone to view yesterday. 'I'm trying to take things one step at a time. If I look at everything I still have to do, I'll start to panic.'

He shook his head. 'You have to remember to take time out to relax and recharge your batteries. That way you'll be able to cope so much better. You're a conscientious, intelligent young woman, and I'm sure you already know far more than you think. The studying is all extra refinement.'

She laughed. 'If only that were true!'

He laid a hand on her waist, an intimate gesture that made her feel slightly uncomfortable. She liked James, but not in the way that he would prefer. 'It is,' he persisted, 'I'm sure of it. And I'm serious about the relaxation bit. Why don't we get together, just you and I, this evening and find a cosy bar overlooking the Thames? Maybe one that has music. It'll do you a world of good to get out and about and forget about work and your studies for a while.'

They'd been here before, and she wondered how she could once again let him down lightly. She hesitated for a second or two, and then said, 'Thanks, James, it sounds like a lovely idea, but you know it's not on, don't you? Like I've said before, I've been down the dating route and it wasn't a good experience. I'm not looking to put my toe in the water again for a while, especially when there are so many other things going on in my life right now.'

He didn't seem to be too put out by what she had said. Instead, she guessed with a feeling of growing frustration that his mind was busy working on a counter-argument.

His gaze moved over her, lingering on the golden hair that fell in a shimmering cloud to her shoulders. 'But you and I would be different. I know it. We get on so well together, we share the same interests… You like the countryside, reading, exploring new places…'

She shook her head. 'I'm sorry, but I can't. I'm sure that going to the pub would be a great evening out— why don't you ask Alice to go with you? I know she enjoys live music.' Alice was the nurse in charge of Neonatal, pretty and dark haired, who put all her energy into the job and worked magic with her young charges. 'She could do with some fun in her life.'

'And Lucy can listen to music every day if she wants,' Matt cut in, coming over to the desk. Tall, fit-looking and vitally energetic, he looked completely at ease in this highly specialised environment. 'She knows I'll be only too glad to play her a tune on my guitar any time she likes.' He tossed a file into the wire tray. 'I do happen to be working on a new song for the students' union disco.' He glanced at Lucy. 'You'd love to hear me practise, wouldn't you, Lucy?'

She rolled her eyes heavenward. 'Uh…if you say so,' she murmured. It was an ongoing bone of contention between them that he strummed his guitar when she was trying to relax or when she was struggling to master a revision topic for her exams. She'd threatened to pull the plug on his amplifier more than once.

James pulled a face, realising that the conversation was over once Matt had joined them. He let his arm slip from her waist. 'I have to go and meet Professor Farnham,' he said, 'so you're in charge, Matt, while I'm away. Perhaps you'd check up on baby Sarah? I persuaded her parents to go outside for a while and get some fresh air, so it gives us a good opportunity to see to her without worrying them.'

'Okay. I'll make her my priority.'

James left the unit, and Matt sent Lucy a thoughtful glance. 'I had the feeling you needed a get-out just then. Was I right, or did I mess things up for you?'

She exhaled slowly. She hadn't realised until then how she'd been holding her breath, keeping a tight rein on her emotions. 'I was hoping he might get the message. I like him, but I'm just not in the mood for going out and living it up right now.'

'Mmm, I got that. Did you mean it when you said dating had been a bad experience for you?'

She nodded. 'It wasn't always that way, but the last time I let my guard down I ended up being trampled. I was hurt pretty badly. I suppose I'm just not keen for that to happen again any time soon.'

'That's understandable.' He studied her curiously. 'I'm surprised anyone would do anything to upset you, though. Most men would be glad just to have won your interest.'

She pressed her lips together briefly, a frown line

working its way into her brow. 'Maybe, but I think it's sometimes better that I don't acknowledge their interest,' she admitted, 'because some men see it as a green light and start an all-out campaign to try to hustle me into bed, whereas, to my mind, I was just trying to be friendly.' Being the focus of male attention was something she lived with, something she was used to by now. 'I want to be appreciated for who I am,' she said, 'not just for my vital statistics.'

He laughed. 'You're probably on a loser there.' He started to walk away from the desk. 'Let's go and take a look at baby Sarah, shall we?' he said.

'Okay.'

She went over to the bay where little Sarah Montgomery lay quietly in an incubator, her stick-thin arms and legs moving restlessly.

Lucy slid her hand into the opening of the incubator and stroked the baby's arm, loving the feel of her downy, soft skin. 'How's she doing?' she asked in a low voice, sending an oblique glance towards Matt. This was the baby that James had been caring for in the Neonatal unit since yesterday morning. She'd been admitted after her heart had stopped and her lips had turned a bluish colour.

'Things aren't looking too good for her, I'm afraid.' Matt was checking the baby's fluid line, but now he stopped for a moment to study the infant. 'She was born prematurely and she's been through an awful lot in these first three weeks of her life. When her heart stopped she wasn't getting enough oxygen, and that could have disastrous consequences. There's a risk of brain damage—always supposing she survives.'

'She's still putting up a fight, though, isn't she?' Lucy's heart went out to this tiny girl. After she'd had a second cardiac arrest in a short space of time James had ordered a CT scan and the results were alarming. There was bleeding in the brain, and that was devastating news for the parents, who were already trying to come to terms with their baby's collapse. 'What caused all these problems, do we know? Is it all down to being born before her proper time?'

'I would think so.' Matt checked the infusion pump and then noted down the baby's vital signs on a chart. 'The blood vessels in a premature baby's brain are fragile and they can bleed easily. It's hard to say what will happen.' A muscle in his jaw flickered, and Lucy could see that he was disturbed by the baby's vulnerable state. 'There's no treatment we can give her to stop the bleeding. All we can do is hope that the situation will resolve itself. We'll keep her on the ventilator to make sure she's getting enough oxygen, and provide support with fluids and medication to stabilise her blood pressure. It all depends how strong she is as to how things will turn out.'

'Her parents are in bits,' Lucy commented, trailing her little finger down to the baby's hand and gently brushing her tiny fingers. 'Professor Farnham tried to prepare her parents for what might happen, but it must be unbearable for them to see her like this.'

'You'd do best not to think about it, if you possibly can,' Matt warned her. 'Paediatrics and Neonatal are difficult specialties—rewarding, in a lot of ways, but they can be harrowing, as well.'

'I know.' Lucy reluctantly withdrew her hand from

the incubator and straightened up. She sighed. 'I know you're right...but it's hard to stay unemotional. Almost impossible, I'd say.'

He nodded. 'You get too involved with your patients for your own good. I saw how anxious you looked when you came back from the intensive-care unit this morning. You went over there to see William, didn't you?'

She hadn't realised he'd noticed her. 'Yes. I was hoping there might be some good news, but he looked so poorly, lying there with all sorts of tubes attached to him and monitors bleeping.' Her expression was bleak. 'I don't know quite what I'd expected, but something a bit more encouraging, perhaps.'

Matt laid an arm around her shoulders. 'At least he came through his operation without having his spleen removed,' he remarked. 'That's something to be thankful for.'

She nodded. He was trying to cheer her up, and she was grateful for that, but when she'd gone along to the intensive-care unit first thing to look in on the boy, she'd been shocked by how white-faced he appeared. Perhaps his peaky, thin face and fair hair emphasised his pallor. He wasn't out of the woods yet, by any means, and he'd been too ill to take much notice of what had been going on around him. He'd lost a lot of blood, and although Professor Farnham had managed to repair his spleen it was a worrying time for everyone as they tried to stabilise his condition.

Matt lightly squeezed her shoulder and then moved away from her to go and write notes on the infant's medication chart. She watched him walk away. She didn't like to admit it, even to herself, but she missed that comforting arm that he'd wrapped around her. She missed the closeness. For just a little while it had made her feel warm and cherished, but now she was alone once more. She didn't know why that bothered her so much, or why she was so aware of Matt's nearness these days, but things were changing, she was changing, and for some reason her emotions were all over the place.

Maybe she was simply tired and overwrought. She'd studied all through her lunch break, taking bites from a sandwich at the computer when the librarian han't been looking. And now that she was due to finish work for the day, she would return home to study some more.

Jade walked with her from the hospital, back to the neat, Georgian house that they all shared. 'I shall be glad when exams are over,' she said. 'The written papers were bad enough, but now there's the practical session to get through. I hate the thought of having to think on my feet and have someone watch me and judge my performance.'

'Me, too. Except that it happens every day, one way or another,' Lucy pointed out. 'I suppose the only difference is that we're not being allocated formal marks for what we do on the wards.'

They arrived home, and Lucy ran the vacuum cleaner around the living areas while Jade disappeared into her room. When she had finished tidying up and seeing to the laundry, Lucy glanced through the paperwork she needed to prepare for her father, and then she, too, went upstairs to revise for her upcoming exams.

She heard Ben and Matt come home an hour later, and after a while, appetising smells began to drift up from the kitchen. It seemed such a long time since lunch. Her mouth watered in anticipation, but she pushed thoughts of food to one side and tried to concentrate instead on the information she was reading on the computer screen. It was Matt's turn to cook this evening. He usually produced straightforward, wholesome meals, anything that could be dished up quickly and without fuss, and his specialty was pizza, with all kinds of different toppings. Today's offering didn't smell like pizza, though.

She tried to shake off those thoughts and dragged her attention back to her studies. It was vital that she go on with her work, and she immersed herself in the lecture notes on screen. She was vaguely aware of hearing Matt's voice a while later, but by then she was deep into learning about things that could go wrong with the renal system. When he shouted up the stairs a few minutes later to say that the meal was ready, she was still engrossed in kidney transplantation and found it hard to prise herself away. Just a minute or two more, and she would be done.

There was a sharp rap on her door some time later, making her jump. 'Are you decent in there?' Matt said in a brisk tone.

'I… Yes…' She frowned, trying to gather her thoughts after the sudden interruption. 'Why?'

He opened the door and glowered at her. 'Because I called you ten minutes ago and, much as I hate to tell you what to do, I can't abide to see good food wasted. If you're not downstairs in two minutes flat, you'll find your dinner inside next door's cat.'

She laughed. 'Yeah, yeah…you wouldn't give your prize concoctions to our furry friend.'

'Wouldn't I? Try me. What's the betting he absolutely loves paella, drools over it, in fact. All that fluffy saffron rice, golden fried chicken, perfectly cooked prawns…?' He was halfway down the stairs when she heard him calling softly, 'Here, kitty, kitty, kitty…'

'No…no,' she shrieked, shutting off the computer and springing to her feet to tear after him. 'You wouldn't dare!'

'Oh, no?' he called back. He was holding her dinner plate aloft when she arrived, breathless, in the kitchen. He was already on his way to the kitchen door. 'Oh, he's going to love this.'

'You do, and I'll…I'll…' She searched her brain to find something suitably heinous. 'My red top will find its way into your laundry,' she threatened.

'Now, that would be a mistake,' he said, smiling, giving her plate a twirl as he turned to face her from the kitchen door. 'I know where you keep the bleach, you see, and you really wouldn't like to see that pretty red top all patchy and sorry looking, would you?'

'Children, children!' Jade cut in, looking on and laughing. 'Settle down. If you two don't sit down and finish your meals like good kiddies, you'll find yourselves doing the washing up.'

'That's a warning and a half,' Ben said with a grin. 'Just look at all those pans that need cleaning.' His grey-blue eyes sparkled. 'Carry on, if you like. I really wasn't looking forward to doing them.'

Matt slid the dinner plate onto the kitchen table. 'Saved in the nick of time,' he said, giving Lucy a triumphant smile. 'Sit. Eat. Be thankful I kept it hot for you.'

He slid into his seat at the table and dipped a spoon into his dessert, a beautifully whipped concoction of strawberry mousse, topped with luscious, fresh strawberries.

Lucy sat down and tried on her best frosty look, but it melted away as the waft of succulent chicken and prawns floated by her nostrils, and she looked down at the bed of golden rice and fresh green peas and felt her mouth beginning to water. She dug in her fork and savoured the taste, trying not to sigh with sheer pleasure.

Matt laughed, seeing her, and she did her best to ignore him.

After dinner, when Ben and Jade had gone to do more work on their house, Matt opened the French doors by the dining area to let in the warm evening breeze, and Lucy decided this would be a good time to phone her parents. Matt poured her a glass of chilled Chardonnay, and she took it with her over to the telephone seat at the far side of the kitchen.

'Thanks,' she said, raising her glass to him.

She chatted with her mother for a while, asking how things were at home and telling her about the babies that tore her heart to shreds in the Neonatal unit. Some time later her father came to the phone, and she told him about the property she'd gone to see the day before.

'It was so lovely,' she said, a hint of excitement in her voice. 'It's right on the waterfront, raised up so there's no danger of flooding, and there's a good bit of land all around so that the gardens can be properly landscaped. There's an old conservatory that's falling down, so that needs to be rebuilt. And, of course, there's quite a bit of work to be done inside, because it's fallen into disrepair. The dividing wall between the kitchen and utility room could be knocked down to make things bigger, but Matt agrees with me that it can all be made to look wonderful. It'll be a fantastic house when it's finished.'

'Matt was with you?'

She could feel the frown in her father's voice. 'Yes, we went to see it together. He actually made some very good points about how it can be renovated.'

'Just how much time are you and he spending together outside the house?' There was an edge of suspicion in his voice.

'Well, quite a lot, actually, since we're working together.' She batted the comment back with a tinge of humour. What did he expect, after they'd been living under the same roof all this time?

'I don't see anything amusing about this conversation,' her father said, grumpily. 'I have your welfare at heart, and I don't want any funny business going on over there. I'm responsible for the people you share a home with, and it wouldn't be right if he was to turn your head.' He warmed to his theme. 'There's too much hanky-panky going on these days, with babies born out of wedlock and couples setting up home together without bothering to tie the knot. You know how I feel about these things.'

She rolled her eyes. This was a conversation they'd had many times. 'Yes, I do…but you have to remember that I'm over twenty-one and quite old enough to do as I please.'

'As if you didn't always.' He sucked in a quick breath, priming himself for the attack.

Lucy cut in before he could get started. 'Anyway,'

she said, 'about this house…I think it's a perfect development opportunity.'

'Hmm.' He thought about it for a second or two. 'I'll bid for it, then, and if it goes through, you could take charge of ordering what's needed since you're familiar with the place.'

She pulled air into her lungs. 'That would be an awful lot of work. I'd have to measure up in all the rooms, find suppliers, try and juggle costs so that we don't go over budget.'

'I'm sure you'll be fine.'

She frowned. How on earth could she take it all on? She had no idea how Jade was managing to pull everything in, but at least she had Ben to help her, and their house was a project close to their hearts.

It was the worst possible time for her to take on anything more. And yet it was something she'd dearly love to do. She'd fallen in love with that house the instant she'd seen it. Perhaps it wouldn't be so difficult, though…after all, she wouldn't need to get started straightaway because it would take quite a while for the building work to be completed, wouldn't it?

'I'll get Matt's father on to the building side of things,' her father added. 'It shouldn't take too long… a few days at most.'

She frowned. 'Matt's father isn't well, you know. Perhaps you should ease off with the work you're putting on him for a while. Everything doesn't have to be done right away, does it?'

'Time's money. How do you think we've managed to become one of the major development companies

hereabouts? Certainly not through sitting still and letting the grass grow around us.'

'Even so, you've taken on a lot of extra work lately,
and Matt's father might not be able to cope with it all
just now. Perhaps you should bear that in mind.'

'I'm sure he'll be fine. He'd say if it was too much for
him. And if he lays off the cheeses and fine wines that
he likes so much, he might do better, cholesterol-wise.
That's probably what's at the root of his problems,' her
father said curtly.

They cut the call a short time later, and Lucy gazed
around the kitchen for a moment, trying to muster
enough enthusiasm to go back to her room and do some
more work. Matt turned around to glance at her from
the patio doors where he'd been standing, looking out
over the garden.

'Why don't you come out onto the terrace for a while
and get some fresh air?' he suggested. 'You've been
cooped up all day, and you look as though you could
do with a break.'

She didn't need much encouragement. Outside, the
sun was setting, but the air was warm and it was still
light. She sat in one of the white wrought-iron chairs
by the table and smiled her thanks as Matt filled her
glass with more wine.

'This is perfect,' she murmured. 'Just what I need
after that lovely food.' She glanced around the garden,
pleased with the lush green lawn and colourful flower-
beds that were filled with exuberant phlox and showy
godetias. A delicate fragrance filled the air, and she
looked over to the fence that was covered with sweet
peas in pale shades of pink and lavender.

She sipped her wine, thankful for a few moments of peace snatched from the frantic pace of the day.

Matt put his own glass down on the table and came to sit in the chair beside her. 'It's been a rough day, one way and another, with William being in a bad way and then the baby. We could both do with some time out.' He gave her a sideways glance and hesitated a moment before saying, 'Is everything all right with you and your father? I couldn't help hearing some of your conversation. It sounded as though he was putting more work on to you.'

'He's full of energy and determination, and he imagines everyone else is the same. It's hard to keep up with him sometimes. It's one thing to plan an orderly approach to jobs, but when they're landed on you out of the blue it can be unsettling.'

'Can't you explain that to him?'

She smiled. 'I've tried. He doesn't see it that way, I'm afraid.'

'Why do you always do as he says? Why can't you say no to him?' Matt asked.

She shrugged. 'Actually, I don't really mind project-managing the development we looked at yesterday. In fact, I'm quite pleased at the opportunity. I just wish it was my property, but, failing that, I'd like to do it up as if it was my dream house…as long as I can take as long as I need and not have to rush into it while I'm in the middle of doing exams. Even Jade will take time out and leave things to Ben while those are going on.'

He nodded. 'I see all that, but the fact is you're always falling in with his plans, aren't you? No matter how much it puts you out, you always do as he asks in the end. Why is that?'

She drank some more wine and thought about it. 'I…I think probably I'm trying to win his approval. I feel as though I'm a disappointment to him.' She made a wry face. 'Well, I know that's true, in some ways.'

Matt studied her, his glance wandering over her troubled features. 'How could that be so? You must be a model daughter, I should think. You make sure everything runs smoothly in this house, that the bills are paid, the garden's in order, you've chosen a rewarding career and you're working hard at succeeding in it. What could he possibly find wrong?'

'I'm not male,' she said flatly. 'I'm not his son.' She put her glass down on the table and pulled in a shuddery breath. 'He wanted a son to follow on in the family business, to take an interest in his life's work, and his father's before him. Failing that, he hoped I would join the company, and when I chose medicine instead, he felt terribly let down. He couldn't hide it. It didn't matter that I chose a worthy career. I'd turned my back on him, as he saw it.'

'So now you do everything you can to please him.' He shook his head. 'You can't go on like that, Lucy. Something's got to give, one way or another.' He frowned. 'So what will you do? Give up on your studies and hope for the best?'

'No way.' Her brows rose in astonishment at the suggestion. Then she sobered and said with conviction, 'I have to do well—at least if I pass my exams with flying colours, he might be proud of me and then it won't matter to him so much that I chose medicine, instead.

If I fail it will just give him another reason to feel that I've let him down.' Her teeth worried at her lower lip and she frowned, hardly bearing to think how it would be if that were to happen.

Matt pulled his chair closer to hers, leaning towards her and wrapping his arms around her. 'I can't get over the fact that you're under so much pressure. How do you stand it? I wish I could take some of the load from you.'

She looked up at him, touched by his obvious concern. 'You did, when you came with me to look at the house. It made everything seem so much better, somehow, because I wasn't doing it on my own. I don't know why that should be, but it helped.'

It felt good, having his arms around her. Even if it was nothing more than a friendly gesture, it was warm and comforting to snuggle up to him this way, in his arms. She could feel the heat coming from his skin, feel the steady beat of his heart next to her own, and she only had to move her head slightly for her cheek to come into contact with his throat and the strong line of his jaw. She was fascinated by his jawline, well-defined, angular, an absolutely perfect example of rugged masculinity. Being this close to him, it would be so easy to gently discover the texture of his skin with the faintest brush of her lips.

'It's probably always better to share things when you can. I'm glad I was of some help to you.'

She closed her eyes and thought about it some more. She was very relaxed, totally at ease, and that was so unusual. Where was it coming from, this sudden longing, this aching desire to press herself against him and feel his bare skin beneath her lips? Had the wine gone to her head? Perhaps it was the dazzling rays of the setting sun that were burning into her, giving her heatstroke or something, and bombarding her with all manner of strange and unaccustomed sensations.

He turned his head towards hers and their lips softly collided, his lips brushing hers with the gentlest touch, a soft caress that was so light, so delicate that for a moment she had to wonder whether it had really happened. Then her lips began to tingle, aching with unbidden desire, and suddenly there was nothing she wanted more than to feel the pressure of his mouth on hers, to have him tenderly nuzzle the small hollow beneath her jaw and taste the smooth creaminess of her skin.

'You taste of fruit and sunshine,' he murmured, kissing her softly then bringing his lips downwards to drift slowly down along the column of her throat.

She gave a tremulous sigh, wanting this to go on and on, and yet…something in her was holding back, and perhaps it was the thought of what had happened to her before that made her feel so guarded, so cautious about simply taking pleasure in the moment.

A dull thud brought them both suddenly, sharply, to their senses.

Then there was a scrabbling sound at the fence, and a small voice said inquisitively, 'What are you doing?'

'Uh…um…' Lucy straightened up in her seat and tried desperately to organise her thoughts. She knew that voice. Where was it coming from?

Matt straightened, moved abruptly away from her and appeared to shake himself slightly, as though he'd been away somewhere and now he was trying to reorientate himself.

'Can I have my ball back?' The voice came from the region of the fence, alongside the pebble patch, and as Lucy pulled herself together she realised that she could see a child's head peering through a hole low down in the fence.

'I thought we'd repaired that gap in the wood,' she said.

'Obviously not well enough to keep a three-year-old at bay,' Matt answered, his tone dry.

He stood up and walked across the grass, swooping down to retrieve a white football.

'Is this what you're looking for?' he asked, showing it to the boy.

Jacob nodded. 'I had it for my birthday. I had jelly and cake, as well, and ice cream and chocolate biscuits. My cat tipped the bowl of cream over, and he licked it all up, and then he was sick all over the kitchen floor. Mum said it served him right, 'cos he'd been pinching the tuna sandwiches when no one was looking.'

'Oh, dear.' Matt was smiling as he dropped the ball over the fence. 'Sounds as though your cat is trouble and a half.'

Jacob looked puzzled, not quite understanding what Matt was saying, but then he must have decided it didn't matter anyway because he eased his head back out of the hole, saying, 'Gotta go. Thanks for giving the ball back.'

Matt watched him over the fence for a while, and then turned back to Lucy. 'He's a livewire, that one.'

She nodded, shading her eyes from the last embers

of the sun as she looked at him. It was just as well that
he'd gone over to the fence to speak to the boy for a
while. It had given her time to get herself together. It
had been madness, kissing Matt that way. They had to
go on working together, sharing this house and trying
to keep a semblance of normality, and how could they
do that when sparks flared at a simple touch?

She had to stop it now, stop that mistake from esca-
lating into something more.

'I…um…I think I'll go up to my room and do some
work.' She paused, gathering her thoughts. 'What happened just now…I…uh…it…'

'I know,' he said, returning her gaze. His eyes were
dark now, his expression unfathomable. 'It shouldn't
have happened. Let's blame it on the wine and the end
of a hard day, shall we?'

She nodded, and hurried to make her escape. Perhaps
he felt as awkward about it as she did. Somehow the
thought didn't exactly please her.

CHAPTER FIVE

'WHATEVER website you've accessed, it must make for very interesting reading,' Matt remarked. 'You've been engrossed in it for the last few minutes. I've been talking to you, and you've heard nothing of what I've said.'

Lucy gave a small start. She was standing at the nurses' station on the children's ward, studying the computer monitor, but now she stopped what she was doing and looked up and said, 'Sorry, what did you say?'

He was standing a little to one side of her, and she turned around to face him properly, just as he moved forward. Their bodies made a soft collision, his long, hard frame gently pressuring the softness of her curves and causing ripples of sensation to catch her unawares, surging through her from head to toe. She sucked in a deep, shaky breath. 'Did you need me for something?'

'Oh, yes,' he said huskily, a hint of humour threading his voice. His hand came to rest on the rounded swell of her hip, as though to steady her. 'All the time.' There was an unusual stillness about him, and it seemed as though he was struggling to keep himself in check. Perhaps their inadvertent, stunning contact had disturbed him every bit as much as it had shaken her.

She sent him a bemused stare. Was it possible that

she could have such a profound effect on him? 'I'm not sure what…I was…' She floundered, completely at a loss. 'I was looking something up,' she tried to explain. For the life of her, she couldn't think straight. Her whole body was hot from that sizzling contact, and even when he moved back a pace, the heat stayed with her, fire coursing through her veins.

'Mmm…I gathered that,' he said in a roughened voice. He cleared his throat and made an effort to pull himself together. 'It was nothing important. I was asking if you wanted to try one of these chocolate éclairs. I picked them up from the bakery at lunchtime.'

He held out a box to her and she looked down at the delectable choux pastries it contained, with their coating of sensuously smooth, dark chocolate.

'Oh, I see…' She struggled to get back on an even keel. 'Um…they look great, don't they?' She gazed at them wistfully for a moment and then said on a sorrowful note, 'But I don't think I could eat a thing right now. I'm far too much on edge. Professor Farnham's expecting me to examine one of his patients and make a diagnosis, and I'm a bit anxious about it. On the face of it, it should be simple, but it always makes me nervous, being put on the spot. And you can never tell with these things. There may be something I'm missing.'

'It's okay. Maybe later, then, when you're not so wound up. I'll ask Mandy if she'll put them in the fridge for me. There are enough for all the staff.' He smiled, putting the box to one side. 'What's the case you're looking at? Perhaps I can help in some way.'

She dragged her thoughts back to the work in hand, trying to be professional about things. It wasn't easy, with Matt standing so close, near enough so that she could see the strong column of his throat and feel the warmth emanating from him.

He was waiting patiently, and she determinedly shut out those errant thoughts and said, 'She's a young girl, twelve years old. When I looked at her notes, I saw that she'd been complaining of a really bad throat and of feeling unwell. Her GP prescribed a course of antibiotics, believing there was an infection, but they don't seem to have worked. She went to see him again this afternoon and he made an urgent appointment for us to see her here.' She frowned. 'Straightaway I thought of tonsillitis, but I suspect there's something more to it, or why would she be here, instead of being treated at home? Apparently, she can hardly bear to open her mouth, and she's having trouble swallowing.'

He was thoughtful for a moment. 'Perhaps you should look for the complications of tonsillitis, such as a middle-ear infection, strep infection or even rheumatic fever. Then again, if one side of the throat is more swollen than the other, you might be dealing with an abscess.'

'Yes.' She nodded. 'I wondered about that. I'll go and have a look at her—if she can stand it.' She made a faint grimace. 'I feel really sorry for her, but at least the professor prescribed some painkillers for her in the meantime. Anyway—' her mouth curved briefly '—thanks for the advice. I just hope I get it right when I present the case to the professor...'

'I'm sure you'll be fine,' he said.

'I hope so.' All these activities and procedures were recorded in her electronic profile and became part of the assessment that would eventually prove her fitness to practise as a doctor. She couldn't afford to make any mistakes.

Matt went with her a few minutes later to the treatment room where the girl was waiting, along with her mother. Professor Farnham was already there, talking to them.

Lucy acknowledged the professor with a smile and a nod, and then explained to the mother and daughter that she was a medical student. She introduced Matt to them, and said, 'Dr Berenger will be looking after you, Melanie, but with your permission I'd like to take a look at your throat.'

The girl agreed, and Lucy said quietly, 'It's very red and inflamed—I can see how painful it must be for you.' To the professor, she added, 'There are no white spots on there, and her throat is closing up so the channel is quite narrow.'

She handed her slim-line torch to Matt, and he took a quick look at the girl's throat, shining the light into her mouth so that he could see her tonsils.

When he had finished, Lucy glanced at her patient and said, 'Thanks, Melanie. You can relax now for a bit. It's uncomfortable for you, I know, but I'm sure we'll get you sorted out very shortly. Just sit back and rest, and let the painkillers do their job. I'll leave you for just a moment or two while I go and have a word with the professor.'

The girl nodded, clearly unwilling to speak because of her discomfort. Her mother sat in a chair beside the treatment couch, and the two of them tried to distract themselves for a while by watching the TV screen that was suspended on the far wall.

Lucy pulled in a deep breath and outlined her findings to her boss. 'She's been unwell for a while, with a sore throat that has become steadily worse. It's very inflamed, more swollen on one side than the other. I can't see any pus escaping at the moment, but even so I believe it's a peritonsillar abscess, otherwise known as quinsy.'

He nodded. 'And what should we do about it?'

'Needle aspiration and intravenous antibiotics.'

'Anything else?'

Lucy's mind went blank for a second or two. Had she forgotten something? A wave of panic hit her, and a rush of heat flowed through her body, bringing small beads of perspiration to her brow. Then she blinked and said on a questioning note, 'We should admit her for an overnight stay, or possibly longer, until we see that the antibiotics are beginning to work?'

'That's it. Good.' Lucy felt an enormous sense of relief and her shoulders relaxed a little. She hadn't quite realised how tense she'd been until then.

The professor smiled and then glanced at Matt, who was standing beside him. 'Perhaps you could see to all that, with Lucy's help?'

'I will.'

The professor left them, and Matt smiled at Lucy. 'See? That wasn't so bad, was it?'

'No, it wasn't. I don't know why I let these things worry me so much.' Calmer now, she helped Matt to set up a trolley with needles and suction equipment.

'The doctor will give you an anaesthetic,' she explained to Melanie, 'so you won't feel any pain when he draws the fluid from the abscess. It shouldn't take more than a few minutes, and then we'll set up an intra-venous line in your arm so that we can give you strong antibiotics to clear up any remaining infection.'

She and Matt worked together to drain the abscess. He chatted to the girl and her mother as he carried out the procedure, putting his patient at ease, and Lucy mar-velled at how gentle he was. He'd said once that he was torn between specialising in A and E or Paediatrics, but after seeing him at work over these last few weeks she was sure he would make a great children's doctor.

Some half an hour later, after they had cleared up and left Mandy to make arrangements for the girl to be admitted, they went over to the staff lounge to take a break.

'Perhaps, now that's over, you'll feel more like eat-ing your éclair,' Matt commented, fetching the cakes from the fridge and sliding the box across the worktop to her. 'I told you everything would be okay. Professor Farnham's a good man. He's on your side—he wants you to succeed.'

'I know. And it was a really simple case. It's just that you're under scrutiny in these situations, and when someone's watching me, everything flies out of my head.'

'It's happened to all of us at some time. You get used to it in the end.' He handed her a plate and poured cof-fee into two mugs, adding cream and sugar.

Lucy bit into the chocolate éclair and gave a sigh of satisfaction. 'Mmm…mmm…mmm, that is so-o-o-o good,' she murmured, savouring the moment.

Matt smiled, giving her a curious sideways look. 'I think Jade used to wonder how you manage to keep that hourglass figure—she thought it was because you watched what you eat all the time, but that isn't true, is it? I've seen you eat fries and cream and all sorts of goodies. You're just naturally made that way, aren't you?' His glance moved over her, gliding over the soft blouse that gently caressed her curves and the skirt whose gentle folds drifted over her long, shapely legs. His gaze came to rest on the honey gold of her hair, the tousled curls held back with two clips.

Lucy paused for a moment, holding the last bit of cream cake aloft. She didn't know what to make of Matt. He'd remarked on her figure in a casual, natural kind of manner, and it was clear he liked the way she looked, but he never pushed the issue. Where other men would have followed up, Matt held back, and yet she knew he wasn't oblivious to her. He'd been shaken when they'd bumped into each other earlier, that much had been obvious. But for the rest…she didn't know what was going on inside his head. He was an enigma.

She finished off the éclair and then licked the remnants of cream from her lips with the tip of her tongue. 'That was so good. Thanks for that. It was really thoughtful of you to bring cakes in.'

He acknowledged that with a smile, but then his mobile phone began to ring, its familiar guitar melody breaking into the silence.

He looked at the display. 'It's my mother,' he said with a frown. 'I hope that doesn't mean something's happened to my father.'

Lucy moved away to give him space to take the call,

but she couldn't help hearing his comments and after the initial exchange of greetings she noted the growing concern in his voice.

'There's no point in getting yourself worked up about it, Mum,' he said. 'Dad's a grown man and he has to be clear about what he can do or can't do, and it's up to him to say if something's too much for him.' There was a pause, then, 'I know…I know…he's always been that way, trying to please everyone and never turning down work. But, as you say, there has to come a point when he must say it can't be done.'

Another pause. Lucy swallowed the rest of her coffee and hoped her father wasn't behind this latest influx of work that was causing problems for Matt's father. Deep down, though, she already knew the answer to that. It was the waterfront house that would have been the straw that had broken the camel's back—her father would have made the bid for it at auction, and what was the betting he had succeeded in getting it?

Matt finished the call, and she glanced at him, seeing the bleak downturn of his mouth.

'I hardly dare ask,' she ventured. 'It sounds as though my father managed to buy the house.'

He nodded. 'So now my dad is trying to work out how to fit it into his schedule. His men are already behind with the work on a new housing development, so this is just one more difficulty to add to the mix. My mother's getting agitated about the whole thing because he suggested delaying their summer holiday, or failing that he wanted her to go on ahead without him, and said he would join her later.' He winced. 'You can imagine her reaction to that, can't you? My mother always had a short fuse. I certainly wouldn't want to mess with her.'

'You can't really blame her, though.' Lucy wished there was something she could say or do to defuse the situation, but she'd already spoken to her father about it, and he wasn't paying her any attention. 'She's thinking about your father's health. That's her priority. She must be very worried. It must be so upsetting to see him snowed under this way.'

'Yes.' He went over to the coffee machine and topped up his mug. 'I don't know what the answer is. I talked to my brother about it, and he said the men are working all hours to get everything done, but the pressure's on, with deadlines and penalty clauses coming into play, and both my brother and my dad tried to talk to your father about this, but he seems oblivious to any of their concerns. He's purely a businessman, looking at the end profit—he seems to think it'll all work itself out.'

She looked at him. 'I'm sorry.'

He shrugged. 'You've done nothing wrong.' He gave a wry grin. 'But you can bet the Clements name is a sore point with my mother right now. You could say she's spitting bricks.'

Lucy pulled a face. 'I'm afraid my father has that effect on some people. I suppose it's understandable if she's not too happy with us right now. Perhaps it's just as well we don't run into her all that often. It'll give her time to cool off.'

She thought back to the time when they had been teenagers and they had all lived in the same Berkshire village. She hadn't known Matt very well back then, but there had been occasions when their parents had organised get-togethers and invited the company's employees over to one or the other's house. Both she and Matt had lived in big country houses, where there had been ample room for these kinds of social functions, and quite often the party had spilled out into the grounds of the estate.

'Do you remember when we used to have those company parties?' she said now. 'We used to alternate, didn't we, with your father hosting the do one year, and the next it would be my father's turn.' She smiled. 'I used to feel really self-conscious at those affairs. One year, especially, when I was about seventeen, I found myself surrounded by a lot of people who were at least ten years older than me, and most of them were talking business. I tried to take an interest and ask all the right questions, but after an hour or two I'd had enough.'

'I remember.' His eyes darkened as he thought back to those days. 'You slipped outside. I saw my brother going after you into the garden, and neither of you reappeared for quite some time.'

She laughed. 'Kyle showed me all the hiding places on your land. We dodged from the summerhouse to the gazebo and even the back of the garden shed, when we saw my father on the prowl, looking for me.'

His gaze flickered. 'I don't suppose he ever caught up with you. Kyle was too canny for that. Back then, he had a huge crush on you. He'd have done anything to keep you with him for as long as possible.'

'We were so young, without a care in the world.' She looked at him curiously. 'What happened to you? I don't remember you coming out to join us.'

His mouth made a wry twist. 'Kyle was my older

brother. He gave me strict instructions to stay out of the way. You were the girl every guy wanted, and those parties were the perfect opportunity for him to cosy up to you, especially the one when you were sweet seventeen.' He frowned. 'I told him he'd better treat you right. You were young and innocent and I was concerned for you. Kyle's changed now, he's decent and straightforward, but back then he was very casual in the way he treated girls. So I wasn't going to make it easy for him. I guessed what was going on in his mind, so I hid all the keys to the outbuildings.'

Lucy's eyes widened. 'You did?' She chuckled. 'I wondered about that. Kyle was so put out when we couldn't get inside any of them.' Why had Matt done it? Was it just, as he'd seemed to imply, that he had been protective, or could it be that he'd had some feelings for her back then?

She shook off the thought. He'd never said anything, either at the time or since. Even so, she couldn't resist saying lightly, 'Perhaps there was a bit of brotherly rivalry going on there?'

'I don't know. I didn't think about it too deeply. I suppose I just acted on instinct.'

Her expression sobered. 'Anyway, perhaps it was for the best. My father was always very uptight about any boys who came near me.'

'I don't think he's changed much on that score.'

'No, you're probably right about that.' She frowned, looking at him oddly. How would he know that? But perhaps he'd caught the gist of telephone conversations she'd had with her father. Her father was ultra-protective of her, and he was always going to try to vet the men in her life, even when she had grown up and was living away from home.

She brushed those thoughts aside and said, 'So if my father's bought the waterfront house, it means he'll be asking me to project-manage the renovations before too long. I ought to go back there sometime soon and take another look and see exactly what needs to be done, just in case your father decides to send someone down there to make a start.' She thought about it some more, trying to work out when she could spare the time. 'Perhaps I'd better go after work today. I'm pretty sure the agent will still have a key so that we can get in. I daren't leave it any longer, because I have my practical exams coming up in a few days' time.'

'You could do without the extra work right now,' Matt pointed out. 'Can't you leave it until the exams are over and done with?'

'I could…but then the workmen will follow the rough draft I gave my father, and they'll add their own interpretation to some of the alterations. I'd sooner they had more detailed instructions—it's my very own project, and I can see it in my mind's eye. I'd hate it not to turn out as I wanted it.'

'What about the revision time you're missing out on? I thought that was important to you, as well?'

'It is, but I can make up for it tomorrow when I have a study session.'

He nodded. 'It sounds as though you have it all worked out. I'll go with you, if you like. You'll need someone to hold the other end of the tape and hoist that creaky loft ladder down so that you can take a look at the attic rooms.' He reflected on that for a while.

'Perhaps your first priority should be to get a proper staircase put in.'

'Yes, you're right. Thanks, Matt. I'd appreciate it if you came along.' She sent him a grateful look and then went to wash her coffee mug at the sink. 'You seem to have a vision for what needs doing.'

The door to the lounge opened then, and Mandy dipped her head into the room. 'We've a seriously ill child coming in,' she said, 'a little boy who was knocked down by a car. He's five years old, with injuries to his head, chest and leg. He's being transferred to us from A and E. He should be in Intensive Care by rights, but they can't take any more patients in there at the moment. Professor Farnham says we can manage him here, instead. I'm going to be with him on a one-to-one basis, and the professor wants you to oversee things when the registrar's not available, Matt.'

'Okay, we're on it.' Matt was already striding towards the door.

Lucy hurried after him, anxious to be part of the team caring for this desperately ill child. A head injury was always serious, with the risk of swelling to the brain and consequent dangerous outcomes.

When she reached the ward, she found that the child's mother was in tears, and the father was white-faced and shaken. 'He ran into the road,' he said. 'I tried to stop him but he pulled away from me to go after a kitten. The driver tried to stop, he slammed his brakes on... but it was too late. Tom was right in his path.'

Lucy did her best to soothe them, but it was hard. She could only imagine the stress they were under. Wouldn't she feel exactly the same if it was her child lying there, unconscious, not moving, not speaking?

'Dr Berenger will make sure that he's well looked after,' she told them. 'Tom's in good hands.' She took them into the office and made a fresh pot of tea, talking to them and answering their questions as best she could while Mandy and Matt checked the boy over and assessed what needed to be done.

'He'll be staying in a side ward,' she said, 'right next to the nurses' station, but one of the nurses will be assigned to watch over him the whole time.' It was difficult for her to know what to say without knowing the particulars of the boy's condition, but the parents told her that their son's right leg had been broken in the accident, and he had been to Theatre to have the fracture fixed and the leg set in a cast.

'I think the doctors were most worried about his head injury, though,' the boy's mother said, her eyes filling with tears all over again. 'He was tossed up in the air and landed first on his leg and then his head came down on the road. I couldn't believe what was happening.' Her voice broke, and her husband laid a comforting arm around her shoulders.

There was a knock on the door, and a nurse said quietly, 'The boy's grandparents are here, a Mr and Mrs Cavendish. Perhaps you'd all be better off in the waiting room. There's more room in there.' She looked apologetic at having to move them on, but Lucy stood up and prepared to show them the way.

The boy's father stiffened at hearing the news. 'They're going to blame me, aren't they? They're going to want to know why I didn't hold on to him more tightly.'

The young woman winced. 'More likely, they'll want to know why they weren't told right away about the accident. All I could think about was Tom. I left everything else to you.'

'I was in shock,' he answered. 'I couldn't think straight. I just knew I had to call an ambulance. The rest of it's a blur.'

Lucy sensed trouble ahead, but she said nothing, leading them instead to the waiting room and standing by as they greeted the woman's parents. 'I'll leave you to talk for a while,' she murmured, conscious of the sombre, tense atmosphere that pervaded the room. 'If you want refreshments, there's a drinks machine in the corridor, and you'll find a cafeteria on the ground floor. Someone will come along in a while and let you know how Tom's doing.'

They weren't paying her much attention. The grandparents' expressions were fraught, while the boy's father was remote, caught up in his own inner battle with guilt and grief.

'How's he doing?' she asked when she reached the side ward. Matt was writing out a medication chart while Mandy set up a drip and checked the infusion meter.

'He's stable for the moment,' Matt answered. 'The chest injury's not serious—it's the head and leg injury we have to worry about.' He handed her the boy's file. 'You might want to read up on this and check the CT scan and X-rays on the computer. The professor will probably quiz you on what's going on.'

'Thanks.' She took the file he offered, but instead of reading it straight away she spent some time looking at the small boy who lay motionless on the bed. It broke her up inside to see a child hurt this way. How could she even think of making Paediatrics her specialty when she couldn't bear to see the awful things that happened to the children in her care?

'We've done all we can for him for now, anyway,' Matt said. 'We'll keep a lookout for any rise in pressure within the brain, and keep our fingers crossed that he remains stable.'

He checked his watch. 'We should have been off duty about half an hour ago, and we should leave now if you want to go over to the house. I'll hand over to James, and then we'll head straight off to the Thames, if you like—or did you want to go home first to get something to eat? I don't suppose a cake is enough to sustain either of us for long, is it?'

'I'd sooner go straight there,' Lucy said, 'if you don't mind. I like to get the work out of the way first, and then I can relax. I know it's my turn to cook tonight, but Ben and Jade won't be there—they're driving over to Jade's parents' home to talk about their wedding plans. It won't be too long for them now...they set the date for straight after the exams are finished.' She shook her head. 'I don't know how Jade manages to fit everything in, though at least she's given up working part time at the café, which is one less thing for her to worry about.'

'I don't think she had any intention of giving it up,' Matt said with a crooked grin. 'It was more that Ben was very persuasive. He said that they were going to be married very soon, and he wanted her to be able to spend more time with him. He told her he'd take care of things so she didn't need to worry.'

Lucy nodded. 'She looks happy, anyway. I expect her mother's helped a good deal by sorting out a lot of the wedding preparations. She was the one who arranged for me to have a fitting for the bridesmaid's dress.'

He smiled. 'I keep forgetting it's going to happen within the next few weeks. I guess it'll be quite an occasion.' He frowned. 'We'll have to think about getting them a wedding present. How do you feel about you and I going into the city to hunt something out? I'd sooner have your input on this.'

'Sounds good to me.' She looked thoughtful. 'I suppose we'd better get on to it fairly soon.'

'Next weekend, then?'

'That's fine by me, but I've no idea what we should get for them.' She screwed up her face, thinking about it.

Matt gave a light shrug. 'Perhaps we'll just generally look around and see what strikes us.'

'Yes. I'm sure between us we'll come up with something.' She left him then, going off to make a quick, final check of all her patients while Matt dealt with the handover to the registrar.

Over in Neonatal, baby Sarah was still on the ventilator, still unable to breathe on her own, while here on the children's ward young William was weak and suffering from low blood pressure, which had a tendency to make him feel dizzy and faint. The trauma of the accident, followed by surgery for a damaged spleen, had taken all his strength away. He didn't have the energy to respond to her light-hearted chat, so she gave his hand an encouraging, gentle squeeze.

'You'll be all right,' she told him. 'Just keep getting plenty of rest.' All she could hope for was that both of them would keep on fighting their way back to health.

'All set?' Matt came to find her as she was once more gazing unhappily down at the small boy with the head injury who had just been admitted to the side ward. Life wasn't fair. It shouldn't be this way. She willed him to recover.

'Yes, I'm ready.'

The journey took about half an hour on the train, and at the end of it Lucy was glad to emerge from the station into the late-afternoon sunshine. The island, with its lush green trees and the wild flowers that grew along the river bank, was as inviting as ever. Lucy felt her spirits lift.

They spent a couple of hours looking around the house, trying to decide where a wall should be displaced here or the plumbing should be altered there, and Lucy took care to write everything down in a notebook.

'There's an awful lot of work to be done,' she said, gazing around when they had finally decided to call it a day.

'But it will be well worth it. It'll be beautiful when it's finished, and your father should get a good price for it. These houses don't come on the market very often, and people will scramble to be in the queue to buy it.'

'Yes, I suppose you're right.' She sighed. 'It's way more than I could ever afford.'

'Are you looking to buy your own place? I thought you were well set up in your father's house.'

'You're right. I'm lucky, I know it, and I should be grateful that I don't have the trouble others have, finding somewhere to live. It's just that I sometimes long to have a place of my own, somewhere that's truly mine. It's silly of me, really, to be even thinking of it, I suppose. That's way ahead in the future.' She frowned, looking around. 'There's something about this place, though. Even as it is, in its rundown state, I feel peaceful here, as though it's a kind of sanctuary where I can leave all my troubles behind.'

He sent her a quizzical glance. 'I can see your point, but you've set your hopes up a bit high, haven't you? It's a shame, because that way you could end up being disappointed.'

'I know.'

He laid a hand around her waist, and somehow the intimate touch was warmly comforting. 'Shall we go and see what the pub down the road is like? I'll buy you dinner. I saw that they do meals when we passed by the other day. Maybe that will help to cheer you up. I get the feeling that this has been a difficult day for you, one way and another.'

'Thanks.' She smiled at him. 'I'd like that.'

The pub was a rambling old building, painted white and set back a little from the riverside. There was a wide footpath alongside the water and a paved area where bench tables had been set out so that people could drink or eat out there on a summer's day.

The evening was still warm, with only a faint breeze to disturb the reeds at the water's edge, and for a while they stood and watched the boats go by and followed the meanderings of a pair of mallard ducks and their offspring, exploring the foliage.

'Do you want to eat out here?' Matt asked, looking around. 'We could sit at one of the tables by the tree over there, if you like.' He pointed to a spot where the sun's rays dappled the leaves of an old beech tree. Nearby, a young couple relaxed with their baby and the family dog, which had stretched out on the towpath, every now and again lifting his head to sniff the air.

'Yes, that's fine.' They went over there and sat down, studying the menus that had been left on the slats of the wooden table. 'Oh, this looks great,' Lucy said. 'I wonder if the food's as good as they make it sound—sun-dried tomatoes, aromatic roasted vegetables and caramelised red-onion chutney—and it all looks so colourful. I didn't realise I was so hungry until I sat down here.'

'Me, too.' He grinned. 'You tend to forget about food when you're busy on the wards. And if things are hectic, it can be several hours before you get to eat again.' He studied the menu, and after a while he stood up and went to place their order.

Lucy gazed at the gently flowing river, watching the damselflies dip and dart over its surface. At the water's edge there were clusters of creamy white meadowsweet, and here and there graceful purple willow herb swayed gently in the evening air.

'This is a crisp and fruity white wine, chilled to perfection, or so I'm told,' Matt said with a smile, placing a wine glass on the table in front of her. He was drinking lager, served in a tall, thin glass that had frosted over, with small rivulets of condensation running down the side.

'Cheers,' she said, raising her glass to him, and he answered, clinking his glass to hers.

'Good times,' he murmured.

'Yes, we could do with some of those.'

The waitress brought their meals—steak, topped with cheddar and grilled bacon for Matt, and chicken-and-bacon salad for Lucy.

'This looks wonderful,' she said. 'I'm glad we decided to come here.'

'I guess we could both do with a break.' He glanced at her. 'I could see you were troubled today, looking in on the children who were so poorly. The fact is we work in a difficult profession. Most people don't ever, in a lifetime, have to deal with the things we come across every day.'

'No, that's true. It's upsetting to see babies on ventilators, fighting for their lives, and as if that isn't bad enough, we see young children coming in with nasty injuries and we have to do our best to patch them up.'

He speared a button mushroom with his fork and then hesitated, studying her expression. 'You didn't seem to have too much of a problem with young William, but when I saw you looking at the small boy who came in today—Tom—you seemed to be more disturbed by his condition than usual. Are you worried about his prospects of recovery?'

'I suppose there's something of that.' She sipped her wine. 'It made me think about why I decided to take up medicine as a career.'

'Are you beginning to have doubts?'

'Yes, I think I am. Now that I'm actually working in a hospital, on the wards, I'm not sure whether I'm cut out for it…for that kind of emergency or the specialist type of medicine.'

She thought he might be shocked or disturbed by what she'd said, but he studied her thoughtfully and asked, 'So what was it that made you want to go to medical school in the first place? Was it just a vague idea about wanting to help people, to make them well again?'

'No, not really.' She sliced off a piece of new potato and swirled it in the mayonnaise at the side of her plate. 'When I was young, around twelve or thirteen, I saw a neighbour's child knocked down by a car. I was with a friend at the time and, of course, we were both horrified by what we saw. The paramedics came and worked with an emergency doctor, getting her onto a spinal board, putting a tube down her throat to help her breathe, starting up an intravenous line. Of course, I didn't understand much of what they were doing back then, but I knew that they saved her life. She would have bled to death on the road if they hadn't acted quickly.'

She paused, thinking back to that time. 'It made me realise what a worthwhile career medicine was, and I wanted to be able to save lives the way those men did that day.' She'd been so impressed by the way the medics had handled the situation, and later, when she'd gone to visit the girl in hospital, she was amazed at her recovery.

'And now you've seen it from the professional side of things, it worries you?'

'It does a bit. Not that I couldn't do what needs to

be done to save a life, but that working with children, working on the emergency side of things, isn't what I want to deal with every day. Does that sound odd to you?' She gave him a worried look. 'I gave up the chance to work with my father when it was what he wanted most of all, and I still don't want to do that, but I'm having doubts about what would be best thing for me to do.' She frowned. 'I'm not explaining myself very well, am I?'

'I think I understand. It doesn't sound odd to me at all. A lot of people have doubts…after all, it's a big step you're taking.' He finished the last of his steak, and swallowed some of his lager. She watched his throat move, and her glance went to his strong forearms, the sleeves of his shirt rolled back, exposing a gold watch on his wrist.

'But I do think you need to have a bit more confidence in yourself,' he went on. 'I haven't seen you put a foot wrong, and I know that one day you'll make a terrific doctor…maybe not a hospital doctor, if that troubles you, but you're certainly cut out for a medical career.' He smiled reassuringly at her. 'Perhaps you might want to work as a GP one day. I think you would probably enjoy working with children at some point. I saw how you were with baby Sarah, and again with William before he went for surgery—you were gentle and involved, and it occurred to me that maybe a mother-and-baby clinic would be more your style, as part of general practice.'

'Oh…' She looked startled, and then, after a second or two, as his words sank in she gave him a dazzling smile. 'I hadn't looked at it that way. I felt like a failure because I was worried about my reactions to these very sick children—but I think you could be right. I can see myself working in a GP's surgery one day. Thank you for that.'

He grinned crookedly. 'Glad to be of service, ma'am. Maybe we should drink to that.' He lifted his glass once more. 'To fulfilling your dreams, whatever they might be.' He looked into her eyes, and as they toasted one another with their drinks it was as though a warm, intimate bond was forged between them.

They chatted over caramelised apple pie, for Lucy, and strawberry cheesecake, for Matt, and then finished off the meal with liqueur coffees.

'That was absolutely perfect—heavenly,' Lucy said on a sigh, as they left the pub sometime later and began walking back along the towpath. 'Thank you.'

Matt started to say something, but his phone rang at that moment and he stopped walking and gave her an apologetic smile as he started to answer it. She waited, wondering who was calling him, then watched as the colour slowly drained from his face.

'What's wrong?' she asked as he slid the phone back into his pocket. 'Has something bad happened?'

'My father's had a heart attack,' he said, in a strained voice. 'I must go and see him.'

'Oh, Matt, I'm so sorry.' She put her arms around him, hugging him. 'Is there anything I can do? Would you like me to go with you?'

He looked distracted. 'No. I'll go alone, thank you.' He hugged her in return and then gently released himself from her embrace, his hands curving lightly around her arms. 'I'll see you home safely and then I must go. If we leave now, I can be at the hospital within the hour.'

'Of course.' She understood that he needed to be with his father right now, and it was clear that he was deeply shocked by the news. He had to go and find out just how bad things were, and he wanted to be able to comfort his mother and offer her his support. Lucy understood all that. Of course he didn't want her there with him. Even so, a tiny part of her felt as though she'd been rejected all the same.

CHAPTER SIX

'Tom, can you hear me?' Lucy gently stroked the small boy's hand. Throughout the morning she had been talking, on and off, to the five-year-old, testing his responses and trying to assess his level of consciousness.

'He's not doing so well,' she told Mandy with a frown, moving away from the bed, out of earshot of the child's mother and grandmother. 'I was getting some kind of a response earlier on, but now nothing much is registering. Perhaps we should give Matt a call.'

'Okay. I'll go and see to it,' the nurse answered, concern showing in her grey eyes. 'He said we should let him know if there was any change in his condition.'

'Thanks, Mandy. He's over in Neonatal, taking a look at baby Sarah.'

She'd been working with Matt for the first part of the morning, but he hadn't been his usual self, and that wasn't surprising, given what had happened to his father. He was distant, locked into a place within himself that she couldn't reach. Last night he'd come back to the house late, after being with his father for most of the evening. He hadn't said much to anyone, and she'd seen that he'd been very worried about his father's sudden collapse. She'd tried to offer him comfort and sympathy, but he'd been distracted, his whole manner strained and very quiet.

Mandy went to make the call, and Lucy studied the monitors by the child's bed, alarmed by the rise in his blood pressure and the slowing down of his heart rate.

'What's happening? Is something wrong?' Mrs Granger had been sitting quietly with her mother by the bedside, but now she called out in alarm as a sudden bleeping came from one of the monitors.

Tom was restless, his arms and legs twitching every now and again. He started to vomit, and Lucy hurried forward with a kidney bowl, holding it in place for him, and then afterwards, when he had finished being sick, she wiped his brow with a cool, damp cloth. She was relieved that his endotracheal tube was firmly in place, protecting his airway, so there was no danger of him choking. In her experience, it was unusual for a child to vomit once the tube was in place, but she was coming across new things every day.

'It seems that there's some swelling inside his skull,' she explained to the anxious women. 'We have to bring that down and try to make him more comfortable.'

Tom's grandmother frowned. The stress she was going through was clearly visible in her eyes, and her back was stiff with tension. 'I'll never forgive Jack for this,' she said tersely, shooting a glance at her daughter. 'He shouldn't have let the boy run ahead of him in the street—it was an accident waiting to happen.'

'He didn't do that. Jack was holding his hand,' the boy's mother answered wearily, close to tears, her voice thickening. 'Tom pulled away from him.'

'So he says. You said you were looking at something

else and not paying much attention, so you only have his word for it.'

Lucy saw the distress in Miriam Granger's eyes and decided it was time to intervene. 'Ladies, Tom may be able to hear you,' she warned softly. 'Either way, the tone of your voices might be enough to upset him and make his condition worse. I think it would be best if you were to try to stay calm around him.'

'Of course,' Mrs Granger said in a guilty tone. She looked uncomfortable, glancing at her mother as though she feared she might disagree. 'I'm sorry.'

Mrs Cavendish remained quiet, pressing her lips together as though she was finding it a struggle to keep to herself all the things she wanted to say, but after a short while, when she said nothing further, Lucy breathed a silent sigh of relief.

Her satisfaction was short-lived, though. In the next moment the little boy began to shake, his body movements becoming stronger and faster paced as a seizure took hold of him. Lucy saw it happen with a growing sense of frustration. She knew what to do, but as a student she wasn't allowed to prescribe medication, and that put her in a quandary. She looked around, ready to call for help, and saw that Matt had already come into the room and was heading their way. Relief flooded through her.

'How long has this been going on?' he asked.

'It just started. I was just about to call for help.'

'That's okay.' He nodded and left the bedside, coming back within a few seconds armed with a syringe. 'I'm going to give him anti-convulsant medication to

try and bring the seizure under control,' he explained
to the boy's mother.

After he had given the medication, he turned to Lucy
and said in a low voice, 'As soon as we have the seizure
under control, I'll sedate him and give him a painkiller
and then we'll try a diuretic to see if we can reduce
some of the swelling in his brain.'

'Will that be enough?' She was worried about this
little boy. He looked so vulnerable, lying there, and she
wished there was more she could do to help him.

'Possibly not. We'll have to consult with the
neurologist—it could be that we'll need to drain off
some of the cerebrospinal fluid to ease the pressure on
his brain.' He checked the catheter that was already in
place in the boy's head, ready for this event, and then
waited for the seizure to come to an end.

He noted Tom's vital signs and prepared the sedative
and diuretic. 'That's good…it looks as though he's coming out of it…the convulsion's stopped,' he murmured
after a while. 'Let's raise the head of the bed slightly
and try to ease some of that pressure.'

Lucy helped him, and together they looked after the
child for the next few minutes, checking the monitors
constantly. Lucy was aware that treating a brain-injured
child was always going to be a delicate balance—they
had to weigh one drug against another, because any one
of them might cause unwanted side effects that could
hinder recovery. Sedation might cause the child's blood
pressure to drop even more, but seizures and restless-
ness placed more demands on him and could cause
pressure to rise dangerously within the brain.

Matt was calm throughout this time, and Lucy mar-velled at how capable and efficient he was as he checked tubes and drips, adjusted the medication dosage and found time to speak to the child's mother and grand-mother. When the neurologist arrived on the ward, he explained what was going on and discussed with him what needed to be done next.

'Keep him under strict observation, Mandy,' he said now. 'Note everything down on his chart at fifteen-minute intervals and call me if there's any sign of his condition deteriorating. I'll finish off the ward round and then, if I'm needed, I'll be in the cardiac-care unit with my father.'

'Okay. I'll take good care of him,' Mandy answered. 'I hope your father's a bit better today when you go and look in on him.'

'So do I.' Matt's expression was grim, and Lucy's heart went out to him.

'Have you been to see him yet this morning?' she asked, as she followed him to the next bay.

He shook his head. 'I was on duty too early, so I haven't had a chance yet, but I phoned for an update. It's not looking good...but I suppose these are still early days. The scans showed a huge clot in one of his arter-ies. My mother's in pieces.'

She touched his arm lightly, wanting to be close to him. 'It must be really difficult for you, having to come into work when you're so worried. I don't know how you're able to cope. I don't think I'd be able to concen-trate if something like that happened to one of my par-ents.'

He exhaled deeply. 'I don't have much choice but to carry on. We're short-handed here, and Administration has been finding it difficult to bring in locums of late because of the holiday period.' He winced. 'Besides, I'm no good at sitting around. Last night I couldn't do anything but watch him lying there in bed, so ill, and I felt helpless, having to sit back and let others take care of him. I was able to comfort my mother, of course, but I can't be there for her twenty-four hours of the day, much as I'd like to help her.'

Lucy shot him a quick, anxious glance. 'I wasn't criticising you in any way, please don't think that…it's just that I've watched you with the children this morning, and you've been so good with them. No matter how bad you're feeling inside, you've managed to stay professional. I really admire you for that.'

He gave her a brief smile that barely touched his lips. 'You've been a great help to me, keeping me on track, alerting me when things were going on with the patients. I've been trying to do my best, but I'll admit my mind's been elsewhere.' He looked at her with a quizzical expression. 'Actually, I'm not quite sure what you're doing here today. You have your clinical examination this afternoon, don't you? I'd have expected you to be at home, swotting up or talking things through with Jade. I know she's really worried about these exams. Ben told me she hasn't been able to concentrate on anything lately, not even their wedding plans.'

'I know.' Lucy sighed. 'She wanted to shut herself in her room to revise this morning, but I was too jittery to sit still and do that, so I decided to come to the hospital instead and keep busy. I'll be meeting Jade in around an hour for lunch, and then we'll go to the exam hall together.'

He gave her a sympathetic glance. 'I'm sure you'll do just fine. Remember you get points for each step of the procedure so you'll pick up easy marks for simple things like washing your hands before and after examining the patient, and for communication skills—so make sure you introduce yourself, and explain what you are going to do. Take a deep breath before you speak, so that you come across clearly. It's as much about your examination technique and the procedures you follow as it is about finding the correct diagnosis.'

'I'll try to bear that in mind.'

'Like I said, I'm sure you'll be all right.' He gently squeezed her shoulder, his long fingers lightly kneading her taut muscles and sending warm, comforting ripples of sensation coursing through her body. 'You've had lots of practice with patients on the wards. Just imagine that each one you come across this afternoon is someone you're treating at this hospital.'

She gave him a smile. 'I'll try. Thanks for the advice, Matt, and the encouragement.' She sobered, studying his strong, angular features. 'This is all the wrong way round. I should be sympathising with you and offering you support. I know how much you care for your father, and this must have come as an awful shock to you.'

She sighed, thinking about Sam Berenger. 'I remember seeing him at home, some years back, at those parties we were talking about the other day, and he was always good to me. He showed an interest in what I was doing and he was keen to know what I wanted out of life. I wish there was something I could do to help. Maybe, one day, when he's up to it, I could perhaps go with you to see him?'

'Thanks. I know you want to help…' His voice took on a cautious note. 'I know you and my dad got on really well together, but let's just see how things go for a while, shall we? He's definitely not up to seeing anyone outside the family just yet.'

Lucy frowned. Perhaps she'd imagined that he'd stiffened slightly as he'd spoken. What he'd said had been perfectly reasonable, but it was so unlike Matt to be reserved and somehow remote from her this way. She looked at him, trying to fathom what lay in the depths of those haunted, deep, blue eyes, but his thoughts were closed to her, and that bothered her more than she cared to admit.

'It's your mother, isn't it?' she said at last. 'She doesn't want anything to do with my family, does she? She blames my father for what's happened, and my mother and I are being dragged into that by association.'

His shoulders lifted, but he didn't try to deny it. 'She'll come around, sooner or later, but for now it's best not to stir things up, I think. She'll only be resentful, and I don't want to subject you to that.'

'I know,' she said on a sigh. 'I understand, I think… but I'm sorry it's come to this. I wish my father had acted differently, but he's a businessman and, like I said before, he expects everyone to have the same drive and ambition that he has. He sees things in terms of production and profit. He's always been like that. I'm sure he didn't expect anything like this to happen.'

'I know. He rang my mother this morning to pass on his good wishes. She didn't want to speak to him, so I took the call for her.' His dark brows drew together as a monitor bleeped in the distance. 'I have to go and see to that. You should go and prepare for your exam, Lucy. I'll see you later.'

Sadness clutched at her, settling deep in the pit of her stomach, making her tense. Somehow he had withdrawn from her in these last few hours, and it felt as though the easy friendship they had shared up to now was marred, shattered by these latest events. She didn't know what to do. It made her ache inside to see Matt brace his shoulders and move away from her. It came as a shock to discover how deeply she cared for him, and it was only now that she was beginning to realise just how much he meant to her. She didn't want to see their relationship fractured.

Those thoughts stayed with her as she went to meet Jade, but all too soon it was time for them to set off for the building where the final exams were to be held, and she made a determined effort to push everything else to the back of her mind.

'Good luck,' she said to Jade, giving her a hug. 'I'll see you back here when it's all over.'

'You, too.' Jade pulled a face, and they went off to find the first of their assessment stations. For the next few hours they would move from one station to another at five-minute intervals, except for a couple of examinations which would last for fifteen minutes, where they were expected to take a patient history and make a more detailed analysis of the situation.

'Your patient requires sutures to a hand wound,' the female examiner said in this first session, and Lucy looked around the room. Of course there was no patient, only specialised material for her to work on. There was a suture pack laid out on the table, along with sterile gloves and everything that she needed to complete the task. What could go wrong? She knew how to do this, but she only had five minutes to show it. She took a deep breath, and explained what she was about to do. Then she opened the suture pack and put on the gloves, ready to make a start.

She had only managed to do two stitches when a bell rang out, signalling the time had come to an end. That should have been enough to show the examiner that she could do the task, so she dropped the needle into the sharps bin, thanked the woman and left the room, moving on to the second station. So far, so good.

'This patient is complaining of palpitations,' the next examiner said, and for a second or two Lucy's mind went blank. Palpitations…heart problems? She took a brief history from the woman who was simulating being a patient, and listened to her chest with her stethoscope. No heart problem there.

'What is the differential diagnosis?' asked the examiner.

Lucy thought about what Matt had said. *You get points for each step along the way...* So she listed the alternatives—stress, panic attacks, thyroid problems, and so on—and concluded with arrhythmia. 'I would need to take blood samples for testing to exclude or confirm these diagnoses and do an ECG,' she told the examiner, but of course there was no time for that, because when five minutes was up she had to move on once again.

It was stressful, and she was alert and running on adrenaline for the whole of the afternoon, but by the time the practical exams had finished she hoped she had done enough to pass. She wouldn't know the result for another week.

'How did it go?' she asked Jade when they met up for coffee in the cafeteria at the end of the session.

'Okay, I think,' Jade answered cautiously. 'There was one examiner who seemed a little uptight and kept barking questions at me, but I think I managed to keep cool and answer properly without getting flustered. And one of the patients kept arguing with me the whole time I was with her.' She shook her head. 'Perhaps she was asked to act up to see how we handle difficult patients.'

Lucy gave a small shudder. There had been one or two hiccups in her meetings with patients that she still found worrying. 'I'm glad it's over with, anyway. Are you thinking of heading for home now?'

'No. Actually, I said I'd meet Ben at the pub at the Bankside. We both have time off this weekend, so we're going to get something to eat and then drive over to my mother's house to sort out a few glitches in the wedding arrangements—there's been a last-minute hitch with the caterers so we have to choose a different menu and the bakery is querying the order for the cake.'

'Nothing too difficult, then,' Lucy said, smiling. 'I'll walk with you, if you like.'

'That'd be great. I was hoping you would stay and eat with us.'

'Oh, no…I wouldn't want to play gooseberry.'

Jade's mouth curved. 'You'd never be that. Anyway, Matt will be there. Ben rang me a few minutes ago to find out how the exams went. He said he'd met up with him after work, or, at least, Ben finished work and Matt had just come from seeing his father. He thought Matt needed cheering up, so he persuaded him to go along with him. We'll make up a foursome.'

'Okay...' Lucy said slowly. 'As long as Matt's going to be there, too.' She wasn't altogether sure Matt would be in any mood for a get-together, but since it looked as though it had all been arranged, she might as well go along with it. Actually, as Ben and Matt knew the girls were together, they'd probably worked out that it would be a good idea for them all to meet up.

The pub was in an ideal setting, by the river Thames. It was really old, dating back some eight hundred years, a grey stone building with brightly painted windows and flower baskets adding bold colour. There were tables and chairs set out on a paved area by the river bank, and inside there were wooden beams, ships' lanterns and old cider flagons set out on high shelves. It looked good, steeped in history, but Ben waved a hand towards the roof terrace and said, 'Shall we see if we can find a table up there?'

They all agreed it was the best idea, to take advantage of the summer sunshine, and after they'd all taken a look at the menu and decided what they wanted to eat, Ben and Jade went to the bar to place their orders.

It was a popular inn, frequented by office workers, professional people and tourists, and Lucy even saw a friend sitting at a table on the terrace, another fifth-year medical student. They waved to one another and signalled their relief at the end of the dreaded exams.

It was warm outside, the blue of the sky broken only by cotton-wool clouds, and from the roof terrace there was a wonderful view over the river. From here Lucy could see a good deal of the city...there was the magnificent dome of St Paul's cathedral and the great Tower Bridge. She watched the river craft slowly edging towards it and then disappearing into the distance.

Matt came to sit beside her, following her glance across the water to the opposite bank. She pointed to the horizon and said softly, 'You could see the Great Fire of London from here, apparently. I read about this place. The writer, John Evelyn, came to the pub with his family and wrote about it. And they say that Samuel Pepys was a regular here, too—I know he wrote in his diary about the fire, and of coming to see it, but I don't know if he was at this pub on that particular night when the city burned.'

'It's hard to imagine, isn't it?' Matt remarked. 'It must have lit up the sky for miles around.'

Lucy glanced at him. He seemed to have relaxed a little, and she was pleased about that. He'd hardly spoken since they'd met up a short time ago, except to ask her how the exam had gone, but perhaps this historic place was working some kind of healing magic on him. She didn't want to spoil any of that by asking him about his father, but it would have been remiss not to say anything.

'Is there any news from the hospital?' she asked.

'Some. My dad's on medication to reduce the blood clot, of course, but the consultant told us he's planning to do a coronary angioplasty to widen the artery and improve the blood flow. It'll be a lot better for Dad than having to undergo heart bypass surgery, anyway. I don't know quite when they'll do it. I suppose it depends on how strong he is…how well he'll withstand the procedure.'

'How has your mother taken it?'

'All right, I think. She feels a bit better now that he's able to talk a little. It means that he's making some kind of a recovery, but of course these next few days are critical.'

Lucy laid her hand on his. 'Mr Sheldon's a brilliant man. He'll take good care of him.'

'I know. It's just that it's…it's still worrying when it's your own dad that's ill.'

'I know.' She wanted to put her arms around him and hold him close, but this was hardly the place to do it, with so many people all around.

Jade and Ben came back, and after they'd chatted for a few minutes the waitress brought their meals to the table. Lucy tucked into lasagne, and she noted that Matt was eating beer-battered fish and chips, taking his time but gradually making inroads into his meal.

'So, how are your plans for the wedding coming along?' she asked, looking at Ben and Jade. 'In general, apart from the minor glitches, I mean. Will you be moving into the house when you come back from your honeymoon?'

'That's what we're hoping to do,' Ben said, tasting a portion of succulent gammon and smiling his satisfaction. 'It should be ready in time. There's only a bit of decorating to be finished off, some walls to be painted in the hall and up the stairs. You and Matt will have to come to our housewarming once we've settled in.'

'I'd love that,' Lucy said with a smile, taking a sip from her glass of chilled white wine. 'You've worked so hard on it between you, you must be longing to move in.' Matt murmured agreement.

Ben nodded. 'Just as soon as we have the wedding out of the way.' He glanced at Jade. 'The biggest problem we're having at the moment is seeing if we can get Jade's father to walk her down the aisle.'

'He seems to have fallen off the radar somehow,' Jade explained. She frowned, her fork hovering over her dish of pasta. 'I've been doing my best to get in touch with him, but so far I've had no luck. My brothers have been trying, as well, but they're coming up blank, too.'

'If we can't find him, Jade's stepfather will do the honours, so it's not a major calamity. It's just that having her father there would have been the icing on the cake for Jade.' Ben squeezed Jade's hand lightly, and she smiled at him, love shining in her eyes.

'If he were to come to my wedding, it would bring him back into the fold, I think,' she explained. 'He was away from us for so long when we were growing up, but I know he felt sorry about that and wanted to be closer to us. It's just that he's not answering my calls or my letters, so I'm not sure what's happened to him.'

'I hope things work out for you,' Lucy said sincerely.

They finished eating, and after a while Jade and Ben decided it was time that they started out for Jade's home in Amersham. 'We'll see you late on Sunday,' Jade said, giving Lucy a hug. 'Thank heaven those exams are over. I'm feeling quite light-headed all at once.'

'Enjoy your weekend,' Matt said.

They watched their friends go, and Lucy said in a low voice, 'We should do something about getting them a wedding present. The wedding will be on us before we know it.' She bit her lip. 'I'll be going home to spend the weekend with my parents, though, so it's going to be difficult to find the time.'

'And I'm on duty at the hospital. What about Monday? Do you have any free time then? I'll have the afternoon off.'

'That sounds good to me. We don't have any lectures now that the exams are over.'

She leaned back in her seat. Matt didn't show any sign of wanting to leave the pub, and Lucy was content with that. She liked being there with him.

'Would you like another drink?' he asked, and when she opted for a second glass of chilled white wine, he left her and went to the bar.

Lucy glanced around, catching sight of her medical-student friend once more. It looked as though the girl and her companions were getting ready to leave. They exchanged smiles once more, and on her way out the girl stopped by the table, sliding into the empty seat beside her. 'It's getting busy in here, isn't it?' she said. 'They must all be like us, wanting to let their hair down after a hectic week.' She laughed. 'Except that we've had more than a week of it, haven't we? I'm glad today's over and done with.'

'I know what you mean,' Lucy agreed. 'Did you get the examiner who seemed determined to catch people out?'

'I did. She really put me through it.' The girl made a face and then stood up. 'I must go. My friends will be waiting for me.'

'Okay, see you.' Lucy gazed around once more. It wouldn't be long before the empty table was filled. There were lots of tourists here, keen to lap up the ambiance of this pub at the centre of Victorian England, and even now she saw a group of people walking onto the roof terrace. She heard snatches of conversation, laughter, and as she glanced towards the steps once more she caught the sound of her own name being spoken. She froze. That voice had a familiar ring to it.

'Lucy?' A tall man, dark haired, immaculately dressed in a grey business suit, was with the group of people heading for the empty table in the corner of the terrace. His jacket hung open because of the heat of the day, and beneath it he wore a fine linen shirt. He walked towards her. 'It's good to see you. How are you? It's been a long time. Too long.'

'Hello, Alex.' She managed to find her voice. 'I'm fine, thanks. How are you?'

'Much better for seeing you.' He sat down next to her. 'I hope your girlfriend doesn't mind me taking her chair for a minute or two.' He smiled. 'I've been in London for about three months, now—I've been trying to call you, but you must have changed your number. I was hoping I might bump into you one day.'

'We both lead busy lives, I guess.' Her mind was reeling with the shock of seeing him. She'd imagined that he still lived in Berkshire.

He leaned closer, his hand resting on the back of her seat. 'Maybe you and I could get together one day? I felt really bad about what happened between us. I always knew, deep down, you were the only girl for me. I made a stupid mistake.' He hesitated, looking at her earnestly, his face just inches away from hers. 'Let me make it up to you.'

That was never going to happen. She gave a slight

shake of her head, her mouth making a downward curve. Out of the corner of her eye, she saw Matt coming towards them, carrying two glasses. 'It's too late for that, Alex,' she said in a sober voice. 'We've both moved on since then.'

'Not me. I can't move on, Lucy...not without you.' He grasped her hand, cupping it with his own, and her heart sank. This was how he'd been before, never wanting to let go after she'd ended their relationship. It was only after she'd moved into her father's student house and had taken up placements at the local hospital that she'd managed to evade him. She'd even had to change her phone number.

'I'm sorry,' she said, trying to draw her hand away from his. She glanced at Matt as he reached the table. 'I'm not a free agent any more,' she stated clearly, turning her attention back to Alex. 'I have a boyfriend.' She waved a hand towards Matt, hoping that he would play along. 'So, you see, I'm not looking to start over.'

Matt's gaze narrowed. He placed the glasses on the table and said in a firm tone, 'I think, perhaps, introductions are in order?'

'Matt, this is Alex Ryder,' she said quickly. 'He used to work for my father.'

'I see.' He laid an arm around her shoulders. 'I have a feeling there's something I'm missing here.' He studied Alex as though he was sizing him up. 'Were you and Lucy an item at one time?'

'I... Yes...that's right...' Alex hastily pulled his hand away from hers as though it was scorching him. 'We were together for a couple of years when she first started medical school.'

'Really?' Matt frowned. 'It's a good thing that's well and truly over with, then, because, as she said, Lucy's with me now. Has been for some time.'

Lucy slowly exhaled, relief washing over her. Alex was still seated, but under Matt's penetrating stare he became uncomfortable and after a second or two he stood up.

'I… Perhaps I should go,' he said, looking hot under the collar. 'I'm glad you're okay, Lucy.'

She nodded. 'Goodbye, Alex.'

Alex moved away, going over to the table in the corner to join his friends, and Lucy looked up at Matt. 'Thank you for that,' she said. 'It was a tricky situation.'

'So I gathered.' He kept his arm around her. 'We've been in this situation before,' he commented dryly, 'with me stepping in at an opportune moment. Perhaps we should make an announcement—Matt and Lucy are an item.'

She laughed. 'Well, there's a thought.'

His gaze trailed over her and he smiled. 'Oh, yes. Definitely.' He didn't say any more, but slowly released her and came to sit down beside her at the table. Lucy was bemused. She never knew whether Matt was for real or whether he was teasing her.

Would it be such a bad idea if they were to be 'an item,' as he put it? She was finding more and more that she wanted to be with him all the time. And yet that was madness, wasn't it? Hadn't she had her fingers burned already? Why would Matt turn out to be any different from all the other men who simply wanted to get her into bed? He hadn't made any moves in that direction so far, but it could be that living in her father's house made him cautious. He knew how difficult her father could be regarding the men in her life.

'So tell me about this Alex,' Matt said, sitting down and swallowing his drink. 'He obviously still hankers after you. What did you do to him to put him in such a tizzy?'

'Me?' She stared at him wide-eyed. 'Nothing. It was the other way round.'

He paused, his glass an inch or so from his lips. 'Is he the one who managed to turn you off men?'

'I wouldn't say I was off men, exactly…I just had a bad experience and I went off the whole dating game for a while. You could say I was disillusioned.'

'Hmm.' He took another swallow. 'So who is he? Is he the one who caused you all those problems?' He put his glass down and looked her over. 'You were as white as a sheet when he was sitting down next to you. What happened with him? You said you were together for a couple of years, so there must have been some kind of rapport.'

'To begin with, yes, there was.' She toyed with her wine glass and then lifted it to her lips and drank as though she needed its invigorating strength. 'He's an architect, and he did quite a lot of work for my father, designing extensions to buildings, organising renovations and so on. That's how we met—I'd go home for the occasional weekend, and he would be at the house.' She gave a wry smile. 'I think my father arranged things that way. He was always vetting the men in my life, but he seemed to think Alex was the one for me, and he made a point of getting us together. To his mind, Alex had the right background, good manners and he seemed personable. So he was really pleased when Alex asked me out. I thought Alex was okay, so I agreed. It all started from there.'

He frowned. 'But it all went wrong?'

'Yes.' She began to fidget. 'Do you think we could get out of here? I can feel him staring at me. I'd like to go.' She drained the last of her wine, and looked at Matt.

'Sure.' He was already getting to his feet, and now he reached for her hand and drew her up from her chair. 'Your wish is my command, princess.'

She shot him a quick glance. She wasn't sure how to take that. Was he poking fun at her again? He seemed serious enough, though, and after a minute or two, when they were walking along the path by the river, she began to relax a little.

It was late evening by now, and a gentle breeze was blowing in off the river, riffling through her hair. Matt glanced at her, watching as she tucked the errant strands behind her ear.

'Are you feeling better now?' he asked. 'At least the colour's back in your cheeks.'

'I'm fine.'

'Good. So, do you want to tell me what happened with Alex?'

She pulled in a deep breath. 'Nothing too unexpected. He was all over me to begin with, even though I was cautious. He bought me flowers, small gifts, anything to try to win me round, but he was always a bit over the top, I thought. I got the feeling he liked being with the boss's daughter, that I was some sort of prize. He kept talking about getting engaged… I just wondered occasionally if marrying into a wealthy family was more important to him than I was. But he could be funny, and charming, and bit by bit I was beginning to think the two of us might make a go of it.'

She hesitated, thinking back to that time, and her vision clouded. 'It took a while before I realised I'd made a mistake.'

'He must have put a foot wrong, somewhere along the line,' Matt remarked.

She shrugged. 'It was partly my fault, I think. My career was important to me, and I was working really hard, studying, wanting to do well. He didn't understand that. He said I didn't need to do it when I could work for my father and not have to worry about anything.'

'But, of course, you couldn't do that?'

'No. He obviously didn't know me very well. Even though I'd tried to explain, he had no real idea how much it meant to me to break away and do what was really important to me. So I carried on studying and he went off and amused himself in the meantime.'

'Ah…' Matt watched her closely. 'By that you mean he found another woman?'

'Women. He played around, and I only found out about it when I dropped by his flat unexpectedly one day and caught him in bed with a girl who worked at the local store. And then I found a receipt for a necklace he'd bought for someone—his sister told me he'd given it to an old flame.' She gave a heavy sigh. 'I felt humiliated, and embarrassed because I was naïve enough to be fooled that way. I'm still embarrassed about it to this day.'

'There's no reason for you to feel that way. He's a

jerk.' Matt put his arm around her and drew her close.
'I'm sorry that happened to you, Lucy.' He looked
around, and waved a hand towards a building in the
distance. 'If I had my way, that's where he'd be.' He
smiled grimly. 'Only I'd have it in its original state, not
the way it is now.'

He was pointing to the Clink Museum, the site of the
old prison where, years ago, ne'er-do-wells had spent
their time contemplating their sins. She laughed. 'You'd
have him thrown in the clink—that's a bit drastic, but I
like it.'

'It's ironic, isn't it?' he mused, 'that a man your father actually approved of should turn out to be so wrong
for you?'

'It just goes to show that my father's only human,'
she said. 'Sometimes he gets things wrong.'

He nodded. 'I wonder if he's come to realise he was
wrong to expect you to stay in the family business?
What does he think, these days, about you becoming a
doctor?'

'He doesn't talk about it. But I suppose he gets to
hear about what I'm up to from my mother. I call her
regularly and let her know what's going on. She's been
worrying about the exams and asking how the revision
was going. I've no idea what my father thinks about it,
apart from the fact he thinks I can spend time on his
projects, as well as doing my revision.' She shrugged.
'Perhaps that says it all.'

'Maybe.' His glance ran over her. 'So you'll be able
to put your mother's mind at rest now that it's all over
bar the waiting?'

Her mouth curved. 'Well, maybe she'll be relaxed

about it—as long as I leave a few things out in the telling.'

They'd reached a quiet part of the walkway by now, and came to stand by railings, looking out over the river. Dusk was falling, and the branches of a tree nearby swayed gently in the faint breeze. The silver moon cast its beams on the water, sprinkling a myriad of sparkling gems over its surface.

Matt sent her a quizzical glance. 'What do you mean?' he asked. 'You said there were a couple of things that bothered you—I took it to mean that there were questions you had trouble with. Was I right? That won't necessarily mean that you've failed.'

'I hope not...only I did mess up a couple of times.'

'What happened?'

She pulled in a quick breath. 'One time, I had to test some blood and urine samples and the examiner kept barking questions at me, and had me so flustered at one stage that I almost knocked them over.' She gave a small shudder. 'But that wasn't the worst of it.' She sighed, thinking back over the afternoon.

Matt put his arms around her. 'It can't have been too bad, can it? From what you told me earlier, things seemed to have gone quite well.'

'Yes, but I didn't tell you about the CPR test, did I?' He shook his head, and she went on, 'There was a medical dummy in the room, a manikin, and the examiner said, "This man has collapsed. What will you do?" So I checked for signs of life and called for a crash team. Then I set to and started chest compressions, just as we've been taught, fifteen compressions, two ventilations. I did two cycles of that and then checked for signs of life again. The examiner came closer to see what I was doing. He was bending over to one side of me as I started the next lot of compressions, and maybe I was too vigorous or something, I don't know, but the manikin's arm suddenly shot up and smacked him in the face.'

'You're joking!' Matt choked.

'I'm not. I wish I was. But that's not all of it. I said, "Oh, I'm sorry. Have I broken it?" And he was holding his nose and said, "No, I don't think it's too bad. It's probably just bruised." And I said, "Um… I was talking about the manikin."'

Matt started to laugh. 'Oh, Lucy, you're priceless. I hope he has a sense of humour.'

'So do I. But I'm not sure really. He just grunted something and then the bell went and I had to move on to the next station.'

He was still laughing and she gave him a playful punch on the arm. 'It isn't funny…well, maybe a bit, but it wasn't at the time.'

He wound his arms more tightly around her and drew her to him. 'I'll keep a lookout for a consultant with a black and blue nose, and I'll know exactly who to blame if he fails you.'

He looked down at her, smiling, his face shadowed in the moonlight, but she could see the glitter of his eyes, and her gaze was so intent on him that she saw the precise moment when laughter turned to contemplation and then slid into passionate intent.

His head lowered, he came closer, so close that his lips were just a breath away from hers, and then, after what seemed to Lucy like an achingly long time, he kissed her, tenderly at first and then as the fever took hold of him he deepened the kiss and his lips pressured hers, tasting, exploring, drinking from her as though she was the fountain of life itself. He eased her backwards against the trunk of the nearby tree, his long body following, moving against her, his thighs tangling with hers, so that sensation after sensation burst in small explosions all over her body, wherever they touched.

It took her breath away. Matt was kissing her, shaping her body with his hands as though he couldn't get enough of her, and she realised that she wanted this, needed it, in fact. She clung to him, kissing him fiercely in return, loving every moment, her body on fire where his hands caressed her, seeking out every dip and curve. She couldn't get enough of him, and he, it seemed, would not be satisfied until he'd kissed every inch of her bare skin, his lips gliding over her throat, the creamy slopes of her shoulders, nudging aside the thin straps of her cotton top, and then returning to dip down and discover the gentle swell of her breasts.

She was aching with need, and reached up to run her fingers through the silky hair at the nape of his neck. A soft groan rumbled deep in his throat, and he said raggedly, 'I've wanted to do this for so long. I've longed to hold you and kiss you like this. You can't imagine how difficult it's been, keeping away from you, when all I wanted to do was hold you in my arms.'

She whispered softly, 'Why did you hold back?'

He sighed, bending his head so that his cheek lay against hers. 'All sorts of reasons…and all of them are just as valid now. I shouldn't have done this…I know I shouldn't…but I couldn't help myself.'

Voices sounded on the night air, and Lucy came to her senses, shocked by the intrusion, and realised that they were out in the open, where people could disturb them at any minute. Matt eased himself away from her, holding her at arm's length as though he couldn't quite bring himself to let her go.

Then a group of young people came to look at the river, and Matt drew her away, walking with her through the quiet streets. They didn't talk much, each busy with their own thoughts.

Matt was right, of course. There were all sorts of reasons why they shouldn't be together, and looming largest among them was his family. His mother was going through a bad time, blaming Lucy's father for what had happened to her husband. She would be horrified to know that Matt was involved with her in any other way than as a tenant of the house where they both lived.

There was no way Lucy could put that right. She had spoken to her father, warned him what might happen, but he had ignored her pleas.

And now circumstances had overtaken them, and Matt's father was desperately ill, just when she had discovered what it was that she really wanted.

She wanted Matt. More than that, she loved him.

CHAPTER SEVEN

'Okay, so which song would you like me to play for you next?' It was Matt's voice, coming from the central area of the children's ward.

Intrigued, Lucy walked towards the nurses' station and saw Matt, sitting on a straight-backed chair, strumming his guitar in front of a rapt audience of children.

The children called out or stuck their hands in the air, all clamouring at once for his attention, and it seemed the majority vote was for a pop song heading the charts right now. Matt cheerfully obliged. He sang, as well as played, and Lucy's legs turned to jelly as she listened to the throbbing lilt of the melody.

He was pitch perfect, and his voice was so sexy, so expressive that she started to come out in goose bumps all over. He'd mastered guitar playing so well that it seemed as though the music was an integral part of him. She closed her eyes and listened, letting the sound flow all around her. It was heavenly. She could have listened to him forever.

But the song came to an end all too soon. A ward assistant brought a trolley round, loaded with milky drinks, and began to serve them to the children, while

Mandy started a second round of blood-pressure and temperature checks.

'I'll play some more for you later,' Matt responded to the children who wanted him to go on with the impromptu concert. 'I have to go and look after those youngsters who are too poorly to listen to music.' He smiled, and ruffled the hair of a boy who came and asked if he could try the guitar for himself. 'Two minutes, then,' Matt said, 'and after that you must hop back into bed or Mandy will be telling me off. I'll let you have another go later on.' He handed the guitar to the twelve-year-old, who plucked happily at the strings for a while.

Matt caught sight of Lucy, waiting by the desk, and his smile instantly made her light up inside. 'It's good to see you,' he said as she walked towards him. 'How are you doing?'

'Suffering from lack of sleep,' she answered ruefully. 'I came home late last night from my parents' house and could have slept for a week. As it was, I snoozed all through the first alarm and couldn't believe it when the second one started shrieking in my ear. I think all my adrenaline's run out now that the exams are over and the medical school term is almost finished.'

'You must have needed the rest,' he murmured, scooting the boy back to bed and placing his guitar behind the desk. He turned to give Lucy his full attention. 'How are you getting on with your father?'

'We're all right, but it would be better for me if I weren't so reliant on him,' she said cautiously, following Matt to a treatment bay.

'You mean, because he pays for the roof over your head?'

She nodded. 'If I pass my exams and become a qualified doctor, at least I'll be able to start paying him back. And he'll be less likely to drop things on me at a moment's notice...or try to check on the men in my life.'

He shook his head. 'I don't think that's going to happen. He loves you. Whatever he does, it's because he cares about you.'

'Even though I didn't stay with the family firm?' Her voice took on a cynical edge. 'I let him down. I don't think he's going to forget that in a hurry.'

'Well, you never know. He might respect you for making a stand.'

'And one day pigs might fly.'

'And that, too.' He laughed. 'Anyway, we've work to do. If we stand here much longer, people will think we've given up on medicine altogether.'

'Yes, you're right.' She looked around, dragging her mind back to the work at hand. 'Are we going to take a look at the new admission?'

'Yes.' Matt was already leafing through the infant's chart. 'Alice Jackson...two-and-a-half years old.' He frowned. 'Her mother says she's been generally unwell, lethargic, with abdominal cramps and irritability. She cries a lot. There seems to be some muscle weakness, too.' He pulled in a deep breath. 'Let's go and find her.'

A couple of minutes later Lucy looked down at the infant in the cot. 'Poor little mite.' The toddler was whimpering to herself, clearly unhappy, her cheeks tear-stained. 'We'll have to hurry up and find out what's going on with you, won't we?' She turned to Matt.

'From the looks of her, she's dehydrated. Shall I set up a normal saline line?'

'Yes, just as soon as I've finished checking her over.' Matt ran his stethoscope over the girl's chest, and when he'd finished he moved to one side to allow Lucy to listen to her chest.

'Her heart rate's seems to be slow,' Lucy said, concentrating on the heartbeat. 'I think we should do an ECG.'

He nodded. 'That was my thought, too. Her blood pressure's high.' He put his stethoscope away and wrote the figures down on the girl's chart. 'We'll get some blood and urine tests done, and see what they come up with.'

Lucy set up the ECG and waited for the printout that would show them if the child's heart was behaving normally.

A few minutes later she tore off a section of the printout and showed it to Matt. 'The heartbeat is definitely irregular,' she pointed out. 'It's too slow. Could there be a problem with the heart muscle, one that's disrupting the electrical signals?'

'It's possible. We'll wait and see what results we get from the tests then we'll be able to decide on a course of action.'

'Okay, what next?'

He glanced at his watch. 'I'm going over to Neonatal to check up on baby Sarah—I'm keeping my fingers crossed that there have been no more setbacks. Her parents can't take much more. They're already worrying about brain damage.' He brooded on that for a moment, and then said, 'I think we'll probably try taking her off the ventilator some time this week. She hasn't had any more seizures and she's managed to put on a little weight. We'll just have to see how it goes and hope that she can manage to breathe on her own.'

'I thought she had a little more colour in her cheeks when I looked at her first thing this morning,' Lucy commented. She glanced around the ward. 'What would you like me to do? I looked in on Tom, the five-year-old, earlier this morning.' The boy's grandmother was still arguing with her son-in-law, and Lucy shuddered inwardly. She felt for the boy's mother. She would hate to have her relationship marred in that way, with the people she loved most at odds with each other. An image of Matt and her father flitted through her mind, only to be replaced by one of Matt's mother frowning at the thought of any liaison between Lucy and her son. It was as though they were doomed at the outset.

She cut off those thoughts and turned her attention back to work. 'The neurosurgeon drained some of the excess fluid from his brain, and he's just waiting to see if he responds to the medication.'

'Hmm. That could take some time.' He glanced through the files on the nearby desk. 'You could look in on young William and take his stitches out. He seemed a lot better yesterday, so with any luck we can get him up and about in a few days. Once his blood count has stabilised he'll be able to go home.'

'All right.' She nodded. 'I can do that.' She sent him a quick look. 'Are we still on for that trip to the shops this afternoon? I thought maybe Jade and Ben might like to have something special, like a set of crystal wine glasses or a beautiful ornament for their new house.

They probably have all the basics already, like towels, duvets, microwave oven, and so on.'

'Yes, of course. I'll have to come back to the hospital to look in on my father when we've finished, though. He really looks forward to having visitors, even though he gets tired afterwards. He hates being cooped up in hospital, but he's too ill to fight it.' He smiled. 'I'll come and find you as soon as I've finished in Neonatal—and I just want to take a quick look at William before we go. Crystal sounds good.'

He left the ward, and Lucy went to look in on the ten-year-old who'd come in after the traffic accident a few weeks ago and ended up needing to go to Theatre for an emergency repair to his spleen.

Now he was sitting up in bed, and she was pleased to see that he looked much brighter today.

'Hi, William,' she greeted him. 'How are you doing?'

'Okay.' He shrugged. 'The doctor said I was going to have my stitches out today.' He sent her a guarded look. 'Will it hurt?'

Lucy smiled and shook her head. 'No. You'll be fine. I'm going to do it myself. I promise you I'll be very gentle and you'll hardly know I'm doing it.'

He cheered up at that, and showed her the game he was playing on his hand-held console. 'I'm on level ten,' he told her.

'Level ten? Heavens, you're good, aren't you?' She pulled a face. She'd borrowed Matt's console last week so that she could have a go, but her efforts were dismal by comparison. 'I only managed to get to level five,' she told him. 'And now Dr Berenger keeps telling me he's the man, 'cos he reached level ten, same as you.'

William laughed. 'I like him. He's way good on the guitar, and he brings me comic books and talks to me about football and stuff.'

'Yes, I've noticed... He always has something or other in his pockets, doesn't he? I expect he'll be along to see you before he goes off for lunch. He'll want to check your operation scar.' She watched him play the game for a few minutes and then went to gather together what she needed to remove the boy's sutures.

'This is easy-peasy,' she told him, as she set out her sterile pack. 'You'll feel a slight pulling sensation, that's all. I'm going to clean the area first of all, so you just have to lie back and relax. Watch television while I do it, if you like.'

'Yeah,' he said, looking up at the screen. '*Robots on Planet Mars* is just starting. That's well good.'

She smiled. It was good to see him looking perky after all he'd been through.

When she had finished removing all the stitches, William looked down at her handiwork. 'That didn't take long,' he commented. 'Mum will be surprised when she comes back from having lunch. She didn't know I was having them out.' He frowned. 'Do you think there'll be a scar?'

Lucy studied the line of stitching. 'Just a faint line, perhaps. I think you'll still be just as handsome and wow the girls.'

He grinned. 'Oh, yeah.'

Matt came along and inspected the healed wound. 'That's looking good,' he said. 'We need to make sure you keep the area clean for a bit longer, so the nurse will come and put a dressing on it once your mother has

had a chance to take a look. I think she'll be pleased.
It's healthy looking, and the surgeon made a very neat
job of it.'

They left William a few minutes later. 'I think we've
done everything that was necessary,' Matt said, glancing at Lucy, 'and I've handed over to the registrar, so if
you're ready, we can go.'

'I'm ready.' She collected her bag and they headed
out of the hospital. 'I think it might be best if we take
the tube and head for Oxford Circus. There are a few
department stores we could check out along Oxford
Street.'

'Okay. That sounds good.'

Sometime later they emerged from the Underground
and walked through the city streets, looking into shop
windows, stopping every now and again to go inside a
store and check out the glassware. Lucy bought a pretty
jewellery box as a gift for her mother's birthday.

Outside, it was a clear, bright day, a little cooler than
usual, but she breathed in the fresh air and was glad that
Matt was by her side. He wore tailored grey trousers and
a crisp shirt that matched the colour of his eyes. He'd
undone the top buttons of his collar, and Lucy's gaze
was drawn to the pale bronze of his skin. She yearned
to gently trail her lips over his warm throat and feel the
throb of his pulse against her cheek.

He sent her an oblique glance, a faint smile playing around his mouth, and a rush of heat flowed along
her cheekbones. Had he seen her looking at him? He
couldn't possibly know what she'd been thinking, could
he?

'How about this store?' Matt said. 'There should be

a pretty good selection of glassware in here. And then, when we've finished looking around, we could go up to the bistro and have some lunch. I'm starving.'

They stepped inside the department store, a complete contrast to the outside world. In here, everything glittered under the bright, artificial lighting, all the surfaces were smooth and polished, and the air was heavy with fragrance from the assortment of perfumes on sale. They took the escalator up to the third floor and wandered around the displays, mulling over vases and decanters and all types of sparkling crystalware.

'What about these?' Matt suggested, pointing out a set of beautiful, elegant champagne flutes with deeply etched lines and an embossed design.

Lucy gazed at them. 'Oh, yes. They're lovely. Absolutely perfect.'

They smiled at one another. 'That was easy enough,' Matt said. 'I thought we might be looking around all afternoon. As it is, we're all done and dusted and it's still not yet three o'clock. There's time for us to go and grab something to eat, and then we can explore for a bit, if you like.'

'Are you sure? What about your father? Will he be expecting you soon?'

He shook his head. 'The consultant will be looking in on him this afternoon, so I'll give him some space.' He gave her a quizzical look. 'Is there anything you'd like to see in particular?'

Lucy gave it some thought. 'The London Eye,' she said. 'I've always wanted to ride on it, but so far I've never had the chance.' She pulled a face. 'And I think usually there's quite a queue.'

'It may not be too bad. I'll phone ahead to see if I can book a couple of tickets—that way we might not have to wait so long.'

'That's a great idea.'

He made the booking then led the way to the bistro, where they had a late lunch, filling up on tapas dishes, delicious Spanish rice and prawns with onion, and spicy chicken wings with salad.

'Mmm…mmm…I love this food,' Lucy murmured, reluctantly putting down her fork, too full to eat any more and quenching her thirst with an ice-cold spritzer. 'This is turning out to be a great day. I never expected it somehow. It's funny how moods can be lightened with a bit of sunshine and retail therapy, isn't it?'

Matt's gaze meshed with hers. 'I think this is the first time in months that I've seen you looking so relaxed. It's good to see you this way.'

She was content for the first time in a long while. Matt knew everything about her. He looked beneath the surface and saw the woman with doubts and uncertainties, and he understood that she was cautious about men who only wanted her for the way she looked. She felt safe with him. She knew him, knew everything about him that was important, and she could easily imagine spending the rest of her life with him. It felt right, as though it was meant to be.

He held her hand as they left the bistro, and Lucy felt a warm surge of happiness flow through her. Maybe something would happen to bring her down to earth again before too long, but for now she was walking on air, and she was going to make the most of it.

They made their way to the London Eye, and she was

surprised to discover that there wasn't a huge queue of people waiting to board. She stepped inside the capsule with Matt, and instead of going over to the central seating area they went to stand by the glass window so that they could enjoy the panoramic view of London.

Matt slipped his arm around her waist, and together they looked for the landmark buildings—the Houses of Parliament on the right, Big Ben, and to the east, St Paul's Cathedral and the 'Gherkin,' one of the tallest buildings in London. 'I love the way the sunlight reflects on the glass,' Lucy said. 'To me it's one of the most beautiful buildings in the city.'

'Mmm, you're right.'

She glanced at him. 'You're not looking at it,' she murmured. Instead, his gaze was fixed steadily on her, gliding over her long, golden hair and coming to rest on the full, pink curve of her mouth.

'That's because I'm feasting my eyes on something far more lovely,' he said huskily against her cheek. 'I just wish we were alone up here so that I could show you how good you make me feel.'

She snuggled into the crook of his arm and looked down at the river flowing beneath them. She wanted this moment to last forever but, of course, it couldn't.

They stepped out of the glass pod at ground level, and walked by the river for a while. The chimes of Big Ben rang out, and Lucy suddenly remembered that Matt had to go back to the hospital. A small wave of sadness hit her. She didn't want the afternoon to end.

Even so, she said, 'You're supposed to be visiting your father, aren't you? It's all right…I'll understand if you need to go.'

'Come with me,' he said.

'Are you sure?' Her heart gave a small leap in her chest. He must have changed his mind about keeping her away from his family and that was altogether re-assuring. He was prepared to let his parents know that she was part of his life.

'I'm sure.'

They took the tube back to the hospital in order to save time. Matt was concerned about his father's con-dition, and as their destination drew closer, the quieter he became.

'Is he strong enough for the operation yet?' she asked, as they left the Underground and walked the short distance to the hospital.

'He's stronger than he was, so there's a good chance the consultant will do it within a few days,' he acknowl-edged. 'The trouble is, my father won't rest. Once he started to feel a bit better, he began to phone the of-fice, checking up on how things were going. Some of his men were due to start work on the waterfront house, just as soon as the materials were delivered, and he's been agitating to give them the go-ahead. Of course, that means keeping an eye on things, making sure the job's done properly and with a decent time frame.'

'But he can't do that, surely?' Lucy was appalled that he would even consider it.

He pulled a face. 'You'd have thought not, wouldn't you? But my father's never been one to stay idle, and he was getting himself worked up about things, so I had to step in. I told him I'd oversee the project and report back to him.'

'Matt, how on earth can you pull that off? You're

working all hours. When you're not at the hospital, you're playing gigs somewhere or other—you need some time to yourself.' They went through the main doors of the hospital and made for the lift bay.

'I've been stopping by the house whenever I had the chance—like this weekend, after work, for instance.' He pressed the button for the lift. 'It's coming along okay, I think, but my father's still agitating. He can't bear to be out of things, away from where it's all going on.'

'I can see why he and my father get on—or rather, used to get on. I'm not sure how they feel about one another now, after what's happened…but they're two of a kind, aren't they? My father pushes, and yours can't say no.'

Matt acknowledged that with a smile. 'One thing's for certain, my dad is going to have to start saying no, or he'll be in deep trouble healthwise.'

By now they had reached his father's ward, and even before they reached his bed it was clear that all was not well. Sam was sitting up in bed, tapping the keyboard of a laptop and pausing every now and again to talk on his mobile phone. He looked harassed, out of breath, and the monitor beside him had started to bleep. Already Lucy sensed the tension building up in Matt.

'What do you think you're doing?' he demanded, going over to his father's bedside. 'Didn't I tell you there was to be no working while you were in hospital?' He glowered at the laptop. 'And what do I find the minute my back's turned?'

His father gave a guilty start. 'Oh, it's nothing.' He fought for breath. 'Just a small thing I needed to clear up.'

'There's no need for you to be clearing anything up.

I told you I would deal with everything. I'm perfectly capable, or don't you trust me?'

'Of course I do, I…' He broke off, unable to speak, and the display on the heart monitor started to show a chaotic, uncoordinated pattern.

'He's gone into V-fib,' Lucy cried, shocked. She called for a crash team at the same time as she saw Matt's father slump against his pillows. His heart had stopped pumping blood around his body, and instead it was quivering in a way that could lead to complete cardiac arrest. She quickly moved the laptop and phone out of the way.

Matt delivered a precordial thump to his father's chest, aiming to stimulate his heart into a normal rhythm, but although the monitor registered a correction for a short time, Sam's heart reverted back to ventricular fibrillation.

Matt began chest compressions, while the crash team prepared the defibrillator. He stood back while the registrar placed the paddles on his father's chest and delivered a shock to the heart. There was no change. The registrar gave Sam a second shock and as they all waited, silent, tense and alert, the monitor blipped and a normal rhythm was established.

Lucy sighed with relief and glanced at Matt. He was drained of colour, standing there, not moving, and she went over to him and laid a hand on his shoulder, wanting to comfort him but conscious of everyone around them.

'He's back,' she said softly. 'It's over…you can relax now.'

He nodded, but still he didn't move. And then Lucy

became aware that his mother had come into the room
and was looking anxiously at her husband, taking in
everything that had happened.

Lorraine Berenger turned to her son. 'It's that house,'
she said. 'He's done nothing but work on it since he
began to recover, and now look at him, barely hanging
on to life.' Her shoulders sagged. 'I can't take much
more of this.' Her expression was bleak, and Matt put
an arm around her, drawing her close.

Lucy stepped back, out of the way. His mother's gaze
followed her, flint sharp, bright with condemnation. She
didn't say anything, but she didn't have to. Lucy knew
that she blamed her every bit as much as her father for
what had happened. The house was Lucy's project, but
it had rapidly become Sam's.

'I'll go,' Lucy said softly.

'You don't need to do that. Stay…' Matt said, but seeing his mother's stony features Lucy shook her head.

'You need to be with your parents,' she murmured.
'I'll see you later, back at the house.'

'I don't know how long I'll be. You don't have to go,'
Matt insisted.

'I know. That's all right. Don't worry about it.'

She left the room and walked back to the lift. She felt
lonely, empty inside, as though she'd been cast adrift
on a cold and choppy sea.

CHAPTER EIGHT

'IS THERE any news about your father?' Ben asked, helping himself to scrambled egg and glancing across the breakfast table towards Matt.

Lucy was spreading butter on her toast, but now she looked up, wanting to hear Matt's answer. More than a week had passed since his father's second collapse, and though she'd regularly asked him how he was doing, so far he'd been noncommittal.

She missed the closeness she'd shared with Matt. Between work, his visits to the hospital to see his father and the gigs that had come up of late, she hadn't been able to spend much time alone with him. And on those occasions when they had been together, Ben and Jade had also been in the house.

Perhaps it was just as well that things were going this way. She longed for things to go back to how they had been before that fateful day, but his mother's reaction to her had shown her that there would always be a barrier to any relationship between her and Matt, especially if his father didn't recover.

'I think he's a little stronger now,' Matt answered. He lifted the coffee pot and looked at Lucy and Jade to see if they wanted their cups topped up. Lucy nodded, sliding her cup forward. 'The consultant is thinking about doing the coronary angioplasty in a couple of days,' he went on, as he poured coffee. 'Having a stent put in to widen the artery will certainly improve his quality of life, and as long as he stops working and gets all the rest he needs, he should do all right.'

Lucy smiled. 'You took his laptop off him, so that must have helped.'

'Yeah…' He grinned. 'And the nurses are monitoring his use of the phone. Not that he'll get any joy from ringing the office, anyway. I've put all the employees under strict instructions not to answer any of his calls. My brother's helping to keep an eye on that, too.'

'It's good news about the operation, anyway,' Lucy said. 'Your mother will be relieved, I imagine. Is she a bit more relaxed about the situation these days?'

'I'm not so sure about that.' He winced. 'She's been working on him to persuade him that he needs to break off the partnership and go it alone. He'd make a go of it because he has a full order book, but he's been with your father for a long time, and I think it would be a wrench for him to leave him behind.'

She drew in a ragged breath. It was much worse than she had imagined. 'I think it would be difficult for both of them after all these years.'

Jade drank her coffee and looked at Matt over the rim of her cup. 'With all this going on, how are you going to be fixed for our wedding? I know Ben wants you to be his best man more than anything.'

Ben nodded agreement. 'But if it's going to be a problem…'

Matt shook his head. 'It'll be fine. I've even been

practising my speech—all those little jokes I have up my sleeve…'

Jade groaned. 'Oh, no, I don't think I want to hear this…'

'Are you sure?' Matt pretended to be disappointed.

'Quite sure.' She laughed, and then said quickly, 'Oh, and while I think of it, my brother James said he'll drive you both back here from Amersham on the night of the wedding, if you like. He and his fiancée live in London, and they have to come back the same day, so it won't be a problem.'

'That's great, thanks,' Lucy said, glancing at Matt to see if it was all right with him. He nodded.

'It'll save us having to get the train,' he commented.

Jade's phone started to ring, and she gave an apologetic smile and answered it. She listened for a moment and then said, 'You've seen them? What did it say? Did you check them all? Oh, wow. Oh, wow…' She clicked off the call a minute or so later and then turned to Lucy. 'The exam results are up on the notice-board in the lecture room,' she told her. 'We passed! Both of us! Oh, wow, wow!'

The two girls jumped up and held on to each other, dancing around the room for a few seconds, then Jade grabbed hold of Ben and kissed him soundly. 'I passed,' she said, her excitement still riding high. 'I passed.'

'Well, of course you did,' he answered calmly, but with a twinkle in his eye. 'What did you expect?'

Lucy was smiling at Matt, and he went over to her, wrapping his arms around her and holding her in a bear hug. 'Well done,' he said. 'I knew you could do it.' As soon as his arms went around her, Lucy's thoughts went into a tailspin. She wanted this, loved being in his arms, but something would surely go wrong. It had been a mistake, falling for Matt. It was a mistake, being in his arms like this. Their families were alienated and she felt responsible for some of that.

But all of that went out of her head when he leaned towards her and kissed her. It was a tender kiss at first, but soon he was moving in closer, deepening the kiss so that she was lost to all sensible thought, and all she wanted was for it to go on and on. Which it did, until they were both wrenched from their cosy little cocoon when they heard a round of applause coming from across the room.

'Well, there's a thing,' Jade said, trying to hide a smile and failing completely. 'I wondered how you two might be getting on in our absence. I thought you might be dividing the house into territories with a barrier in between to keep you apart, but this is good, very good.' She was grinning widely now, and so was Ben, and Lucy didn't know where to put her face. She was sure she was blushing fiercely.

'I'm glad things are working out for you two,' Ben said. 'But enough of this frivolity, I'm on duty in half an hour. I have to go.'

'Me, too.' Matt held Lucy for just a while longer, as though he couldn't bring himself to let go, but then he slowly released her and went to get ready for work.

Lucy dragged her mind back to mundane things, glad that Jade had gone to find her bag and she didn't have to talk to anyone just then. She'd been overwhelmed by that kiss, and now she had to shore up her defences all over again. She couldn't get involved with someone whose mother hated her and her family. It wouldn't be fair to Matt if he had to constantly work at keeping the peace between them. And sooner or later wouldn't it cause friction between them, too?

And what of Matt's feelings for her? Where was their relationship going? He'd kissed her, and he definitely cared for her, that was for sure, but he'd never actually spoken to her about how he felt. Perhaps she wanted more from him than he was prepared to give.

She broke up the remains of the toast into crumbs and then went out into the garden and dropped them onto the bird table, looking around as, out of the corner of her eye, she spotted a sleek white cat.

'He likes your garden,' a small voice said, and her glance flicked to where Jacob was peering at her, resting his chin on the top of the wooden fence.

'It looks like it, doesn't it?' The cat was searching in the undergrowth for a good place to settle down, and Lucy smiled, looking back at the boy. 'My word, you've suddenly grown,' she said, sounding astonished. 'Look at you, able to see over the fence. Have you been eating lots of dinners?'

Matt came to join her in the garden, and she pointed out the boy to him. 'He must have grown a foot in two weeks,' she mused.

'Hmm…strange, that,' Matt said on a thoughtful note. 'I've seen his mum watering the carrots with plant food just lately. I wonder if she's been watering him, as well?'

They both shook their heads in puzzlement, and Jacob giggled. 'I'm standing on a box,' he said, his voice rising with glee. 'A big wooden box.'

'Oh, well, that's it, then. And I thought you were as big as the fence.' Lucy chuckled. She moved away from the bird table. 'We have to go to work now, Jacob.' She waved at him. 'Perhaps we'll see you later.'

'Okay.'

Matt put his arm around her as they walked back to the house. 'We should set off for the hospital,' he said. 'Jade and Ben have already gone.'

She nodded. With his arm around her shoulders and his body next to hers, she was in seventh heaven. The only thing that would have made it better would be for him to kiss her, but that wouldn't do at all, would it? She was having enough trouble getting over the last time.

She looked up at him, her blue eyes quizzical.

'Don't even think about it,' he said, his eyes gleaming. 'Or I won't be responsible for my actions.'

'I can't think what you mean,' she murmured. That last kiss had been a spur-of-the-moment thing, hadn't it? She couldn't read anything into it. Matt had been going through a rash of temptation lately, and it was only because they'd been thrown together over these last few weeks. He cared about her, but he didn't love her, did he? He'd never said that he loved her.

They walked to the hospital a few minutes later, and as soon as she entered the Neonatal unit Lucy's nerves were on edge. Matt was going to take baby Sarah off the ventilator this morning, and everything depended on whether she could breathe on her own.

Lucy looked at her, a tiny infant with thin little arms and legs, wearing a knitted cap to keep the warmth from escaping at the top of her head. Matt could probably hold her comfortably in one hand.

'Are you ready?' He looked at her, and he must have guessed that she was overwhelmed by misgivings. What if the baby couldn't breathe on her own? Would she be distressed, or choke? Just the thought of it bothered her.

'Yes, I'm ready.' She could do this…she had to do this. She'd almost finished her five years of medical training, she'd passed all her exams over the years, and now there was nothing standing in the way of her becoming a pre-registration doctor. She even had her next stage of training arranged—the first year of a three-year course to enable her to become a GP, a family doctor. How could she look anyone in the eye if she couldn't bear to watch a small baby being taken off a ventilator?

'Do you want to do it?' Matt asked. 'You've seen it done before, haven't you, and you've practiced on manikins before this? She'll be fine. We've been monitoring her all the while, and I feel she's ready for this. We'll continue with oxygen afterwards, but it'll be delivered through an oxygen tent rather than through a tube down her throat.'

'All right. I'll do it.'

She followed the procedure she'd been shown many times before, and switched off the machine before carefully withdrawing the tube. The baby coughed, retched and for a few interminable seconds seemed to choke, but Lucy was ready with suction to clear any secretions from her throat. Then the infant took a spontaneous breath and began to wail lustily.

Lucy exhaled deeply. It had worked, and the baby was breathing by herself. She turned to Matt, her mouth curving in a relieved smile.

'That wasn't so bad, was it?' he said.

She shook her head. 'Now we have to wait and see how well she does on her own.' She frowned. 'We won't know the extent of any brain damage for some time, will we?'

He pressed his lips together briefly. 'We'll do a CT scan at some point. That will give us an idea of what's going on. But after suffering from bleeding on the brain, it's hard to imagine that there'll be no problems ahead. Anyway,' he said, becoming businesslike once more, 'in the meantime, we'll keep her on medication to regulate the heartbeat and watch to see if she starts to put on weight and generally gain strength.'

They left the Neonatal unit and went to check on their patients on the children's ward.

'I'll catch up with you in a few minutes,' Matt said. 'I want to go and look up some X-ray films on the computer.'

'Okay. I'll go and see how Tom is doing.' She was worried about the boy with the head injury. He had a broken leg, too, and although it had been treated and put into a cast, the healing wouldn't be complete until he could start to put some weight on it.

She hesitated as she approached his bay, though, because she could hear raised voices coming from there.

'I wish your mother would keep her opinions to herself,' Tom's father was saying. 'She's always having a go at me.'

'It's only because she's upset, and worried about Tom,' his wife answered.

'Sure, make excuses for her, why don't you? That's all you ever do...side with her.'

'She's my mother, for heaven's sake. I don't want to

take sides. I just want you both to sort yourselves out and let me concentrate on our child.'

Lucy closed her eyes briefly, trying to shut out the image that circled in her mind. She didn't want to see or hear this couple arguing, especially when their child was so desperately ill. But neither could she rid herself of the other vision that rose up clear and sharp in her head. Was this how it would be for her and Matt? Would his mother's animosity taint any relationship they might have?

She walked towards the bedside, clearing her throat to alert the couple to her presence, and they both fell silent. 'I've come to see how Tom's getting on,' she said, glancing at the monitors and then leafing through the boy's file. 'Since the pressure inside his head has gone down, we've started to gradually reduce the sedation. He might start to show signs of coming round so you need to be aware and alert one of the nurses if that happens. It might not be very much, just be the twitch of a finger or a slight movement of his good leg to begin with.'

Mrs Granger brightened. 'That's all we need,' she said softly. 'Anything to give us a sign that he's coming back to us.'

'I don't think it will be too long now,' she told them. She inspected the various catheters to make sure all was well, and then added a few notes to the boy's file before taking one final look at him. He wasn't moving, but he looked serene and peaceful.

Taking her leave of them, she went over to the nurses' station. She was looking through the wire tray on the desk for any test results that had come in when Matt came to join her.

'Alice's results are here,' she told Matt. 'The two-year-old with abdominal cramps and slow heartbeat,' she reminded him. 'The serum calcium and parathyroid hormone are both elevated, and serum phosphate is decreased. Sounds as though her parathyroid gland isn't working properly and she's overloaded with calcium. That means we should look out for kidney stones.'

He nodded. 'Let's go and take a look at her. We'll do a scan, but we can give her a potassium supplement to help prevent stones. She's still on normal saline, so we'll add a diuretic, furosemide, to help eliminate any excess calcium, and she'll need an injection of calcitonin to strengthen her bones.'

She walked with him to the child's cot. 'Should we try her on bisphosphonates to stop the breakdown of bone?'

'Yes. You can set up an infusion.' He looked at the infant, an unhappy little girl, fretful and restless, and said softly, 'We'll soon have you feeling better, little one.' He stroked her hand and then waggled his fingers at her, making funny noises and puffing his cheeks so that after a while she stopped whimpering and began to chuckle. 'That's the way,' he murmured. 'I'll get the play leader to come and find something to amuse you.'

Turning back to Lucy, he said, 'I'll call for a consultation with the endocrinologist. If the illness is due to a problem with the parathyroid gland, such as a tumour of some kind, she'll need surgery.'

'Poor little thing. I hope we can sort her problems out fairly quickly.'

'So do I.'

Lucy's mobile phone rang at that moment, and she went to a quiet corner of the room to answer it. Matt stayed where he was, setting up the child's medication.

'Dad, what is it?' she asked, concerned all at once. He sounded agitated. He rarely rang her at work, so something must be bothering him quite badly. 'Is everything all right? Is Mum okay?' Matt glanced at her, hearing the concern in her voice, and she lifted her shoulders in answer to his unspoken query, showing her bewilderment.

'She's fine,' her father said. 'It's this business with Matt's father I'm ringing about. Apparently, he's been talking to a lawyer about ending the partnership. I had a letter from the solicitor this morning. Can you talk to him for me? I can't reach him by phone, and his email's not working. As for his wife, she won't speak to me at all—she just puts the phone down on me. He can't be serious. I don't think he can have thought this through.'

'I'm sorry,' she said. 'It must have come as an awful shock to you. You've worked together for so long. How many years is it? About twenty?' She looked at Matt, willing him to come over to her. This concerned him. It was about his father, after all.

Matt finished what he was doing and checked that everything was in order before he joined her in the seating area.

'It's about that, yes…a long time. I'm sure we could work something out between us. We've always worked well together, and I just don't want to lose him as a partner.' Beside her, Matt pulled in a deep breath. Clearly, he could hear what was being said. 'Will you talk to him for me, Lucy? See if you can get him to change his mind?'

'I don't see how I can do that,' Lucy said honestly. 'I get the feeling Matt's mother doesn't like me being there. And she's encouraging him to make the break so she won't thank me for going along and trying to persuade him otherwise.'

'You could try, though.'

She shook her head, even though he couldn't see her. 'I don't think so. It wouldn't have any weight coming from me, anyway. I don't have much to do with the business, apart from helping to find development sites and dealing with suppliers. I don't see what arguments I can put forward to persuade him to stay.'

He didn't like her answer. She knew it. She sensed his disapproval even before he spoke, and when he did, he ground his words out through his teeth. 'That's been the trouble all along, hasn't it? You never wanted to be part of the business. You insisted on going ahead with a career in medicine when you could have had a ready-made partnership on your doorstep. But, no, you took it into your head to take off instead and get yourself involved in years of study—expensive study, mind you—and for what? So that you can set yourself up as a family doctor and listen to people coming in with their coughs and sniffles and whatever other piffling ailments they can think of.'

'And what about those people who have hidden heart problems or kidney diseases?' she asked. 'I can be their first port of call. I might be the one who discovers what's wrong and starts them on the path to treatment. It's not just about sniffles and hypochondria.'

She could feel her temper rising, and made an effort to calm down. Her father often had this effect on her, and she ought to know better than to rise to his bait.

Matt put his arm around her, squeezing her gently. 'Stick to your guns,' he mouthed.

'Are you going to talk to Sam or not?' her father pressed.

'Like I said, I don't think I can do that,' she said firmly.

'So you want me to come all the way over there when I'm up to my eyes in work? I have men working at full tilt, and we're still facing penalty clauses. I have to go and talk to site managers and electrical installers and you won't do one simple thing for me.'

She sucked in a deep breath. 'You can't shift the responsibility to me like that. How important is this partnership to you? If it's as significant as you're making it out to be, then it ought to be worth your while to come down here to see him and talk things through personally. It seems to me you've both been so caught up in work that you've lost the ability to communicate with one another.'

Matt's palm slid over her back, reassuringly warm and comforting, signalling his support.

Her father made an exasperated snort and cut the call.

'Oh, dear.' Lucy sighed. 'It's not good, is it? I mean, it sounds as though your father's decided to go ahead with quitting, but I always had the feeling he was in his element when he was working with my dad.'

'So did I.' Matt agreed. 'My mother's obviously been putting pressure on him, and while he's ill and vulnerable he doesn't have the energy to think things through properly.' His glance trailed over her in concern. 'Don't let it worry you. I think you did the right thing, standing up to your father. He strikes me as the sort of man who'll walk all over you if you show any sign of weakness. Perhaps that's where my father went wrong. He tries to fulfil people's expectations.'

'Maybe.' She was still smarting at her father's easy dismissal of her career. Of course he didn't mean it. He couldn't. After all, he'd been lucky so far, but he might well need a doctor's services one day. And wasn't his partner on the receiving end right now?

'I'll talk to my dad about it,' Matt promised, 'if it will put your mind at ease. He might want to delay making any moves until he's out of hospital and working under his own steam.'

'Thanks,' she said gratefully.

They went back to their patients, doing what they could to make them comfortable. Young William was ready to be discharged from hospital, and Lucy gave him a hug and wished him well. She was glad to see him looking so much stronger. 'You take care,' she said.

'Yeah, I will. See you.' Walking with a jaunty stride he left the ward with his mother a few minutes later, and Lucy went once more to see how Alice was doing.

After work that day, she went for a last fitting for her bridesmaid dress, and was thrilled with the result. What would Matt think when he saw her in it at the weekend? A small ripple of excitement ran through her. Perversely, despite all her worries about them being together, she wanted him to think she looked good.

* * *

On the day of the wedding she was filled with unexpected nerves mingled with the thrill of anticipation.
She'd travelled to Amersham on the train with Matt that
morning, and while he went off to find Ben at a local
hotel to carry out his best-man duties, she'd gone to
Jade's house to help the bride get ready. The wedding
was scheduled for mid-afternoon, so they had ample
time.

'You look beautiful,' she told Jade, when the preparations were complete and they were ready to set off for
the church. Her friend's white dress clung in all the right
places, emphasising her slender curves, while her hair
was simply but perfectly styled, with a band of flowers
for a headdress and finished off with an exquisite lace
veil.

'The taxi's arrived,' Jade's mother said, and began to
help Lucy shepherd the two small bridesmaids, Jade's
cousins ages around six and seven years, and the page
boy, age four, another cousin, into the waiting car.

'Don't they look adorable?' Mrs Blythe exclaimed. 'I
love their dresses, with those wonderful overskirts and
the pretty flowers in their hair. And as for you, Ryan,'
she said, looking at her nephew, 'you look gorgeous in
your trousers and waistcoat.' Ryan was shy, but Lucy
saw that his cheeks dimpled as he clambered into the
car.

A few minutes later, outside the church, Lucy gathered the youngsters together in readiness for the bride's
appearance. 'Here she comes,' she whispered.

Music filled the church, with Wagner's triumphant
wedding march playing as Jade walked down the aisle,
her hand on her father's arm. Lucy smiled. They'd fi-

nally managed to get in touch with him after he'd sorted out a house move and he'd been overjoyed to come and 'give his daughter away.'

Ben turned to look at his bride, love and pride in his expression, and as the small procession moved level with the front set of pews, Lucy's gaze tangled with Matt's. She saw the widening of his eyes as she drew near, the look of wonder that sparked in their depths, but it was his arrested expression that said it all, and a warm glow came over her. He liked the way she looked.

She was wearing a dusky pink strapless dress with a sweetheart neckline and ruched bodice, and the skirt had a draped, gently flowing wrap-over effect. It floated as she moved, brushing against her ankles, and it made her feel ultra-feminine.

Throughout the service, she was conscious of Matt's intense blue gaze moving over her, and afterwards, when the congregation assembled in the churchyard, he came to stand with her as she and her small charges threw confetti over the happy couple.

'You take my breath away,' he said huskily. 'I was trying to follow the service in the church, but I couldn't take my eyes off you.'

'You don't look so bad yourself.' He looked terrific, in fact, with his dark, expensively tailored suit emphasising the breadth of his shoulders, and crisp, immaculate cuffs setting off the pale bronze of his skin. He wore a silk tie, and a stylish waistcoat, its deep red-wine colour matching the rose in his buttonhole.

'Well, thank you, ma'am,' he said with a flourish. 'Perhaps I could escort you to the ball?'

'I think that would be an excellent idea.' She looked

down at the children in their bridal finery. 'How do you feel about our little entourage? I've a notion they're expecting all sorts of goodies when we get to the reception.'

He laughed. 'I'm pretty sure I can handle three little ones. Do you think they take bribes?'

She chuckled with him, and just at that moment they both looked up, into the flash of a camera lens. 'That was a beauty,' the cameraman said. 'Now let's have one of you both with the pageboy and younger bridesmaids.'

As soon as the wedding photos had been taken outside the church, they all went to the country house hotel where the reception was being held. They sat down to a wonderful wedding supper of prime rib beef, gratin potatoes, glazed parsnips and cracked peppercorn sauce, and just before dessert was served Matt stood up to make his best man's speech.

He was good, Lucy thought, watching him deliver his speech. He did it with wit and charm, causing everyone to break into laughter every now and again. He toasted the bride and groom, read out the cards, and then handed out gifts from the bride and groom to the mothers of both parties, and to the pageboy and bridesmaids.

Lucy opened her gift when Matt sat down beside her once more and the guests were starting on their dessert. The black, silk-lined box revealed an intricately designed gold bracelet decorated with glistening gemstones. 'Oh, it's lovely!' she exclaimed, turning to thank Jade and Ben for the beautiful present.

'Let me help you with it,' Matt said, and she held out her wrist to him, conscious of a pulse beginning to flutter at the base of her throat when his fingers brushed her arm and touched her skin with fire.

He must have sensed her reaction, or perhaps he felt it, too, because he held her hand for a fraction longer than was necessary and only let go when the young bridesmaids demanded that he help them, too. He gave Lucy a wry smile, but obliged them cheerfully enough.

Later in the evening, when the lights were dimmed and the disco started, they joined Jade and Ben with their guests on the dance floor, moving to the fast rhythm of the music, their bodies bathed in multi-coloured darting lights that were projected from around the room. Perhaps she'd had a little too much wine, because the heavy beat echoed through her and filled her with exhilaration. Matt drew her close when the tempo slowed, lowering his head so that his cheek rested against her temple, and a thrill of sweet anticipation swirled through her from head to toe. She loved the feel of him, his hand at the base of her spine, the brush of his strong thighs against hers. She wanted more.

When the bride and groom left, about an hour later, they waved them off, and instead of going back into the reception room Matt took hold of Lucy's hand and they walked together in the moonlight, following a path that wound its way through the hotel's landscaped gardens. He led her though a narrow archway and they came upon a secluded arbour, where white, star-shaped jasmine clambered over a rustic frame and filled the air with a heady, sweet scent.

He pulled her into his arms and her breath caught in her throat. Alone with him in this sheltered nook, she was conscious of the music throbbing in the distance, reverberating through her head, building to a crescendo of sound. She lifted her face to him and his mouth came down on hers, kissing her fiercely, feverishly, as though he couldn't help himself, couldn't wait any longer. He ran his hands over her soft curves, urging her closer, so that his thighs locked with hers and it seemed their bodies melded into one. His breathing was ragged. 'You're pure temptation,' he murmured against her throat, a groan starting up in the back of his throat as he moved against her. 'I tried to resist you…but I can't, I'm only human, Lucy…I need you.'

His heart was thumping so heavily that she could feel it against her breasts, a thunderous beat like a drum roll building to an explosive climax. She wanted him, desperately, needed to feel his body against hers, his lips trailing fire over her throat, the creamy slope of her shoulder, and lower, tracing the full, ripe curve of her breast. He let the tip of his tongue glide and dip beneath the bodice of her dress, and sensation ripped through her like the lick of flame.

The rush of blood roared in her ears, making her temples throb. His hand slid beneath her skirt, sliding over the velvet softness of her thigh, and heat shot through her. And then, out of the darkness, she heard the crunch of pebbles underfoot, scuffling sounds, followed by a moment of silence, and then the high-pitched sound of children's voices, coming closer.

'Lucy…where are you? Lucy?' a girl's voice called out in the semi darkness. 'My aunty sent me to find you. Where are you?'

Lucy swallowed hard, tried to stem the tide of desire that washed over her. 'I must answer her,' she whispered, the tips of her fingers moving shakily over Matt's chest.

Matt gave a shuddering, almost pained, groan. 'I know. I just…give me a minute.'

'Lucy?' Another voice called her name and there was a whispered conversation from the other side of the hedge. 'She must be out here. We've looked everywhere else.'

Lucy made a supreme effort and wrenched herself away from Matt, pulling air deep into her lungs, before saying in an even tone, 'It's all right. I'm here, girls.' She walked through the archway and looked down at her small nieces. 'Is it about the lift home?'

'Yes.' Both girls nodded. 'Aunty says if you and Matt can be ready in ten minutes, Jade's brother will drive you both back to London.'

'That's brilliant. Thanks, girls. Will you tell your aunty that we're coming now?'

'Okay.' The girls darted off along the path, without looking back.

Matt came through the archway to join her. 'I'd forgotten all about the lift home,' he said. He shot her a wry smile. 'Perhaps it's just as well the girls came along when they did. Things might have got a bit out of hand.'

'Yes.' She didn't know whether to be disappointed or relieved. Matt had been overcome with desire for her, and that was intensely exciting, thrilling her to the core, but ought she to tread more warily, think before she took that ultimate step of going to bed with him? She wasn't the kind of girl who took lovers indiscriminately. For her, sex had to be meaningful, based on love. And yet, so many times, she came across men who wanted her, told her they needed her, that she was the only woman they could ever desire. She'd learned to sift them out, the men who were just after one thing.

With Matt, the difference was he'd never acted that way, until now. Just a few moments ago they would have both thrown caution to the wind. But now she'd had time to cool down, she was able to think more clearly. She wanted him, longed to have him make love to her, and yet…he hadn't mentioned the one thing she needed to hear. Love. It was the one word that would have made everything all right, but he hadn't said it. At the back of her mind there was an insistent thrumming, a warning bell that she tried to ignore. She could so easily be hurt if she gave everything to this relationship and then Matt decided to move on. She'd been hurt when Alex had betrayed her, but if the same thing happened with Matt, her life would fall apart.

'Are you all right?' Matt glanced at her as they walked back along the path towards the hotel. 'You're very quiet.'

'I'm okay. Perhaps I'm just a bit shocked by the interruption…it's left me feeling a bit shaky.'

He reached for her hand, tucking it into his palm. 'I got carried away. I never meant to come on so strong, but you look unbelievably beautiful. I'm burning up, aching for you.' He gave a short laugh. 'Lord knows what your father would think if he found out. He'd probably have a fit.'

She acknowledged that with a rueful smile. 'More than likely.'

They went back to the reception and met up with Jade's brother James and his fiancée. 'It was a great day for them, wasn't it?' James said, looking back at the wedding debris, scattered petals of confetti, balloons and party poppers. 'They looked really happy.'

Lucy smiled. 'They did.'

They said their goodbyes and set off for home. It was well after midnight by now, and the street was dark and quiet when James dropped them off outside the London house. Sitting next to Matt in the intimacy of the back of the car, both of them hidden in the shadows, she'd been in a constant state of hyper-awareness. He held her hand in his, his long legs nudging hers, and for all her doubts and uncertainties she wanted the journey to end so that she could be alone with him once more. She was overcome by a heightened sense of expectancy.

They waved off James and his fiancée and went into the house, shutting the front door behind them. The glow from the security light threw soft shadows across the hallway, and in the darkness they brushed against one another. She heard Matt's sharp intake of breath and she reached for him, running her hand along his arm. She knew it was adding the spark to his tinder, but she couldn't help herself, and when Matt gently urged her against the wall, leaning over her and kissing her soundly, she was glad. She wound her arms around his neck and pressed her body to his, throwing caution to the wind. His breathing was coming in soft, short bursts, as though he was struggling to get air into his lungs.

'You know exactly what that does to me, don't you?' He trailed kisses over her cheek, her throat, and gave a shuddery sigh. 'Ah, Lucy, you drive me crazy with wanting you…but…' He gently eased himself away from her, holding her lightly, at arm's length. 'Here,' he whispered, 'in this place…it feels wrong.'

All at once, without warning, the hall light snapped on, and they broke apart in startled surprise. Lucy's father stood in the hallway, glowering at both of them.

'So this is how you keep your word, huh?' he shot at Matt, grinding the words between his teeth. 'You're quite happy to take advantage of my daughter under my own roof?'

'That's not how it is,' Matt answered, his tone clipped. 'I'm not taking advantage of her.'

'It's how I see it. It's not enough that your father let me down, is it? It must be a family trait.'

'What are you doing here, Dad?' Lucy interrupted, bracing herself.

'I'm staying the night. I had to come over here to see Sam as you wouldn't help out.' He continued to glower at her. 'I can see why that was now. You're too busy cavorting with the tenants.'

'Tenants…in the plural?' Lucy said, her mouth curling around the word with contempt. 'Did you mean to be so insulting? No, don't answer that. I can see you're in no mood for a logical discussion.' She glared at him. 'As to Matt and I…I'm old enough to decide for myself how I live my life. It's time you understood that. And if I choose to be with Matt, I don't see that it's any business of yours.'

'I'm still your father, and you owe me some respect, don't forget that. In fact, you owe me a whole lot more, but you seem to take it all for granted.' His dark eyes glittered with anger. 'We'll talk about this in the morning. I'm going to bed.'

He marched up the stairs, leaving Matt and Lucy to face each other in the hallway.

'I'm sorry about that,' she said. 'He'll get over it. It must have been a shock to him to find us, that's all.'

'You always defend him, but there are times when he goes too far.' Matt's jaw set in a hard line, and his eyes were dark with anger. 'He talks about my father as though Dad owes him something, when in reality he's probably pushed him way beyond what was reasonable.'

She couldn't let him get away with that. 'I don't believe it's just that he pushed him. Your father was perfectly capable of setting limits on what he would, or wouldn't, do and he obviously chose not to do that.'

Matt's mouth made a flat line. 'I still don't think he was able to stand up to the pressure. I've seen how your father treats you, and it's wrong. He can't go on doing this, dictating how people live their lives. And if he's intent on causing trouble at the hospital, I'll have to stop him. I'll not have him upset my father.'

'He won't do that, I'm sure of it.' His anger was fuelling her own, and she spoke firmly, emphasising each point. 'He's not perfect, he's never been perfect, but he talks without thinking. He'll come round by morning and see that he's not being fair. My father's not a bad man. He makes mistakes. We all make mistakes sometimes.'

'Perhaps he makes more than most,' Matt said flatly.

'That's unfair.' She frowned, wishing they could lay this to rest, wishing her father had never turned up. 'Matt, you're not even trying to understand him. He says what's on his mind, but that's not necessarily a bad thing. He's always been blunt and to the point, but he can be reasonable, too.'

He shook his head. 'Perhaps he's the one who needs to understand. You, too. You're always making excuses for him. Well, I can't do this any more, Lucy. I won't do it. I'm not going to be one of his tenants any longer. I'm moving out.'

She stared at him, shocked to the core. 'But where will you go? You don't have to do this, surely? I don't want you to go, Matt.'

'I'm sorry, but that's how it is. I'm not staying. It's over. I'll get my things together and leave in the morning.' Grim faced, he turned away from her. He went to the kitchen and rummaged in one of the cupboards, coming back with a holdall. She realised he meant to start packing that very night, and she suddenly felt as though she couldn't breathe. Her stomach felt like lead. How would she go on without him?

CHAPTER NINE

'It's over.' Those words echoed through Lucy's mind again and again over the next couple of days. She'd been hurt beyond belief when Matt had moved out the next morning, with hardly a word spoken between them. It made her feel ill to see him go.

And even though she saw him at work the following day, he was preoccupied, busy making phone calls to various people, and she guessed he was sorting out a place to stay.

It was strange to wander through the rooms of the empty house now that he had gone. She was desolate without him. She didn't want to eat. She couldn't sleep. It was a miserable way to go on, but she didn't know what she could do to put things right.

'Is you going off to work soon?' Jacob peered over the top of the fence as she broke up pieces of stale scones and spread them out on the bird table.

'Yes, in a few minutes,' she answered. She glanced at him. He looked as unhappy as she felt, and from the tear streaks running down his cheeks, she guessed he had been crying. 'What's wrong, Jacob?' she asked, going over to him. 'Has something upset you?'

He nodded. 'We can't find Henry,' he said, his voice breaking up. 'He's lost.'

'Henry?' she repeated, at a loss. 'Oh, do you mean your cat?'

He nodded. 'He didn't come in this morning for his breakfast. He always comes when I rattle the box of biscuits, but today he didn't.' Tears ran down his cheeks, and Lucy wanted to hug him tight and console him.

'Perhaps he's just gone on a little adventure,' she said. 'I'm sure he'll turn up. He's not been missing for too long, after all.' She had a quick look around the garden, but there was no sign of the white cat. 'If he doesn't turn up soon, your mum and dad can perhaps put up some posters in the neighbourhood. I'm sure someone will find him and bring him home to you.'

He perked up a bit at that, but Lucy was sombre as she made her way to work. The boy's distress had been genuine, and it seemed to be on a par with her own. If only she could put up posters and have Matt returned to her...

She'd reached the hospital's main entrance when her phone rang. Her father's name came up on the display and she winced. They hadn't spoken since he'd gone to see Matt's father, and she had no idea of the outcome of that visit because he'd gone straight back to Berkshire afterwards. She hadn't had it in her to phone him.

'How are you?' she asked. 'Did you manage to sort out your problems with Sam?'

'We're working on it,' he said briefly. 'I heard that Matt is moving out. His father told me. Is it true?'

'Yes. He's already gone.'

'I see.'

He fell silent, and Lucy said in a sombre tone, 'Why would he stay, in the circumstances?'

'Why wouldn't he? I didn't expect him to leave. He's the son of my oldest friend.'

She didn't answer him and he said gruffly, 'I said some things I shouldn't—to you—the other night. It was late, I was worried about this partnership thing— you know I don't mean those things, don't you?'

'I know.'

She walked to the lift bay, and her father said, 'You'd better advertise for more students to take over the accommodation. Jade and Ben won't be coming back, of course. As to Matt, he might reconsider, if you put it to him.'

'No, he won't.' She stepped into the lift as the doors opened. 'I have to go to work now, Dad. Was there anything else you wanted?'

'No. No, that was all.'

'Okay. Bye. Give my love to Mum.'

'I will.'

She found Matt on the children's ward, looking through the files at the nurses' station.

'Hi,' he said. 'Will it be all right with you if I come back to the house later on this evening to fetch some of the things I left behind?'

'Yes, of course.'

'I didn't have room to take them with me when I moved out. There's a spare amplifier, some medical books and a lamp, and so on. Bits and pieces.'

'Yes, that's fine.' She didn't know how to talk to him. It felt wrong, as though they were strangers, not two people who had shared passionate, exhilarating kisses just a couple of days ago. How could things have gone so wrong between them? She said slowly, 'Where are you living now? You managed to find a place quickly enough.'

'I'm looking after a friend's flat while he's away on holiday for the next fortnight. It'll be long enough for me to sort things out.'

'Yes, I suppose it will.' She frowned. 'How is your father? I hope my dad's visit didn't set him back in any way?'

'No, it didn't. He's feeling much better, actually. Mr Sheldon did the angioplasty yesterday, and everything went really well. He'll be on medication now, to keep his blood pressure down and make sure his blood doesn't clot easily, and generally they'll keep an eye on him in Outpatients from now on.'

'Your mother must be pleased about that.'

'Yes, she is. She's much more relaxed. Of course, she'll be watching his diet like a hawk, to make sure he keeps off the fatty foods and doesn't overdo the drink.' He smiled. 'He's happy with the way things are going, and he seems to have learned a lesson about doing too much work. He's promised her that he'll learn to delegate and keep work things from nine to five now, five days a week. Kyle's going to step in as a manager—my father hadn't wanted to let go of the reins until now, but I think that will probably work out well.'

'I'm glad for you.'

He gave her a quizzical look. 'How are you? Have you patched things up with your father?'

She nodded. 'He's already phoned and apologised to

me. I knew he didn't mean what he said. You perhaps overreacted, walking out like that.'

His eyes darkened. 'It was for the best, Lucy. I've thought for a while that I should be looking for a place of my own.'

'So you'd have gone anyway?' she asked disconsolately.

'Yes, eventually.'

Mandy came over to the desk just then and handed him a file. 'It's the endocrinologist's report on Alice,' she said, 'the toddler with the parathyroid problem.'

'Ah, yes. She had the operation yesterday, didn't she?'

'She did,' Mandy said. 'And I thought you might like to know—I went over to Neonatal, and they have the CT scan results on baby Sarah. She's fine. It doesn't look as though there's going to be any brain damage... nothing lasting, anyway.'

'That's brilliant, Mandy. Thanks for checking.' He smiled at Lucy, who breathed a sigh of relief, and then he glanced through the report on Alice.

He handed it to her. 'Apparently the tumour was benign. The surgeon took it out—no problems, and she seems to be doing well. We'll need to keep an eye on her medication over the next week or two, but once things settle down, she should be fine.'

'Oh, that's brilliant news. Her parents will be so relieved.' Lucy read through the consultant's report, glad that things had turned out so well for the little girl.

She spent the rest of the morning helping Matt with the children on the ward, and she was pleased that all of them seemed to be doing all right. There were a couple of new admissions, and Matt went to examine them and write up their notes, while she went to see how Tom was getting on.

His level of sedation had gradually been reduced, and yesterday, once he had opened his eyes, Matt had removed his endotracheal tube. He had been sleepy, though, and they'd had no real chance to assess whether he had suffered any brain damage.

Over the course of the morning Lucy had noticed more restless movements in his limbs, and for her that was good news, but the boy's parents didn't seem to have noticed. Tom's grandmother sat with them, and the atmosphere between the three of them was tense.

'The coffee in those machines is too bitter,' Tom's father was saying. 'I didn't choose black, but that's more or less what came out.'

'Why don't you try the cafeteria?' Mrs Cavendish suggested. 'I don't think it's too bad in there.'

'Why do you think?' he snapped. 'I don't want to have to leave my boy's bedside.'

'It was only a suggestion,' his mother-in-law said, her voice rising.

'Why are you shouting at each other?' It was barely above a whisper, but all three of them turned in sudden shock to see that the child was watching them, his eyes open, blinking at the hospital lights.

'Oh, sweetheart…you're awake!' His mother was overjoyed, reaching for his hand and holding it between hers.

His father could barely speak for a moment or two because he was so choked up. Then he said, 'Well done, lad. You're back with us.'

'You were cross with Gran,' the boy said.

'Oh, that was nothing. We were just upset, that's all. We've been so worried about you. Your gran and I will get on fine, won't we?' He turned to look at his wife's mother, and she nodded.

'Of course we will. I'm so glad you're all right, Tom.' She glanced at Jack. 'I'm sorry if I've been hard on you these last few days. It was the shock, I think.'

'It's okay. Forget it. It doesn't matter now.'

Lucy quietly went about her work, checking the monitors, making sure that Tom was comfortable. It seemed that he would be all right. And perhaps his family would be okay, too.

She went home with Matt at the end of the day, and it was almost like old times. He was still the same with her, joking, teasing, as though nothing had happened. She didn't understand it. How could he be the same when she was breaking up inside?

She made coffee for them both, and Matt made one of his pizzas, and they sat and ate together and everything was so normal she wanted to cry for all that she'd lost. Instead, she steeled herself to act as though nothing at all was amiss.

Afterwards, she went with him out into the garden, so that he could rummage about in the shed for the bits and pieces he wanted to take to his new place.

'Have you any idea where you'll live when your friend comes back from his holiday?' she asked. 'I suppose there are plenty of flats to rent in the city. They might be a bit pricey, though.'

'I won't be renting,' he said. 'I'm looking to buy a house.'

'Oh, I see,' she said in surprise. 'Still, I suppose you might as well. Better to put money into property than waste it on rent.' She frowned. 'Do you have somewhere in mind?'

He nodded. 'I wanted to talk to you about that.' They stopped by the old apple tree, heavy with slowly ripening fruit. 'I've been looking at the waterfront house. I know how much you want it, and I thought maybe we could put in an offer.'

Her mouth dropped open. 'We?' She stared at him. 'What are you suggesting? That we live together?'

'Now, there's a thought.' He grinned. 'I can just imagine your father's reaction to that. No, of course not.'

'Then I don't understand. Saturday night you told me it was over between us. I was devastated, and now...' Her voice broke on the words. 'And now you're suggesting we buy a house together—a house I can't even afford?'

He frowned, looking at her oddly. 'Over between us? I didn't say anything of the sort. Where did you get that idea from?'

'"I'm not staying. It's over. I'll get my things together..." That's what you said.' She'd been so upset she remembered his exact words and now she threw them back at him.

'I meant, it's over, me living in this house—your father's house.' He put his arms around her, holding her close. 'How could it possibly be over between us when I care about you so much?'

'But...' Relief washed over her. He hadn't meant what she'd thought. She gazed at him in bewilderment. 'You do?'

'Of course. Surely you know that?'

'Well, I...' Her brows drew together. 'The other day...in the hallway, after the wedding, you didn't seem to want me. And then you said you were leaving. I didn't know what to think.'

'Ah, Lucy, you don't know how hard it's been for me. I've wanted you so badly it hurt. Being with you here, day after day, wanting you and not being able to do anything about it—you can't imagine how difficult it was for me.'

'I didn't know. You never said...'

'How could I?' He gave a wry smile. 'I know how you feel about men constantly making a play for you. I didn't want to be like all the others. I want you for who you are, not just for the way you look.' He hesitated. 'Besides, it wouldn't have been right to take advantage of you while I was a tenant in your house, would it? It would have felt all wrong.' He smiled wryly again. 'And if he'd had his way, your father would have booted me from here to Timbuktu if I'd so much as breathed too close to you.'

'Surely not?' She was stunned by the revelation. He'd never said a word, given her no inkling of the intensity of what he'd been feeling. And as for her father's involvement... 'He wouldn't do that—you're like part of the family, his partner's son.'

He gave a short laugh. 'Don't you believe it. You said yourself he vets everyone who has anything whatever to do with you. And that means everyone. He did it to me.'

She pulled in a shaky breath. 'I can hardly believe what you're saying. Did he really warn you off? When?'

He nodded. 'Way back, when I first moved into the house. I understood that he had your welfare at heart, but he needn't have worried. I would never have taken advantage of our situation. It would have felt wrong somehow.'

She was still shocked by his revelation, but after a moment she said sorrowfully, 'I thought he would let go when I was twenty one, but now, three years later, it's beginning to look as though it's never going to happen.'

'Oh, I don't know about that. I think the process has already started. After all, you stood up to him, didn't you? That's why he came over on the day of the wedding, because you finally stood your ground. And you did the same again that night in the hallway. Perhaps that was what I was waiting for—for you to be ready to break away and finally make decisions for yourself. I hoped you'd decide that you wanted me. Anyway, it made me realise I had to leave and prepare the way for both of us to be together.'

She glanced at him fleetingly, her silky lashes veiling her eyes. 'I'd no idea you felt that way about me... that you were holding back.'

'I didn't want to do anything to upset the apple cart. But it was hard. I cared so much for you. I wanted to show you how I felt, I wanted to put my arms around you, hold you—and those mornings, when you were half-asleep, wandering along the corridor with your hair all tousled and your robe slipping down off your shoulders…'

His voice became rough around the edges, his gaze wandering over her, while Lucy simply stared at him, wide-eyed, as he added, 'More and more, I'd find myself fighting the urge to slide it off you completely.'

Startled, her eyes widened and her lips parted a fraction. 'You did?' The words came out on a silent breath of air, and warm colour filled her cheeks. 'So…so why leave it until now to tell me?' She couldn't get to grips with what was happening. Things had changed so much in these last few weeks. The man she'd known had always been there, part of the gang, a fixture in her everyday life, and yet it seemed as though she hadn't really known him at all. These last few weeks had been a huge learning curve. She was finding out more and more about him as every day passed.

He sighed. 'Now, that's a difficult one.' His mouth made a flat line, briefly. 'I think, deep down, I didn't want to frighten you off. I knew how you felt about men in general and, as long as I was kind of invisible around you, I guessed it probably wouldn't matter. Then there were the exams coming up. You had so much on your mind, and I knew how important they were to you. I didn't want to do anything to ruin that for you.'

'And now?'

'Now it's getting too hard for me to handle. Working with you throughout the day, being at home alone with you when Jade and Ben were away, it's brought us closer together, and all the time temptation's just an arm's length away.' His eyes darkened as he moved closer to her. 'I've realised I'm not made of stone. I want you… I want to hold you and kiss you, and show you how much I care for you.'

She gazed up at him, her blue eyes glimmering with invitation. He cared for her, wanted her...wasn't that how she felt about him? 'Then why not give in to temptation?'

He exhaled raggedly, his body jerking as though she'd just touched him with a live wire. Then he shook himself down and said softly, 'You're a temptress, a seductive, alluring woman, and I'm just a helpless man. I've been on a slow burn for months, and now, when you look at me that way, I feel I'm sliding into a meltdown. How am I supposed to find the strength to resist you?'

He ran his hand lightly down her arm and leaned towards her, bending his head so that his forehead gently rested against hers for a second or two.

Her mind was in a whirl. He wanted her, and it wasn't just a passing fancy, it had been building up for a long while. She put her arms around him and held him close. 'I want you, too,' she whispered.

He kissed her then, a fierce, achingly sweet kiss that made her feel as though she was burning up with fever. Her soft curves were crushed against his strong body, and she drank him in, wanting everything he had to offer. A soft sigh escaped her lips and she looked into his eyes, 'I love you,' she murmured.

'Ah...you don't know how good that makes me feel.' He kissed her again, his hands moving over her, caressing, stroking along the length of her spine. Then he said in a soft, questioning tone, 'So...maybe I was right in thinking about buying the house?'

'I'm not sure I understand about that.'

He tilted her chin with his fingers. 'I meant it to be for us. I love you, Lucy. I don't even know when I first realised it. It sort of grew on me. I think that's when I first started thinking I ought to move out. And then we saw the waterfront house, and I knew you wanted it more than anything. So I told your father I wanted to buy it.'

She was stunned. 'But how? What did he say to that? You and he haven't exactly been getting on like a house on fire just lately, have you?'

He smiled, gently tucking a golden strand of her hair back behind her ear when it fell across her cheek. 'Well, you could call it a kind of deal-breaker, I suppose. My father suggested he would consider staying in the partnership if I had first option on the house—at a reasonable price, of course.'

'And my father agreed to that?'

'Strangely enough, he did.'

She let out a long, slow breath, trying to think this through. 'But your mother would never be happy about that, would she? She doesn't want your father back in partnership, and she certainly wouldn't want to do business with my father.' A sudden thought struck her. 'Does she know about you and me?'

She looked up at him, and he dropped a kiss onto her forehead. 'Yes.' He smiled. 'She's actually softened up quite a bit since my dad had his operation. She was wound up very tightly, you know, and I think she was looking for someone to blame. I've talked to her about it, and she realises things got out of hand.'

'So she doesn't mind about you and me?'

'She doesn't mind. I think she'll actually be quite pleased when she has more time to think about it. I know my dad is happy about you and I getting together.'

'Mmm... About that, what exactly did you have in mind?'

'Marriage?' It was a question as much as a statement, and he must have realised that he was doing things all the wrong way around because he said gently, 'Will you marry me, Lucy? Please say yes, because I have the future all planned out, and I need you to go along with it because you're an integral part of it.'

She laughed. 'So that's what I'm to tell our children, is it? I had to marry you because your plan wouldn't work without me?'

'Well, sort of, yes. I hadn't thought much beyond buying the house and then getting married. I can't imagine the future, my future, without you.' He frowned. 'Did you just mention our children?'

She wrapped her arms around his neck. 'I did. And of course they'll need a wonderful house where they can grow up happy...with a few safety measures built in around the waterfront, of course. How on earth can we afford it?'

'That's all right. I've made quite a lot of money over the years, selling my songs and music and playing gigs here and there. I've invested most of it, with my father's advice—he's pretty shrewd at these sorts of things—and I've made enough for us to be comfortable. So it's not a problem. All I need is for you to say that you'll marry me, and the rest will follow.'

'Yes,' she said, reaching up to kiss him tenderly. 'Oh, yes, please.'

He bent his head to hers and he kissed her, wrapping his arms even more firmly about her. But in the silence of those few minutes, when they were locked in each other's embrace, they heard a strange mewling sound.

Slowly, they broke off the kiss and looked around. 'It's coming from the shed,' she murmured. 'It sounds like Jacob's cat, Henry. He said he'd lost him.'

'If it is him, perhaps he got in through the open windows—or maybe it was when you put the watering cans away. You do that every evening, don't you, after you've watered the plants?'

'Oh, heavens, what have I done?' Lucy was aghast at the thought she might have unwittingly locked up the poor cat.

Matt opened the shed door and peered inside. 'Well, well,' he said. 'You just have to come and see this.'

'What is it?' She followed him to the door.

'I think Henry must be a Henrietta...otherwise something very strange is going on. Are those five kittens I see? Or is it six?'

'Oh, let me see.' She looked inside the shed, and there were six kittens, snuggled up inside an old basket, with Henry-etta. She was licking each of them in turn. 'Oh, they're so sweet, aren't they?' she exclaimed. 'I can't wait to tell Jacob. He'll be so thrilled.'

'Mmm... Can we put a hold on that for a minute or two? I think we were in the middle of sealing a very special bargain.'

She laughed, gazing up at him. They propped open the shed door with their bodies as they held one another close and kissed once more. Lucy was in a state of sheer bliss, loving the way he dropped soft kisses on her cheek, her throat and then traced his way back to her mouth once more.

'I love you,' she murmured.

'Mmm…me, too. I'll love you forever and a day.' He kissed her again and for the next few minutes there was quiet throughout the garden, except for the gentle sound of birdsong.

And then… 'What you doing?' a small voice piped up from the side of the garden, and they both began to laugh.

* * * * *

SUMMER WITH A
FRENCH SURGEON

BY
MARGARET BARKER

First published in Great Britain 2012
by Mills & Boon, an imprint of Harlequin (UK) Limited.
Harlequin (UK) Limited, Eton House, 18-24 Paradise Road,
Richmond, Surrey TW9 1SR

© Margaret Barker 2012

ISBN: 978 0 263 89165 2

Harlequin (UK) policy is to use papers that are natural, renewable and recyclable products and made from wood grown in sustainable forests. The logging and manufacturing process conform to the legal environmental regulations of the country of origin.

Printed and bound in Spain
by Blackprint CPI, Barcelona

Dear Reader

I've returned once more to my favourite part of France for the setting of SUMMER WITH A FRENCH SURGEON. I fell in love with the area when I strolled hand in hand one summer's day along a favourite beach with my boyfriend John, who was soon to be my husband. Later we took our children. Now some of our children and grandchildren live not far from this beach.

I still walk along the same beach if I'm searching for a new romantic story. Although my husband died a few years ago I still feel the inspiration he used to give me when I needed to conjure up a romantic hero.

The beach is set in a beautiful area of hills and valleys near fashionable Le Touquet and the picturesque old town of Montreuil-sur-mer. It's a perfect background for the romance of Julia and Bernard, two doctors who initially fight against the attraction that pulls them together. There are many obstacles to overcome before they can give in to the romantic love that finally claims them for ever.

I hope you enjoy reading their story as much as I enjoyed writing it.

Margaret

To my wonderful family, who give me continual love,
inspiration and happiness.

CHAPTER ONE

EVER since she'd been tiny, Julia had always made a special point of trying to appear confident. Well, with three older brothers to boss her around she'd had to be tough to survive. Still, glancing around now at her fellow trainee surgeons, she felt decidedly nervous. Since her disastrous marriage to Tony—who'd done his best to destroy whatever confidence she'd had—her life had been an uphill struggle to even get back to how she'd felt as a teenager, competing against her brilliant medical-student and qualified brothers.

Coming here, to France, to further her surgical career was the first step on her long journey back to self-confidence. And, in fact, looking out of the taxi as she had been driven down the hill just now towards St Martin sur Mer, she'd been in seventh heaven as she'd absorbed the wonderful scenery spread out in front of her. The stunning view had made her forget any apprehension she'd had about taking this big step.

She'd found herself overwhelmed with nostalgia as she'd seen the undulating sand dunes spilling down onto the beach and behind them the small, typically French hotels, cafés *tabac*, restaurants, shops and houses clustered near the high-tech hospital. She'd felt the excitement she'd known as a child when her French mother and English father, both doctors, had brought the whole family here for a couple of weeks every summer holiday.

She brought her thoughts back to the present as the eminent professor of orthopaedic surgery strode into the room. She caught her breath. Wow! Bernard Cappelle looked much younger than she'd expected and very… handsome? She paused, surprised by the turn of her wicked thoughts. It had been a very long time since she'd noticed any man in that way.

He was more than handsome, he was charismatic. Yes, that was more like it. He was oozing the sort of confidence she longed to acquire. Well, maybe, just maybe in another ten years, when she was an eminent surgeon, she would stride into a room and silence would descend as her students stared in awe at their professor of surgery, as was happening now with the great Bernard Cappelle.

If she hadn't made a concrete decision to hold off relationships since Tony had bled her dry of all desire for emotional commitment of any kind she would have allowed herself to fancy Bernard Cappelle.

In your dreams, girl! No chance! She wouldn't let herself even fantasise about him. Good! That meant she could concentrate on making the most of the six-month course without wasting her energy on emotional dreams about an unattainable man who wouldn't even notice her.

The awesome man cleared his throat as he looked around the assembled doctors. Ah, so he was possibly a bit nervous? At least that meant he had a human side.

'Hello, and welcome, ladies and gentlemen. I hope that…'

Bernard Cappelle began by welcoming them to the Hopital de la Plage, which would be their place of study and work for the six-month course. He explained they would study an orthopaedic operation theoretically before they moved on to the practical aspect of observing and assisting in Theatre. They would also be expected to assist with the pre- and post-operative care of the patients and also work in *Urgences*, the accident and emergency department, on occasion if required.

Julia took notes but realised soon enough that she'd read most of this in the brochure she'd studied carefully before applying. So she allowed herself to study the man who was to lead them all to the final exams, which would give them a prestigious qualification that would be a definite help to her in her desire to become a first-class orthopaedic surgeon.

She sat back in her hard and uncomfortable chair, probably designed to keep students awake. There were ten students on the course, Dr Cappelle explained. He'd chosen them from their CVs and was confident from their qualifications and experience that they were all going to give the next six months one hundred per cent of their available effort. He paused for a moment and his eyes swept the room before alighting on Julia in the front row.

'Are you happy for me to speak French all the time, Dr Montgomery?' he asked in heavily accented but charming English.

She was taken aback by suddenly being the centre of attention. Everyone was waiting for her reply. She swallowed hard. 'Yes, yes, of course. My mother is French, my father English, so I'm bilingual.'

'Then if you are happy I will speak in French...' He went on to explain that he was much happier when speaking French. 'And you are not intimidated by being the only lady in the class?'

She sat up straight, trying to look bigger than she actually was. 'Not at all. I was brought up with three brothers who did their best to intimidate me but without success.'

There was a scattering of sympathetic laughter. She was quaking in her shoes but making a valiant effort not to show it. She wished he would take his eyes off her and attention would focus on someone else.

'Excellent!'

A student sitting nearby spoke out in a clear distinct voice. 'Why is it, sir, that women orthopaedic surgeons are few and far between?'

Bernard Cappelle appeared to be giving the matter some thought. 'Good question. Could it be that the fairer sex are more delicate and possibly wary of taking on a profession that requires a certain amount of strength on occasions? What is your view, Dr Montgomery?'

'I have to say,' she continued boldly, forcing herself to display a confidence she didn't feel, 'I'm surprised to be the only woman on the course. I've never found, during my early career so far in orthopaedics, that being female is a disadvantage. When you're operating the patient is usually sedated in some way...I mean they're not likely to struggle with you or...'

Her voice trailed away as her depleted confidence ebbed and flowed.

The student who'd begun the discussion broke in. 'And there's always some hunky big, strong male doctor hovering around a fragile lady, hoping she'll ask for his help so that he can muscle in and...'

She missed the end of his sentence because the entire group was now laughing loudly. Ha, ha, very funny... she didn't think. She waited until the laughter died down before taking a deep breath and speaking in the clear, concise, correct French her well-spoken mother had always insisted she use.

'Gentlemen, you can be assured that I never take advantage of my so-called fragility. My brothers took me to judo classes when I was very young. I was awarded a black belt as soon as I was old enough to qualify and the skills I learned have often come in handy. So, as you can see, I only need to call for help when it's absolutely necessary.'

'Bravo!' Dr Cappelle said, admiration showing in his eyes. From her position in the front row she could see they were sensitive, a distinctive shade of hazel. Phew, she was glad she'd had to practise the art of being strong from an early age. Her show of pseudo-confidence was turning into the real thing, although she realised that had she known she would be the only woman on the course she might have hesitated before signing up.

Well, probably only hesitated for a short while. Looking around, she knew she could handle these young doctors, whatever they tried on. She'd learned a lot about men in the last few years. Basically, they were still boys, feeling as daunted as she was at the prospect of the exacting course they'd signed up to.

'I'm now going to give you a tour of the operating

theatres we use here at the Hopital de la Plage. Some of
them will be in use and we won't be able to go inside
en masse. May I suggest you make a note of the areas
you aren't able to see today so that you can find a more
suitable time to inspect them at a later date?'

Before they all filed out, the professor asked them to
call him Bernard. He said that he didn't hold with titles
in a teaching situation, explaining that it was easier for
him to get to know his students if there was always a
warm atmosphere, especially in tutorials like today. He
looked around the room as if to judge the collective reaction of his students to this unexpected statement.

There was a stunned silence. Julia felt slightly more
at ease with the great man when he said that but as
she glanced around the room she knew that her fellow students weren't taken in. Bernard Cappelle somehow managed to remain aloof even while he spoke.
She sensed an aura of mystery surrounding him, which
made him seem distant, brooding, definitely enigmatic,
approachable in a professional situation but with caution. Yes, his students would call him Bernard because
he'd requested they do so but at the same time they
would be wary of him. So would she but for several
reasons, some of them decidedly inadvisable given her
past history!

Being in the front row, she went out first and found
Bernard walking beside her. He seemed very tall. She
wished she'd put her heels on but hadn't realised they
were going to trek round the hospital.

'You don't mind if I call you Julia, do you?'

He had such a deep, sexy, mellifluous voice. She was
going to have to be very firm with herself to eliminate

any sign that she felt an attraction to him. There, she'd admitted it. Well, power plus charisma, plus a barely discernible twinkle in the eye, which undoubtedly accompanied a wicked sense of humour, all added up to a desirable package that she certainly wasn't going to attempt to unwrap. Bernard could teach her his professional skills and knowledge and that was all she wanted from him.

Besides, he was probably married, bound to have a stunning wife waiting for him at home. Although married men were often ready for a fling and flings were another thing totally off her agenda.

'Yes, you can call me Julia.' She didn't even smile, making it seem as if she was doing him a favour.

'Good.'

They were now going inside one of the theatres, which Bernard had told them was not in use that afternoon. There was gleaming, bright high-tech equipment everywhere she looked. She was really going to enjoy working in a place like this.

At the end of the afternoon tour Bernard took them down to the staff cafeteria, where the conversation drifted from the equipment they'd viewed and the endless possibilities of a teaching hospital of this calibre to their previous experience and what they hoped to get out of the course that would be relevant to their future careers.

Somehow she found herself next to Bernard again. She wondered if he felt he had to protect her from the attentions of her fellow students in spite of the fact that she'd made it quite clear she wanted to be treated in the same way as all the men on the course.

'So, do you think you're going to enjoy working here, Julia?'

'I don't know whether *enjoy* is quite the right word.' She took a sip of her coffee. 'I intend to get the most out of it but I realise it's going to be hard work.'

'You look like the sort of person who enjoys hard work—determined, tough, doesn't give up easily. From your CV you seem to have led a busy life both in and outside hospital. Am I right, Julia?'

She nodded. 'I suppose so—at least, that's what people have told me concerning my professional life. I've been focussed on my medical career throughout my adult life.'

'Did that give you enough time for your private life?'

'My private life? Well…'

She broke off. She wasn't going to notify her teacher that she'd come to the conclusion she had a serious flaw in her personality—her inability to handle her time outside the pursuit of her career. Especially in her inability to recognise a complete and utter swine when she thought she'd picked the man of her dreams. She turned her head away from him so that he wouldn't notice the misty, damp expression in her eyes that would give him an inkling of her intense vulnerability since the suffering Tony had inflicted on her.

Looking round the almost deserted cafeteria, she noticed that the majority of her fellow doctors were drifting out through the door, having been told that the rest of the day was theirs to orientate themselves around the hospital or do whatever they wanted.

She had been planning to escape back to the small study-bedroom she'd been assigned in the medical quarters and sort out her luggage. She felt that would be the safest option open to her now, instead of having a discussion about her least favourite subject.

She stood up. 'If you'll excuse me, Bernard, I'm going to make use of this free time to get my room sorted out.'

It sounded trite to her own ears but the last thing she wanted so early in the course was to be interrogated by her boss on the delicate subject of her private life.

As he rose to his full height there was an enigmatic expression on his face. 'Of course, Julia.'

He escorted her to the door. She turned left towards the medical residents' quarters. He turned right towards the theatre block.

She walked swiftly down the corridor. At the entrance to the door to the residents' quarters she found one of her colleagues waiting for her. She recognised him as the one who'd had most to say for himself. Tall, dark and good looking in a rugged sort of way, very self-assured.

He smiled, displaying strong white teeth as he stretched out a hand towards her.

'Dominic,' he said, as he shook her hand in a firm grip.

She reclaimed her hand. 'Julia.'

'I know. Some of us are having an impromptu meeting at the bar round the corner and we'd like you to join us if you could spare the time.'

'Well, my room needs sorting and—'

'Julia, we've all got things to do but…' He broke off and began speaking in English. 'All work and no play isn't good for you.'

She smiled at him. She needed to stop taking herself so seriously and it would be good to get to know her colleagues.

'OK. I'll come but I mustn't stay too long.'

'Don't worry. We're all in the same boat.'

'Ah, it's good to be outside in the fresh air.' Julia revelled in the warm early evening sunshine as they walked out through the hospital gates.

Across the road there were still families on the beach, children running into the sea, which she knew would still be a little chilly in the spring.

'Café Maurice Chevalier,' she read from the sign outside the café restaurant Dominic took her to.

She could see some of her fellow students grouped around a large table outside. Two of them were already pulling up another small table and a couple of chairs. There was a bottle of wine on the table. Someone poured her a glass. Dominic went inside to the bar, returning with another bottle and some more glasses.

Dominic went round the table, topping up wine glasses. They all raised their glasses to cries of '*Santé!*'

'Cheers!' said Dominic, proud of his English.

'Cheers!' everybody repeated, laughing loudly.

Names were bandied about and she managed to put names to faces. Pierre, Christophe, Daniel, Jacques, Gerard and Paul were the most vociferous. Dominic seemed to have been elected leader of the group. Julia was secretly glad she'd got brothers who'd shown her how to join in when she found herself in all-male company.

'This place was here when I was a child,' she said,

during an unusually quiet moment. 'I used to sit outside and watch the sun going down with my parents and my brothers. It's good to be back here.'

'I should think it's good to escape from the attentions of our grumpy old tutor,' Dominic said. 'I saw him deep in conversation with you. How did he come across on a one-to-one basis?'

'To be honest, I don't know what to make of him. All I hope is that he's a good teacher.'

'Oh, he's a good teacher,' Dominic said vehemently. 'But he's a hard taskmaster. Apparently, he went through a difficult divorce and he's sorting out custody of his six-year-old son at the moment.'

'How do you know?' Pierre asked, screwing up his eyes against the glare of the setting sun.

Dominic grinned. 'I came here a week early to get the feel of the place. Unlike Julia, I've never been to this part of France before. I was born in Marseilles. I chatted up one of the nurses—'

Loud guffaws around the table greeted this.

'And found out a lot about Professor Grumpy. There's a rumour that he's going through a bad time at the moment, touchy about his divorce and tends to take it out on his students if they don't come up to scratch. But he's a brilliant surgeon and teacher, much admired by his colleagues.'

'Well, that's all I need to know,' Julia said, putting her hand over her glass as Christophe came round with another bottle.

'Ah, don't be too complacent,' Dominic told her. 'It's also rumoured that he doesn't think women make good surgeons.'

All eyes were on her now. She found herself filled with dread. Not only was she desperate to make a good impression on her new teacher but she was battling with an insane attraction towards him. Could it be true he didn't like women surgeons? So why had she been the only woman chosen for his exclusive course?

She looked out over the beach to the sand dunes at the corner of the bay, breathing slowly until the feeling of dread disappeared. She would cope. She would have to. She turned her head to look up at the magnificent hill behind them. She didn't want negative thoughts to spoil the beautiful sunset that was casting a glow over the hills, just as she remembered from her childhood.

She glanced round the table. 'My tutor in England told me I'm a good surgeon,' she said quietly. 'It's what I want to do with my life. And I'm not going to let a grumpy tutor spoil my career plans.'

A cheer went round the table. She felt she'd been accepted, just as her brothers' friends accepted her.

She stood up, smiling at her colleagues who had now become her friends. 'I've really enjoyed myself but I must go.'

'I'll come with you, escort you back.'

'No, you stay and have another drink, Dominic. It's not far.'

He pulled a wry face, but let her go off by herself.

She walked quickly, pausing as she went round the corner to look up at the sun dipping behind the hills. It had almost disappeared but a pink and mauve colour was diffusing over the skyline. She remembered how she'd once thought it was a miracle that the sun could disappear behind the hills and reappear from the depths of the sea in the morning. Her father had explained about the earth being round and so on but she'd still thought it was a miracle. Still did!

She turned her head and looked out at the darkening sea. There were fireflies dancing on the black waves, illuminating the scene. It was truly romantic, though not if you were all alone surrounded by strolling couples and families taking their children home to bed. She reminded herself that this was the life she'd now chosen, to ensure that she pursued her chosen career to the height of her destiny.

A smile flitted across her lips as she told herself to lighten up. It was a bit early to be having grand thoughts about her destiny.

Oh, yes, she was going to enjoy her evening now that she'd calmed her wicked thoughts and got herself back on the journey that she'd set herself. There would be time enough for romance, marriage, babies and everything else she wouldn't allow herself until she'd established her career.

CHAPTER TWO

ALMOST three weeks later Julia was sitting outside Bernard's office, waiting for her turn to have a one-on-one meeting with him about her progress to date. She was studying the printed sheets that Bernard had handed out at the last tutorial. It was difficult to believe that the first month of their course was almost over. The days had flown by during which they'd all been bombarded with work assignments, essays to write on the theories behind various orthopaedic operations and actual operations to observe in Theatre.

Whilst in Theatre they had to make copious notes, all of which needed to be written up in their own time. The notes then had to be transformed into a coherent observation of the operation, including their own comments and criticisms. These were emailed to Bernard as soon as possible. In no time at all they received an assessment of their work with much criticism from him. She knew she wasn't alone in being the recipient of his scathing comments.

They'd also undertaken sessions in the *Urgences* department, the French equivalent of Accident and Emergency, where they had to do minor operations and treatments on emergency cases, observed and assessed by the director of *Urgences*, Michel Devine. He in turn reported back to the twitchy Bernard.

When Dominic had told everybody that Bernard was reputed to be a hard taskmaster, he had been spot on! She'd been so naive three weeks ago. She hadn't believed she would have to work under such pressure.

Just at that moment Dominic arrived in the corridor and plonked himself down beside her.

'What time's your endurance test?'

She frowned at him. 'Shh. He'll hear you.'

'Don't care if he does. I feel like walking out. It's time he cut us some slack. We're all qualified and experienced doctors, for heaven's sake. Who does he think he is, treating us like—?'

The door opened. 'Good morning, Julia. Dominic,' their taskmaster said, glancing severely at Dominic.

Julia followed Bernard inside and sat down on the upright chair in front of the desk. She wasn't afraid of him, she told herself as he went round to the other side and glanced at the screen of his computer. She reckoned all the information on her was there. Everything she'd ever done since aspiring to take on this arduous course.

He looked across the desk at her and at last there was eye contact with him. She couldn't help the frisson of excitement that ran through her as she looked directly into those dark hazel eyes. Why was she being so perverse in finding herself attracted to this man who'd made the past three weeks such an endurance test for her?

'How are you finding the course, Julia?'

No smile, just that piercing stare that was causing

shivers to run down her spine. Shivers she couldn't possibly analyse.

She took a deep breath. 'It's relentlessly tiring…but exceptionally interesting and frustrating at the same time.'

He frowned. 'In what way is it frustrating?'

'Well, you haven't yet let me loose in Theatre so I can do some actual surgery. I'm getting withdrawal symptoms from all this theorising.'

Was that a brief twitching of the lips or the beginnings of a contemptuous smile on his face? Whatever it was, it died immediately as he looked intensely displeased with her.

'Julia, you will appreciate that I have to make absolutely sure that if I let one of my students 'loose in Theatre', as you put it, that the patient will be in capable hands.'

'Yes, of course, I do appreciate that, but I've had a great deal of experience in Theatre and—'

'So I'm told,' he interrupted dryly. 'Your tutor in London, Don Grainger, gave you an extremely glowing reference, outlining some of the orthopaedic operations you have performed.'

She brightened up at this piece of news. What a treasure Don Grainger had been during her medical-school days and after graduation.

'So,' Bernard continued in the same dour tone, 'during this illustrious career you're pursuing, how much experience have you had of hip replacements?'

Oh, joy! At last she was definitely on home ground! She began to elaborate at length on the hip replacements she'd undertaken, at first assisting before moving on to operating under supervision.

He interrupted to ask questions as she enthused about how she loved to remove the static, painful joint and re-place it with a prosthesis. His questions concerned the types of prostheses she'd used, which she preferred and if she enjoyed following up the after-care of her patients.

'But of course I enjoy seeing my patients after I've spent so much time with them in Theatre. Seeing the patient before and after surgery, making sure they're getting the best possible after-care, is all part of the buzz a surgeon gets.'

'Buzz? What do you mean by this?'

In her enthusiasm for the subject she'd gone into English. Embarrassed at getting so carried away, she began to speak French again to dispel the wrinkles of concern that had appeared on his brow. 'It's the won-derful excitement of taking away pain and suffering and restoring a new, more active lifestyle to a patient. Not exactly what I meant but something like that.'

They were both silent for a few moments. The clock on the wall ticked away the seconds, reminding Bernard he had another student to see. He wished he didn't find this one so fascinating. Was it her enthusiasm for the subject or was it something he shouldn't even be think-ing about every time he met up with her? She was his student, a career woman, and he was a family man. Never the twain should meet!

He put on his stern tutor expression as he stood up to indicate the interview was over.

'Send Dominic in, please.'

She turned and walked to the door, anxious to escape from the inquisition and the conflict of emotions she was experiencing.

'How was it?' Dominic asked as she came out.

She shrugged her shoulders. 'I've no idea how it went,' she whispered. 'Good luck!'

The next day she was still none the wiser. If anything, she was now feeling even more frustrated. She really was getting withdrawal symptoms from being just a cog in the machinery of this difficult course. She needed to actually make a major contribution to an interesting operation in Theatre, feel the buzz of satisfaction she was used to getting when an operation was a success and the patient's state of health vastly improved.

She looked up from the notes she'd been studying as Bernard walked in and took his place at the front of the tutorial room. The chattering between the students died down as ten pairs of eyes focussed on their professor. She thought he looked slightly worried this morning as he glanced around the room.

'Good morning.' A slight nod of the head in her direction as he acknowledged her, seated, as she had been so far this course, in the front row.

Bernard's serious expression didn't change as he began to explain what would happen that morning. They had admitted a patient three days before who had been on the waiting list for a hip replacement. Apparently, the lady in question was from a medical background herself. She had elected to have her operation under general anaesthetic and in the interests of furthering the education of the budding surgeons in Bernard's group she had agreed that her operation should be used for teaching purposes.

'Surgery begins at eleven this morning.' He seemed to be directing his statement right at her.

Why was he still looking at her? She tried to shrink down in her seat. He raised his eyes again to address the now apprehensive students.

'I shall be performing the operation with the help of a qualified and experienced junior surgeon and one of my students.'

He was looking at her again. She swallowed hard.

'I have deliberately given you no warning of this because there will be times in your future careers when you will be called upon to operate at short notice and I wanted to see how you handle the added adrenalin that sometimes causes panic amongst the less suitable candidates.'

He smiled. Thank goodness! It was as if the sun had come out. She shifted awkwardly in her seat, sensing that he was about to make an important announcement.

'The reason I sent out a questionnaire before you arrived here, asking about previous experience of hip replacement surgery, was to ascertain who might be a likely candidate for the first operation of the course. Several of you indicated varying degrees of competence. I consider that some of you would be perfectly capable of being my second assistant this morning.'

He read from a list, Julia holding her breath apprehensively after she heard her name read out.

'There's no need to be worried. We are a teaching hospital with excellent insurance.' His smile broadened. 'There is a stipulation that patients must be chosen with care and must agree to everything that might happen during their surgery. The patient we will operate on this morning is a retired surgeon herself and fully co-operative. Now...'

He paused and looked around the class. 'Who would like the opportunity to work with me this morning?'

Talk about adrenalin pumping! Her heart was pounding so quickly she felt everyone in the room would hear it. This was the opportunity she should seize on. The opportunity she'd asked Bernard for. The old Julia would have been leaping to her feet, desperate for the experience. These days she could feel real fear whenever opportunity knocked.

Seconds dragged by. Nobody had moved. Several throats had been cleared, including Bernard's. She could feel his eyes boring into her. What had her father always told her? Feel the fear and do it anyway.

Her hand shot up, seemingly having a life of its own. Every fibre of her body was warning her to hold off, not to stick her neck out, but this was why she'd come here. To challenge herself and banish her insecurities. She could do this! Raising her eyes tentatively towards the rostrum, she was rewarded by a look of intense pride.

Bernard knew he'd goaded her on that morning. He'd deliberately put her to the test and she hadn't failed him. He'd already seen for himself how knowledge-able she was about her passion but, from what he'd learned during their brief time since she arrived, she was a student who needed her confidence boosted. And this could only be done by subjecting her to difficult and demanding situations that required top-class skills, diligent training, impeccable qualifications and endless energy. The ability to carry on long after your whole body was experiencing real physical weariness, if required.

Though he didn't doubt that intellectually she was probably streets ahead of her louder colleagues he worried that she might not be physically strong enough at times. He would have the same concerns with any female student. A fact that had made him consider hard about offering her a place on this course. If he was honest with himself, he'd only admitted her to the course as a favour to his old friend Don Grainger. Don was no fool. He wouldn't have put her forward to take the course if he didn't think she was a natural surgeon.

But Julia still had to prove herself to him. Although he trusted his old friend, he needed to be in Theatre with her himself to actually make a sound judgement.

He composed his features back to the completely objective, professional tutor he was supposed to be. But it was difficult to hold back the elation he felt now that his plan had worked. The teacher in him wanted to build up her confidence, which he surmised had for some reason taken a knock somewhere along the way. The fact that he found her impossibly attractive must be dealt with as a separate issue, which couldn't in any way colour his professional judgement of her.

'Thank you, Julia. Would you meet me in the ante-theatre at ten-thirty, please? We shall be using the teaching theatre where those of you not required on the lower surgery area will sit on the raised seats behind the transparent screens. You will be able to hear everything, take notes and ask questions at the end of the operation.'

Julia dealt with the moment of panic that suddenly

came over her. She needed to escape and scan her notes. She mustn't leave anything to chance during her debut in Theatre. And she wanted time to check out the patient. That was always important. She wasn't dealing with an abstract. This was a human being who deserved respect so perhaps it would be possible to…

Thoughts tumbled through her mind as she hurried to the door, only to find that Bernard was waiting there for her.

'Would you like to meet the patient?'

She gave a sigh of relief. 'That's definitely on my check list…along with everything else I need to do.'

'Don't worry. There's plenty of time.'

She revelled in his smooth, soothing voice and remembered that he must have had to go through difficult situations to reach the heights of his profession. She had a lot to prove to him so she felt intensely nervous because he still hadn't thawed out with her. Could she work alongside him without making a fool of herself?

She squared her shoulders. She would do the best for the patient, as she had always done, and Bernard's opinion of her didn't matter. Oh, but his opinion of you does matter, said a small, nagging voice in her head.

'You look nervous, Julia,' he said, as if reading her thoughts. 'Take a deep breath. Now let it out. That's better. I wouldn't let you operate on my patient if I didn't think you were capable, extremely capable according to your previous tutor.'

She felt as if she'd grown taller already and much stronger. Her thoughts were clearing and she could feel a list of priorities forming in her head.

He led her along the corridor, speaking now in a gentler tone than he usually used. She felt comforted, supported both physically and mentally. His arm brushed hers as they walked together and she was surprised by the sparks of attraction his close proximity aroused. Not an easy situation to be in. Nervous of Bernard because he would be judging her performance in Theatre, concerned about their patient and surprised at the frequent frissons of attraction towards her boss. This was going to be an intensely difficult situation.

He had a difficult job as tutor to ten students who had begun to regard him as the enemy. But she was beginning to view Bernard differently. Again she felt a tingling down her spine and knew she mustn't give in to this strange insane feeling that was forcing itself upon her.

'You see, Julia, in most hospital situations the surgical team meet the patient before they operate, don't they? So I do like my students to be involved in the pre-operative and post-operative care of their patients, working alongside the full-time hospital staff.'

She felt her clinical interest rising along with the added interest engendered by simply being alongside this charismatic man. On this, her surgical debut day, when she wanted to use her skills and knowledge as best she could, she was also trying so hard not to let her personal interest in him get in the way.

'Yes, as I told you, I would very much like to meet our patient. You said she was a surgeon?'

'An extremely eminent surgeon here in France. As a student I was very much in awe of her.'

'So you've known her a long time?'

He smiled as he looked sideways at his demure companion, looking so fresh, so young, so infinitely…he checked his thoughts…capable. Yes, she was capable. That was all that mattered.

He composed his thoughts again. 'I feel we shall experience full co-operation from our learned colleague. She was a great help when I was a young student in Paris.'

They walked together along the corridor, he adapting his stride to her slower pace. In the orthopaedic ward Bernard led her into one of the single rooms.

'Hello, Brigitte. How are you this morning?'

The patient, who was seated in a comfortable armchair by the window, smiled and put down her newspaper.

'Bernard! I'm very well, thank you, and so relieved that I'm going to have my operation today.'

He introduced Julia as a well-qualified doctor from England who was working towards a career in orthopaedic surgery.

'Julia has had a great deal of surgical experience. She has been mentored by our esteemed colleague Don Grainger and comes to us with his own high recommendations.'

The patient smiled. 'High praise indeed from Don.'

'Well, he's been Julia's tutor since medical school and he wrote in glowing terms about her capabilities. So much so that I've decided to tell my designated assistant to remain on standby in the theatre. I may or may not need him. How would you both feel about that?'

Brigitte leaned forward towards Julia. 'I would be delighted to help you up the career ladder in any way I can, Julia. After the operation—at which, of course, you must assist—we must have a long chat. I truly miss my days in surgery but my arthritis cut my career short. I like to keep up with the latest developments, though.'

Bernard was waiting for Julia's answer. 'And how do you feel about assisting with the surgery, Julia?'

'Very honoured.' She felt confident. Why shouldn't she be, with such generous support from the patient and professor?

'Excellent!' Bernard smiled.

Jeanine, the orthopaedic sister, came in to explain that they were about to prepare their patient for surgery. Did Bernard wish to do a further examination? He said he would like a few minutes to show his assistant the extent of the arthritic damage to the hip. Brigitte, walking with a stick, made her way back to her bed and lay down with a thankful sigh of relief.

She pointed out the most painful areas of her leg, which were around the the head of the right femur. Bernard held up the X-rays so that Julia could see the extent of the arthritic erosion and they discussed the method they were going to use to remove the damaged bone and replace it with a prosthesis.

Leaving the patient to be prepared for Theatre by the nursing staff, Julia still felt slightly apprehensive but at the same time she realised how lucky she was to be given an ideal situation like this in which to move forward, gathering confidence along the way. At the same time she would not only be furthering her career, she would be easing the pain and improving the health of a patient, which was why she and all the members of her family had joined the medical profession.

She walked towards the medical quarters. She needed

a few minutes of peace and quiet to gather her thoughts and focus on the operation in front of her. She no longer felt the need to check her notes. Every bit of knowledge she needed was stored in her brain. She'd assisted at a hip replacement before on several occasions, actually performing part of the surgery with an experienced surgeon hovering nearby, watching her every move, ready to stop or correct anything he didn't approve of.

It wouldn't be any different this time, except that it would be Bernard who would be doing the hovering. And this affinity she felt with him, this desperation to please him was something that unnerved her. It wasn't just that he was her chief in this situation. It was something more than that. Something definitely emotional. An emotional connection. And she was trying to avoid emotion.

Where relationships were concerned she didn't trust herself, judging by her track record. At least she should leave all emotion outside the door of the theatre and concentrate all her training and expertise on doing the best for her patient.

Bernard was waiting for her when she nervously pushed open the swing doors of the ante-theatre. He gave her a smile of encouragement.

'OK?'

She smiled back with a confidence she didn't feel— yet! It would come back to her as soon as she started working. Concentrate on the patient, she told herself. Don't think about yourself. Remember the last time you assisted at a hip replacement. The outcome was excellent. The patient survived to live a useful life—and so did you!

She scrubbed up. A nurse helped her into her sterile gown.

'We're ready to begin, Bernard,' the anaesthetist said over the intercom.

They were ready. Julia was aware of the bright lights as she followed Bernard into the theatre. Indistinguishable faces appeared as blurs through the transparent screen. She made her way towards the motionless figure on the theatre table aware, not for the first time, that going into Theatre felt very much like going on stage.

She was so involved during the operation that she had no time to worry about herself. Her concentration was taken up completely by the task in hand. She found herself working harmoniously with Bernard. Sometimes he would nod to her across the shrouded figure on the table, indicating that she should perform the next stage while he supervised. All the procedures came back to her immediately as her fingers deftly performed what was required.

Time flew by and it seemed only minutes before she was finishing the final sutures. At that point she suddenly became aware of Bernard's eyes on her as they had been during the entire operation. She placed her final used instrument on the unsterile tray, which a theatre nurse was preparing to remove. As she did so she glanced up at Bernard's eagle eyes above his mask. She thought he was smiling but she couldn't be sure as he turned to speak to the theatre sister and began giving her instructions on the immediate after-care of their patient.

There was nothing more for her to do in Theatre. It was all over and she'd survived, and more importantly so had Brigitte. The patient was now being wheeled into the recovery room. As she made her way out through the swing doors, Bernard came up to speak to her.

'I think a debriefing session would be a good idea this evening, Julia.'

As he held open the swing door and followed her out, she allowed herself to admit that the sparks of attraction she'd felt as his gloved hand had brushed hers during the operation had been difficult to ignore. And when she'd looked up once to the eyes above the mask she'd had to take a deep breath to remain focussed and professional.

She looked up at him as they walked together along the corridor. 'Yes, that would be very helpful.'

'Come along to my office about six.'

He was pushing open the door of his office as he spoke as if anxious to be alone again. The door closed behind him and he walked across to his chair. He had to admit to himself that Julia really was a natural. Everything that Don had said about her was true. What Don had failed to mention about his prize student was how attractive she was.

What was it about Julia that made him feel so physically moved when they were together? Even in Theatre, the place where usually he was at his most professional, he'd felt sparks of attraction. That time when he'd passed her an instrument and their gloved hands had briefly touched... He shouldn't be thinking like this!

He had a difficult ex-wife to deal with, a wonderful six-year-old son who should be his priority. He
shouldn't even be allowing these insane thoughts to
enter his mind. He leaned back in his chair and took a
deep breath. That made it worse because he was sure
he could still smell that subtle perfume that lingered
around her.

Was he going mad? He switched on his computer
and forced himself to begin writing up his notes on the
operation.

Walking down the corridor, Julia had no idea what impression she'd given Bernard during the operation. He'd
given her no indication of his assessment of her performance as he'd closed the door, seemingly anxious to
get away from her.

Her confidence, which had been high in Theatre,
was now wavering but she reminded herself of the way
he'd reassured her all the way through the operation.
Now that she had time to reflect, she thought he'd even
smiled into his mask on occasion and nodded approval
as she'd used her initiative. And she was almost sure
she'd heard him whisper, 'Well done!' as she'd finished
the final suture—or had she imagined that?

But did it matter what Bernard thought of her performance? If she was satisfied that she'd given it one
hundred per cent and made life easier for her patient
then that was what really mattered, wasn't it? Seeking
approbation from Bernard was not why she'd come here.

She walked away purposefully. She would make
notes, be ready to ask questions and take the criticisms
that would help make her a better surgeon in the future.

At six o'clock she was standing outside Bernard's office, waiting for the second hand to reach the top of her watch.

'Come in!'

He was sitting at his desk. He stood up and came towards her as she closed the door, motioning her to sit in one of the armchairs placed near the window. He took the other one and opened a file of notes. She put her briefcase on the floor at the side of her chair after taking out her own small laptop.

'So how do you think the operation went, Julia?'

She cleared her throat and launched into the questions she'd prepared, going through all the steps of the operation from the first incision to the final suture.

He answered all her questions carefully and lucidly while she made notes on her laptop.

She leaned back against the back of the armchair as he answered her final question, and looked across at him. The expression on his face gave nothing away for a few seconds until he relaxed and gave her a studied smile.

'Excellent! I like a student who has everything under control both during and after the operation. I've no doubt you'll make a first-class surgeon.'

She breathed a sigh of relief. She'd sensed his approval but until that moment she couldn't be sure she hadn't been imagining it.

She smiled back. 'Thank you, Bernard. So, do you have any questions for me?'

'Just one.' He hesitated. He really shouldn't say what was uppermost in his mind. But he planned to be very careful if he felt himself giving in to the wrong emotions.

'It's been a long and intense day. Your trip shouldn't all be about work, however. You are a visitor to France after all, so may I buy you a drink at the Maurice Chevalier?'

She hesitated for a couple of seconds. She doubted very much that Bernard had extended this invitation to any of her fellow students, but his offer had been very formal. She would be foolish to try and read too much into it. Finally she smiled and nodded her agreement.

As she closed her laptop and put it back in its case she was aware of the now familiar tingling feeling running down her spine. Apprehension?

Yes, but it was something more than that, she admitted as she felt the light touch of Bernard's arm as he ushered her out through the door.

CHAPTER THREE

THE Maurice Chevalier was deserted when they first arrived. Julia breathed a sigh of relief. The last thing she wanted was to seen by her fellow students social-ising with their tyrannical boss. She had mixed feel-ings about her motivation in accepting his offer to buy her a drink. Yes, he was thawing out towards her. But would her colleagues think this was favouritism? And should she be alone with him in a social situation given the insane feelings she'd been experiencing?

Very soon a trickle of sunset worshippers gradually filled up most of the tables overlooking the sea. She folded her white cashmere sweater on her lap as she sat down and breathed in the scent of the sea and this unspoiled stretch of the coast that she loved so much.

It was turning a bit chilly now that the sun had dis-appeared behind a cloud so she would soon have an ex-cuse to wear the new sweater that she'd fallen in love with when she'd been doing some last-minute panic buying in London . She didn't usually spend so much on clothes but she'd salved her conscience by convinc-ing herself that anything that would boost her depleted confidence was a definite asset.

'What would you like to drink, Julia?'

'I'll have a Kir please, Bernard.'

He nodded before going inside to the bar, returning shortly with her crème de cassis and white wine aperitif and a pastis with ice and water for himself.

She smiled as he placed the drinks on the table. 'Thank you. I used to come here as a child with my parents and brothers when we were on holiday. My mother used to drink Kir. I knew it was a very grown-up drink but she allowed me a small sip. I loved the taste of the blackcurrant juice mixed in with white wine. As soon as I was old enough I tried one for myself and that became my favourite aperitif in the evenings.'

'To your grown-up Kir, Julia.' Bernard smiled as he raised his glass to her. He thought she looked so lovely now with the sun low in the sky on her face. What an enigma she was! To think that she had performed so self-assuredly in Theatre today and yet here she was reminiscing so naively about her childhood.

She smiled back as she took her first sip. 'Mmm! So reviving after a long day in hospital!'

'You deserve it after your performance this morning. I was proud of you—I mean, you're one of the students I selected from a large number of applicants who wanted a place on the course so it's good to know you didn't let me down.'

He hastily drank from his glass of pastis with ice, adding some water so that he wouldn't become too exuberant. He didn't want Julia to misinterpret his remarks. She might think he…well, he fancied her in some way. Perish the thought, he lied to himself, knowing full well that she was a most attractive woman and he'd better be careful or he might go overboard in his admiration.

But putting that aside, he told himself sharply, trying to leave his admiration out of the equation, whenever he discovered a talented student he found it very satisfying, euphoric almost! But he'd better hold back with the praise so that Julia would work hard throughout the course and not let him down. And he must also be aware that his delight in her achievements had to remain totally without emotional attachment.

Nevertheless, it was certainly true that he found himself drawn towards her in a way that a professor shouldn't think of his student. They were both adults, yes, but he mustn't let this attraction he felt affect his professional judgement of her during the months of hard work ahead.

He looked across the table. 'So tell me, Julia, what made you apply for this course?'

She hesitated before answering. 'Well…er…having survived a disastrous marriage that had been a total mistake, I felt it was time to make a fresh start and get on with my career. My family background also contributed to my decision. Mum and Dad, who'd planned to be surgeons when they were in medical school, had then taken a more practical route to become general practitioners because they fell in love, married when my eldest brother was on the way and…'

She broke off and took a deep breath. 'Sorry, Bernard, you don't need to know all this.'

'Oh, but I do. It's fascinating! Your story is similar to mine, in fact. I too come from a medical background where my parents gave up their ambitions in favour of family life. Please go on.'

She felt relieved she wasn't boring him. 'Well, as I

told you before, GP parents and three brothers, now surgeons, meant I had to be a high achiever to get myself heard in the family. Fortunately I enjoyed studying my favourite subjects. Only when I hastily married Tony after a whirlwind courtship and found it so difficult to find the time for study did I question the sanity of becoming a surgeon.'

She leaned back against her chair, her eyes temporarily blinded by the sun low in the sky, setting behind the hillside that swooped down into the sea. She delved into her bag for her sunglasses.

'That's better.'

She paused to gather her thoughts. How much should she tell him? He was a good listener, seemed interested, but was he simply being polite?

'At times I despaired of my exhausting role of wife, stepmother, medical student…'

'So you hadn't qualified when you married. Why didn't you wait until…?'

'I thought I was madly in love! I'd never been in love before and the wonderful euphoric sensations I experienced when I first met Tony swept me along. For the first time in my life I entered a world that was quite different from my own.'

Bernard looked puzzled as he watched the vibrant expressions on her face. 'In what way was it different?'

'Tony was a very successful man, having made enormous profits in the building and property business, proud of the fact that he'd come from a deprived background and made something of himself. Money meant everything to him. He lived and breathed doing deals, buying expensive clothes for himself, for the children and for me. He told me he'd outgrown his first wife, she was lazy, an ex-model who'd let herself go and wouldn't keep up with his aspirations so he'd set her up in an expensive house where she could bring up their two children. He'd bought a luxurious flat in London where he could continue his wheeling and dealing.

'I found out later that his wife had divorced him because of his womanising, realising that she was happier without him. She'd been hoping for a huge divorce settlement but she was still waiting. Of course, I didn't know any of this when I first saw him at the opera.'

'The opera?'

She smiled. 'Oh, it was a business deal he was doing with a client and he clinched it by taking this man and his wife to a performance of *La Bohème*. Anyway, I'd gone along with a group of fellow medical students and we were queuing at the bar in the interval, trying to get a drink.

'Tony was in front of me and put on the charm when he gathered that we were all medical students. He insisted on buying everybody a drink before whisking me off to his table and introducing me to his business friends as a young doctor. With the benefit of hindsight I know I shouldn't have allowed myself to be swept away by an unknown man who liked to flash his cash but I was still young, impressionable, and having had a cloistered childhood this whirlwind from another exciting world seemed the epitome of sophistication.'

'But what about your own friends? Didn't they think…?'

'Oh, they were happy to accept the free drinks but they thought I'd gone mad…which actually I had, for the first time in my life! I'd always been so careful to toe the line and do everything my mother and father told me…especially my mother. She'd insisted I mustn't marry until I was well established in my career. She used to constantly tell me about how she'd sacrificed her ambitions and forced herself to be content with life as a country GP, married to a GP, struggling with a huge workload whilst bringing up a family.'

She looked across the table at Bernard, who was hanging on her every word. She took a deep breath as she remembered her totally out-of-character stupidity in those early days of her relationship with the charismatic but totally unreliable Tony.

'You see, I was totally blown away by Tony's charismatic aura. I'd never seen anyone like him before except on TV or in a film. Looking back and remembering, I can't believe how gullible I was in those days. I feel as if I'm remembering something that happened to someone else, a little sister if I'd had one, someone with no experience of real life—which, in a way, was exactly how I was. I couldn't take my eyes off this tall, handsome character in the well-cut, expensive suit who seemed to demand attention from everybody who was listening to his deep, sexy voice.'

She paused as the weird memories from her past came back to her.

She took a deep breath as she watched Bernard's reaction. Yes, he was a good listener and definitely seemed to want her to continue.

'Tony was proud of the fact that he was a self-made man who'd come from a poor background. At the time I just couldn't help admiring him and then the admira-

tion blossomed into something more dangerous and I
fell for him, hook, line and sinker, whilst enjoying the
fact that he seemed attracted to me.'

'So he was impressed by the fact that you were a
medical student?'

'Oh, he thought I was a good catch. He told me during our disastrous marriage that he'd thought I must
be from a wealthy family because we were all doctors.
How wrong he was! Our education was the top priority to my parents and that made a big hole in the family budget.

'What I didn't realise was that his business deals
were getting fewer and further between and he needed
to find a wealthy wife to help keep him in the lifestyle
he'd got used to during his successful years. My parents
met him for the first time at our registry office wedding. My mother could hardly disguise her dislike of
him and she made no secret of the fact that I'd let her
down badly. That hurt…that really hurt.'

Her voice faltered as she remembered the angst she'd
suffered, knowing full well that it was all her fault,
knowing she'd hurt her mother who'd given up so much
to raise her family. She shifted in her seat, pulling the
sweater around her shoulders as she glanced away from
Bernard towards the beautiful seascape in front of them.
Maybe she should stop talking about her past and give
him a chance to recover from his busy day.

'Bernard, you're a good listener but I don't want to
bore you.'

'Please continue! I'm fascinated. I can see where
you're coming from now. I do like to take an interest in

the background of my students. As you say in England, it helps if I know what makes them tick, isn't it, Julia?'

'Yes, you got that exactly right, Bernard. You're finding out what makes me tick.'

He leaned across the table. 'I can tell you already, having known you only a couple of days. You're aiming for the top and it isn't easy, believe me. You'll reach the next peak and what will you find? Another peak to climb!'

He broke off. 'Please do go on. So you married this man from a different world? Were you happy at first?'

'Well, for the first few weeks of our marriage Tony boasted to all his associates—I won't call them friends because they were mostly hangers-on intent on helping themselves to his dwindling cash—about his clever young wife who was going to be a doctor. But the problem was that he thought I could pass my exams without spending time studying, be the perfect stepmother to his children when they came to stay at weekends, be a good hostess to his clients—and I quickly realised it wasn't possible. That's when it all turned nasty. His attitude completely changed. He seemed to think that by shouting at me he could turn me into superwoman, perfect in everything he wanted me to do for him.'

'You have another saying in England—marry in haste, repent at leisure. Isn't that right?' Bernard was watching her reaction. 'Was that what happened?'

'Exactly! He changed completely once the ring was on my finger and he realised my family hadn't endowed me with money. One of the things he told me before we married was that having fathered twins who were then five, a boy and a girl, he didn't want any more children.

It was a struggle to come to terms with that because I'd always hoped I would have children of my own when I'd established my career.

'I subjugated my own desires for parenthood by immersing myself in taking care of my stepchildren. I loved those two as if they were my own and it was a terrible wrench when we split up and I lost all contact with them.'

Bernard noticed the emotional waver in her voice as she said this. Yes, he could see she would adore starting a family. Warning bells were ringing in his head. He mustn't get too familiar with her.

'So what caused you to split up?'

'It was pressures of my work and trying to take care of my stepchildren. Tony, not being from a medical background, just didn't understand. I adored the children, bonded with them and began to put them before my medical studies, but Tony was still dissatisfied with the amount of time I could spare him. He began to look elsewhere.

'Everything came to a head one fateful weekend just six months after we were married. I was trying to get to grips with some revision in the study and was working on my computer when he flung open the door and told me to leave all that medical stuff and get into some expensive clothes. It was important that I should get out of my scruffy tracksuit and tart myself up so that I looked drop-dead gorgeous. He'd been speaking to a prospective client and he was taking him and his wife out for lunch. The wife, apparently, was a real doll and knew how to dress so I'd better make the effort.'

She took another deep breath as the awful memories of that occasion came flooding back.

'I pointed out that I had an exam on the Monday and I needed to study...'

She broke off as she remembered how miserable she'd felt. Bernard put his hand across the table and laid it over her slender fingers. 'Julia, you don't have to tell me if it's too awful to remember.'

She swallowed hard. The touch of his fingers and his obvious concern for her unnerved her. Careful! Be very careful. Don't mistake sympathy with emotional involvement.

'Tony told me he was fed up with seeing me studying. I was no fun any more. And then he blurted out that he'd met somebody else. He wanted a divorce.'

'So...what did you do?'

'To be honest, I'd had enough and it was a blessed relief to think that I could walk away from the hell that my life had become. I asked him to have my things sent to the medical school. He said he would make all the necessary arrangements for my stuff to be sent wherever I wanted. I took my laptop and a few books, went back to the medical school and tried to concentrate on the exams looming after that disastrous weekend.'

'You must have felt...'

'I felt relieved to escape from Tony.' She shivered at the bad memories that still haunted her, often preventing her from sleeping in the night. 'But terribly sad to lose contact with the children.'

They sat for a few moments in silence. Bernard had been deeply moved by the story of her marriage. He could see how she would need her confidence to be boosted at every possible moment. But he mustn't go overboard. Mustn't allow emotion to take over. Yet he didn't want to cut short the evening and they both needed a meal after their long day.

'Let's go inside and have something to eat. That's if you'd like to,' he added. 'Maybe you've got other plans tonight, meeting up with friends from the group or…'

'No plans tonight except to relax.' She smiled up at him. He was already standing, looking down at her.

He led the way. Inside, the warmth of the sun had made the place feel cosy and inviting. He held out her chair for her. The waiter came along and Bernard asked what the *plat du jour* was.

'Always best to get the main dish that's been cooked that day in these small places, don't you think?'

She felt very comfortable with him as he ordered the coq au vin for them. It came in a large casserole dish. Bernard dug the large serving spoon into the centre and helped her to a generous portion.

'Hey, steady on!' she said, reaching across to touch his wrist. A shiver went down her spine, a quite different shiver to the cold one she'd experienced outside. She felt they must have met somewhere before in a former life. She put both hands back in her lap.

'Did you live near here when you were a child, Bernard?'

He passed her plate across to her. 'I was born just five miles from here, up there in the valley beyond the hills. My grandparents were farmers. The farm is still there, but my father decided he wanted to be a doctor. He went off to medical school in Paris—like I did—and after qualifying he did a course in general practice so that he could come back to our village and fill a very real need. He set up practice in a room at the end of the house and my mother acted as receptionist and nurse besides running the family. She had trained as a nurse in Boulogne but she was born in the village.'

She swallowed a spoonful of the delicious chicken casserole. 'Did you have brothers and sisters?'

He shook his head sadly. 'No, my mother wanted to have more children but it didn't happen. She died of ovarian cancer when I was six.'

'That must have been awful for you and your father. However did you cope?'

'My father employed a lady from the village to help out as nurse, receptionist and housekeeper but it was hard for him to adapt. He also employed her daughter Marianne to help her mother with the housekeeping and look after me. She's still working up there at the farm just as she did when she was sixteen. She took care of me from the time I was six and when she married in her late teens her husband moved in to work on the farm. They became part of the family.'

He hesitated for a moment as if to compose himself. 'I was fifteen when my father died. He'd never been the same since my mother's death. He went through the motions of being a competent doctor but one harsh winter he succumbed to a bout of influenza that turned to pneumonia. I think he simply lost the will to live without my mother.'

They were both silent for a while, engrossed in their own thoughts as the delicious, home-cooked food revived them.

Bernard cleared his throat and put down his spoon.

'I always wanted to marry someone who would be my soul mate as my parents had been together,' he said huskily. 'But it didn't happen. Like you, I was mistaken about the partner I chose—or did she choose me?'

He gave her a whimsical smile. 'If only I could turn the clock back. Apart from the fact that I wouldn't have had my wonderful son, Philippe, if I hadn't met Gabrielle.'

She leaned back in her chair, watching the sad expression that flitted across his face. The young families around them were departing now, mothers ushering their offspring out of the door as fathers paid the bills. It was all so nostalgic. Why couldn't she have replicated something like this? Why couldn't Bernard?

It wasn't just that both of them were career minded, both aiming to climb the peaks to the top of their chosen profession. It was possible to have a career and a family—but not yet! The timing was wrong. She mustn't get ideas about the rapport building up between them. She mustn't fantasise about developing a meaningful relationship with Bernard.

'How often do you see your son?'

'As often as I can escape from my work. I'm going to Paris this weekend to see him. Philippe lives with Gabrielle in her mother's house, which is very convenient. His grandmother dotes on him and has been a tower of strength to all of us when my wife was…well, lacking in maternal instinct and hell bent on—'

He broke off. 'No, you don't want to hear all the sordid details of our less than perfect marriage.'

She wanted to say, Oh yes, I do. She liked to hear about other people making mistakes in their lives. It

made her feel in some way that she wasn't the only
naive idiot where relationships were concerned. But
she remained silent

'I'll get the bill.' He signalled for the waiter. Suddenly
he was turning back into the professional as his thoughts
turned to the work ahead.

'I've asked Dominic to assist me tomorrow in
Theatre. He came to me this afternoon and said he
would be happy to assist. It just so happens I've got to
do a knee replacement tomorrow morning so I'll be able
to put him through his paces. He's had a lot of experience but wasn't brave enough to volunteer for the first
operation of the class.' He stood up and moved round to
hold the back of her chair. As they walked to the door
he said, 'Thank you for setting the ball rolling today,
Julia. You'll be a difficult act to follow.'

As they walked back together towards the hospital
she was aware of his hand hanging loosely by his side.
She so wished he would take hold of hers but she realised he was in professional mode again. Just as well
when she'd decided to keep a rein on her own emotions.

'I've got to do some work,' he said briskly, not trust-
ing himself to relax his guard as they stood together outside the main door of the hospital. He did have work to
do in his consulting room but he was trying to ignore
his real feelings. What he wanted to do was whisk her
back to his rooms in the medics' quarters and… No,
don't go there, he told himself as he looked down at her
beautiful face turned up towards his.

'So have I,' she said quickly, knowing full well that
all she wanted to do was have a hot shower and climb
into bed. The shower should help to take away the mad

emotions running through her mind and her body, but would she be able to sleep?

'Goodnight, Julia. See you tomorrow.'

He bent down and brushed the side of her face with his lips, telling himself they were off duty now and hospital protocol had no place in this private moment. He mustn't give anyone cause to think that he was favouring one of his students because he wasn't. But he couldn't bear to let her go without some brief contact. Anyway, it was normal to exchange kisses on the cheek in France after spending the evening with a pleasant companion.

She walked quickly in the opposite direction from his consulting room, taking the long way round to her study-bedroom in the medics' quarters. She didn't look back.

He watched the slight, slim figure in the beautiful white sweater and figure-hugging black trousers turning the corner at the end of the corridor. He'd better wait a few moments before he made his way to his own study-bedroom, where he planned to sleep that night. He felt too tired to drive out to the farm and he'd had a couple of glasses of wine with the meal. He could go and do some work in his consulting rooms but he didn't think it would be easy to concentrate tonight.

He realised the nurse on Reception was watching him. He hoped he'd given Julia enough time to disappear into her room.

He let the water cascade over him as he soaped himself with shower gel. His mind was buzzing with conflicting ideas. It was going to be so difficult to keep his growing admiration for Julia under control. He had to remain totally professional. But that was easier said than done.

He stepped out of the shower and reached for a towel. He'd hoped the hot water would help to put him in a steadier mood. It had been a long time since he'd felt like this. As he dried himself and threw the towel towards the laundry bin he recognised the symptoms only too well. It wasn't necessary to have medical qualifications to recognise that he was very attracted to Julia. And he wanted to go along with this mad, wonderful feeling. But it could be disastrous!

He climbed between the cool sheets, kicking at the corners where the maid had tucked them in. That was better. One of the perks of being a consultant was that you had daily maid service and a decent-sized room. He thought of the tiny room where Julia would be cloistered and hoped she was comfortable. She would have forgotten all about him and knowing how conscientious she was she would be reading up about knee-replacement operations.

He put his hands behind his head and leaned back against the pillow as he thought about how she had suffered with her marriage. He would have liked to talk about his own marriage with her but had decided against it even though he just knew she would have lent him a sympathetic ear. But he'd never told anyone the full story of what had gone wrong with Gabrielle. He'd been every bit as gullible as Julia! But at least he had his adorable son, Philippe, to dote on—the one good thing to have come from that ill-advised union.

Which reminded him about the latest bombshell his ex-wife had dropped recently. She was planning to get married again. The prospective husband was rich apparently but also considerably older than she was with grown-up children from a previous marriage and he didn't want a young child around the house. So she'd asked him to have Philippe live with him.

Bernard knew he would be absolutely thrilled at having Philippe with him. He'd already planned ahead so that the new arrangement would work. Philippe could stay at the farm during the day with Marianne, go to the local school as he'd done, make friends in the village. He felt the excitement rising at the prospect. But it was tinged with apprehension about how Veronique, Gabrielle's mother, would react.

His ex-wife hadn't yet told her mother of her plans. It would be too cruel to simply take Philippe away. He was like her own son and she'd poured all her considerable maternal love into his upbringing to the age of six. He would have to make sure Veronique came over to see Philippe and that he took his son to Paris as often as he could.

He could feel the doubts creeping in already and knew that if he was really honest with himself the situation was far from solved. Ah, well, he'd have to contend with that problem this weekend when he went to Paris. Meanwhile, he'd better try to get some sleep.

He allowed himself to think about Julia as he closed his eyes, alarmed at the physical reaction surging through his body. If only he'd been able to bring her back here, make love to her and then fall asleep with her in his arms.

He knew that it was going to take an effort on his part but he had to stop thinking like this, definitely try to see her only in a professional situation. Yes, that was what he should do. But whether he could keep to this resolution was a different matter.

CHAPTER FOUR

As Julia showered in the tiny bathroom tucked away in the corner of her study-bedroom her thoughts turned to the day ahead. Hard to believe she'd been here more than a month. The last five weeks had flown by so quickly as she'd tried hard to put all her energy into adapting to her new situation.

She stepped out of the shower and grabbed a large fluffy towel. A whole weekend stretched ahead of her. Two whole days when she was going to try and catch up on her sleep, do some work on the notes she'd taken during Bernard's tutorials and then spend some time outside in the glorious June sunshine.

For the past few weeks she'd spent far too much time indoors, in Theatre and in the wards, seeing the pre-operative and post-operative patients in her care. On two occasions she'd been called in to help out in the *Urgences* department, the French equivalent of Accident and Emergency. She'd enjoyed all her work, giving all her energies and expertise to the patients and ensuring she learned and made notes on every important medical experience to store up for future reference.

But as she pulled on her jeans and a favourite old black T-shirt she knew she'd neglected her own health and strength in her desire to embrace every situation in her new life. It was something her parents had constantly chided her about. But it had been a case of 'Do as I say, not do as I do.' She'd long ago realised she was inherently disposed to using up her energy and then falling back on her frazzled nerves with an empty tank of petrol—just like her parents and brothers.

Nevertheless, she had work to do this morning before she could play. She sat down at her desk and reached for her laptop and the notebook that was always in her bag. She tried to put as much information straight onto the laptop but in many situations where she had a hands-on approach this was impossible.

She particularly enjoyed Bernard's tutorials because they seemed to be the only times she saw him nowadays—when they were in a professional situation. He'd definitely thawed out with all of his students and she'd noticed he'd gained their respect now that they appreciated how much he wanted them all to succeed.

She'd been particularly amazed—and gratified!—when he'd praised her in front of all the students, saying she'd made him reassess his opinion of female orthopaedic surgeons. 'I've no doubt now that Julia is inherently talented and a natural at this type of surgery.'

She'd been delighted by his praise, but slightly apprehensive. She worried that her fellow students would tease her for being teacher's pet. She needn't have worried on that score because they crowded aound her at the end of the tutorial, congratulating her. Those who'd watched her debut performance were especially complimentary.

Dominic had actually kissed her on both cheeks,

and as she glanced at their tutor on the rostrum she'd seen him frowning with disapproval. Strange. She didn't know what to make of that. Dominic was ever the flamboyant one of the crowd and she'd made a point of discouraging any advances. While she enjoyed spending time in Dominic's company, if she was honest with herself it was Bernard's attentions she longed for.

She wondered what he was doing this weekend. She knew he'd been off to Paris to see his son on the weekend after they'd enjoyed supper together at the Maurice Chevalier. She'd looked forward to his return but on the Monday morning, as they'd worked together, he'd seemed distant, preoccupied even. During a coffee break, when all her colleagues had been with them, she'd plucked up courage, hoping to break the ice, and asked him if he'd enjoyed his weekend. He'd answered briefly that, yes, it had made a change from hospital life.

From the pained expression on his face she'd deduced it hadn't been a total success. But there had been something else in his manner towards her. Without being overtly cold, he was putting her at arm's length, as it were. Making it obvious that perhaps he regretted being so warm towards her after her debut performance in Theatre. At least, that was how she'd taken it. So she'd thrown herself into her work and reined in her emotions, which, yes, she admitted it now, had been getting out of control.

But it hadn't been easy. She was still plagued by embarrassing thoughts about him. Thoughts that had nothing to do with real life and never could become reality…could they? She was like a teenager with a crush on the teacher! She should get out more, which she was definitely going to do this morning after she'd done some work on her notes.She sighed as she opened up and began reading the scribbled notes, remembering how she'd hung on every word as Bernard had delivered an off-the-cuff mini-lecture about performing amputations a couple of days ago. The importance of preparing the patient both physically and mentally. And then the after-care, the importance of listening, referring the patient to the best professional care. She'd been totally enthralled by his sympathetic approach, by the stories he'd told them about his secondment as an army surgeon in a war zone overseas. Some of his descriptions of what that had entailed had brought tears to her eyes because she'd found herself thinking she was so glad that he hadn't had to have a limb amputated.

That beautiful body of his—well, she assumed it was magnificent beneath the well-cut suits. Occasionally when he took off his jacket and rolled up his sleeves in a practical situation she'd seen muscles that looked as if they should be on one of those statues she'd seen when she'd wandered around the Louvre in Paris.

She made a determined effort to gather her thoughts and get back to the real work in hand.

A couple of hours later she got up from her desk and pulled on her jeans and a T-shirt. Scraping her long blonde hair into a ponytail, she hurried out of her room, anxious to get on the beach before it got too hot.

In a room not too far away down the corridor that was reserved for senior staff Bernard was also working on his laptop. He was transcribing notes for a paper he had to deliver at a conference in Paris soon. He'd been putting it off as he'd had to spend a lot of time with his students during the last month. They were an intelligent group and the work was enjoyable but time consuming.

He glanced at his watch. Good thing he'd started early that morning. He'd still have to finish off the paper while Philippe was here. He'd promised to take him to the beach. Perhaps if he took him there this morning they could go up to the farm, have lunch and then he could work for a couple of hours while Marianne took care of Philippe.

He phoned the farm. Marianne was delighted with the arrangement he proposed. 'Yes, take Philippe to the beach for the good sea air before you come out here for lunch. Your rooms are ready, of course. See you soon, Bernard!'

He started to get ready for the arrival of his son. Philippe's car, driven by the uniformed chauffeur, would arrive soon from Paris. This was one of the perks that Gabrielle had got used to since she'd begun dating the wealthy Frederic—her soon-to-be husband.

Julia walked briskly down to the beach. As the warm summer breeze fanned her cheeks she felt reinvigorated. This was exactly what she needed today. Fresh air. No work. No worries!

She skipped down the wooden steps that led onto the sand and broke into a gentle jog. As her breathing improved to a steady rhythm she increased her pace to a gentle run. Mmm, it was good to know her limbs hadn't seized up as she worked endlessly in hospital! She ran towards the sea and began to follow the shoreline.

'Julia?'

She turned at the sound of a man's voice. A little way up the beach a man in a T-shirt and shorts was digging a moat round a sandcastle. A child was helping him.

'Bernard?' She stood still, panting to get her breath back.

Bernard stopped digging and leaned on his spade. 'I don't mean to disturb your run but I'd love you to meet my son.'

She smiled as she walked up the beach towards him. He came towards her. Her heart, which had increased its rate due to her running, was now beating even more rapidly.

The young boy followed behind.

'Hello.' She smiled down at the young boy who turned to his father, looking up at him adoringly whilst waiting to be enlightened as to who the lady was.

'This is Julia, Philippe.'

Philippe extended his hand towards her. 'Hello, *mademoiselle*.'

She gave the charming boy a big smile. 'Oh, please call me Julia,' she said in French. 'Have you come from Paris this morning?'

Bernard watched her easy rapport with his son. It gave him a warm feeling but warning bells rang. Julia was only here for six months. He mustn't allow a rapport to build up between them. Philippe would be sad when she had to leave. So would he!

'Yes, I came by car. Are you a doctor here, like Papa?'

'Yes, I'm a doctor but I'm also a student on the course

that your father is in charge of. I'm learning how to improve my surgical skills.'

'Oh, yes, Papa has told me all about it. I'm going to be a surgeon when I grow up.'

'Are you?'

'Papa tells me I'll have to work very hard if I want to be a surgeon. Papa works hard all the time. Look at the castle he's building for me, Julia.'

'It's beautiful! A real work of art.'

'What's a work of art?'

'Well, it's something that's beautiful.'

'I've been digging the moat round it and piling the sand on the castle while Papa made the work-of-art bit at the top. I'm going to run down to the sea now and bring back some water in my bucket.'

Julia smiled down at the eager young boy. 'If you start digging a channel down to the sea, the incoming tide will flow into it and come all the way up to the moat round your castle.'

Wide eyes stared up at her in amazement. 'Will it really, Julia? Will you help me?'

She'd been totally unaware that Bernard had been watching with mixed emotions the two of them getting on so well together. He could feel the poignancy of the encounter and the feelings he was experiencing were difficult to understand.

She glanced across at him, her maternal instincts making her want to spend time with this adorable child but at the same time wondering how Bernard would feel. To her relief he was smiling fondly at the pair of them.

'That's a brilliant idea, Julia. Are you sure you can

spare the time? I know your tutor has a reputation for pushing you hard!'

She smiled back at him. 'I'm giving myself the whole day off to recharge my batteries.' She turned back to the little boy, who was still waiting for her answer. 'I'd love to help you, Philippe. Have you got a spare spade?'

Bernard picked up a large plastic bag and passed her a spare spade.

'Thank you.'

His hand, covered in sand, felt rough as it touched hers. She looked up at him and her heart seemed to stand still. She allowed herself to look into his eyes for a second longer before she turned back to his son.

'Come on, Philippe. Let's show Papa how hard we can work together.'

Bernard leaned against his spade as he watched Julia take his son to the edge of the sea. As they sprinted together she looked so young. Her long blonde hair had escaped the band she'd tied round it and was flowing over her shoulders. He couldn't help thinking how much more attractive she looked now than when she had to imprison it in a theatre cap. And, heaven knew, she had a serious effect on him in Theatre even without that tantalising hair showing!

He shouldn't be thinking like this. How many times had he reprimanded himself for breaking his self-made rule of no commitment ever again? And before his eyes he could see the rapport developing between Julia and Philippe.

They were digging their channel now. The tide was coming in and beginning to trickle into it. Throwing aside all his reservations about relationships, he ran down the beach to join them. This was what he needed. Some carefree relaxation. If Julia could give herself a day off, so could he.

The channel grew much quicker now with three of them working together. In no time at all it had reached the moat of the castle and water was trickling in, slowly at first and then more quickly.

Bernard put the finishing touches to the crenellated edge at the top of the castle before reaching into the bag for a small boat.

'Here you are, Philippe. See if your boat will sail round the castle now.'

'Oh, it's brilliant! Look at my boat, Papa!' The little boy was clapping his hands with delight, stopping occasionally to push the boat if it got stuck in the side of the castle. 'Round and round and round and…'

'That was a brainwave of yours, Julia,' Bernard said quietly. 'I can see you've done this a few times.'

She smiled. 'I have indeed. And on this very beach. But the tide's coming in very quickly now so Philippe had better make the most of it. Not long before you'll have to pack up and leave. I'll help gather up your things.'

Together they gathered up the plastic beach toys and Bernard stuffed them back into the large bag. A particularly strong surge of water flooded the moat and he called out to Philippe that they would have to go now.

'No, Papa, I don't want to go!'

Another surge of water swirled around Philippe's ankles. 'OK! I'm coming.'

Philippe ran to his father for safety, putting his arms around his legs. Bernard hoisted him up onto his shoulders and picked up the bag then they all hurried up the beach.

'I've got my car parked on the promenade. I'm taking Philippe up to my farm. Julia, can I give you a lift back to hospital or are you going to keep running on the path up there now that the tide will soon be in? Alternatively…'

He hesitated only a second before putting to her the idea that had been forming in his mind.

'Would you like to come up to the farm with us as you've given yourself a day off from the tyranny of your endless work schedule?'

'Oh, Julia, please say you'll come! I can show you the sheep and the cows and the—'

'That sounds really exciting, Philippe.' She shouldn't accept this invitation but she desperately wanted to. She salved her conscience by telling herself that it would be good for Philippe to have someone other than his father to amuse him. 'Thank you, Bernard, I'd love to see your farm.'

'Hurrah!'

Bernard had already justified his invitation by telling himself that Julia obviously loved children and might like to amuse Philippe while he got on with some work that afternoon. He led the way up the steps and along the promenade to the car.

Philippe had slipped his little hand inside Julia's and was chatting happily to her about the farm, the animals and all the other delights of the place that was his home when he was with his beloved Papa.

'You don't mind sitting in the back, I hope? Philippe

is happier there if he's got someone to talk to and you both seem to have a lot to discuss.'

'Oh, we've got a lot to talk about, haven't we, Philippe? So, did you drive yourself over from Paris this morning?'

Philippe giggled. 'I'm only six.'

'Oh, I thought you were much older.'

'Philippe is six going on sixteen, actually.'

She smiled, positively glowing at the attentions of father and son. Bernard was leaning through the door of the car, checking on Philippe's seat belt and pointing out hers. He was very close as he leaned across to check on both of them. As he straightened up and prepared to close the car door their eyes met and Julia felt a frisson of pure excitement mingled with apprehension running through her. She felt emotionally warm and cosseted and decided to simply go with the flow for a few hours. No point worrying too much about where all this might be leading

There was absolutely nothing wrong with them being friends, she decided. But as she looked up at the expression on Bernard's face she held her breath.

His expression was one of total admiration as he looked at her and she could feel her confidence zooming higher. Bernard was so good for her professional confidence. She remembered how he'd praised her in front of her colleagues. That had given her ego a much-needed boost after the knocks she'd taken in the past. This was what she needed, a totally platonic friendship. The fact that she was only here for just over four more months and shouldn't be building a rapport with Bernard's son was still at the back of mind, but for today she shelved the problem. A day off was a day off from worry.

Bernard drove them out onto the main road.

'I'm going to drive as soon as I'm old enough, Julia. Thomas was explaining about his car this morning when we came down this hill. It's such a clever car, it changes gears all by itself. Papa has to change his own gears in this car, don't you?'

'It makes me feel more in control.' Bernard shifted down a gear as the hill grew steeper.

'Thomas says he'll teach me to drive when I'm older.'

Bernard remained quiet. Who knew what the future held? There were so many hurdles to negotiate in the new situation that his ex-wife had thrust upon them.

Julia was also confused about the man Thomas but she didn't want to ask questions. It was Philippe who provided a clue.

'Thomas took his cap off when we got outside Paris. Mummy likes him to wear it when he takes us shopping. He's Frederic's chauffeur.' He leaned towards Julia. 'I think Mummy is going to marry him soon—well, she keeps telling me she is. I hope we don't have to move into his house. It's so quiet and Frederic won't let me use his computer. I was only looking at it one day when he came in and he got really cross with me. I wasn't going to play games on it or anything like that.'

Bernard pulled into a parking area saying that this was a good place to admire the view. There was a tight feeling in his chest. The revelations that his son made every time he saw him made his heart bleed. The sooner he finalised the custody preparations and got Philippe over here, the better. He got out of the car and opened the back doors.

'Wonderful view, isn't it?'

Julia heard the emotion in his voice and saw the sad expression in his eyes. She could only guess at the situation that had developed in Bernard's life and he was obviously deeply concerned about his son's welfare.

Bernard was taking hold of Philippe's hand as he jumped out onto the grass. 'Keep hold of my hand, Philippe. I don't want you to roll down the hillside and end up in the sea.'

Philippe giggled. 'That would be fun!'

'Do you know, Philippe, I used to stand here admiring the view with my *papa* and mummy when I was younger?' Julia said.

'Really! Papa told me that you live in England.'

'Oh, I do live in England but we used to spend our holidays in France. My mother is French and my father is English. My mother was keen we should speak French all the time when we were in France so we would enlarge our French vocabulary.'

She broke off as she noticed the puzzled expression on the young boy's face. 'Sorry, Philippe, I keep forgetting you're only six. What I'm trying to say is that we needed as much practice as we could get to make sure we spoke good French. My grandmother lived over those hills there in Montreuil sur Mer.'

She pointed her finger towards the hills they'd travelled over so often.

'We used to stay with her when I was small and after she died we continued coming over to France and staying here on the coast for our holidays.'

Bernard was smiling across at her appraisingly.

She smiled back. He looked like a man who was also taking a day off from his worries.

'Philippe is so intelligent I'm speaking to him as if he were much older,' she said quietly.

'I entirely approve. I do the same myself. Expand his knowledge as much as you can if he's interested. If he gets bored he'll switch off. It's a fascinating world if he's with the right people while he's growing up.'

Philippe was anxious to be included in the conversation again. 'So, Julia, when did you learn to speak French properly like you do now?'

She thought hard. 'I sort of learned it alongside learning to speak English—as a child. It seemed natural to speak English to my father and French to my mother. My brothers learned in the same way.'

'How many brothers have you got?'

'Three brothers, all older than me.'

'They must be very old. Are they as old as Papa?'

'My eldest brother, John, is about the same age as your father, I think. One time when we were standing here John started walking down that steep slope when my parents weren't looking. His trainers slipped on the wet grass and he tumbled a long way down the field until he managed to stop.'

'Was he hurt?'

'No, but his clothes were all grass stained and muddy. My mother wasn't too pleased.'

Philippe giggled. 'It must be fun, having brothers to play with. Frederic, Maman's fiancé, has got a few grown-up children but I don't think he likes them very

much. They don't come to see him. He's very old, you
see, and he gets tired.'

Julia looked across at Bernard. As their eyes met she
could see his desolate expression deepen. Poor Bernard!
She wanted to lean across the top of Philippe's head and
give him a big hug—in a totally platonic, friendly way,
of course. She mustn't lose sight of the fact that she'd
come out to France for a fresh start and here she was
becoming involved with another ready-made family,
just as she had with Tony.

But Bernard wasn't like Tony. Nobody could be as
bad as Tony. But what did she know about men? Only
that if they wanted you they were charming and at-
tentive at first. When they were fed up with you they
moved on to someone else.

'Come on, let's all get back in the car. There's a
storm brewing up over the sea.' Bernard was pointing
out towards the horizon. 'Can you see the white flecks
on the top of the waves, Philippe?'

'Yes, it's so exciting. The white flecks on the waves
look like white horses riding over the waves. Oh, look
up there, Papa! The sky's getting all dark. Where's the
sun gone? Can't we wait here till it really arrives, Papa?'

'It's better to get to the farm so we don't get wet.'

Bernard drove over the brow of the steep hill and
started down the other side. The road was narrow with
tortuous bends. He drove carefully because the rain was
now pelting down and hailstones were bouncing on the
slippery road.

'I remember coming over into this valley as a child
and seeing that village down there! Difficult to see it
in all this rain but I know it's there.'

Bernard switched on the car lights, hoping that if another vehicle drove towards him it would also have its lights on.

'We can't see the farm in this bad weather but we'll soon be there. It's on the other side of the village.'

It was a difficult but short drive down the hill. The rain began to ease off as they drove through the village. Bernard pointed out various landmarks—the village school, the *tabac*, the *alimentation*, which sold groceries.

'There's no *boulangerie* these days. A van comes over from the next village and delivers the bread to the *dépôt de pain*—that building over there, which doubles as the newsagent.'

They were soon driving out of the village towards the farm. The gate was open. Smoke was curling from a chimney.

'Strange to see smoke from a chimney in June,' Julia said.

'We have an ancient wood stove in the kitchen, which is never allowed to go out.'

'I help Marianne put wood on the stove when I come to stay with Papa. Look, there she is.'

A plump, middle-aged lady was coming towards the car, carrying a large umbrella.

Bernard got out and took charge of the umbrella. 'Philippe, you go into the house with Marianne. I'll bring Julia under the umbrella I've got in the boot of the car.'

She felt a firm arm going around her waist as she moved towards the kitchen door. They were sheltered from the rain by the umbrella but as she splashed through the puddles she glanced down at her mud-splashed workout clothes.

'Oh, dear,' said Bernard. 'Looks like your clothes have taken a bit of a beating.'

Julia laughed. 'Are you trying to say I look a mess?'

His grip tightened around her waist as he steadied her advance towards the kitchen door. Rain was dripping from the edge of the umbrella all around them but for a brief moment she felt as if they were the only people in the world. He'd pulled her to a halt and was looking down at her with such a strange expression on his handsome face. She felt her heart beating madly.

She knew this was another of those magic moments in life that she would never ever forget. For a brief moment she allowed herself to think that nothing else mattered except this magic feeling that was running through her.

'Papa, hurry up!'

'We're coming, Philippe.'

CHAPTER FIVE

JULIA wiggled her bare toes in front of the lively flames in the wood-burning stove as she sipped the mug of hot coffee that Bernard had just put into her hands before settling himself amongst the squashy cushions beside his son.

'I can do that, Julia!'

'Do what, Philippe?'

She looked across at the other side of the stove and watched as the small boy wiggled his toes much faster than she could. He was curled up in a corner of the old sofa, snuggling up to Bernard, who was looking more relaxed than she'd ever seen him.

She smiled at the pair of them. 'You're much more supple than me, Philippe.'

The young boy giggled. 'That's because I like running about in my bare feet. Maman won't let me go without shoes in Paris but when I come home—I mean to this home, my real home—Papa doesn't mind, do you?'

Bernard put his coffee mug in a safe place on the hearth out of reach of Philippe's arms, which rarely stayed still when he was enjoying himself.

'That just depends on the weather. It wouldn't be a

good idea to wade across the farmyard while it's still raining, would it? You saw the state of Julia's jeans and shoes when she came in, didn't you?'

Philippe put his head on one side while he considered his father's words. 'You know, Papa, I think Julia should have taken off her things in the car so she wouldn't have spoiled them.'

'Maybe I didn't want to arrive in the kitchen half-dressed.' She took another sip of her coffee, feeling a nice, warm, thawed-out feeling creeping over her.

'Oh, it wouldn't have mattered, would it, Papa? You see people with no clothes on all the time, don't you?'

Bernard looked across at Julia with a whimsical expression on his handsome face. 'I do indeed, son. But not usually beautiful young ladies like Julia. I have to say, though, that Julia's own trousers are a much better fit. Kind as it was of Marianne to wash them, these baggy jeans tied up with an old belt look most comical on her.'

She gave him a wry smile. 'Oh, very funny! Are you trying to tell me I look frumpish now?'

'Julia, you would look good in an old sack.'

She felt overwhelmed by the admiration that shone from his eyes. She realised he was flirting with her, probably feeling safe because his son was with them.

Philippe was obviously enjoying being part of a grown-up conversation. Suddenly, he jumped up.

'Shall I get a sack, Papa? I know where Gaston keeps a whole pile of them in the barn. We could cut some holes for her arms and then Julia could put it over her head. Then we could all play at dressing-up, couldn't we? Would you like that, Julia?'

She pretended to be considering the offer, keeping half an eye on Bernard, who looked as if he was going to say something outrageous. Keeping a serious expression on her face, she said, 'I think you might get a bit wet, Philippe, if you go out to the barn.'

'Oh, yes, the rain!' Philippe stared across at the kitchen window where the drops of rain seemed even bigger as they lashed at the panes of glass. 'When will the rain stop, Papa?'

Bernard shrugged. 'Soon, I hope. We'll have to play a game that doesn't involve going outside until the weather improves. Would you like to find one of your board games that the three of us could play together?'

He looked up at Marianne, who'd just returned from organising the washing in the utility room alongside the kitchen and was waiting to say something to him.

'Bernard, I heard you talking about the weather. I was about to suggest we have an early lunch because the weather report says things are likely to improve...'

Julia gathered that the weather report on television had predicted there would be dry weather and sunshine in the afternoon. Marianne had a chicken casserole in the oven, which she could serve up in a few minutes.

'Excellent! Let's have an early lunch.' Bernard stood up and moved across to Julia. 'Be careful you don't trip up in those baggy pants.'

He held out his hand, which she took, not because it was required to steady herself but simply for the feel of those firm, enticingly capable fingers in an off-duty situation. Marianne said she'd laid the table in the dining room. Bernard, still holding her hand, led her down a stone-flagged corridor to the front of the house, which had a good view of the garden.

Philippe skipped along beside her, chattering all the time. She was glad none of the young boy's conversation required an answer because she had suddenly become overwhelmed by the warm feeling of the intimacy that was developing between the three of them. She felt she was enveloped in a family situation that seemed perfectly natural.

'I want to sit next to Julia, Papa!'

'That's strange, so do I.'

'She can sit between us, can't she?'

Bernard led her to the table where a beautifully laundered white cloth had been placed. The silver cutlery shone in the light from the chandelier hanging over the centre of the large round table.

'It's not often we need to have the light on during the day,' Bernard said, glancing out at the darkened garden with low black clouds overhead.

He held out a chair for her. Philippe sat down quickly beside her. Bernard smiled. 'It's a good thing we have a round table. My grandparents bought this table for my parents when they were first married.'

Marianne bustled in and placed the chicken casserole in front of Bernard.

'Enjoy your lunch!'

'Thank you!'

Bernard began serving out portions of the delicious casserole. Throughout the meal the warm rapport between the three of them continued. The conversation flowed, the food was exceptionally good and only

Philippe noticed, as he put down his dessert spoon, preparing to leave the table, that the rain had stopped.

'Papa, the weather report was correct. Here's the sun!'

He waved his arms excitedly at the sun, which was now shining through the windows as they left their places in the dining room.

Julia was feeling replete, having enjoyed a good helping of the chicken casserole and farm-grown vegetables followed by a home-made apple pie. Philippe had enjoyed joining in the conversation and she found she loved the sound of his young voice making interesting comments, asking questions, always giving a positive aspect to what they were discussing.

He seemed older than six but that was possibly because he'd had to get used to different situations during his short life. She hoped Bernard would elaborate at some point about why his marriage had been as disastrous as he'd implied. It couldn't have been his fault. He couldn't have brought about a divorce...not with his generous personality and wonderful parenting skills. His wife must have been in the wrong.

She remembered how, glancing up at Bernard as she'd finished her apple pie, she'd seen him looking at her with an enigmatic expression. Had he any idea how overwhelmed she was by the warmth of the situation they'd created that day, just the three of them? It was the first time she'd felt she belonged somewhere since she'd left her own family home.

Bernard suggested a grand tour of the farm, if he could enlist the help of his son as a fellow guide perhaps? After all, he knew the interesting places as well

as his father now that it had become second home
to him.

Philippe readily agreed to help his father show Julia
around. They started with the barns. The smell of the
hay in one barn took her right back to her own childhood.

'My brothers and I had some friends who lived on a
farm. We used to spend lots of time there in the school
holidays and the barns were wonderful places to play
hide and seek in.'

Philippe said children in France also played that
game but he hadn't got any friends to play it with when
he was here and there weren't any barns in Paris.

Oh, dear! Julia wished she hadn't started talking
about her childhood. Obviously, neither Bernard nor his
son had experienced the enjoyable if sometimes chaotic
family situations she'd had. Once more she thought how
sad for Bernard that his marriage had been a disaster.
He was a brilliant father.

They walked up the hill to see the sheep grazing on
the hillside and talked to Gaston, Marianne's husband,
who was mending a wall. The affable, middle-aged man
was happy to show them his wall-making techniques
and smiled encouragingly at Philippe, who was a willing pupil.

'We'll have you up here, helping me out, when you're
a bit bigger,' he told Philippe. 'Would you like that?'

'I'd like to stay here all the time. It's much better
here than in Paris.'

As they were going back down the hill, Philippe
skipping happily ahead of them, Bernard spoke quietly to Julia.

'You've no idea how relieved I was when Philippe just said he'd love to live here.'

'I'm sure he would. It's a wonderful place for a child.' She hesitated. 'You aren't thinking of...?'

'I'll tell you later.'

Philippe was running back up the hill. 'Papa, Julia, look, there's a rabbit by the side of that wall. Can you see it? Oh, look, there's another one.'

She couldn't help thinking that she didn't want this day to end. How wonderful it would be to spend more time with Bernard and his son. She tried not to think too far ahead. This was a one-off day. A day to cherish and not to look into the future.

Bernard handed her a glass of Kir as they sat together in the conservatory, which was bathed in the evening sunlight. Philippe had gone to bed without protest, being completely exhausted by the activities of the day. But not too exhausted to listen to the bedtime story he'd requested from Julia.

She took a sip of her Kir before placing the glass on the small table beside her wicker chair. 'You know, Bernard, little Philippe fell asleep when I was only two minutes into the story. Doesn't say much for my reading, does it?'

'Oh, I don't know. He was almost asleep when I lifted him out of the bath. I gathered you'd be downstairs in the land of the grown-ups within half an hour. What took you so long?'

She raised an eyebrow. 'Need you ask? Marianne intercepted me to check I had everything I need in the guest room. You are all being so kind. I hadn't intended to stay but you both convinced me I had to.

'Then there was your son beseeching me to have breakfast with him and you telling me that you didn't want to drive back to the hospital and… I could have got a taxi, you know.'

'I know,' he said languidly. 'But I wanted you to stay and I got the casting vote.'

He moved his chair closer to hers. 'I wanted to have time to talk to you in an off-duty situation. I don't want to think about the hospital tonight. And…well, I just wanted to be with you. I like being with you.'

He leaned across and cupped her chin with his hands. Slowly, he lowered his head and kissed her on the lips, a long, lingering, deliciously wicked kiss.

As he drew back she reflected that she would have preferred the kiss to have lasted much longer, but that would do for now. It had whetted her appetite for more, more of…well, more of everything where that had come from. But she conceded it really was not part of the plan for a new start in life. Except men like Bernard wouldn't wait for ever while she achieved all her ambitions and then told him he was definitely the man for her.

'What are you thinking?' he breathed.

She looked up into his expressive hazel eyes. For a brief moment she longed to tell him. To ask him if he could possibly understand her yearning to start a relationship with him whilst having to cope with her sensible reluctance to change her ambitious plans. She couldn't have it both ways…or could she?

She hesitated before moving on from her impossibly romantic thoughts. 'I was thinking how peaceful it is out here. This afternoon you said you were glad Philippe loves this place. Are you planning he should spend more time here?'

He leaned back in his chair. 'The fact is, the situation has been rather thrust upon me. Gabrielle is going to marry Frederic, a rich, retired businessman much older than she is. He's got grown-up children and finds Philippe too much trouble when he's around their Paris house. Gabrielle has asked me to have Philippe to stay with me permanently.'

'But that would be good for you, wouldn't it?'

He gave a big, contemplative sigh. 'It is my dearest wish to have my son living with me. There are a few problems to be sorted before we can go ahead. Gabrielle, of course, is anxious to be able to get on with her wedding plans without having to think about what to do with Philippe.'

'But surely, as his mother… I mean I don't understand. Bernard, you've hinted that your marriage was a disaster but you haven't told me why. Is your ex-wife to blame for…?'

'I should never have married Gabrielle. She was totally wrong for me right from the start and for that I blame myself.'

He splashed some more iced water in his pastis and raised it to his lips, the ice clinking as he took a much-needed drink. If he was going to be seeing more of Julia in an off-duty situation then he owed it to her to fill her in on his background. She was watching him now with a wary expression on her face, as well she might if she suspected half of what he was going to tell her.

He trusted her implicitly. He didn't know why because he hadn't known her for very long. But it was long enough to know she was his kind of woman. Whereas Gabrielle certainly was not and never had been.

He leaned back against the cushions and stared up at the ceiling where a fan was whirling round above his chair, bringing welcome cool air to the warm evening.

'My only excuse for even talking to Gabrielle was that I was young and inexperienced. I met Gabrielle Sabatier in Montmartre. I'd gone with a crowd of fellow doctors to celebrate the fact that we'd all qualified in our final exams. Gabrielle was working as a waitress in the restaurant where we were having supper. She told me later that evening…' he paused as a sudden vivid recollection of that seedy flat in a narrow street forced itself upon him '…that she needed a wage to pay her rent while she was searching for employment as an actress, having just finished drama school.'

He got up and walked over to the window, looking out across the lovely garden so lovingly cared for by Marianne and Gaston, and beyond the garden wall the hills bathed in evening sunlight. He'd always loved beautiful things in his life. How could he have fallen victim to the tawdry life that Gabrielle had introduced him to?

Julia moved swiftly across the room and stood in front of Bernard, looking up at him, her eyes full of emotion as she recognised he was undergoing some sort of crisis.

'Bernard, you don't need to tell me about your past life if it distresses you. Come and sit down again.'

'If only…' He enfolded her in his arms, bending his head so that their cheeks were together.

She could feel the dampness of his cheek as he struggled to contain his emotions. She remained silent for a few seconds, feeling his heart beating against hers, experiencing a longing she'd never known before.

And then he kissed her with an urgency that thrilled her through her whole being. This was the man for her, with all his past problems, with all his future ahead of him to sort out which way he would turn. She longed to be a part of his life.

Gently he released her from his arms and stood looking down at her, the evening sunlight bathing the two of them as if blessing their emotional embrace.

'Julia, I want to tell you everything about my liaison with Gabrielle. Things I've never discussed with anyone before. I feel…I feel you will understand why I have such a lot of emotional baggage to contend with.'

He took hold of her hand and together they walked back to their seats. He settled her and moved his chair even closer. She took a sip from her glass and he reached for the bottle of crème de cassis to top her glass up.

'You see, I'd never met anyone like Gabrielle in my life. I thought I'd fallen in love with her even while she was serving on at the crowded table in Montmartre. My friends were joking, saying she fancied me. Well, I was overwhelmed by this vivacious, sexy creature, as were all my friends.'

Julia couldn't help jealous vibes disturbing her. Oh, dear, she was becoming more involved than she'd ever meant to be. Maybe she should insist he keep it all to himself? His past was something she didn't want to think about.

'Gabrielle asked me to wait until she'd finished work

and go back to her flat with her.' He paused and drew in his breath. 'I knew what would happen. I wanted it to happen. Yes, we became lovers that night and I was too enamoured to see what she was planning.'

'Which was?' As if she couldn't guess!

'She thought I was a good catch. A young doctor with a safe, well paid career ahead of him. A meal ticket for life! Sorry, I don't want to sound bitter but…anyway, weeks later when she told me she was pregnant, like the idiot I was, I agreed to marry her.'

Julia felt a pang of sympathy for the young, inexperienced Bernard. She leaned across and squeezed his hand. 'It often happens to young men, even experienced men.'

He flashed her an endearing smile of gratitude. 'I hope Philippe has more sense when he starts growing up. Anyway, it transpired she'd been brought up in relative luxury in the sixteenth arrondissement of Paris, in between the Bois de Boulogne and the river Seine— in a very pricy house. Her father had been a successful businessman until he overextended himself, went bankrupt and took an overdose, after ensuring that his widow would keep the house, albeit living a frugal lifestyle with Gabrielle, her only child.'

'Did you ever think that Gabrielle had been traumatised by the death of her father?'

'Oh, I'm sure she was. Her response to the tragedy had been to turn herself into an even harder, more ruthless character. But I didn't know that when I agreed to marry her.'

He splashed more water into his glass as he tried to remember exactly how it had been. Julia was right in saying that Gabrielle must have been traumatised by the suicide of her father.

'Believe me, I've made so many allowances for her behaviour…but each time she disappointed me with her responses. Anyway, a few weeks after we were married Gabrielle told me she'd miscarried. I insisted on taking her into hospital where tests proved that she'd never been pregnant in the first place. She knew I'd seen through her plan. We became like strangers when we were together. She began to show her true colours, nagging me to rent a house in the prestigious area where she'd grown up and her mother still lived. I told her I couldn't afford it. I was at the very beginning of my medical career, working all hours I could, and I couldn't take on any more expense. I was exhausted most of the time.'

There was a sound of someone coming down the corridor. Bernard sat up his chair as Marianne appeared in the doorway.

'I'm going to prepare supper for Gaston now, Bernard. You're absolutely sure you don't want me to cook supper for you?'

Bernard smiled. 'We're not hungry yet, Marianne. I'm going to make an omelette and salad later on.'

'Well, if you're sure.' Marianne turned to Julia. 'I've put your jeans in the guest room. I do hope you have everything you need in there.'

'Thank you so much, Marianne, for everything.'

'You are most welcome. See you tomorrow.'

As the footsteps receded down the corridor Julia asked Bernard where Marianne lived.

'She and Gaston live in the old surgery at the end

of the house. After my father died we had it converted for them so they could be on site while I finished my schooling and moved to Paris to train as a doctor.'

They were both silent as Julia digested this information, thinking to herself that Bernard hadn't had an easy life. Perhaps that was one reason why he'd fallen in love so easily and so quickly with someone who'd appeared on the surface to be the girl of his dreams.

'So what happened after Gabrielle knew you'd seen through her machinations?'

'Oh, she started to make my life hell. There was I, trying to establish myself as a reliable junior doctor at the hospital and she just never stopped nagging while I was with her. I tell you, I was tempted to walk away from this disastrous marriage but I decided the honourable thing to do was to stick it out. In our family background marriage was a lifelong contract, not to be broken.'

'Didn't she work?'

'She got a small part in a TV soap and told me she'd got a long contract. But actually it was only for three months, to be reviewed. On the strength of that I gave in to her demands that I rent the house she wanted. We moved into the house. Two weeks later Gabrielle admitted her contract had been terminated. I phoned her director to enquire what had happened. He said she was temperamental and unreliable. Hah! What a wise man. If only I'd had the sense to see through her earlier.

'Anyway, I continued to work long hours and began to climb the career ladder. I was earning more and just able to scrape the rent together. Then one day when I returned home there was a note saying she'd left me.'

'How did you feel about that?'

He looked across and smiled. 'If I'm honest, I felt relieved. It was as if a burden had lifted from my shoulders. I assumed she'd met somebody…and I was right. But two months later she returned. She'd had an affair with a married man who'd promised to leave his wife but he'd gone back to her. She begged me to forgive her. I was too busy with my all-absorbing work at the hospital to contemplate divorce.' His voice dipped as he resumed a tone of resignation. 'I took her back.'

'Was she grateful?'

'She seemed to have changed. She even turned on the charm. I should have realised she was up to something. She began begging me to make love to her. I insisted she stay on the Pill. A baby at this stage of our fragile relationship would have been unthinkable.' He breathed out. 'And guess what?'

'She stopped taking the Pill and became pregnant?'

He gave her a wry grin of resignation. 'Why weren't you there to say that when I took her back! I saw right through her but it was too late. It was the last straw. Even though I'd always longed for a family, I knew I couldn't afford the added expense unless I earned more. I told her I was going to apply for a prestigious surgical appointment in St Martin sur Mer. If I was successful we would move there.'

'How did she feel about that?'

'She said she wouldn't leave Paris. I told her that if I was successful in getting this appointment I would support her and the baby, whether she came or not. When I told her I'd been successful she flounced out and went to live with her mother but not until after she'd demanded a large monthly sum to be paid into her bank account. The one good thing that came out of her move back to her mother was that there was a steadying influence in her life. Veronique Sabatier is a saint! How on earth she came to give birth to a daughter like Gabrielle I cannot imagine.'

'So Philippe has had a good grandmother to care for him?'

'Absolutely! What a relief. As soon as he was born I loved him with the all-consuming love that only a parent knows. And now…'

He spread his hands wide. 'I'm going to be able to have him with me always—well, until he's a grown man and leaves the family nest.'

She saw the loving expression in his eyes as he drew her to her feet, holding her close to him. 'Thank you for listening to me. I've never told anyone the full story of my disastrous marriage.'

And then he kissed her, this time more slowly, taking time to savour the joy of being with her. Neither of them was thinking beyond the next moment. The present was all that mattered.

He released her from his embrace, looking down at her with an expression of love on his face.

'Let's go and have supper together,' he said, his voice husky as he struggled to come to terms with the fact that all he wanted to do was lift her into his arms and carry her upstairs.

He put his arm around her as they walked towards the kitchen. She revelled in the connection that existed between them, wondering at how much their relationship had developed during the day. How much more could it develop before she found herself hopelessly in love and unable to sort out her conflicting emotions?

CHAPTER SIX

JULIA lay back against the goosedown pillows. She'd been able to tell it was goosedown as soon as she'd laid her head on the softness that had moulded itself around her head. Mmm. Everything about this room was luxurious, well appointed, but probably rarely used—she hoped! The idea of Bernard having a guest room like this made her think that he wanted to impress the girls he showed in here.

But then did he leave them here all by themselves to admire the room? Almost as soon as he'd shown her the superb bathroom, fluffy towels and expensive soap he had left!

But not before that goodnight kiss. Her legs began to feel weak again, even though she was now lying down. She'd been hanging on to her excited emotions, trying hard not to show her real feelings because she knew she simply couldn't have controlled her desire to make love with him.

When he'd taken her in his arms once more, just outside the door to her bedroom, she'd gathered her thoughts together in something of a panic. She'd wanted him physically, desperately, but her rational self had told her not to go there, not to upset the relative calm of their relationship, which worked with the current situation of professor and student. She'd made mistakes before when she'd allowed herself to give in to her passionate nature.

Yes, he'd kissed her gently at first and her wickedly fluid body had reacted with instinctive longing. Oh, yes, she wanted this man…oh, so desperately. But almost as soon as he'd started to kiss her with real urgency he'd pulled away and whispered, 'Goodnight, Julia,' in that deep, sexy voice. And before she'd known what had happened he had been striding away from her to his own room.

Shortly afterwards, in his room not too far away, Bernard, lying back against the pillows, was wondering why he hadn't stayed to make love with Julia, cursing himself for doing what he'd considered to be the right thing. He remembered how she'd felt in his arms. She'd given every indication that she'd wanted him to make love to her. He hadn't misread the signals. Would it really have complicated their relationship too much at this stage if he'd given in to his true feelings?

He rolled onto his side, waiting for the waves of desire to calm down. The cold shower he'd just taken hadn't helped as much as he'd hoped. He'd only known Julia a few weeks but he knew that he was falling in love. Being in love with a student—any student—wasn't an easy situation to be in.

Yes, they were both adults, so there was nothing untoward about the situation. Nothing that the hospital board of governors could possibly frown upon so long as they were discreet. It was more the problem of handling the emotion for the next few months before Julia finished the course and took the final exams.

For the final month he would find it easier. With the exams over he could relax. He would already have assessed her performance as a student during the course. A panel of external examiners would mark the exam papers and listen to her answers to their questions in the viva voce exam.

Thinking rationally, as he hoped he was doing now, helped to sort out his confusing thoughts. He realised she was the most talented student he'd ever had to deal with. He mustn't do anything to put her off track because she was obviously very ambitious and had a lot to live up to, coming from a prestigious family background like hers.

There was also the problem of her having been hurt by that dreadful ex-husband who seemed to have been hell bent on destroying her confidence. Since she'd arrived here, he'd been trying to build up her confidence again so she could realise her full potential.

Yes, he'd seen her blossoming into an excellent surgeon, relaxing with her fellow students and having an easygoing friendship with him. She already seemed to be more in control of her own life. He'd admired her when she'd first arrived but this increasingly self-confident woman was becoming more and more irresistible to him.

He turned on the bedside light again, knowing that it would be impossible to sleep, with Julia only a short distance away. The moon was shining through the open window onto his huge bed where he should have brought Julia if he'd given in to his true feelings. He gave an audible sigh as he wondered if she was lying awake staring at this same moon and if so, what was she thinking?

He'd been flirting with her all day so why did he have to rationalise himself out of going ahead with his natural instincts? He didn't even know how she would have felt if he'd suggested she sleep with him. As he'd held her in his arms on the pretence that he had simply been saying goodnight she'd been so wonderfully pliant. He'd felt every curve in that vibrant body reacting to his caresses. But he'd forced himself to leave her.

With the occasional dalliance making his off-duty time more interesting for a while he wouldn't usually have thought twice about making it obvious he wanted to sleep with her. If the woman was willing, they would go ahead. But it didn't mean anything. It was an experience that they both enjoyed as mature adults free of any committed relationship. He'd always checked that they weren't involved with a partner.

But Julia was special, the most wonderful woman he'd ever met. The only woman in his life who made him feel that he had to sacrifice his own feelings so that he wouldn't spoil her future potential. She was like a precious flower that he had to nurture.

The sun was shining in through the gaps in the chiffon drapes at her window. Julia stirred and cautiously opened her eyes, unsure of her surroundings. She'd lain awake half the night but the sleep that she'd just been enjoying had been very deep and she was reluctant to return to reality. Somewhere in a nearby room she could hear a child's voice singing.

So, she hadn't dreamed she was in Bernard's farmhouse. She hadn't imagined that wonderful day they'd spent together.

She sat up quickly as she heard gentle tapping on her door.

'Julia, can I come in?'

'Of course, Philippe!'

She pulled the robe from the bedside chair to cover her shoulders. Even as she did so she remembered how impressed she'd been when Bernard had produced the cream silk, extremely feminine robe last night. But then the inevitable moment of jealousy as to who'd worn it before her had threatened to invade her happy mood.

Philippe stood beside her bed, smiling. 'Marianne has sent me to tell you that breakfast is ready.'

The young boy described the delicious breakfast that Marianne had prepared and Julia listened, smiling at him. She raised her head as she became aware that Bernard was now standing in the doorway. He was wearing a dark blue towelling robe that covered most of him except for his athletic, muscular calves and bare feet. His dark, sleep-tousled hair was still damp from his shower and he was looking wonderfully handsome with the sunlight on his lightly tanned face.

'No need to hurry, Julia. I've brought you some coffee. Marianne is still making preparations downstairs so take your time.' Bernard placed a small tray with a cafetière and a delicate porcelain cup and saucer on her bedside table. 'Philippe insisted it was time to wake you.'

'Julia was awake when I knocked on the door, weren't you?'

'I was indeed, Philippe.'

Her eyes met Bernard's over the top of the small head and she felt her heart turn over. The warmth and love she'd felt yesterday had returned as she became wrapped up once again in this idyllic family situation.

Bernard retreated again to the doorway and held out his hand towards his son. 'Philippe, come with me while Julia gets herself ready.'

'Can't I stay and run her bath for her, like I do for you, Papa?'

'I think Julia will be happy to have a few quiet moments to gather her thoughts for the day ahead, so we'll see her when she comes downstairs.'

After they'd gone, she enjoyed a leisurely soak in the bath, balancing the delicate coffee cup in the small tiled alcove of the wall. It made a welcome change from the hurried shower she took most mornings in her tiny en suite.

When she got herself downstairs fully clothed in her workout gear from the previous day, the smell of freshly baked croissants drew her to the kitchen. Bernard was reawakening the dormant flames in the wood-burning stove. He closed the stove door and turned as he heard her coming in.

He put down the poker on the hearth and came across to pull out a chair for her at the table. Philippe ran inside from the kitchen garden and jumped up onto the chair beside her and began to eat enthusiastically. He urged Julia to join him and, smiling, she reached for a still warm croissant.

Julia was halfway through her croissant, spread liberally with the home-made apricot jam, when she saw Bernard answer his mobile.

'Bernard Cappelle.'

She saw him frowning. From the ensuing conversation she gathered it was an urgent call from the hospital.

'Of course. I'll be there as soon as I can.'

He looked across the table at her. 'That was Michel Devine from the emergency department. There's been a road traffic accident on the motorway, involving several vehicles. He's asked permission to call in as many of my students as possible to help with the patients who will be treated at the hospital. Are you willing to…?'

'Of course.' She was already pushing back her chair.

'Michel, I've just spoken to Dr Julia Montgomery and she says she's available.'

Minutes later they were driving down the hill towards St Martin sur Mer. Bernard had asked Marianne to take charge of Philippe, who would have to stay at the farm for another day. Philippe had been delighted at the prospect of a whole day with Marianne and Gaston on the farm and another night with his father.

Julia could see a couple of ambulances arriving outside the hospital as Bernard carefully negotiated his way through the traffic at the foot of the hill. The porter in charge of the hospital gateway directed several vehicles to the side so that Bernard could come through and park.

Inside, Michel was organising his staff. A triage system was being set up so that patients were assessed as soon as possible after their arrival.

A nurse was handing out white coats to the arriving medical staff. Julia pulled hers on and reported to Michel Devine for instructions. He asked her to check out the patient in the first cubicle.

'The paramedics have put a tourniquet round his bleeding leg to stem the flow but we need to do something more effective now we've got him here,' he told her tersely. 'There's a nurse in there who'll help you while you assess what needs to be done, Dr Montgomery. It's obviously a serious orthopaedic problem, which is in your field of expertise.'

She moved through the curtain to the cubicle and went in to take charge of the situation. The young man's eyes pleaded with her to help him as she took hold of his hand. He was lying on his back, his hands clenched over the bloodstained sheet that covered him.

She spoke to him in French, making her voice as soothing as she could. He was obviously in deep shock. Glancing down at the notes the nurse handed to her, she saw that his name was Pierre. She noted that sedation that had already been given at the scene of the traffic accident.

Gently peeling back the sheet that covered his injured right leg, she could see that this was a very serious problem. The right leg had been badly damaged and would require immediate surgery. She was already making a swift examination of the damaged tibia and surrounding tissues when she sensed that someone else had joined her in the cubicle.

Relief shot through her when she heard Bernard's voice behind her. He moved to her side and leaned across the patient so he could form his own opinion.

'I'll make arrangements for immediate surgery,' he told her.

She nodded in agreement. 'Are those Pierre's X-rays?'

Bernard was already flashing them up on the wall screen. She swallowed hard as she tried to make sense of the crushed pieces of bone. From the knee downwards, the leg seemed to resemble a jigsaw puzzle. Was it still viable? It was going to require some expert surgery and after-care if their patient was to be able to walk on it again. Maybe amputation followed by the fitting of a prosthesis might be the only option. A decision would have to be made during surgery.

She held Pierre's hand as Bernard made a swift call to the surgical wing.

'*Ma femme*, my wife,' the young man whispered. 'Monique. *Je veux*...' His faint voice trailed away as tears started trickling down his bloodstained face.

Even as Pierre was asking for his wife, the nurse, at the other side of the cubicle, was looking directly at Julia. 'The information is in the notes, Doctor.'

Glancing briefly down at the notes, Julia learned that his wife, who was seven months pregnant, had been unconscious since the accident. She'd been sitting beside Pierre in the passenger seat when the vehicle had crashed through. Their patient had cradled her in his arms until a doctor had arrived and taken her away in the first ambulance. She was already in the obstetric suite, undergoing an emergency Caesarean.

'Julia, I'd like you to assist me. Theatre Sister is making preparations for us.' Bernard went on to instruct the nurse about premedication for the patient. Julia was glad he was cool and calm because she knew that was how she must be—totally professional so that she could do her best for the patient.

Bernard came across to speak to Pierre, explaining the serious condition of his leg. Julia held her breath as the subject of possible amputation was broached. Pierre looked at her and then at Bernard.

'Is that a possibility? Can't you…?' His voice trailed away.

'Pierre, we'll do all we can to save the leg, but if it's too badly damaged it would make more sense to amputate. Prostheses these days are excellent and you would be taught to walk. I hope it won't come to that but the decision can't be made until we find the full extent of your injuries. Do you understand?' he added gently.

Their patient closed his eyes for a moment. Then in a clear voice he declared that he fully understood and would accept their decision, whatever it was.

Carefully, Julia withdrew her hand from the patient's grasp. 'I've got to leave you for a short time, Pierre. You'll soon be going to sleep but I'll be up there in Theatre with you and I'll see you when you come round from the anaesthetic.'

'*Merci*,' he whispered. 'Thank you, Doctor.'

She swallowed hard to force herself to be totally professional, aware of his sad eyes on her as she followed Bernard out of the cubicle.

There was no time for a break during the day. Julia assisted Bernard with Pierre's long operation and found herself scrubbing up for the next patient almost immediately. They were supported by a good team from the surgical orthopaedic department, each member adding their expertise to the operations that were performed.

In the early evening, when she and Bernard could finally take a break, he drew her to one side for a quiet debriefing. They were still both in theatre greens up in the recovery room, having just despatched their final patient to one of the orthopaedic wards.

As Bernard started to speak she sank down onto a plastic chair at the side of the water cooler and reached out to take a plastic cup.

'Here, let me do that for you.'

'Thank you.' She flashed him a grateful smile as she took the cold water from him.

Their hands touched and she felt a frisson of energy running through her at the contact. She drank deeply and didn't stop until she'd finished all of it.

'That's better! I feel almost human again.'

Bernard smiled. 'Michel just called to say the emergency department has dealt with all the accident patients that were assigned to this hospital. He's very grateful for our help and suggests we go off duty.'

'Well, if you're sure they can cope, I'd love to go off duty.'

'I'm absolutely sure. Besides, you look completely whacked, Julia.'

'Thanks very much! That's just what a girl needs, to be told she looks as exhausted as she feels. Still...' She sat upright, threw the plastic cup into the bin and stood up. 'There's nothing that a shower and a change of clothes can't put right.'

'How about supper? That would be reviving, wouldn't it?'

What exactly was he suggesting? She couldn't do anything to stop the anticipation running through her.

'Well, what do you say, Julia? Why don't you come back to the farm with me? I've got to return there as soon as possible because Philippe will be getting impatient. If you're with me, he'll be over the moon.'

He was waiting for her answer. She was very tempted at the prospect.

'Well?'

'Why not?' She didn't like the sound of her breathless voice, which completely gave away her confused emotions. She'd meant to sound so cool, as if this was just an invitation to a friend's tea party.

'Good! I'll call Marianne and tell her you're coming so she can get your room ready.'

'Oh, there's no need to—'

'Yes, there is! Because if you think I'm driving back to the hospital again, you're mistaken. And don't start talking about taxis. There aren't any out in the countryside. This isn't London or Paris, you know.'

She laughed and suddenly it was as if the sun had come out from behind the clouds. They'd been in a windowless theatre all day but she could almost breathe the vibrant country air that she would experience when they escaped together.

He put a hand in the small of her back. 'Can you be ready to leave in half an hour?'

'I'll try. I've got to spend a few minutes in Intensive Care with Pierre. I promised I would when he came round from the anaesthetic at the end of his operation.'

'I'll come with you to make sure you don't stay too long. The intensive care staff are experts, you know, and the orthopaedic staff are also checking on our patient.'

'Oh, I know he's in good hands but a promise to a patient is a promise.'

He bent down, cupping her face in his hands and kissing her gently on the cheek. 'You're not becoming emotionally involved with a patient, are you, Doctor?'

She felt a fluttering of desire running through her body. That was only a chaste kiss, for heaven's sake. She moved to one side as the swing door opened and a nurse walked in.

'We can continue this discussion as we go along to see our patient,' Bernard said gravely, leading the way out into the corridor.

Sister in Intensive Care gave them a brief update on Pierre's condition as soon as they arrived. He was on continual intravenous infusions of blood and breathing normally now after the initial difficulties following the general anaesthetic.

'It was a long operation,' Bernard said. 'Has he asked for details?'

'He's still very confused and the morphine keeps him semi-sedated. But he'll be pleased to see you so that you can explain what you actually did.'

Julia picked up the notes. 'Let's go and see him.'

Pierre's eyes were closed and he was lying on his back. His injured leg was up on pillows, covered by a cradle.

'Pierre,' Julia said gently.

Their patient opened his eyes and a slow smile spread across his face.

'Thank you,' he whispered. 'You did save my leg, didn't you?'

'Yes, we did,' Bernard said.

'And my wife, *ma femme*?'

Sister smiled broadly. 'I was just coming to tell you. I've had a call from Obstetrics. You have a beautiful little daughter, Pierre. She's very tiny because of being premature so she'll need to stay in hospital for a few weeks.'

'Et ma femme?'

'Monique is very weak so she'll be staying in hospital for a while until her strength returns.'

'You'll all be in hospital for a while,' Julia said. 'We'll arrange who can visit who as soon as possible.'

Pierre breathed a deep sigh of contentment. 'You've all been so good to us.'

As they walked back down the corridor and out through the front door, Julia looked up at Bernard. When they'd left Intensive Care he'd waited while Julia popped back to her room to change and pack some nightclothes. She met him at the hospital entrance.

'It's at times like this I remember that I love being a doctor,' she said quietly, lengthening her stride to keep pace with him.

He took hold of her hand as they continued walking towards the car park.

She glanced around to see if anyone was watching.

'Don't worry,' he said, as if reading her mind. 'We're off duty. We can do anything we like.'

'Anything?'

He grinned. 'Why not?'

CHAPTER SEVEN

AS BERNARD drove up the narrow, winding road that led to the top of the hill above St Martin sur Mer, Julia could feel herself relaxing already. She leaned back, studying Bernard's firm hands turning the steering-wheel as he negotiated one of the bends. A white sports car was coming towards them, a young couple laughing together as they passed within inches of their car, driving much too fast on that potentially dangerous section of the road.

Bernard eased off the accelerator just in time as he realised the other car was going to encroach on their side of the road. The blaring music from the young couple's car became fainter as it disappeared down the hill.

He breathed a sigh of relief as he continued up to the top of the hill. 'They wouldn't drive with such abandon if they'd seen the damage that sort of driving can do.'

'I was thinking exactly the same. Michel told me the multiple crash we assisted with was caused by a van driver using a mobile phone as he was overtaking a car. He lost control of his van, ploughed through the central barrier and vehicles piled up around him.'

'Including our Pierre and his wife,' Bernard said

quietly. 'I'm so relieved it was possible to save them. The result of good teamwork throughout the day— paramedics, nurses, doctors, everybody.'

He took a deep breath as the enormity of the events finally hit him now that he'd left hospital and was able to assess the situation.

His voice wavered with emotion when he spoke again. 'Pierre and Monique had only been married a few months and that precious baby was a much-wanted child.'

Julia swallowed hard. 'All babies are precious.'

Bernard could hear the gentle, emotional tone in her voice as she said this.

'You love babies, don't you?'

'Yes, of course I do.' She hesitated. 'I'd love to have my own baby. But not until the right time,' she added quickly. 'I need to feel I'm in charge of my own life first.'

He eased the car over the brow of the hill. 'Since you arrived I've sensed you're becoming more and more in charge.' He changed gear as the road flattened out. 'But, Julia, you mustn't be too inflexible. Who was it that said life is what happens when you're making other plans?'

Julia thought for a few moments. 'I don't know who said it but it's very true.'

They were sailing down the other side of the hill now, into the green, spring-awakened valley. She could feel the connection between them growing stronger by the minute.

She clenched her hands as the truth of everything that had happened since she'd met Bernard hit her. This was the sort of man she wanted in her life. She drew in her breath. This was the actual man she wanted in her life. But even as the realisation came to her she reminded herself that the timing wasn't right.

She'd planned to make a fresh start. This was why she'd left the old life behind. She shouldn't be thinking of veering off course. She'd done that before and look where that had landed her!

But she needn't change direction if she was careful. There was no harm in enjoying the present without taking too much thought about the future. She needed the fun and enjoyment of being with Bernard. He lifted her spirits. So, all things considered, she could make her present situation work...couldn't she?

As they drove through the farmyard gates, she determined to enjoy the evening whatever happened. She was going to focus on the present and let the future take care of itself for now.

Bernard switched off the engine and reached a hand across to take hold of hers. 'You're very quiet all of a sudden. What are you thinking?'

'I was thinking about how much I'm looking forward to seeing Philippe.'

A little whirlwind dashed out through the kitchen door, tearing towards the car.

Bernard laughed. 'You've got your wish.'

'Papa! Julia! I was waiting for you to arrive. Marianne! They're here.'

Bernard suggested the three of them have an early supper together at the kitchen table. He explained to Marianne that both he and Julia hadn't had time for lunch and also they both wanted to spend as much quality time with Philippe as possible before he went to bed.

The supper was a riotous success with Philippe excited and happy to have the undivided attention of two doting adults.

'Would you like some more pie, Philippe?'

Bernard was already slicing through the pastry to the succulent guinea fowl underneath in anticipation of his son's answer. Marianne's pie was a family favourite.

Philippe grinned and held out his plate. 'Yes, please.'

'You must have had a busy day to give you a good appetite like this.' Bernard put a generous slice on Philippe's plate.

'It was brilliant!' Philippe recounted the day's happenings, including feeding the hens, collecting the eggs still warm from the nests, helping Gaston mend a wall and milking the cows.

'And you helped me with the pastry,' Marianne said as she came in with a platter of cheeses from the larder and placed it on the sideboard. 'I'll leave this here, Bernard, for when you're ready for your cheese course. I've also left some desserts in the fridge, if you wouldn't mind helping yourselves. I'm going over to see my sister in the village tonight.'

'Of course, I remember now. It's her birthday. You should have reminded me and gone earlier. Thank you for this excellent supper. Go off and have a great evening.'

Julia came down to the kitchen after putting Philippe to bed to find that Bernard had finished clearing up.

The dishwasher was whirring away in the background as he came towards her and handed her a glass of wine.

She gave him a wry grin as she took the glass from his hands. 'I try to stick to the rule that I don't drink after supper if tomorrow is a work day.'

'Ah, rules were made to be broken. This is only a *digestif*. Something to round off a delightful dinner.' He raised his glass to his lips. 'Here's to good food, excellent wine and congenial company.'

She took a sip of her wine, feeling suddenly shy now that they were alone.

'How was Philippe when you left him?' he asked.

'Trying hard not to fall asleep before you've been up to see him.'

He put his glass down on the sideboard. 'Don't go away. Take your wine into the conservatory and I'll be back shortly. And, Julia…?'

'Yes?'

'Don't fall asleep. I know you must be tired but…'

She laughed. 'I've no intention of falling asleep.'

As she settled herself on the comfortable, squashy-cushioned sofa she knew she hadn't felt this happy for a long time. Yes, she would go with the flow again tonight. She'd seen enough misery during the day. She was going to seize the moment and not think about tomorrow. If Bernard held her in his arms tonight as he'd done last night, she was going to make sure that this time she gave him the right message. She wasn't going to let him give her a goodnight kiss and leave her languishing in her lonely bed, thinking about what might have been.

* * *

'Philippe's asleep,' Bernard whispered as he sat down beside her on the sofa a few minutes later, putting his arm around her and drawing her against him.

She could feel the instantaneous awakening of her whole body. In the short time he'd been away from her she'd been fighting against weariness. But as soon as she felt his arm around her she was totally wide awake. She could feel every fibre of her body quivering with anticipation as he bent his head and kissed her, oh, so gently. She parted her lips to savour the moment. His kiss deepened.

This was the first time he'd kissed her with such glorious abandon. She responded in equal measure. She gave an ecstatic moan as his hands began to caress her breasts. Deep down inside her she felt herself melting, becoming entirely sensual, fluid, unwilling and unable to control the rising desires inside her.

Suddenly he broke off and leaned back against the sofa. His breathing was ragged as he looked questioningly into her eyes.

'Julia, I want to make love to you so much but we need to discuss what this will mean to our relationship. I'd love to settle into a serious long-term relationship with you but I don't think that either of us could make the commitment necessary. You've got your career to think of and eventually you will want a husband and a family of your own. I'm not sure after my last experience that I will ever be able to offer that to you, and I know that would be a great disappointment to you.'

She hesitated. 'Yes, it would. You have your son. I've always wanted children when I've established my career. My first marriage was a disaster but I adored my stepchildren. It was so hard to walk away and never see them again.'

Her eyes misted over. Bernard moved closer again, taking hold of her hand and kissing the palm very gently. 'I want you to have the experience of your own children because you have so much maternal instinct to draw on. Philippe already adores you.'

'I know. Getting close to Philippe worries me in many ways. Not only will I miss him terribly when the course finishes and I have to return to London, I'm also concerned about him getting used to me being with you. After what he's experienced with his own mother, I'd hate to cause him any more upset.'

'We could have a compromise relationship, don't you think? A short-term affair while you're here in France?'

He put his arms around her, drawing her closer, his eyes probing hers, willing her to agree.

She gave him a gentle smile. 'I think a short no-commitment affair would be fun. We should live one day at a time, enjoy being together and not think too far ahead.'

'Oh, my darling Julia...'

His lips claimed hers and the passion of his embrace deepened.

Briefly, he paused and looked into her eyes, silently questioning if she wanted him as much as he wanted her.

'Yes, oh, yes,' she whispered.

He smiled, the most wickedly sexy smile she'd ever hoped to see on his handsome face as he scooped her up into his arms.

* * *

Julia opened her eyes and for a brief moment she felt unsure of her surroundings as she struggled to leave the dream she'd just enjoyed. Moonlight was flooding through the open window and there was a scent of roses, damp with dew. This room looked out over the garden.

And then she remembered. It hadn't been a dream. The lovemaking had all been real. The gentle caresses that had become more and more irresistible to her. Her own hands had explored that wonderful athletic, muscular body, longing for Bernard to take her completely. And then when she'd felt him inside her she'd felt completely at one with this wonderful man who had been taking her towards the ultimate ecstasy. They had climaxed together in a heavenly experience when they'd clung to each other, feeling that they would never be separated.

'Are you awake?'

She heard his deep, sexy voice from the other side of her pillow. They'd slept together, very, very close. His bed was enormous and there was space all around them.

Gently he pulled a crumpled sheet around her. She realised they were both naked. The rose-scented breeze had probably wakened her.

He raised himself up on one elbow, looking down at her with a heart-melting expression in his eyes that made her feel she was absolutely special to him.

'Your skin feels chilly,' he murmured, his hands roaming over her in the most tantalisingly erotic way.

For a brief moment she thought he might leave her and go across the room to close the window. But, no, he'd had a better idea!

She moaned with desire as he covered her body with his own. This time their lovemaking took her to heights of ecstasy she'd never imagined existed.

As they lay back against the pillows, their arms still around each other, she could feel her body tingling with the excitement of a joyful consummation.

'Are you still cold?' he whispered.

She laughed. 'I think we should both run barefoot on the dewy grass outside to cool off.'

'You look wonderful when you're totally abandoned. You should stay like this all the time, no problems, no rules…'

'No tomorrow,' she whispered, as she realised they were both longing to make love again…

It was the early morning sun shining in through the still open window that woke her up this time. And this time she knew immediately where she was because she was still clasped loosely in his arms. Mmm, what a night! It had definitely not been a dream. In her wildest dreams she could never have imagined all that. Maybe she'd died and gone to heaven.

So, what now?

CHAPTER EIGHT

JULIA switched off her computer. In the past few weeks since that idyllic night she'd spent with Bernard her life had revolved around work. He seemed intent on working through the syllabus in great detail, with her and the rest of the students using practical sessions in Theatre and theoretical tutorials.

Her mobile was ringing.

'Julia, are you free this evening?'

Was she free? If she wasn't she would make sure she cancelled whatever it was that stood between her and an evening with Bernard. She'd seen precious little of him recently in an off-duty situation and was beginning to think he regretted suggesting a short-term affair. Or maybe he just didn't have the time.

'I'll just check.' She paused just long enough to flick to the right page in her diary. Totally devoid of any social engagement. 'What did you have in mind?'

'I need to talk something over with you. Actually, I feel I owe you an explanation as to why I've been a bit distant recently.'

He paused and cleared his throat.

She waited. Was he going to explain why he'd seemed somewhat distracted whenever they'd been together?

He sounded unusually nervous when he spoke again. 'It was a pity I had that phone call from Gabrielle so early in the morning when you were staying with me. Having to take Philippe back to Paris that day wasn't what I'd planned but my ex-wife can be very difficult if she doesn't get her own way.'

She waited again as he paused, not wanting to interrupt the flow. She remembered she'd crept out of his bed and gone to the guest room early in the morning before anyone else had woken up. So she'd been surprised when Bernard announced at breakfast he had to take his son back to Paris and had cleared his commitments at the hospital for a couple of days. Michel would be in charge of his students—who, of course, included her—and he would give them on-the-spot tuition in the emergency department.

'Frederic, Gabrielle's future husband, wanted to legally clarify the situation on custody of Philippe, to make sure that he wasn't going to be involved in any way and that I was going to take charge of my son. It's been hell sorting everything out for the past few weeks. I don't know who's worse to deal with, Gabrielle or Frederic. They deserve each other! Anyway, are you free to have dinner with me this evening?'

'Yes…I'd love to.'

No point in hiding her feelings. He sounded much more like the man she'd found so intriguingly irresistible when she'd first arrived.

'Are you in your room?'

'Yes, I've been working.'

'I'll reserve a table at the hotel restaurant for eight o'clock. Meet me in Reception about half past seven.'

* * *

He breathed a sigh of relief as he put the phone down. The past few weeks had been difficult for him. Besides coping with Gabrielle and Frederic's demands, going over to Paris every weekend, he'd also been trying to sort out his feelings for Julia. He'd had to make sure he remained dispassionate about her in his professional dealings. The fact that he'd convinced himself he could handle a short-term relationship before they'd made love that night didn't make it any easier. The practicalities of a relationship between professor and student took some careful handling.

Also she'd had a disastrous marriage. He couldn't be flippant about any relationship that grew between them. It had to be what they both wanted. Now there were other practical considerations. With Philippe's imminent arrival it was going to be difficult for them to see each other. Julia had spoken the truth before as well—if she became an item in his life Philippe would come to regard her as a mother figure. He suspected he already did but to what extent he couldn't be sure. So if she walked out of their lives—as well she might now that her confidence had returned and she was very much in demand—his son's heart could be broken as well as his own!

The fact remained that they ultimately wanted different things out of life. She deserved a husband devoted to her and children of her own. Was he the man to take that risk again? He'd vowed to himself while he was going through the hell that Gabrielle had created during Philippe's early childhood that he would never have another child. Even though he adored Philippe he still remembered the problems associated with having

a baby. Could any partnership remain a loving relationship while the parents coped with the problems that
babies posed, especially career-minded parents battling
with everyday work situations?

He sighed as he went into the shower to prepare for
this important date. He'd decided he would stay in the
medics' quarters tonight and had brought a casual suit
to change into.

He was relieved to see her welcoming smile when he
went into Reception. He'd almost forgotten how beautiful she was when she wasn't shrouded in a white coat or
a green theatre gown, or else frowning over a problem
that needed explaining in a tutorial. She was wearing
some kind of silky-looking cream dress and heels. That
made a change from the T-shirt, jeans and trainers that
seemed to be standard uniform among his students.

He felt a flicker of desire running through him as
he noticed how sexy she looked with the dress accen-
tuating her slim figure yet clinging to the curves of her
breasts and hips.

He took a deep breath to steady his emotions as she
began to move towards him. She seemed to glide in
those strappy high-heeled sandals that made her ankles
look so slim. The skirt skimmed her knees, hiding those
fabulous thighs, which he knew were oh, so tantalising.

'Julia, you look stunning!'

He rested his hand on the back of her slim waist to
guide her out through the door, aware that they were
being watched by various members of staff. He would
reserve his kiss of welcome till later.

He raised his hand. 'I think that should be our taxi.'

Checking with the driver, he helped her inside. They sat slightly apart on the back seat as the taxi drove off towards the seafront.

Julia could feel her excitement mounting. Glancing sideways, she saw her handsome escort was watching her. She smiled at him. He moved closer, took hold of her hand and kissed her briefly on the lips.

Her fingers tingled as his hand closed around hers. Mmm, they were on course again! She didn't know where they'd been but she knew, or rather she hoped she knew, where they were going.

The hotel was one of the older buildings at the far end of St Martin's seafront. She remembered reading about it in a good-food guide. It certainly looked like a very smart sort of place from the outside.

A uniformed man came to open the car door for her as Bernard was paying off the cab. Inside the ambience was relaxed and welcoming. They were shown into the dining room with a small discreet bar near the entrance. Their table by the window was ready. She sat down, her eyes catching a glimpse of the darkening sky over the sea. The sun had already dipped into the sea and the pink and blue twilight seemed so romantic.

She looked across the table at Bernard, her heart brimming with emotion, feeling so close to him again. He was ordering a bottle of champagne.

'What are we celebrating?'

He smiled. 'The end of an era.'

She gave him a questioning look.

'I'll tell you when the champagne arrives…ah, here we are.' He was glancing at the label. 'Fine. Yes, open it, please.'

The popping of the cork, the fizzing in her glass. She was intrigued, impatient for him to enlighten her.

'Here's to the future,' he said enigmatically, holding his glass towards hers. 'I've finally settled everything with Gabrielle and Frederic but it's been difficult dealing with them. They're going to be married next week and Philippe is safely tucked up in bed at the farm. Marianne is over the moon to have him finally living back home where he should be.'

'So, what was the problem?'

'Problems!' he corrected her. 'Where shall I start? Everything had to be legally sanctioned as regards Philippe. Gabrielle wanted him to be privately educated but I insisted I wanted him to have the same upbringing I'd had out here at the village school. I want him to enjoy the countryside. To bring his friends back to the farm whenever he wants to.'

'What did Gabrielle think of that idea?'

'Well, of course, neither she nor Frederic want to be involved in bringing him up themselves but they wanted him to be taken each day to a private school about twenty kilometres from the village where he would mix with "decent children," was how she described it to me. She pointed out that she wanted him to have the best education possible so he would be a success in life.'

Julia watched him take a drink from his glass, noticing the perspiration on his brow and the set of his jaw as he swallowed hard. It hadn't been an easy time for him, she surmised.

He put down his glass. 'I pointed out that Philippe had set his heart on being a surgeon like me and the village school had given me a good education, preparing me for eventual admission to the excellent lycée in Montreuil.'

'Did that satisfy her?'

'Well, Frederic and I had to convince her that the medical profession was well regarded. She pointed out that we'd had money problems when we were first married. I explained that the early days of a profession are always difficult financially but unless Philippe becomes hampered by a difficult marital relationship—as I was—he would be a success.'

'I bet you enjoyed saying that to her!'

'I certainly did. It also shut her up. She didn't want me to start making revelations to Frederic of how she'd made my life hell when we were first married. Oh, the poor man doesn't know what he's in for. I actually feel sorry for him. Still, it's not my problem any more!'

He smiled across the table at her. 'Anyway, let's order. What are you going to have, Julia?'

She picked up the menu that the waiter had left with her. She chose moules marinières as a starter, followed by a locally caught fish, with added prawns.

'This is pure nostalgia for me, Bernard. As a child I loved the fish dishes I ate when we were here on holiday—unlike my brothers, who always asked for steak frites.'

'Ah, yes, there used to be a small wooden café on the edge of the beach that served the most delicious steak and chips.'

'That's the one!'

They relaxed into their memories of St Martin sur

Mer, which they both agreed had been an idyllic place for children.

'It still is,' Bernard said. 'And the surrounding countryside is the healthiest environment to bring up a child. You've no idea what a relief it is for me to know that Philippe will breathe in clean air every day when he goes to school instead of fumes from traffic.'

'You're very lucky.'

'I am now,' he said, his voice husky.

He reached across the table and squeezed her hand. She felt desire rising up inside her. Did he mean what she hoped he meant?

Their meal was beautifully served. They took their time, caught up once more in their conversation, which flowed so easily.

Bernard told the waiter they would take coffee on the terrace. He took her hand as they went out of the dining room and relaxed in the cushioned wicker chairs by a small table overlooking the sea.

He was intensely aware that this was the first time they'd been alone since they'd made love on that idyllic night they'd spent together. It had been almost too perfect for him. She could be the woman of his dreams, but there were so many reasons why he had to be careful with her.

He took a sip of his coffee. 'You know, you've changed a great deal since you first arrived, Julia.'

'Have I?'

'You've become much more confident and your confidence seems to grow day by day.'

'I'm certainly enjoying the course…in an exhausting kind of way. So much work to get through and then the exams looming at the end of it all.'

'I don't think you need to worry. Hard work plus natural talent for your chosen profession will bring success.' He paused, trying to make his question sound as innocent as possible. 'What have you planned to do after the exams?'

The question, out of the blue, threw her completely. 'Well, I'd planned to go back to London. Don arranged for me to have a six-month sabbatical from the orthopaedic department. I enjoy my work there and it's a good springboard from which to climb higher up the ladder, either in my own hospital or wherever a promotion should arise. I've always been ambitious but...'

He waited, watching her struggle to find the right words. He sensed what she would say even before she spoke again.

'I can't help my longing to have a child, well, a whole family really. And fitting that in with the demanding career I've also set my heart on is confusing. I'm really beginning to appreciate my parents' dilemma. I wonder if I'll have time to fit in everything I want to do with my life.'

He watched her trying to deal with the conflicting thoughts running through her mind. Since telling Julia he wasn't sure about being able to marry again and have more children, he'd had time to think. Marriage and parenting with Julia would be a totally different experience from what he'd had with Gabrielle. If they split the responsibilities fifty-fifty, they could both continue their careers.

But such a situation would require total commitment

to each other as well as the child. Marriage really was the only way. But if he told her he'd changed his mind about children and asked her to marry him, would she agree simply to have him father a child? He had to be sure she loved him first and foremost before he thought so far ahead.

That was why he'd needed some space from her after falling so hopelessly in love during that night they'd spent together at the farm. The struggles he'd endured with his ex-wife and her new partner had given him time to think about his relationship with Julia.

She was watching his serious expression. 'You're very quiet. Is something troubling you?'

'No, definitely not. Except…' He took a deep breath, almost frightened to say what was on his mind. His feelings were intense and raw, he could even feel them manifesting themselves in every part of his vibrantly awakening body. Would she feel the same way?

'Will you excuse me for a moment?'

He was already walking back into the dining room. She sat very still. Through the open door she could see him talking to the head waiter and decided he was paying the bill.

Darkness had fallen. She looked out across the bright lights beside the seafront. There were palm trees planted at the edge of the beach, which looked wonderful in summer but took a beating sometimes during the winter.

She was so captivated by the view that she didn't notice him come back to the terrace. He took her hands and drew her to her feet. He was grinning in a boyish, mischievous way.

'I've got the option on the bridal suite for tonight. I thought it would be a perfect place to relax at the end of our busy day. You won't have to creep out before dawn so as to avoid being seen in my bed either. A discreet chambermaid will bring breakfast in bed too, if you'd like. What do you say?'

She giggled. 'I'd say you'd gone mad. Why the bridal suite?'

'Because that's the only room vacant tonight.'

'Oh, don't spoil it. I thought you wanted to lavish loads of money on me because I'm worth it.'

If she only knew! He wasn't going to tell her the real truth—that there actually were a couple of much cheaper rooms available.

'So, you're happy to stay here?'

'I'd love to check out the bridal suite. I've never slept in anything like a bridal suite in my life.'

He put his arm around her waist and led her to the door. 'Who said anything about sleeping?'

She really was confused this time when she awoke in the middle of the night. At first she thought she was in Bernard's bed at the farm. His head was certainly on the edge of her pillow. She put out her hand to touch the thick, dark hair. And then she remembered.

The first and last time they'd spent the night together had been fabulous but this time…! Her body was still tingling with the most consummately passionate experience…or was it experiences? They had been in each other's arms from the moment they'd stepped across the threshold of this sumptuously exotic room.

By the time she'd reached the top of the stairs with

his arm around her waist her legs had turned to jelly. Every fibre of her body had been crying out for his love-making, his wonderful, creative, heavenly lovemaking.

He opened his eyes and smiled his slow, sexy smile that told her the night was still young. They had hours and hours before daybreak and reality. When they would both try to come back to earth. But for the moment there was no tomorrow...

Julia said that, yes, she would love to have breakfast in their room when he asked her.

He picked up the bedside phone in one hand and reached for her with the other. 'Oh, no, you don't escape this time. Room service, please. We'd like to order two breakfasts please to room... Oh, great, thank you.'

He put down the phone. 'They knew we were in the bridal suite. We didn't make that much noise, did we?'

She laughed. 'I don't remember.'

'Oh, well, in that case, let me remind you...'

'Not now. What about the chambermaid?'

'Oh, never mind the chambermaid.'

'I'm going for a quick shower.'

'Spoilsport,' he said carefully in English.

She waved a towel at him from the door to the bathroom. 'Your English is definitely improving. You must have a good teacher.'

'And your surgical skills aren't too bad either since you found yourself a good teacher.'

'Sorry, what was that?'

'Not important.'

He settled back against the pillows to await her return, feeling blissfully happy with the way things had gone since his sudden daring idea to take a room here. If he could ever be sure that she really and truly loved him for himself and didn't just regard him as a baby maker, he would ask her to marry him. He'd been very careful to ensure she knew he believed in using a condom. An unplanned pregnancy wasn't what either of them needed.

But what about his dread of going through the early days of a new baby? Even the most loving relationship must be affected. His parents had survived and remained in love, but would he and Julia be able to replicate that when they were both ambitious and in difficult and demanding work situations?

For the moment Julia needed to concentrate on her work at the hospital and her exams. But a little light relief in her off-duty time would help to relax her and prevent too much tension, wouldn't it? He smiled to himself as he heard the taps had stopped flowing in the bathroom. She would soon be back in his bed and he would be able to check she wasn't becoming tense again.

There was a knock at the door. He'd have to wait.

Groaning with frustration, he rose to admit the waiter...

CHAPTER NINE

THE summer was moving along too quickly. As she switched off her computer Julia realised that they were more than halfway through the surgical syllabus that Bernard had set for them.

She got up from her chair and walked across her small room, which was now so familiar. It had become home to her and apart from the occasional night up at the farm this was where she'd lived all the time.

And there'd been that completely heavenly night in the bridal suite! She would never forget that. She was beginning to think it might have been a one-off but she hoped not.

She bent to straighten the sheet on her bed, which was exactly as she'd left it that morning before she'd gone down for a practical tutorial in Theatre. As she leaned across the bed to take hold of the sheet she decided to lie down and take a short break before the evening. It had been a long day, a hot day apart from her time in Theatre when Bernard had insisted the air-conditioning be turned up to full.

She stared up at the ceiling. He'd seemed sort of tetchy today. He often seemed a bit irritable when he was teaching and operating at the same time. She could understand it. She could well imagine how she would feel if she had to do the same. Maybe that would happen when she became a more qualified and experienced surgeon.

The life of a surgeon was a demanding one for sure. No wonder Bernard seemed like two people sometimes. There was the man who could relax when they were together. Ah, she loved him so much when they were alone! But she worried about him when he was working. Was that natural when she wasn't sure where this relationship was going? Worrying about her man with a kind of wifely instinct? Also worrying about his child, who was becoming more and more attached to her every time she saw him?

Her mobile was ringing. Maybe it was Bernard, cancelling their date for tomorrow. It had happened when he'd told her there was an emergency he had to deal with.

'Julia, are you free this evening?'

She sat up, alert and excited by this turn of events.

'Yes; just finished writing up this morning's op. Do you think you could explain that new way you demonstrated of closing up the patient? When I was writing it up just now I—'

'Of course I'll explain but not now. I've just finished so I'm driving home in ten minutes. I thought we could all make an early start together on our day off tomorrow. Can you make it?'

'Yes, but I'll need to pack a bag. Where are we going tomorrow?'

'Oh, let's decide this evening. See you in ten, OK?'

She leapt off the bed and started throwing things

into her overnight bag. Typical Bernard! He could be so impulsive at times—like booking them into the bridal suite.

She forced her mind not to think about that particular occasion because she wouldn't be ready in ten minutes if she did. She could think about that later when they were alone in his bed.

He smiled and came towards her as she arrived in Reception.

'Well done! I knew you could do it.'

'Why the rush?'

'No reason. Just impatient to leave my daytime self behind and put on my off-duty persona.'

He put a hand on her back as they walked out towards the staff parking area.

'Ah, so you admit you're a different person in hospital from the impulsive man you can be off duty?'

'Absolutely! Guilty as charged. And to think you noticed!'

'Difficult not to.' She got into the passenger seat.

Bernard closed her door and went round to the driver's side. He started the engine and then placed a hand over hers. 'Which of my personalities do you prefer?'

She smiled up at him, feeling the familiar stirrings of desire simply by being close to him.

'Definitely the off-duty man. The other one can be a bit of a temperamental tyrant when he's in Theatre.'

He bent his head and kissed her on the lips. Drawing away slightly he murmured, 'Ah, so you noticed? It's only an act I put on to keep the students on their toes.'

'Well, this student was certainly on her toes today.'

'I noticed. That's good!'

He put the car in gear and moved out towards the front gates. 'So the work's going well, is it?'

'Exceptionally well. If you could give me a few minutes' private tuition tonight on that point I mentioned when you phoned?'

'Oh, I can certainly give you my full attention later on when we're alone.' He changed gear as they began a steep ascent.

She felt her body reacting already to the thought of the night ahead and she sensed he was in a similar mood. His voice had been definitely sexy as he'd said 'when we're alone'. She couldn't wait for the personal tuition.

Sitting around the kitchen table with the excitable Philippe chattering to her, she relaxed completely.

Marianne had bought mussels from the fish merchant who delivered to the village on Fridays and she'd been delighted when Bernard had phoned to say that Julia was coming that evening. The housekeeper placed the steaming, aromatic dish of moules marinières in front of them now.

'Bernard, I think this is one of Julia's favourite dishes, am I right?'

'Marianne, you're amazing!' Julia said. 'You remembered!'

'Well, it's my favourite, also,' Philippe said. 'May I have that big one there, Papa?'

'Of course!'

Bernard beamed round the table, a feeling of total happiness descending upon him. This was how every working week should end. Sitting at the table with his son and his beautiful, talented…what was Julia to him exactly? Certainly he shouldn't take anything for granted. There was nothing permanent about the situation, even though he wished it could go on for ever.

He glanced across at her and saw she was watching him with those eyes that sometimes looked so questioning, as if she wasn't sure of something, as well she might be. She was the most wonderful woman he'd ever met but he still couldn't allow himself to think of her as being a permanent fixture in his life. He still felt unsure of the future. There were still so many problems to iron out before he could be sure she would always be there.

Bernard put the pencil down on his notepad. 'So, does that answer your question?'

'Yes it does, Professor. That's what I put in my notes but I had to be sure.'

He gave her a sexy grin. 'So may I forget my academic commitment to a demanding student and relax again, Dr Montgomery?'

She giggled as he put his arms around her and drew her into their first embrace of the evening. They were still downstairs in the conservatory but they were alone at last with the whole of the night ahead of them.

'Marianne has put your things in the guest room,' he said solemnly.

'Do you think she understands the situation?'

'Well, if she does understand what's going on, she's more clued up than I am,' he said enigmatically.

He took a deep breath. 'Of course she assumes we sleep together at the beginning of the night…well, not so much sleep but… Yes, of course she understands the situation. She also understands that you creep along to the guest room in the early hours before Philippe wakes up.' He hesitated. 'You don't have to do that, you know.'

'I just feel that…it's simpler this way. I don't want to confuse him.'

Bernard drew in his breath. He surmised she didn't want it to be taken for granted that she would always be there. She'd come out to France to make a new start, hadn't she? That had been her initial idea. Now that she'd found her confidence, she may well decide to spread her wings and fly away at the end of the course. She had the whole of her life in front of her. He must never take her for granted.

He drew her closer in his arms. 'Let's go to bed.'

Their lovemaking had been unbelievably tender. Afterwards he held her in his arms so tightly it had almost been as if he was going to keep her there, safe, in the place she loved to be. But there was something different tonight. She sensed a certain melancholy in the moment.

Bernard lay with his arms around her, trying not to dispel the mood. Their consummation had been heavenly as always but almost immediately afterwards reality had forced itself upon him. This relationship was all too good to be true so far. He wanted to make it go on for ever…but only if that was what she wanted. He couldn't burden her with the question of commitment to him when she was coming up to the difficult weeks before the exams and the end of the course.

And he could definitely not bring up the subject of

babies. If he told her he was beginning to think he'd love to father a baby with her, how could he be sure it would be him she wanted or a baby? She could be very loving, but so had Gabrielle been when she'd wanted her own way.

But the wounds of his suffering still hadn't healed properly. The thought of spoiling their idyllic relationship by commitment, pregnancy and a small baby to care for, along with dual careers in surgery, was a very daunting one. Julia had come over to France to make a fresh start on her own. Did he have the right to impose a different kind of life on her? He couldn't bear to spoil the brilliant future that lay ahead of someone so talented.

Julia woke in the early morning and stretched out her hand under the sheet. Bernard wasn't there. Of course he wasn't. She'd made an early departure from his bed last night. He'd seemed tired, less communicative after they'd made love, so she'd decided to come along here to the guest room to get a whole night's sleep before their day out.

He'd kissed her tenderly, lovingly when she'd explained, but he'd seemed somewhat distant, as if he was standing outside their relationship and being totally dispassionate. Maybe she should have asked him if he was worrying about something but she'd sensed he wouldn't have told her. He could be a very private person when he wanted to be. But she loved him, oh, how she loved every facet of his enigmatic character.

She sighed as she switched on the bedside light. Almost seven o'clock. The little whirlwind would come charging in soon.

Bernard had heard Philippe chattering to Julia in the guest room. He'd woken very early today, which was unusual. Last night had been wonderful, holding her in his arms, making love to her, knowing they would be together today. He wasn't going to worry about where their relationship was going. He would simply accept that they made each other happy and now wasn't the time to think too far ahead.

'So where are we going today, Papa?'

Philippe stretched his little arm across the table. Bernard reached forward and wiped away some of the jam and croissant crumbs that had collected on the palm of his son's hand with his napkin. Then he gave the still sticky hand a squeeze.

'Would you like to go out in the boat?'

'Yes, oh, yes, let's go in the boat, Papa! Out to the island?'

As Bernard steered his boat across the sea he could feel the cares of the past week disappearing. He could hear Philippe chattering happily to Julia, who was pointing out landmarks on the now distant shore. She too seemed happy to be out in the boat, reminiscing with his son about her childhood holidays in this area.

'Oh, we didn't have our own boat,' Julia was explaining to Philippe. 'We didn't live over here in France so my father used to hire one sometimes. My brothers always wanted to steer it and I was always the last to have a go…and then only under strict supervision.'

'What's supervision?'

'It's when a grown-up watches you the whole time you're holding onto the wheel and—'

'Papa, will you supervision me while I'm steering the boat? Or Julia could supervision me, couldn't she?'

Bernard turned, one hand still on the wheel. 'Pass me that wooden box. If you stand on that, I'll supervise you while you hold on to the wheel. At least we've got a clear route ahead of us. Nothing for you to bump into at the moment.'

Julia helped Philippe onto the box and stood at the other side of him while Bernard kept a light hand on the wheel.

'No need to turn the wheel, Philippe. We're going straight ahead towards that island.'

'That's our island, isn't it, Papa?'

'Technically, no, but…'

'What's technically?'

'We don't own it but we're allowed to go there.'

'But we've been there lots of times so we can pretend it's ours.'

Bernard stooped and planted a kiss on his son's head. 'We can pretend anything we like today.'

His eyes met Julia's as he raised his head. He could feel a lump rising in his throat as he saw the wistful expression in her eyes. Did she feel the same way as he did about the day ahead? Just the three of them, pretending to be a family?

As they neared the shore, Julia helped Philippe down off the box again so that Bernard had full control of the boat. As they reached the shallows she took over the wheel, as they'd discussed, so that Bernard could jump out and tie up the mooring rope.

'I always wanted to tie up,' she said to Philippe. 'But my brothers got there first. My father would be steering the boat and my mother holding tightly to my hand.'

'It's more fun being a boy, I think.'

'Well, I did used to think my older brothers had a lot of fun. But I always had fun too.' She was holding the young boy's hand as they stepped barefoot into the shallows, holding their sandals so they didn't get wet.

Bernard was holding out his hand to take their sandals as they reached the shore. They walked up the beach to settle themselves under the shade of the trees. Bernard started bringing their things from the boat.

Philippe was already stripped off and running into the sea. He'd insisted on wearing his swimming trunks from the moment he'd got dressed that morning.

'Come on!' he shouted happily.

'Is the sea warm?' Julia asked as she stripped to the bikini she was wearing under her shorts.

'Very hot, hot, hot. Come and try it.'

'OK, I will.'

Bernard took hold of her hand. 'It's going to be a scorcher today.'

She revelled in the touch of his fingers enclosing hers. 'Last time I was here it rained all day and we played under the trees, wearing our mackintoshes.'

He drew her closer, feeling a frisson of desire at the closeness of her bikini-clad figure. 'How old were you?'

'It was years ago! I don't remember. I…' She glanced

at the small boy in the sea. 'We'd better go and supervise Philippe.'

Bernard laughed. 'Supervise seems to be the word of the day. I'm glad there's nobody to supervise you and me today. I'm feeling positively reckless.'

She laughed as, still holding her hand tightly, he set off down the beach.

'If only the rest of your students could see you now, Professor!'

'Papa, there are some little fish nibbling at my toes. Look, look, they're everywhere in the water. Julia, come here, can you see them? What are they?'

'Well, my English father used to call them sticklebacks. My French mother simply called them little fish, like you do.' She wiggled her toes. 'They tickle, don't they?'

'Let's swim, Papa. I can swim, Julia. Watch me!'

One each side of him, he proudly swam out towards the deeper water. 'We won't go too far out,' Bernard said to Julia as they swam alongside. 'Philippe loves swimming but he'd go on swimming till he felt tired. He forgets he's got to go back.'

'Yes, but you always put me on your chest, Papa.'

'See what I mean?'

Bernard's arm brushed against hers. The water further out was colder than nearer the shore but even so she felt a warm glow stealing over her. Just being close to him in any situation was one of the joys of their relationship. Again she found herself wondering how long they could be together like this before decisions about the future had to be made. Well, there were no decisions to be made today. Enjoying the moment was her primary concern.

'Time to go back.' Bernard steered the other two around so that they were all swimming back towards the shore.

Bernard had brought everything they needed for a barbecue. He quickly built up the sides with the large stones they'd gathered and got the fire going underneath before placing the metal rack over it.

'I've never tasted such delicious chicken drumsticks,' Julia said, tearing at a piece with her teeth. She looked across at Bernard, who'd just put more chicken on to grill. 'Mmm, you must be a very experienced chef, sir.'

'Papa always cooks lunch when we come here. Why does lunch taste much better out in the open air than inside, Julia?'

She laughed. 'Good question! I've often wondered about it.'

Bernard dropped some more food on Philippe's plate. 'On this particular island it's because we've all been swimming, which is marvellous for inducing an appetite, and the sun is shining through the trees and we're all happy.'

'And we're going to stay here all night in Papa's tent and wake up in the morning to start swimming as soon as the sun comes up.'

'Oh, not this time, Philippe. I didn't bring the tent. Anyway, it wouldn't be big enough for three of us.'

'Yes, it would! Julia and I don't take up very much room, do we? Well, do we really need a tent? It's warm enough to sleep here under the trees.'

Philippe snuggled up to Julia, wiping his sticky hands on a nearby patch of grass. 'You'd like to stay here, wouldn't you, Julia? I bet you stayed here all night when you were here on holiday, didn't you?'

'No, I'm afraid we didn't. Why don't you just close your eyes now, pretend it's night-time and have a short sleep? You look sleepy to me.'

Philippe stared at her. 'How did you know I feel sleepy?'

'Because you got up very early and you've had a busy day that included a long swim. That's always exhausting.'

She was already tucking a dry towel around the small boy and lowering her voice. He snuggled closer into her side. 'You will wake me, won't you, Julia? I don't want to wake up and find it's all dark and I've missed the rest of the day. It's such a nice day. I don't want to miss anything. Don't leave me, Julia…'

His voice drifted away as his breathing steadied and his eyelids drooped.

Watching her, Bernard felt the urge to put his arms round his two favourite people and keep them here with him for ever. He could build a camp here under the trees and blot out the rest of the world and its problems. What a wonderful mother Julia would make when she had children of her own. But she was also born to be a talented surgeon. He forced himself away from the problem. Today they belonged together and the future was the future, something to think about tomorrow.

He sat down on the sandy, grassy slope and reached towards her, careful not to disturb his son sleeping nearby, visible to them through the long grassy fronds.

Lowering his head, he kissed her gently on the lips. His kiss deepened. She clung to him, aware of the poignancy of this tender moment. One day in a family situation with Bernard had made her sure of what she wanted in life—career and motherhood, hand in hand. If she could have both options with Bernard that would be perfect. But there were so many obstacles to clear before that could happen. Could she convince Bernard to take a chance on them?

He was pulling her to her feet, leading her to a shadier spot a short way into the trees.

'It's OK, we can see Philippe from here. He's exhausted so he'll sleep until we wake him up.'

She couldn't dispute that even if she'd wanted to, which she didn't! Her passion and desires were rising up inside her as his hands caressed her into a mounting frenzy of uninhibited lovemaking.

Only as she felt the onset of her climax did she attempt to stifle the moans that were rising in her throat. She mustn't cry out, mustn't wake the sleeping child…

'Julia, it's time to wake up.'

She opened her eyes to see Bernard kneeling beside her. The sun was slanting down in the sky. She glanced across at the still sleeping Philippe.

'How long have we been asleep?'

He gave her a sexy grin. 'Too long. There's a boat coming over. Look. I've started packing up. Would you wake Philippe?'

As she sat at supper much later that night in the kitchen, she knew she would remember this day for the rest of her life. Whatever happened in the future, the days, months and years of uncertainty stretching ahead of them, she would never forget what a blissful day she'd enjoyed before she had to go back to reality and deal with the problems that lay ahead.

CHAPTER TEN

THE end of the course was fast approaching and exams were looming. Concerned as she was about the state of her relationship with Bernard, Julia was just as worried about her performance in these tests. Succeeding at this course had been her reason for coming to France. Bernard had proved a delicious distraction.

As the warm water from the shower cascaded over her body she allowed herself to look back on those halcyon days of high summer when Bernard had taken her out in his boat to 'their' island. Mostly Philippe had been with them, which was always fun. On two occasions he'd been in Paris for the weekend, staying with his grandmother who was always asking for a visit. So they'd gone alone to the island, sleeping overnight in the small cabin on the boat.

She sighed as she patted herself dry with her towel. For the last couple of weeks it had been nose to the grindstone the whole time, revision for the written exams and preparation for practical theatre work. There wasn't much she could do about preparing for the viva voce where a panel of examiners would ask her questions. Either she would satisfy them with her answers or she wouldn't.

She glanced out of the window as she finished dressing. The branches of the tall oak tree at the side of the hospital garden were being buffeted around by a high wind. The leaves had turned an autumnal gold in the past week and some of them had been blown away already. Here in the hospital, where the air-conditioning had been switched to central heating, she would be warm.

After a quick coffee and croissant in the cafeteria, she made her way along the corridor to the orthopaedic ward to see the patient she was to operate on that morning. This was the part she really enjoyed; meeting with the patient, the human aspect of surgery. When he was anaesthetised on the table the situation would change. Especially this morning when there would be an examiner watching her every move.

'Good morning, Vincent. How are you?'

Her patient, a middle-aged man who looked younger than his age and had told her he still wished he could play football, smiled broadly as she arrived at his bedside.

'I'm good, thank you. But I will be happier when the surgery is over.'

She patted his hand in sympathy, secretly thinking exactly the same as he did. How happy she'd be when the operation was over!

'I just called in to check you're OK about everything. We really do appreciate you giving your consent to allow your operation to be assessed by an examiner and performed by someone who is currently qualified to do the surgery but aiming for a higher qualification.'

'Of course it's my pleasure! I'm happy to be of service to the hospital in any way I can. Professor Bernard explained to me about… Ah, but here he is.'

Julia glanced up and saw that Bernard had joined them. 'Hello, Vincent, hello, Julia. Yes, I've explained the exam situation to Vincent.'

Vincent pulled himself up against his pillows. 'Yes, I know I'm in capable hands. Dr Julia will do my knee replacement, with a more senior surgeon by her side, who I hope will be you, Professor.'

Bernard smiled. 'Yes, that's correct. Theoretically I could intervene and take over if I felt it necessary. But in this case I'm sure that won't happen. I've worked with Dr Julia many times and she is exceptionally experienced and talented.'

Vincent gave him a cheeky grin. 'And also very beautiful!'

The two men laughed together boyishly.

'Without doubt,' Bernard said, his eyes meeting with Julia's. 'Beauty isn't a prerequisite for a surgeon but I think it helps the patient to be cared for by someone beautiful on the morning of their operation.'

To her dismay she could feel a blush rising on her cheeks as her eyes met his. 'I was just about to check that the results of all our pre-op investigations will be made available to the examiner.'

'You're in charge,' Bernard said solemnly. 'I'll leave you to it.'

She was carrying copies of her patient's notes as she left the ward some time later. Everything was in order. The left knee had been prepared for surgery. The paperwork concluded. The results of Pierre's blood tests were to hand. No problems with his haemoglobin or electrolyte balance. He was a man in excellent health apart from the knee injury, which he'd told her had meant he couldn't play football any more, not even for the local team in his village.

As soon as she walked into Theatre a feeling of confidence and capability flooded through her. She was vaguely aware of a stranger at the back of the room who was obviously the examiner. But there was no reason for that to make any difference to her performance. She'd performed a total knee replacement before. No need to worry about the outcome.

The anaesthetist nodded. Everything was OK with the patient's breathing under the anaesthetic.

With a steady, sterile, gloved hand she took the scalpel she'd asked for from Bernard and made the first incision.

'How did it go?'

She looked up at Dominic, her fellow student, who was walking towards her in the corridor as she tried to slip away for a desperately needed coffee at the end of the operation.

She stopped to chat to him. He looked terribly worried and nervous.

'It went well. No need to worry. You'll be fine. I was introduced to the examiner at the end. He was absolutely charming but he gave nothing away.'

'Didn't you ask him how you'd done?'

'Of course I didn't! Bernard's talking to him now. I needed to get away. You're on this afternoon, aren't you?'

'Can't wait!' he said gloomily. 'Can't wait till it's all over.'

'Have you got a nice, co-operative patient?'

He smiled. 'Oh, she's very nice. Couldn't be more helpful. And I know I can do a good job. I'm just on my way to check on her. Thanks for the pep talk, Julia. Just one more question.'

'Yes?'

He hesitated. 'Will you be staying on in France or going back to England once this course is over?'

She drew in her breath. 'I'm still not sure. My consultant in England is waiting for me to let him know. He's still under the impression I'll be rejoining the orthopaedic firm.'

Dominic grinned. 'And your consultant in France is hoping you'll stay here?'

'No comment! Good luck!'

She turned and walked away. She had to make a decision soon about what she should do. But she was still not sure where Bernard stood on their future and she was afraid to ask. She knew she wanted to continue with her career but she also wanted to continue her affair with Bernard. If he would only put into words how he felt about her. Give her hope that their affair could become more permanent...possibly leading to marriage?

She walked on, head down so that she could think without having to break off and talk to someone. Marriage would be a step too far for Bernard. He didn't want children and she did. Could she persuade him to change his mind about that? But then he might think she only wanted him to father a child, wouldn't he?

She banished the thoughts from her head. If only Dominic hadn't opened up all her doubts and fears about where she and Bernard were heading. Perhaps she should phone Don in London and talk it over with him. And if Bernard was still keeping her guessing she'd book a seat on the train and go back to London. Couldn't do any harm. It might even make Bernard tell her how he really felt about her.

Her confidence about her career prospects continued to grow as the exam period continued. It had been a couple of weeks since she'd operated on Vincent and he'd made excellent post-operative progress. In fact, the orthopaedic consultant in charge of his outpatient care had told her earlier that day that he'd seen him in his clinic, walking extremely well with the aid of a stick in physiotherapy. The consultant had told her he wouldn't need the stick for much longer.

Yes, she was delighted with the news. And also relieved that the other operation she'd performed under examination, which had been the required emergency operation, had also gone very well.

She'd known that she was theoretically on call for the whole of the examination period except when she was actually doing a written exam, doing an exam operation or taking the viva voce. She'd been relieved that when the actual emergency call had come she'd been well rested after a good night's sleep in her room and ready to spring into action.

As soon as the call had come from Michel in *Urgences*, asking her to go immediately to Theatre where an emergency case and an examiner were waiting for her, she'd felt herself to be on top form. A teenage girl had been rescued from a burning car. Unable to move from the damaged passenger seat, she'd been pulled out by her friends through the side window. Her patient's ankle was badly shattered as part of the engine had smashed through the front of the car, crushing her foot.

Quickly assessing that she would have to pin the ankle to realign the shattered bone, she'd simply got on with the job, hardly aware until later that she'd been examined.

After that, the written exams hadn't caused her any problems. Everything in the syllabus had been covered by the questions, which meant there was a variety of choice.

Her phone was ringing. 'How did the viva voce go this morning?'

'Bernard, I thought you would know more than I do!'

'Well, if I did I wouldn't be asking, would I?'

'And if you did you wouldn't be telling either! Oh, the distinguished panel were very civil, very cool, didn't ask me anything I couldn't answer. All in all I actually enjoyed it.'

'Good! You haven't forgotten the party tonight, have you?'

'Of course not.' She sprang off the bed and dashed over to her wardrobe, flinging wide the door. 'I hadn't forgotten but I'm running late. What would you like me to wear?'

'How about that sexy nightdress you brought with you the last time you were here?'

'Oh, you mean that flimsy bit of silk I picked up in the boutique on the seafront? It's still in the bag it came in, as well you know. One day I'll wear it—when I'm allowed to take it out of the packaging!'

'I thought there wasn't much point when I was only going to take it off as soon as you got within reach.'

She heard him chuckling down the line. That was more like the Bernard she knew and loved. The last few weeks had been a tense time for both of them with little time for frivolous exchanges that had nothing to do with exams.

'I'll drive you over to the farm in about half an hour. OK?'

'Fine! How are my fellow students getting out?'

'I've paid for a minibus there and back. I don't want to have to worry about drunk driving amongst my students. I want everybody to enjoy themselves now that the exams are finished.'

Marianne had done them proud! As Julia surveyed the buffet supper the housekeeper had laid on for them she felt she had to quietly congratulate her.

'Oh, I enjoyed it, Julia,' Marianne said as they whispered together in the kitchen. 'And two of my friends from the village came out to help me.'

'They're the ladies who were serving drinks earlier, I presume? Honestly, Marianne, I would have been out to help you today but I didn't finish my last exam until this morning.'

'Julia, I didn't expect you to help when you've been so busy at the hospital. Bernard told me you were giving all your energy to the exam. That's why we haven't seen you out here for a while. Philippe was so excited when he knew you were coming. And I'm glad you read his bedtime story before he went to sleep. I'd hoped you'd give him some time.'

'I've missed him so much. I just love him to bits. He's…very special.'

Marianne gave her a searching look. 'He feels exactly the same about you, Julia.'

Julia swallowed hard. She knew the implication was that she shouldn't take that love lightly, that she shouldn't break a young boy's heart. Now that she'd finished her exams, all the emotional problems of her relationship with Bernard had begun crowding in on her again.

'Are there any more of those canapés, Marianne?'

It was Bernard, putting an arm round her waist as he rescued her just in time.

'Lots more in the oven ready to come out.' She raised her voice. 'Gaston, get the canapés out, please!'

'What were you two whispering about?' Bernard handed her another glass of wine as he steered her towards the window seat in the sitting room.

Julia smiled. 'I was congratulating Marianne on the marvellous buffet supper.'

'Oh, she loves having a party here. It doesn't happen as often as she would like. Thanks for putting Philippe to bed. He'd been waiting to see you all day, apparently, and I was too tied up with my guests to help you. I popped upstairs to his room just now and he's out for the count. I don't think we'll hear from him, in spite of the noise, until the morning.'

He wondered if she knew how nervous he'd been feeling when he'd said that. He'd decided, really decided, against all the odds that he was going to tell her how he really felt about their relationship tonight. He found himself holding back on the wine. He wanted to remember this night even if...no, he was going to be positive. He had to know the truth, whatever it turned out to be.

'I want to make a toast, everybody!' Dominic was standing in the middle of the room, raising his glass in the air. 'I think I know I speak for all of us on the course when I say that we've had the best professor guiding us every step of the way. I've learned a lot, rediscovered areas of surgical technique I'd forgotten and grappled with the new techniques Bernard has taught us. Whatever my exam results, I'll always be a better surgeon than I would have been and a much better all-round doctor. So, fellow students, please raise your glasses to Bernard, the finest surgical professor we could possibly have wished for!'

Glasses were raised high. The wine flowed. The conversation turned to what everybody was going to do now it was all over. Most of them were going back to the hospitals that were still holding their jobs open for them. The general consensus was that promotions were imminent if their exam results were good. Others were more pragmatic. They would pick up where they'd left off, happy that they'd had the experience to widen their knowledge of surgery.

'How about you, Julia?' Dominic asked. 'Have you made up your mind at last?'

She cleared her throat. She felt nervous with Bernard standing so close to her, listening to every word she was saying. They'd moved to be with the group in the centre of the room but his hand was still lightly on the small of her back.

'I'm keeping my options open for the moment,' she

said quietly. 'I'll have to return to London to discuss my future with my tutor, whatever I decide to do.'

'When will you go?' Dominique asked.

She hesitated. They were all looking at her, including Bernard whose expression was totally enigmatic. They hadn't discussed this and she now wished they had. She hadn't had time…or had she simply been avoiding this conversation?

'Well…I've reserved my seat on the Eurostar tomorrow. I'm going to London for a few days to talk things over with Don.'

Bernard swallowed hard, trying not to convey any emotion at the announcement. He should have known this would happen. This now confident young woman who'd come out here for a fresh start and made such an impression on all her colleagues. She was ready now to fly away and get on with her successful life. She was ready to combine career and motherhood whenever the time was right. And even if he'd told her he'd changed his mind about having a commited relationship again, it wouldn't have made any difference.

She didn't need him to be her husband and father her child. She was so charismatic, so utterly desirable, so talented, so sexy she could take her time in choosing the right partner for herself.

As he watched her fellow students crowding round her, wishing her well in the future, he knew that he'd lost her. She was going back to London tomorrow and she hadn't told him. Just for a few days, she'd said. But once she got back there she wouldn't return. Her colleagues over in London would gather around her, just as her French colleagues were doing now, and Don

Grainger would persuade her to return and climb the career ladder under his tutelage.

He had to let her go back to London. He mustn't try to dissuade her. It would be selfish of him to try. She was off the course now. Her reason for being here finished. Her exam results would reach her electronically, wherever she happened to be.

CHAPTER ELEVEN

JULIA breathed a sigh of relief as Dominic finally weaved his way across the farmyard to join his colleagues in the waiting minibus. She thought he'd never go so she could be alone with Bernard and explain why she hadn't told him she was leaving for London tomorrow.

She looked around the room but Bernard had disappeared while she'd been listening to Dominic's endless talking. Where was he?

'Ah, there you are, Bernard.'

He was coming through the door. She smiled and moved towards him but stopped in her tracks when she saw he was carrying her overnight bag.

His expression gave nothing away. 'I think it's best for you to go back to the hospital tonight. You've got an early start tomorrow. I've told the driver of the minibus you'll be going back to the hospital and will be with them as quickly as you can.'

'Bernard, I wanted to explain the situation to you tonight. I'm only going to London for a few days.'

'So you said. I'll wait to hear from you. Let me know your plans when you've discussed things with Don.'

He was moving closer, still holding her bag. 'I'll take you to the coach.'

He really meant it! She'd better go gracefully without trying to explain now. Maybe this was his way of ending their short-term relationship. Perhaps he was relieved to have an excuse to end it so easily.

She'd never thought it would end like this. But she'd never been any good at understanding men. She must have got it wrong again!

Her colleagues in the minibus had started to sing now.

Julia winced at the noise disturbing the peace and quiet of the valley but she needn't have worried. Everyone fell silent as she and Bernard reached them. Dominic made a space on the front seat for her and took her bag. For the sake of appearances she smiled at Bernard. He smiled back but it was a wintry smile that was there to pretend that all was well.

The driver was anxious to get going. Everyone started calling their thank-yous and goodbyes.

She doubted very much that Bernard could hear her saying goodbye to him. He gave a wave of his hand and walked back up the farmyard.

She woke in the early morning of a grey dawn. Even the clouds through the window added to her dark feelings. She stretched out her hand towards the other side of the bed. The sheet was cold. She knew he wasn't there. She'd come back to her room at the hospital. Correction! He'd sent her back to her room.

She propped herself up on her pillows and checked the time. She'd set her alarm when she'd got back last night. It would soon be time to get up and make final preparations for the journey.

She remembered the awful journey in the minibus last night. Her friends had become mercifully quiet after she'd joined them. They'd had the decency not to ask questions and they hadn't sung any more. But she'd been very relieved to get to her room and close the door on her own little sanctuary.

Her alarm was sounding. Time to get up. She threw back the duvet. She'd asked the hospital domestic staff to keep her room for a further week until she got back from London. But now she was unsure whether she would return. Her emotions were in turmoil and now wasn't the time to try and sort them out. She determined to go back to London to make her decision.

CHAPTER TWELVE

SHE stepped down from the Eurostar at St Pancras, marvelling at the speed with which she'd been transported from Calais–Frethun. Only an hour ago she was stepping on the Eurostar in France and now here she was making her way through the crowds, hearing English voices. She got a taxi after only a short wait and gave him the name of her hospital.

'Are you visiting a patient?' he asked her conversationally.

'No.' She climbed into the back seat.

Usually she enjoyed chatting with cab drivers as they struggled through the London traffic jams but today was different. She felt different, spaced out, unreal. Maybe when she was back amongst her colleagues in the orthopaedic department she would be able to make sense of her future. She'd gone away with such high, ambitious hopes. She hadn't been looking for an all-consuming relationship that had turned her world upside down and forced her to examine her dreams.

She wished she'd been able to say goodbye to Philippe. She forced herself to ignore her feelings of guilt about him. He'd come to regard her as a second mother figure and if she stayed in England he would feel she'd abandoned him. And she would miss him more than she dared think about just now. And as for Bernard... If their affair was over...

Her eyes misted over as she searched in her bag for a tissue to blow her nose.

One step at a time.

She felt a surge of apprehension as she paid the driver and looked up at the tall façade of the building that had been her home and workplace as a medical student and then a qualified doctor. It usually felt as if she was coming home again but this time was different.

'So, you'll get your exam results in a couple of weeks, I understand?' Don smiled across the desk at her. 'I was so relieved to get your email this week to say you were coming back to report on the course.'

'Thanks for your reply. I'm glad you were free to see me this morning.'

'I would have made time for you, Julia.' The consultant hesitated, running a hand through his steel-grey hair as he observed his star pupil. Something told him that she wasn't feeling her usual positive self.

'Would you like more coffee? You must be tired after your early start this morning.'

'No, thanks.'

She sat up straight against the back of her chair as she tried to brighten herself up. In the background she could hear the hum of the endless traffic outside on the forecourt of the hospital. An ambulance screeched to a halt and the siren stopped. It was weird. She should be feeling nostalgic by now.

'I've kept in touch with your progress over in France,' Don told her in a casual, friendly tone.

She managed a tight smile. 'I thought you might.'

'Oh, yes. I wasn't going to let you slip through my fingers. I've invested a lot in your training. Seen you grow up from student days. I'll be retiring soon, you know, well, in a couple of years.'

'No, I didn't know. You'll be missed here.'

'Oh, nobody is indispensable. Anyway, to go back to my progress reports from France, your professor, Bernard Cappelle, seems to think very highly of you. When I spoke to him a few days ago he told me you'd made excellent progress and he had high hopes for your exam results. From the way he spoke it seemed you might be staying on in France.'

Her heart gave a little leap of excitement but she remained silent, waiting for him to continue.

He carried on, wondering why she wasn't making any comment.

'That's why I'm so delighted to see you here in London today. There's the possibility of a promotion in the department, and then when I retire in two years my vacancy will be up for grabs. I've no doubt that, having excelled on the prestigious course at St Martin, you would be a strong candidate.'

He broke off. 'Julia, I think you should take a rest for a few hours to recover from the journey. I've asked Housekeeping to prepare your old room in the medics' quarters. My secretary has the keys. Let's meet up here in my office about four this afternoon.'

He stood and walked round the desk. She remembered how he'd been a father figure to her when she'd gone through the messy divorce days. He wasn't fooled by the brave face she was trying to effect. He held out his hand as she stood up, making a valiant effort to keep going.

She grasped his hand. 'Yes, you're quite right, a rest would be a good idea. I'll be back at four. Thanks, Don, for—'

'For treating you like one of my daughters.' He grinned. 'When you've got four girls at home you become an expert at sensing when something is not quite right.'

She smiled back, knowing she hadn't fooled him. She would have to sort out her problems, emotional and career-wise, before she came back.

She fell into a troubled sleep the moment her head hit the pillow. But the dreams that haunted her throughout were worse than being awake. She was dreaming that Philippe was seriously ill, that Bernard wasn't there with him, that he was on the island looking for her, calling her name, but she was calling out to him from the sea where she felt as if she was drowning. The water was over her head but her arms and legs weren't working properly… She managed to struggle up from the depths of her sleep. Relief flooded through her as she realised she was safe in her room. She was wide awake now and her mind had cleared. She knew she had to speak to Bernard as soon as possible.

He wasn't answering his phone. She tried several times. She'd get hold of Michel Devine in *Urgences*.

'Michel?'

'Michel Devine.'

His abrupt manner and the background noise told her he was on duty.

'It's Julia.'

'Ah, Julia. I thought you were in England. Bernard told me—'

'I'm trying to call him but he's not answering.'

'He's up in Paediatrics with Philippe—that's why he's not answering. I'll get a message to him if—'

'Is Philippe OK?'

'We're not sure. Bernard brought him in this morning. He's going through tests for meningitis.'

'Oh, no!'

'Don't worry, Julia. Philippe is in safe hands and Bernard is constantly with him at his bedside. What message shall I give Bernard?'

'Tell him…tell him I…tell him I'm coming back tonight. Thanks, Michel.'

She glanced at her watch as she zipped up her bag. Good thing she hadn't unpacked anything except her toothbrush. She went out into the corridor. She'd contacted Don, who'd agreed to see her earlier that afternoon.

He was waiting for her in his consulting room in Outpatients. A couple of patients were waiting outside as she went in and closed the door.

'Thanks for seeing me at such short notice. I'll make it brief because I know you've got patients waiting.'

'So why the change of plan, Julia?' He got up from his desk and moved over to the window where there were a couple of armchairs and a small table. 'Have you had any lunch?'

'I'll get something on the train.'

'The train?'

'I'm going back. Bernard Cappelle's son is ill with suspected meningitis. I have to be there with them. Sorry, Don, but it's put everything in perspective, coming back to England. I wasn't sure what it was I wanted but now I am.'

For a moment the consultant stared at her before he realised the reason behind her strange behaviour.

'Ah, I get the full picture now. I have to say I wondered if there was something going on between you and Bernard. So you're an item, to quote my daughters, are you?'

She hesitated. 'Yes, we've built up a relationship, a complicated relationship, and I don't know where it's going, but…' She stared across the small table at Don. 'I shouldn't be burdening you with all this.'

'Julia, you are talking to an expert in the affairs of the heart and in my opinion you've got it pretty bad. So I'm all agog to hear what you're going to do about it.'

She hesitated. 'I've got to think about it.'

'What's there to think about? You're obviously head over heels in love with the man. Call me an old romantic but you shouldn't turn your back on that sort of relationship.'

'But, Don, remember when I was going through that awful divorce and I told you I'd never trust my own judgement of character again? I was trying to be rational this time, taking my time to think through the problems of marrying Bernard and carrying on with my career.'

'You were too young when you married that obnoxious man. You'd had no experience of people like that.

Now you're an extremely intelligent and experienced woman. I'm sad to see you going back because I had great plans for your future here. But you've got to go back and stay there with Bernard. You obviously love both him and his young son. Let me know as soon as the boy has been through all his tests at the hospital.'

The journey seemed much longer on the way back. She was amazed to see Michel Devine waiting for her at St Martin station. She'd told him the time her train from Calais–Frethun would arrive.

'How's Philippe?'

'Still having tests.' He opened the car door for her. 'Bernard is with him the whole time but the paediatric department is firmly in charge.'

'I just hope it's not meningitis.'

'If it is, he's in the best hospital to deal with it. And he's got the best father to lavish attention on him.'

'Thanks for picking me up, Michel.'

'I thought you might be shattered after going there and back in the space of a few hours. I thought of sending a taxi for you but I'm going off duty now and I can get you back to the hospital myself.'

'Well, it's much appreciated.'

'I'm so glad you've come back. You definitely belong over here…with Bernard. As a widower of three years, I was pleased when I saw you and Bernard getting on so well. A good relationship like yours is worth sticking to. My wife and I were only married for three years before she lost her battle with cancer. While she was alive were the happiest days of my life.'

She swallowed hard as she heard the raw emotion in

his voice. They were drawing into the forecourt of the hospital.

'Thanks, Michel. I'll go straight up to Paediatrics.'

He switched off the engine and came round to help her out. 'I'll put your bag in Reception till you need it, then I'll go off duty.'

'Thanks for the advice.'

He gave her a sad smile. 'What advice?'

'Not in so many words but you nudged me in the right direction.'

'I hope so.'

CHAPTER THIRTEEN

JULIA pushed open the swing doors that led into the paediatric ward. It was late in the evening now and most of
the children had been settled down for sleep. The lights
had been dimmed in the main ward. She could see the
ward sister walking towards her now.

'Ah, Caroline!'

She was glad they'd met socially during the summer.
She also knew that she was one of the most experienced
and well-qualified sisters in the hospital.

She began to relax. 'How is Philippe?'

Caroline frowned. 'I'm afraid the tests are still in-
conclusive. Bernard is with him. He's been here all day.
I thought you were in England, Julia.'

'I made a brief visit to see the boss of my department. I'm back now. Change of plan. Where is…?'

'Let me take you to his room.'

Caroline took her to a room near the nurses' station.
The door was slightly ajar. She pushed it open.

'A visitor for you, Bernard.'

He was sitting by Philippe's bed, hunched over his
son, his head resting in his hands, his elbows on the
sheet. He turned his head and for an instant she saw a

flash of welcoming light in his eyes before the mask of total dejection returned.

'I thought you were in England.'

Sister went out and closed the door behind her as Julia approached the sick child's bed. Bernard stood up, running a hand through his dishevelled hair. She could see that he hadn't shaved that day. The dark stubble she'd noticed he always had in the mornings was now much more prominent—positively designer stubble, she couldn't help thinking. She longed to draw him against her and hold him there but sensed the cold aura surrounding him.

'I came back,' she said lamely. 'I was worried about Philippe.'

She leaned across the small patient now, automatically reaching for his pulse. It was racing along too fast, almost impossible to count the beats. His skin was dangerously hot.

'What's the latest?'

Bernard handed her the notes. She was still scanning the test results as one of the doctors on the paediatric firm came in.

'What's the latest news from Pathology, Thibault?' Bernard asked, his calm voice belying the obvious anxiety that cloaked the rest of him.

'A glimmer of hope, Bernard. The latest blood sample gave negative results for meningitis. I'm going to take another sample now.'

She stood beside Bernard as the blood sample was taken.

'It could be septicaemia, couldn't it?' he said to the

young doctor as he prepared to return to the pathology laboratory.

'Or it could be the antibiotics beginning to kick in,' Julia said quietly, thinking out loud.

The three of them pooled their ideas, each anxious that the dreaded diagnosis of suspected meningitis should be proved to be wrong.

'We'll just have to hope, Bernard,' Dr. Thibault said gently. 'Tonight is the crucial time. As you know, if we don't have an improvement in your son's condition by tomorrow morning there is a chance that—'

'Yes, yes,' Bernard said, his voice wavering now. He didn't want to contemplate that his son's illness could be fatal. 'We can beat it! This is the twenty-first century and we'll pool our skills to save Philippe.'

'If I might suggest, Bernard,' the young doctor said, carefully, 'you've been here all day and you must be tired. I think I could arrange for you to take a break if you would approve of that?'

'I can't leave Philippe at this stage.'

'I'll call the path lab and ask them to collect this blood immediately. I can stay here with your son for the next hour.'

Julia looked across the small table at Bernard. The canteen had been deserted when they'd arrived but she had phoned the kitchen and the staff cook on night duty had turned up to prepare some food.

Chicken and vegetable soup had been placed in front of them, along with a crusty baguette heated up in the oven and a basket of fresh fruit—apples, oranges and bananas.

It wasn't until they'd started to eat the soup that they both realised how hungry they were.

'Did you have lunch over in England?'

She put down her spoon, having polished off her first helping. 'There wasn't time. I meant to get a sandwich on the train but I wasn't hungry. I'm hungry now.'

'There's more soup in this casserole,' Bernard said, dipping in with the soup ladle the waitress had left on the table.

It was only when she'd finished the last piece of her apple that her brain seemed to function again.

'Dr Thibault was quite right to send you off for a break. You looked terrible when I first got here.'

'Thanks! You weren't looking your usual self either.' His eyes seemed to be boring into her. 'Care to tell me why you're here?'

'I told you; I was worried about Philippe.'

'And?'

'Bernard, I don't think we should talk about this until we've got through tonight.'

'We? You don't have to stay, Julia.'

'Oh, but I do. I can't rest until I know that…that he's out of danger.'

Bernard stood up. 'Neither can I.'

She must have dozed off in the high-backed armchair beside Philippe's bed. Bernard, at the other side, was wide awake, she could see, sponging his son's chest with cold water.

As he dabbed it dry he looked across at her. 'The rash isn't so pronounced. It's disappearing in places. I'm beginning to hope it's septicaemia.'

'Still dangerous,' Julia said quietly. 'But easier to treat than meningitis.'

Bernard nodded. 'He's opening his eyes… Julia!'

She jumped up from the chair and went round the bed. 'Philippe?'

'Where am I?'

Julia could feel tears of joy pricking her eyes as she heard the weak little voice. A tear trickled down her cheek as she leaned over Philippe, taking hold of his tiny hand. She'd been right to come back here. This was where she belonged.

Philippe was propped up against the pillows, eating a small carton of yoghurt. It was what he'd asked for as soon as he'd begun to feel stronger. Since the amazing recovery in the early morning he'd gradually gathered strength. The diagnosis was confirmed, septicaemia. His treatment and medication had been adjusted accordingly and there was every chance now that he was going to have a full recovery within days.

'Papa, can we go home? I want to see the cows. Gaston will need some help with the milking today.'

'We'll need to stay here for another night at least.'

'But you'll both stay with me, won't you? Julia, you can stay, can't you? You won't leave me, will you?'

She looked at the anxious eyes of this young boy who meant so much to her and across the bed to his father whom she loved more than she'd ever imagined possible.

What would she do if he didn't want her any more?

CHAPTER FOURTEEN

SHE'D spent the night in the guest room. On Bernard's instructions Gaston had moved another bed into Philippe's room before they'd all arrived back from the hospital yesterday. Bernard had insisted she get a good night's sleep.

'You've spent the last three nights in an armchair so you must get a proper rest tonight,' he'd told her.

She'd argued that so had he. They could take turns at caring for Philippe during the night.

But Bernard had been adamant that he wanted to do the night watch. As she pulled the curtains fully back and fixed the ties, she raised her face to the morning sun. There was little heat now in the late autumnal rays but it was soothing to her nerves. Bernard had been right. She did need a good rest. Her nerves had been totally frazzled over the last few days since Philippe had become ill.

And the journey to London and back had tired her more than usual. Well, the discussion with Don Grainger had set her thinking.

She sighed as she looked out over the garden. The fallen leaves on the lawn. The roses drooping and waiting to be dead-headed. She'd pushed the emotional problems that still existed between Bernard and herself to the back of her mind until they were absolutely sure Philippe was out of danger. And she didn't want a discussion while Philippe was the main priority in Bernard's life.

Maybe she should simply go back to her room in the medics' quarters at St Martin? Marianne and Gaston were taking care of all the practicalities of the situation. Was she really needed here?

'Julia, I've brought you some coffee.'

She raced to the door at the welcome sound of Bernard's voice.

He was standing outside in the corridor, carrying a small tray, the expression on his face totally unreadable.

'How's Philippe?'

'He had a good night. In fact, so did I. I slept until Marianne brought the coffee tray just now. She's taken over to give me a break. I feel that now Philippe is out of danger and you're back from London we should talk. My place or yours?'

For the first time for days he looked relaxed again. There was a half-smile on his face but still that awkward coolness that had to be resolved if she was to convince him that she'd made a mistake in returning to London without discussing it with him first.

She'd had time to think and she knew that she wanted Bernard on any terms. She could be happy with him without them marrying or having a child of their own. Philippe felt like her own child already and if Bernard didn't want more children, neither did she. But did he want her? Had the short-term affair been enough for him to decide to go back to his independent lifestyle?

She moved towards him. 'Which room would you prefer?'

'I'd like to install myself back in my bedroom so let's go there. I need to shave and everything is in my bathroom. We can talk while I'm in there before I arrange my schedule at the hospital for today. I plan to go in for a couple of hours this morning. I've arranged for a nurse to come out from the hospital to be with Philippe, and Marianne and Gaston will be in charge here.'

She followed behind him. This wasn't how she'd planned to discuss her change of heart—in a bathroom!

He held the tray in one hand and pushed open his door with the other, walking swiftly over to the small round table by the window. She sank down into one of the armchairs and watched as he poured the coffee into the cups. He took a sip and swallowed. 'Mmm, that first coffee taste of the morning. Nothing like it!'

She watched, mesmerised, as he began to walk towards the bathroom, the cup firmly clenched in his fingers.

'Bernard! You're not really going to shave while we have the most important discussion of our lives!'

He turned, a half-smile again on his face. 'Ah, so you do have something to tell me? Don said you might have.'

He moved swiftly back to the table and stretched his long legs out in the armchair across from her.

'Don?'

'Who else knows you almost as well as I do? Well, professionally anyway. He phoned me last night to check how Philippe was but also to fill me in about your discussions. He said he thought you would be staying in France and conceded that his loss was my gain. He'd hoped to guide you up the career ladder in London until his retirement and he was sad to lose you.'

'So you were simply talking professionally?'

'What else?'

She was beginning to feel alarmed. The two men who'd been most influential in her career had been discussing her.

'He didn't touch on anything…er…well, personal?'

He feigned surprise at her question. 'Such as?'

'Oh, Bernard, you can be so infuriating at times!'

She leapt out of her seat and went across so she would have the advantage of looking down at him. 'Such as whether our relationship was over or not?'

'Ah, that.' He half rose from his seat and pulled her down onto his lap. 'Well, he might have mentioned it.'

She turned her head and looked up at him. He had the advantage now and she'd really wanted a discussion. She needed to convince him that she'd come to the right decision at last.

'I've had time to think over the last few days,' she said quietly. 'I know you don't want another child but I've realised that I can live as a surgeon so long as I have you…and Philippe, of course…in my life. I don't need a baby any more.'

'But I do,' he replied gently, drawing her so close that she could feel his heart beating. 'I've known for some time now that, contrary to how I used to feel, I would love to have a baby…but only with you. I've watched you caring for Philippe and I realised that you would be the most wonderful mother to our baby.'

'So why didn't you tell me you'd had a change of heart?'

'I wanted to be sure you wouldn't choose to have a baby with me just because I could fulfil one of your dearest wishes. I had to be sure that you loved me as much as I love you.'

'But I thought that was obvious!' She put her hands against his cheeks and drew his lips against hers.

She felt his response deepening, his hands gently caressing her body. Gently, he lifted her up into his arms and carried her over to the bed.

'Can I make my love any more obvious?' she whispered as they both lay back, exhausted by their lovemaking and panting for breath.

She turned her head on the pillow to look at him as she curled her toes against his, one of the positions she loved to adopt after they'd made love.

He smiled. 'I think you've convinced me… But, then again, I just might be having doubts.'

He rested on his elbow, looking down into her eyes. 'I'll need convincing often if we're going to stay together for the rest of our lives.'

She gazed up into his face. 'And are we going to stay together for the rest of our lives?'

Before she realised what he was doing he was on his knees beside the bed, looking up at her with those devastatingly sexy eyes that were expressing the love he felt for her.

'Julia, will you marry me?'

His voice was husky, full of emotion as he asked her the question she'd thought he might never ask. She'd had her doubts before but now that they'd sorted out the problems that had been holding them back she was free to commit herself.

She leaned forward and put her hands over his. 'Of course I will.'

He was in bed beside her, drawing her into his arms. 'Oh, Julia, my love…'

'Bernard, the nurse is here to look after Philippe.'

Julia struggled up through the tangle of sheets as she heard Marianne's voice outside in the corridor. She swung her legs over the side of the bed.

Bernard put out a restraining hand. 'I'll go,' he whispered. 'Stay here and rest. There's no hurry. Take your time before you come downstairs.'

He was smiling fondly down at her. 'As soon as Marianne hears our news, you'll need all your energy to cope with her. She'll be thinking ahead to the wedding and all the plans that will be needed.'

'Please don't tell her till I come downstairs.'

His smile broadened. 'I won't need to. That woman is psychic, I'm sure. She's been expecting an announcement ever since you stayed that first night here.'

It was only as she climbed out of the bath and reached for a towel a little later that she realised the enormity of the tasks ahead of her. There were phone calls to make to her parents—that must be a priority. How would her mother take it? Last time she'd announced she was going to be married her mother had been very unsure. She'd gone ahead with it defiantly and had lived to regret it. But this time she was absolutely sure of her man.

But the practicalities had to be dealt with. Where would they have the wedding? France? England? There'd have to be a long list of guests. How much easier if would be if they could just sneak away, the three of them.

As she thought of the three of them making a real family unit at last she felt a great longing to see her soon-to-be stepchild as soon as possible.

Hurrying along to his room, she slowed down to check that she was presentable. It was still early but so much had happened, so much had been resolved and so much needed to be sorted out. As her mother would say, she should gather her wits about her.

Yes, there would be a nurse from the hospital taking care of Philippe and she didn't want to look as if she'd been rolling about in Bernard's bed all night. It had only been this morning when she'd given herself completely to the joy of being finally sure that their future was well and truly together.

She smiled as she recognised one of the nurses from Paediatrics. 'Hello, Florence.'

'Julia!' Philippe's voice was croaky and weak but his happiness at seeing her again was expressed in the way he held out his thin little arms towards her.

She leaned down and clasped him against her. 'Oh, Philippe, it's good to see you looking so much better.'

'Can I come down and have breakfast with you and Papa? I'm feeling hungry now.'

'You said you didn't want to eat anything,' Florence said gently. 'Let me bring something up from the kitchen for you. I don't think you're strong enough to go downstairs yet.'

As if on cue, Bernard chose that moment to come in. 'What's this about breakfast, Philippe?'

He reached down and picked up his small son in his arms. Julia grabbed a blanket from the end of the bed and wrapped it round him. He snuggled happily against his father.

'Take a break, Florence,' Bernard said. 'Come down and have some breakfast with us. The more the merrier around the table today!'

Marianne was waiting for them in the kitchen, cafetière in her hand. The delicious smell of coffee had wafted up the stairs as Julia had walked behind Bernard, followed by Florence. Julia sat down beside Bernard, as close as she could to Philippe so that she could make sure he was comfortable in Bernard's arms. She doubted he would eat much, if anything, after the ordeal he'd been through, but it was the experience of being once more part of the family that he needed.

Their family! Her heart seemed to turn over at the implications of what was happening.

What a momentous occasion. Was Bernard going to make an announcement here at the breakfast table? With Florence here the news would spread like wildfire at the hospital. Was that what he wanted?

She glanced up at him as he cleared his throat. He was looking oh, so pleased with himself, happiness oozing from every fibre of his muscular, athletic, tantalisingly sexy body. His happiness was infectious. There was a feeling of total unreality about the situation but she'd never felt as happy as she did at that moment. Yes, she wanted to tell the whole world that she was soon to be married to the most wonderful man on the planet.

'Come and sit down, Marianne,' Bernard said. 'I want everybody here because I've got an announcement to make. Where's Gaston?'

'He's just finished the milking. He's going to take a shower as soon as—'

'Ask him to come in here, Marianne, if he's still out there, taking off his boots.'

Gaston glanced around the table as he walked in, treading carefully across the room in his socks to sit next to his wife.

'I haven't even washed my hands,' he complained to his wife before looking across at Bernard. 'What's this all about? I need to clean up.'

'Julia has just consented to become my wife. I want you all to share in our happiness.'

'And about time too,' Gaston said, now grinning from ear to ear. 'Creeping around in the middle of the night when the two of you—'

'Gaston!' his wife hissed at him. 'Be quiet.'

'No, I won't be quiet. This is the best news we've had in this house since I came to work here and told you that Marianne had set a date for our wedding.'

'And that was a long time ago, wasn't it, Gaston? I was much younger but I remember it well because my father opened one of his special bottles of champagne so we could drink a toast. I haven't been down to the cellar recently. Do you know if there's still a bottle of that vintage?'

Gaston struggled to his feet. 'I checked a few weeks ago because I was hoping you'd get a move on, Bernard. Shall I put a bottle on ice?'

'Bring a couple. We'll have a glass now and drink

some more this evening when we can all relax at the end of the day.'

'Julia, are you going to be my new mother?' Philippe asked shyly.

She swallowed hard. 'I'm going to be Papa's wife. You can carry on calling me Julia because I'll never replace your real mother, will I?'

'I suppose not. Well, you can be my second mother, then, but I'd like to still call you Julia.'

Gaston arrived with the champagne. 'It's freezing cold down there in the cellar. I've brought the ice bucket but we don't really need it. And it needs polishing. Hasn't been used for years. I cleared away the cobwebs but...'

He glanced across at his wife, who was already holding a duster.

Julia gathered Philippe into her arms as Bernard stood to do the honours. The cork was expertly removed with barely a hiss, the champagne was poured, the glasses raised.

Marianne was in tears now that she'd got the situation she'd hoped for. It was almost too much for her as she raised her glass to the happy pair.

'Congratulations!' she said, through her tears.

Florence was overwhelmed at being the first to acknowledge that there was some truth in the rumours that had been circulating in the hospital. Just wait until she got back there at the end of the week!

'Well, that all went very well today,' Bernard said, as he climbed into bed. 'Do you think you could put that list down and give me some attention? There can't be that much to do when you're organising a wedding, can there?'

'You must be joking! Not for the groom perhaps. So long as you write a good speech and…'

'Oh, do I have to give a speech? I'd better start now, then. Just lend me that notepad you're still scribbling in.'

He reached across and grabbed it from her, glancing down as he did so. 'Oh, how did your mother take the news?'

'Very well, actually. I gathered that you'd phoned Don this morning and he'd phoned Mum to prepare her for the news. They're old friends from way back at medical school. He'd also given you a very good character reference, I believe, because she said she was looking forward to meeting you.'

'And did you agree on where the wedding should take place?'

'The church where my grandmother and my mother were married in Montreuil sur Mer. I was baptised there because my mother insisted on keeping our French family connection going.'

'So, a very interesting family choice.'

'And do you approve?'

'Absolutely!' He drew her into his arms. 'Is that all the business for the day completed? The night nurse has taken over from Florence in Philippe's room so we're free to go to sleep or…'

As she gave herself up to the delights of their lovemaking she knew she was going to be the happiest bride ever.

EPILOGUE

THE day of the wedding dawned with a flurry of snow-flakes drifting outside the window. Julia had spent the night in a hotel in the village with her parents in line with the tradition of not seeing her groom before the wedding. It had been hard to be separated from Bernard but as he'd reminded her when he kissed her goodnight it was only one night apart and then they would be together for the rest of their lives.

After Julia had eaten breakfast in bed, her mother arrived with Claudine, the dressmaker, and Monique, a hairdresser who was going to shampoo and arrange her long blonde hair so that it would fall over her shoulders underneath the delicate lace veil.

Claudine was going to dress her and make sure that the stunning silk dress they'd designed between them was shown off to perfection. The dressmaker held out the stiff petticoat and Julia stepped into it, one hand on Claudine's shoulder to steady herself. It looked gorgeous!

The ladies in the room asked for her to give them a twirl. She obliged. It didn't feel at all stiff and starchy as she'd thought it might.

Finally, she stood in front of the mirror fully dressed

in the superbly beautiful dress while her mother, Claudine and Monique stood around to admire her. Behind her reflection she could see her mother wiping away a tear. She turned and hugged her.

Her mother hugged her back, but gently. 'Careful of your dress, darling. I'm so happy for you. This time you're going to be very happy.'

And as she walked into the church on her father's arm she knew she really was going to be happy for the rest of her life. She'd chosen and been chosen by the most wonderful man in the world.

Walking down the aisle, she felt like a fairy-tale princess on her way to marry her prince. He was there in front of the altar, her own Prince Charming. He turned as she was nearing him, his eyes shining with love and admiration at this vision of perfection, his soon-to-be wife.

As she reached his side she realised there was someone else with her in front of the altar. Glancing down, she saw Philippe smiling up at her. He'd left his place in the procession of bridesmaids behind her and come to join her and his father. He looked adorable in his tailor-made suit.

'Let him stay with us,' she whispered to Bernard, who smiled and nodded in agreement.

The organist stopped playing. The congregation fell silent. The marriage service began.

There was another flurry of snowflakes as they came out of the church and stood on the steps for the photographs. Julia and Bernard smiled for the cameras. Her parents joined them with her brothers and their families. Philippe joined them and then agreed to leave the bridal pair to join Julia's parents, who were going to take him back to the farm. The photo shoot would have gone on longer but the descending snow put an end to that.

'The kiss!' everyone was calling out.

Bernard took her in his arms and they kissed to loud shouts of approval.

'Encore! Another kiss!'

'Just one more,' Bernard whispered. 'I want you all to myself now.'

As soon as they could get away into the car, they did so.

'See you back at the farm,' Bernard called out to everybody as he drove away. He'd insisted on going against tradition by driving his own car over to the church so that they could be really alone on the way back home.

'I wanted you to myself for the first few minutes of our marriage,' he said, pulling the car in behind a tractor on the narrow country lane. 'I'm taking a short cut, which should be quicker than the main road so we'll be back at the farm before our guests arrive, I hope. We'll have to be sociable for the rest of the day.'

She smiled. 'It's been such a whirlwind of organisation for the last few weeks. I'll be so glad to have some normal married life.'

'Do you think we'll ever have a normal married life, whatever that is?'

'I know we're both continuing with our careers but as we both understand what the other's going through we can pull together, help each other…until we have a baby, when it might get a bit harder.'

She glanced across at him. His eyes were on the narrow road ahead. The tractor had turned into a gate and left the road clear at last. The snowflakes had stopped now and the pale wintry sun was peeping out from behind a cloud.

He changed gear as they went down into the valley where he could see smoke spiralling from the farm chimneys. 'I wonder when that will be?'

'Well, it could be sooner than we expected. I promised I would tell you if…well, don't get too excited but I'm seven days late.'

'My darling! Why didn't you tell me?'

'I'm telling you now! But it could just be the excitement of the wedding and all the preparations. Don't, for heaven's sake, start getting your hopes up.'

He pulled into the farmyard and switched the engine off.

'Come here, you gorgeous girl, my wonderful bride.'

He kissed her gently on the lips. As his kiss deepened she moved in his arms.

'Later, darling. Our guests are arriving.'

'Keep me informed, won't you?' he whispered as a car pulled in behind them.

'Of course.' She smiled happily as Gaston opened a door for her to climb out. A long strip of red carpet had been laid in front of her leading to the kitchen door. Bernard was already there for her holding out his hand to guide her indoors.

Bernard's speech was hilarious. Everybody was still laughing as they raised their glasses for another toast. They were all crowded into the dining room, the food spread out as a buffet.

'There's more food in the kitchen, Julia,' Marianne said quietly. 'Shall I bring the desserts yet?'

'I'll tell everybody the desserts are in the kitchen when they would like to help themselves. Nobody's standing on ceremony here. Everybody seems to be getting on well.'

'I should think so,' Gaston said, topping up her wine glass. 'Good thing we've got plenty of bottles in the cellar.'

She moved through the guests, trying to have a word with everybody. They all complimented her on her dress, especially her cousin Chantal. They'd been great friends as children and nothing ever changed when they met up again.

'Your dress is absolutely gorgeous, Julia! It fits you perfectly.'

'I had it made in Montreuil by the daughter of the dressmaker who made the wedding dresses of our grandmother and my mother, who's over there looking very happy to be the mother of the bride, don't you think?'

'She's also happy to be chatting to my mother. You can tell they're twins. They're so alike, aren't they? And they don't see enough of each other nowadays so they never stop talking when they do meet!'

'Just like we do!'

They both laughed.

Chantal turned back to admire Julia again. 'You're so slim. That dress fits you like a glove.'

'I suppose I am…at the moment.' Now, why had she said that? Was it because Chantal had always been more like a sister when they'd been small? The antidote to all those brothers bossing her around?

Chantal moved nearer and put a hand on her arm, guiding her through the throng of guests to a small window seat where they could whisper together. 'You're not…? Are you?'

Julia smiled. 'Maybe. Too early to say but I hope so.'

'So do I! Please remember me when you're choosing godparents.'

'Chantal, you would be my first choice! I'm so glad we're going to see more of each other now that I'm going to be living in France. It's easy for you to come over from Paris by train, isn't it?'

'I may be coming back to this area sooner than you think. I've split up with Jacques.'

'No! But I thought you two had the most perfect relationship.'

'So did I. He's gone back to his wife. He'd managed to fool me completely for a whole year. I didn't realise I was his mistress. I felt such a fool when he told me.'

'So are you thinking of leaving the hospital?'

'I've left! Couldn't stand working alongside him when all the time—'

Chantal broke off as Bernard arrived.

'Not interrupting anything, am I?'

'No! Well, actually Chantal was just telling me she's leaving Paris and moving back to this area.'

'I'll be looking for a job, Bernard. Any vacancies for a well-qualified and experienced doctor?'

'Send me your CV and I'll see what I can do, Chantal.'

'I'll do that!'

Philippe came running across the room to join them. 'Papa, I've got an idea. You see my friend Jules over there with his parents? Well, he got a little brother during the summer. Now that Julia and you are married, does that mean I can have a baby brother or sister? Maybe as a Christmas present?'

He was looking up beseechingly now at Julia.

She looked across at Bernard, who was smiling happily. 'We'll have to see what happens, won't we?' he told his son. 'These things take time.'

Philippe looked pleased. Papa hadn't ruled the idea out. He ran back to his friend Jules to say he might get a baby brother or sister but probably not for Christmas.

'These things take time,' he told Jules airily.

'I didn't think they would stay so late,' Julia said as she slipped into bed beside Bernard.

'Sign of a good party! I'd say it was a huge success.'

'It was wonderful to see my parents and all three of my brothers again but I'm glad they're staying at the hotel in the village, otherwise we'd still be downstairs, having supper.'

'Today has been a wonderful day!' he said, drawing her against him.

'It's been the happiest day of my life. Wasn't Philippe sweet when he asked for a baby brother? I don't know about Christmas but he might get one for his birthday!'

'Wonder woman!'

She laughed.

Bernard drew her closer. 'Just one request.'

'Yes?'

'You're not going to leave me in the early morning and go to the guest room, are you?'

'Not now that you've made an honest woman of me.'

'Any regrets?'

She sighed as she felt his arms drawing her even closer.

'Only that we didn't get together like this sooner.'

'You mean like this…or like this…or like this…?'

She laughed. 'You know what I mean.'

'I certainly do…'

* * * * *

A sneaky peek at next month...

Medical Romance™

CAPTIVATING MEDICAL DRAMA—WITH HEART

My wish list for next month's titles...

In stores from 4th May 2012:

❏ Sydney Harbour Hospital: Lexi's Secret — Melanie Milburne

❑ West Wing to Maternity Wing! — Scarlet Wilson

❏ Diamond Ring for the Ice Queen — Lucy Clark

❑ No.1 Dad in Texas — Dianne Drake

❏ The Dangers of Dating Your Boss — Sue MacKay

❑ The Doctor, His Daughter and Me — Leonie Knight

Available at WHSmith, Tesco, Asda, Eason, Amazon and Apple

Just can't wait?

0412/03

Special Offers

Every month we put together collections and longer reads written by your favourite authors.

Here are some of next month's highlights— and don't miss our fabulous discount online!

On sale 20th April

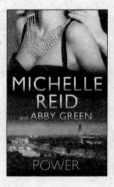

On sale 20th April

On sale 20th April

Save 20% on all Special Releases

Find out more at
www.millsandboon.co.uk/specialreleases

Visit us
Online

0412/ST/MB3

The World of Mills & Boon®

There's a Mills & Boon® series that's perfect for you. We publish ten series and with new titles every month, you never have to wait long for your favourite to come along.

Blaze® Scorching hot, sexy reads

By Request Relive the romance with the best of the best

Cherish™ Romance to melt the heart every time

Desire™ Passionate and dramatic love stories

Visit us Online | Browse our books before you buy online at **www.millsandboon.co.uk**

Have Your Say

You've just finished your book.
So what did you think?

We'd love to hear your thoughts on our
'Have your say' online panel
www.millsandboon.co.uk/haveyoursay

- Easy to use
- Short questionnaire
- Chance to win Mills & Boon® goodies

Visit us Online
Tell us what you thought of this book now at
www.millsandboon.co.uk/haveyoursay

YOUR_S